The Dance of the Dead

Also by James Maxwell

The Gateway Saga
Blood and Empire
Wrath and Ruin

The Firewall Trilogy
A Girl From Nowhere
A World of Secrets
A Search for Starlight

The Evermen Saga
Enchantress
The Hidden Relic
The Path of the Storm
The Lore of the Evermen
Seven Words of Power

The Shifting Tides
Golden Age
Silver Road
Copper Chain
Iron Will

Published by Everlast Books

www.jamesmaxwell.com

ISBN-13: 978-0-646-71802-6

Cover design by EGA

Printed in the United States of America

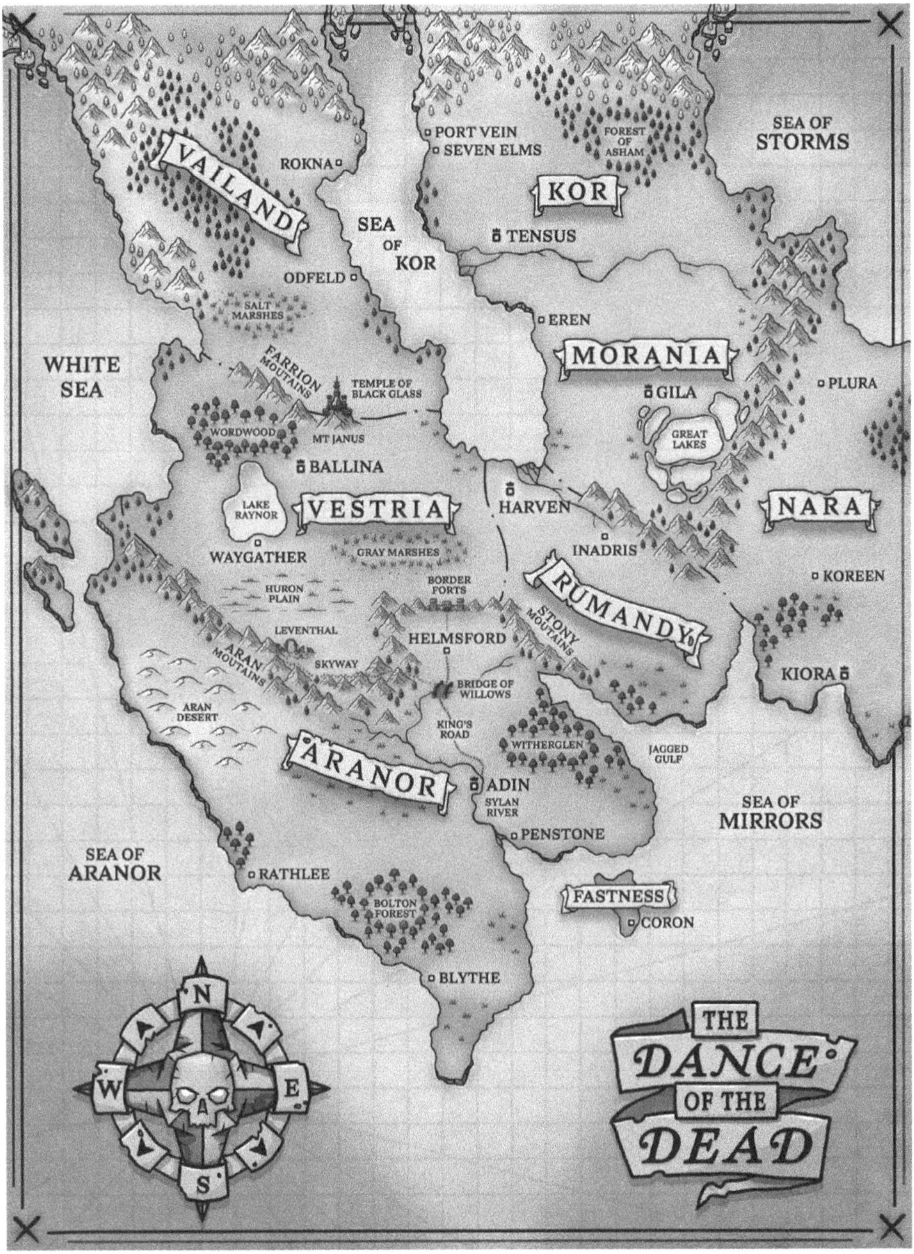
VAILAND
ROKNA
PORT VEIN
SEVEN ELMS
FOREST OF ASHAM
SEA OF STORMS
KOR
SEA OF KOR
TENSUS
ODFELD
SALT MARSHES
EREN
MORANIA
WHITE SEA
FARRION MOUTAINS
TEMPLE OF BLACK GLASS
GILA
PLURA
GREAT LAKES
WORDWOOD
MT JANUS
BALLINA
HARVEN
LAKE RAYNOR
VESTRIA
NARA
WAYGATHER
GRAY MARSHES
INADRIS
HURON PLAIN
BORDER FORTS
RUMANDY
KOREEN
LEVENTHAL
HELMSFORD
STONY MOUNTAINS
ARAN MOUTAINS
SKYWAY
BRIDGE OF WILLOWS
KIORA
ARAN DESERT
KING'S ROAD
WITHERGLEN
JAGGED GULF
ARANOR
ADIN
SYLAN RIVER
SEA OF MIRRORS
PENSTONE
SEA OF ARANOR
RATHLEE
FASTNESS
BOLTON FOREST
CORON
BLYTHE
N
W
E
S
THE DANCE OF THE DEAD

For Alicia, with all my love and gratitude

Chapter 1

THERE WAS NOTHING restful about death.

He paced, back and forth, boots crunching on the bone-dry gravel. His jaw tightened and relaxed, over and over. He roamed like a despairing animal tied to a stake in the ground.

But his eyes were lifeless... and they didn't move at all.

As his toil continued, he kept his head turned in the same direction, with his gaze fixed on a hulking structure. The wooden building was too big and forbidding to be a house, but also too ugly to be a manor. With its corner towers and high walls, it almost looked like a fortress.

The building was once called Seven Elms Convent, and most of it was burned. The gate leaned off its hinges. One of the four towers had crumbled into a charcoal mess.

The convent had a hold on him. He couldn't look away.

The ruin was in a lonely place of barren, windswept hills, which made the nearby circle of trees all the more striking. Frequent gusts of wind tore at the grass and blew his long, graying hair in front of his face. He was on high ground, near an ancient lighthouse and cliffs that towered over the Sea of Kor. The wind carried the smell of salt, burned wood, and decay.

His attention remained on the convent. Clouds came and went, but there was never any sun and it never rained. This was a world of shadow.

His haunting had a rhythm. Part of his cycle was to stop. He stood with his legs apart, watched the ruin, and cracked his knuckles. Darker storm clouds began to gather overhead.

He heard a whine and glanced down. A skinny dog with brown ears panted and looked up at him. He bent to rub behind the dog's ears, then gave a firmer pat on the flank. Where had the dog come from? Searching his memory gave him nothing. Perhaps it didn't matter.

He just knew that he needed to do his penance. To atone.

It was time to move. He didn't know how he knew, he just started to walk, leaving the road behind. Grass swished past his legs as he took a path away from the ruin, in the rough direction of the lighthouse.

He now headed toward an abrupt drop.

Approaching the clifftop, he had an all-encompassing view of the Sea of Kor. Whitecaps flung spray above the surface of the sea far below. Mist floated on top of the midnight water. He stopped on the very edge of the precipice, despite a surge of vertigo.

He sensed movement. As his eye followed the cliff edge, he spied a figure approaching.

The figure was lean and tall and wore a black hooded cloak that was tattered at the edges. The frame was that of a man, but nothing could be seen of his face, and he walked with an odd, jerky manner.

He returned his attention to the sea, even as he was aware of the ghoul coming closer and then halting, a few paces from where he was standing.

A hoarse voice croaked out. "Still you are here," the ghoul said, head kept down.

"As I should be," he replied. "Such is my fate." He avoided glancing at the ghoul.

"Important events are taking place in the world, events that you could be in a position to influence."

"You should already know. I do not care."

"You were once a man of courage. A shaper of things. You could have been a king." The ghoul's tone became more insistent. "You do not need to remain trapped here in the shadow world, Malgannis Vandryden. Come, you must have deeds left undone. I can end this unceasing restlessness."

Malgannis said nothing.

"Perhaps I am not making myself clear. The lord of the underworld has already agreed to it. You can return. You should return." The ghoul paused, waiting for a response, before pressing on. "All you must do is pay the price. Life can be yours once more. Let us strike a bargain."

Malgannis finally turned his head to look at the face contained within the black hood. A skeleton stared back at him, a pale visage of empty eye sockets and oversized teeth.

“The umbra is no place to dwell,” the ghoul pressed. “This is an in-between world. In exchange for your soul, I can offer—”

“Hell?” Malgannis challenged. “A short burst of life and then an eternity in the underworld, so my soul can turn in flame while you harvest whatever life force remains? No,” he said firmly. “This is where I belong.”

“If I cannot appeal to your aspirations, then what of pleasure? Sell me your soul, and I will give you a taste of mortality once more. Think of it. Perhaps you would like a woman. Or a feast. Or you might have loved ones you wish to see—”

“Anyone I loved is long dead, and anyone who wishes to see me doesn’t know me. Enough. How many times must you try to buy what I refuse to give? My soul is my own. Leave me be.”

The ghoul waited a few moments longer, giving Malgannis a chance to change his mind, even though he knew he never would. With no deal to be made, the creature then bowed, before turning and departing. Malgannis watched the ghoul head back along the cliff edge and become swallowed in the haze. At last he was alone and stood with his feet close to the precipice, staring out to sea.

Then, once again, it was time to keep moving.

He walked back toward the road, and soon the blackened ruin appeared ahead. He reached a particular place, and with his boots on the gravel, he turned to face the remains of Seven Elms Convent. With his eyes fixed on the ruin, the cycle was complete, and he started again.

He began to pace, his gaze on the convent, making a short journey before he turned on his heel and strode back to his earlier position. His tread made a regular grinding sound. His tight jaw worked soundlessly.

There was nothing restful about death.

A smoky, salty wind blew at his hair. After some time, he stopped and cracked his knuckles while he inspected the ruin. Dark clouds gathered overhead. A dog whined, and he bent to scratch the scrawny creature behind the brown ears, before giving it a firm pat.

He knew it was time to go elsewhere, and so he abandoned the road to take his first steps toward the cliff.

But he stopped.

This time was different.

A strong sense of foreboding came over him. The scent of decay was much stronger as his tongue tasted ash and dust. The wind’s fingers on his cheeks were colder, and the storm clouds were multiplying, circling each other as they darkened and thickened.

Something was terribly wrong.

Lighting sparked on the clouds. The sky flashed white, and then did it again. The clouds moved together and began to spin like a whirlpool in the sky, directly over his head. From darkness and haze there was suddenly color. Jagged blue lines forked from one cloud to another. The sky became washed with green and black. His skin tingled.

A bright spear of lightning shot to the ground and struck him with instant force.

He screamed. He sizzled from head to toe, along the length of all four limbs. His teeth smashed together. A metallic taste filled his mouth. As his eyes burned with tears, he found himself in darkness, blind.

The vortex of swirling air took hold of him, grabbing hard in an attempt to yank him into the sky. His toes were soon the only part of him still touching the ground. He wanted to resist. He was going somewhere, and he didn't have a choice.

His body flew upward. There was emptiness below him as his feet left the ground.

✦

Something was smothering him. The air around him was thick, like a cocoon of softest silk wrapped around his body, entangling his limbs and filling his vision with darkness.

He couldn't understand where he was. He wanted to open his mouth and try to breathe but every sense told him not to. A glimmer broke through the black. The light was gone as soon as it appeared, but it had an unusual quality. Long buried memories resurfaced. The light rippled and shifted. The sight was familiar.

Water. He was looking through water. He was drowning!

He forced his eyes to stay open and searched for more glimmers of light. His chest was burning. Ribs convulsed inward. His throat longed to open and suck air through his mouth. If he allowed it to happen, only water would fill his lungs.

There. Up there. A brighter area, and farther still, a slick and shimmering surface.

He clawed at the water and kicked with his legs. The light was so far away. He couldn't help it. His lips inadvertently parted and he swallowed some water before his mouth slammed shut. His chest gave another series of spasms. It had been so long since he had felt real pain. Everything hurt.

He could do this. Focusing his attention on the light above, he synchronized the movements of his arms and legs. The rippling surface was closer now. Heave. Kick. Heave. Kick. Air. There was air up there.

With one last heave and kick, he thrust his head above the surface. His first gasp sent stars sparkling across his vision. He concentrated on keeping his head up as he spluttered and coughed. It was painful to breathe at first, but then it felt good. He blinked water out of his eyes. His scraggly hair was in the way, so he pulled it to the side. Taking stock, he saw he was in daylight and the glimpse of rock meant solid land. He was in a wide pool, facing three tall peaks like hulking monoliths, fancifully carved in places, rough in others.

Yet he knew his limbs had lost their strength. As soon as he had the thought, he began to sink.

Searching across the pool's surface, he summoned one last effort. More kicking and crawling in the water took him to the rocky edge, but his legs couldn't find purchase below, and he grabbed hold of a knob to pull himself up. He grunted as he attempted to get his body out of the water. His first try failed and he plunged back into wetness. He made a second try, groaning as he hauled at whatever he could grip, scrabbling with his feet.

And then he was up on the rock. He rolled onto his back and stared up at the pale blue sky as his chest sucked in and out. He gasped and waited to recover.

At last, his breathing evened out, and he sat up, coughing and swallowing when his head swam. He closed his eyes and rested his fingers on his temples until the sensation passed. Bile rose to the back of his throat. He stayed in place until the feeling went away. It was only then that he climbed to his feet, staggering, before at last he stood tall.

He tried to make sense of where he had found himself. He was under the towering height of the three rocky peaks that faced the irregular pool, with the middle one nearly twice the size of the other two. On the other side of the pool, tall columns of glossy black stone formed a perimeter around the water's edge. In between the columns, the sight of manlike figures made him start, until he realized he was looking at statues: grotesque creatures with wings and fangs; hairy men with horns; ghouls in cloaks.

The place was eerie. He checked in all directions but had the sense that he was completely alone.

The surface of the pool was now smooth and mirrored the black columns, the statues, and the three tall peaks. Standing by the water's edge, he leaned over the pool to stare down at the surface.

He watched his reflection. By the gods, he had forgotten how old he was.

His face had more than a few wrinkles, but at least he still looked strong, with shoulders wide enough to match his height—he was taller than most men. His dark hair fell to his shoulders and was threaded with silver. Angry, piercing dark eyes stared back at him. He glanced down at himself; he was clothed in a jerkin and gray doublet, black trousers, and high boots with leather laces. It was practical clothing, the kind he always wore.

He inspected his hands, turning them over, seeing the weathered hands he knew so well, the hands of a warrior. Even the battle scars were still there, pink lines made by sharp blades and then faded by time.

He turned back to the three looming peaks, huddling together like close companions. With its sinister statues and midnight columns of stone, this place felt connected to the world he had just come from, and yet the sky was blue and color filled the landscape. He knew in his bones that he was somewhere special, somewhere anyone with sense would stay away from. He was beginning to understand where he might be, and what it must mean.

One moment he was in the shadow world, where he had believed he needed to stay. He had refused the ghoul's offers, time and again. He couldn't move on to the afterlife. No matter how much he wanted it. Not after what he had done. But then everything had changed.

He had never been here before, but people told stories. The pool... The glossy columns and statues... The three ugly pillars of dark rock... He could only be at the Temple of Black Glass, high on the summit of Mount Janus. This place was special to the black priests and their dark arts. Like ghouls, they represented the lord of the underworld, except that their domain was the realm of the living. Like ghouls, they had power over life and death.

Somewhere, a bird chirped. Another bird replied with a burst of song. He definitely wasn't in the shadow world.

He had been dead, a shade haunting the umbra. His memories were clear. He knew who he was, and how he had died. But now, somehow, he was alive.

"What is this? Am I being tested?" he asked aloud.

As if in response to his question, different, jarring sounds made his head jerk to the side. In a loud burst, he heard shouts and screams. The cries had a familiar quality; they rekindled long-buried memories. His sense of isolation was broken in an instant. He wasn't alone in the world.

The screams were violent. Someone was dying.

Chapter 2

MALGANNIS STOOD WITH HIS EYES UNFOCUSED as the shouts continued. The cries were distant, but close enough. More jangling noises reached his ears: loud clinks of metal on metal.

He had to find out if he was hearing what he thought he was.

He hurried to leave the pool behind, passing the three hulking peaks. A few lonely trees gave way to open, rocky ground that swiftly fell away to form the plummeting slope of the barren mountainside. He knew he was on top of a mountain by the lofty view; in the distance, he saw green plains filling valleys and a wide river, along with forests and smaller mountains. A gust of wind threw itself at him, bringing cold air that smelled of recent rain.

He leaned out to look down as his gaze moved from one place to the next.

The metallic tones of hand to hand fighting rang across the hills as two forces fought each other in the valleys below. Mounted warriors in blue cloaks charged, scattering a group of soldiers in black and red. Arrows arced through the sky. Men screamed and fell. Knights slashed down from horseback, bringing their swords up and down as they tore through the infantry trying to spear them.

A battle was underway, on the mountainside below. Malgannis was familiar with battles. War and fighting were what he knew best. Both groups were trying to seize and hold Mount Janus, the very place where he was standing.

His apprehension spiked with every cry as he watched the different forces. Blue and gold: the colors of Aranor. The soldiers in black and red were from Morania. He searched for the commanders. Why were the two nations fighting? He found the Aranese commander first, in the process of leading a charge with his knights arrayed behind him.

The mounted warrior's armor was bright silver and etched into his helmet was a crown—not only was he the commander, he was the king. From the distance, Malgannis made out brown facial hair, and as the man rode his white courser, twice the size of a normal riding horse, his blue cloak snapped in the wind.

For a fleeting moment, Malgannis felt a burst of hope, but this king was much too young, he couldn't be the son Malgannis had left behind. From the cold and the color of the sky, he guessed it might be winter, but he had no idea how much time had passed. Could the king be his grandson? Or had his line ended?

The king crashed into a group of infantry and fought with skill, wielding a sword from horseback. His enemies cried out as they fell. Yet he couldn't be everywhere, and from what Malgannis could see, the Moranians' numbers were greater, and the soldiers in black and red were beginning to dig in on Mount Janus's upper slopes where they would be difficult to dislodge.

Moving his gaze, Malgannis struggled to locate the commander of the other army among so many soldiers, until his attention was drawn to another warrior, watching the battle from a high ridge where he would be able to give orders.

The Moranian commander sat on the back of a gray warhorse. Tall and imposing, his only insignia was a crisp red symbol on his cloak: the letter 'V'. He wore full plate armor with greaves and mailed gauntlets, along with a striking helmet that revealed nothing of his face, fashioned with facets and a thin slit for his eyes to create a hard, angular impression.

As Malgannis looked on, the Moranian commander pointed and called out to one of his men. Soon after, another wave of soldiers in black and red surged up the slopes of Mount Janus. Archers lined up and loosed a volley of arrows, which sailed through the air toward the soldiers of Aranor.

The Moranians continued to gain ground, and with a growing sense of dread, Malgannis took in the number of soldiers in black and red heading toward him. As he realized the situation was lost, the king of Aranor waved his arm over his head, gathering his forces as he rode away.

"Is this him?"

"Who else could it be?"

The male voices were harsh and loud. Malgannis whirled. He saw three fighters on the open ground, men in black and crimson who were approaching him with swords drawn.

"Remember, we split the gold."

"What if I'm the one who kills him?"

"It doesn't matter. We split the gold. That's the deal."

Malgannis searched the ground for a weapon. He had nothing to fight with and a steep drop at his back.

His strange return to life might not last long at all.

✦

Graven Callow waited impatiently. With great effort, he had seized Mount Janus and the black temple at its summit. For the risk to be worthwhile, he now had to learn the answer to his burning question.

From a distance, he had seen the whirling clouds above the mountain. He had also questioned a black priest. Someone dead had come back to life. Someone important.

Underneath Graven's body, his dappled gray warhorse snorted and pawed at the ground. The stallion was from Nara – all the best horses came from Nara – and Graven had never seen his like. Graven was wearing steel plate armor. His sword was double-edged and it wasn't his only weapon; he also had a couple of spears and a crossbow close at hand. His helmet covered his head completely. Yet with all the weight upon him, the stallion could ride for hour after hour.

As he watched the mountain, Graven heard a series of thuds as another, even heavier horse approached. He sensed movement, and then a deep, rumbling voice spoke at his side.

"Mount Janus was not supposed to be our next target."

Graven glanced at the man speaking. Halvar was a Vailander, and despite his own height, Graven looked small compared to his loyal companion. People were often surprised when they heard that Graven's second was a Vailander, but then they saw his size; the man was a giant. Halvar was no fool either. Anyone who underestimated his intelligence would regret it.

Halvar wore no helmet, revealing black hair cut close to his scalp. His neck and torso were twice the thickness of any other man, and Graven had seen him break a soldier's arm simply by grabbing him too roughly. Along with his bone-white skin, he had the characteristic wide-set eyes of all Vailanders. He rode a draught horse, the only creature big enough to carry his weight, but in battle he preferred to fight on foot.

Halvar continued, "This attack was not planned as it should have been. The enemy almost outmaneuvered us."

"But they didn't, and we were victorious," Graven replied. "Patrick is a new king, young and inexperienced. We were bold and we now hold the mountain. Aranor's army has fled."

"What use is a mountain?"

"Our attack was not about the mountain," Graven said. He kept his focus on the top of Mount Janus, although he could only see a hint of a tall rocky pillar on its summit. "This is about the temple. Someone has returned."

"And your curiosity is worth risking the entire war?" Halvar asked.

Graven raised an eyebrow at the man beside him. "Careful, my friend. I value your service, but remember the colors you wear. My men come mostly from Morania, and you are a stranger here." He returned his gaze to the mountain. "We will soon know if the risk was worthwhile. It must be someone important. Powerful magic demands a high price, and there is nothing more powerful than a rebirth. Whoever he or she is, bringing them back must have come at a terrible cost. And one thing I know is that it was not us. Whoever has come back is an enemy, Halvar. Perhaps someone with the potential to change this war."

"We will see," Halvar said. "I must return to the men."

Halvar jerked at his reins, and as the draft horse lumbered away, Graven continued to watch Mount Janus, an impatient frown creasing his forehead. On the mountain's lower slopes, a cluster of bodies in Moranian colors showed the aftermath of a charge by some knights. Graven didn't feel sorrow for them. Freedom for all was worth the sacrifices of a few.

How close was he now? As long as nothing unexpected took him by surprise, he knew he was winning this war that he had been fighting for months. When he had final victory, it would be worth the struggle.

If there was one thing Graven hated it was exploitation, the idea of a dominating power taking advantage of those unable to fight back. Aranor had long oppressed any weaker nation—which, until now, had been all of them. Their so-called peace required rules to follow and agents to enforce them, and they all needed to be paid. The world had transformed; rather than the honest professions, the farmers and workers, wealth was now concentrated among the lawmakers and arbiters, moneylenders and tax collectors. The soldiers protecting the exploiters also needed to be paid, which meant that Aranor's system for the world was nothing more than a great larceny. Taxes for Aranor. No large national armies. No liberty. No independence. A self-perpetuating machine.

The problem for Aranor was that Morania was no longer weak, and the time for liberation was now at hand. Graven was going to free not just Morania, but all the world's nations. Nothing could go wrong.

He had issued his men with the necessary instructions. Soon they would come back, hopefully with a captive but with a body if they were forced to kill.

He had no qualms about destroying his opponents. The calculation was a simple one—every enemy killed saved lives on his own side. The larger his army was, the faster the war would be over. If he was known as ruthless, he could use fear as a weapon, and force his enemies to surrender, bringing the end forward.

While he waited, he couldn't look away.

✦

Erik sighted along his arrow, even as the muscles in his arms burned. He held his bowstring to his ear, making tiny movements of the stock and arrow, lifting it up and then to the right. His arrow was pointing straight between an enemy's shoulder blades, and he had to hope that when he released it, that was where it ended up.

Through the screen of trees, Erik watched as the tall man with long graying hair turned, clearly surprised to see the three fighters heading his way. Erik heard the three men discuss their prize money and recognized the clipped accent of Morania.

"What if I'm the one who kills him?"

"It doesn't matter. We split the gold. That's the deal."

Erik watched the three fighters spread out, all with naked blades held in front of them. He swore under his breath, knowing he couldn't hold his bowstring tensed for much longer. He had found the man he had been trying to locate, but someone else had reached him first.

The tall man scanned the ground, searching for a weapon. His expression was grim as his hunt was fruitless, but he shifted his body into fighting posture; he wasn't going to be taken easily.

Erik loosed his arrow.

His bowstring thrummed and his arrow sped through the air. One of the three fighters cried out and convulsed, before clawing behind himself to reach the shaft plunged deep into his own back, until he sank to his knees and toppled. The other two Moranians spun around, eyes wide as they tried to find the source of the threat.

Erik threw his bow to the ground and wrapped his hand around the sword hilt at his waist, drawing it swiftly as he burst into a run and left the protection of the trees.

As soon as he saw Erik, the tall man charged. He struck the nearest fighter and they both went down in a tangle. The Moranian lost his sword. In an instant the two men were both rolling as they each tried to gain the upper hand, grabbing at each other's throats, punching with clenched fists.

The last fighter saw Erik coming and readied his sword defensively. Erik knocked the man's blade to the side and attempted a thrust, but the Moranian side-stepped to take himself out of harm's way. The Moranian then hacked down from above, and Erik barred his weapon in front of his face. Steel scraped against steel. Erik disengaged, saw an opening, and stabbed into his opponent's torso. The Moranian gasped and his sword fell out of his hands. He stared down at Erik's blade, before the life left his eyes and he crumpled.

As Erik's attention went straight to the tall man, he realized the brief struggle was over. The stranger stood panting. He was scowling and watching the departing figure of the last of the fighters, who was running hard until in seconds he was gone altogether.

Erik swore, knowing more of them would return. He glanced at the tall man again, and continued to inspect him warily as he wiped his blade clean on the nearest dead man's clothing.

Erik hadn't been given the man's name, but the description he had been given was accurate, or at least accurate enough to know he had found the man he'd been looking for. The stranger wasn't just tall, he was big, with muscled arms and a thick torso. His eyes were dark and piercing and his skin was heavily weathered. Erik had been told he would be old, but he had been expecting a man a man in his fifties, a few decades older than he was. Instead, the stranger looked haggard, like he had been left out in the sun and rain for far too long.

As Erik returned his sword to his scabbard, and then went back to the trees to retrieve his bow, he wondered how long they had before more enemies appeared. He had come armed, but he had thought his mission was a covert one, a quest of stealth and secrets, and he wasn't even wearing armor. He hadn't expected to find the mountain swarming with Moranians, evidently after the same man he had been trying to find.

When he returned to the stranger, Erik couldn't help reveal his frustration. "Why did you let him get away?"

The tall man was rubbing his chin, where a red mark showed where he had been struck. As Erik spoke, his hand stopped moving. "You do realize I am unarmed?"

And too old for running, Erik thought, although he didn't say it out loud. "He's going to come back with more of his friends."

"Then why didn't you stay hidden with your bow?" the stranger growled. "They didn't know where you were. You could have had all three."

"I had to come in fast. They could have killed you."

"You fool, they had forgotten all about me. All they were thinking about was where to take cover. You made the wrong choice."

"I just saved your life." Erik waited for a meaningful length of time. "You are most welcome."

The tall man ignored the comment. "Who are you, anyway?" He glanced past Erik's shoulder, toward the temple. "And what am I doing here?"

"I've been looking for you. I was told to meet you here, today, at the Temple of Black Glass." When the stranger didn't say anything, Erik frowned. "I've come here from Adin."

"Adin?" the stranger asked slowly. "So you're from Aranor?"

"Of course I am. And from your accent, so are you."

The stranger looked again in the direction of the three mysterious peaks and the wide pool in front of them. "Do you know? About..." he trailed off.

"I've been sent to help you, but I haven't been told much."

"Sent? Who sent you?"

Erik's frown deepened. "The king's sister." He paused again. "Princess Coraline?"

"This princess..."

"Princess Coraline."

"Aye, Princess Coraline. What did she say?"

"She said I was to meet you at the Temple of Black Glass. If I didn't find you right away, to search for you. She didn't mention anything else. Such as the fact that you don't seem to know her, but she knows you. I assume it's something to do with the war—" Erik interrupted himself when he remembered something. "Wait. Don't tell me. She said you aren't to reveal your name, or anything about who you are. Not even to me. It's critically important, she said. There are enemies everywhere, and if I'm captured, she doesn't want me to reveal more than I must. All I know is you're someone important." He shot a glance to the side when he heard a loud voice calling for some men to split up. "Now... we're in danger, me as much as you. Where are your things?"

"Eh?"

The stranger's confusion was making Erik increasingly irritated. "Your pack. Where's your weapon? Don't you know there's a war going on?"

"I... I lost my possessions." The stranger gave Erik a calculating look. "They mentioned a bounty, which means I'm a target. Tell me, lad. What's your plan?"

"We need to go to Aranor. That's why I'm here. To get you there."

"Aye, I plan to go home, to Aranor. But what's your plan to get off this mountain?" The calls of searching soldiers grew louder, but still the tall man facing Erik didn't move. "Well, My Lord?"

"I'm not a lord."

The stranger inspected Erik up and down. "You look like you spend more time with scissors than a sword... Whatever you are, you're close enough to a lord to be the same thing." He stood with legs apart and thumbs hooked in his belt. "If we're going to travel together, I want to know your plan. I've only just got here and I'm not quite ready to leave."

Erik's nostrils flared but he fought to remain calm. "King Patrick isn't far from here. He can give us a proper escort. We'll go to him."

The stranger raised an eyebrow. "Are you trying to get killed? They'll be expecting us to try to get to the army. By now, there's a horde of Moranians in the way."

Erik scowled. He had come here with a purpose. He was a long way from home, and in no mood to argue. Not only was the stubborn old man confused and unprepared, he was bedraggled and unkempt. "Well that's where I'm going."

"Off you go, then." The stranger nodded toward where the two armies had been fighting. "On your way."

"You're being hunted, and you would rather travel alone?"

"I don't know you. And I don't like your plan."

"My name is Erik. Erik Wallace." Erik waited, but the stranger didn't give him a name. "You think you can do better without me?"

"If you're going to try to get to that king and his army, then yes, I do."

"Fine," Erik said. He nodded toward one of the fallen Moranian fighters. "Grab yourself a sword. And good luck. I suggest you hide until I return with more men."

Erik strode away, while the old fool watched his back.

Chapter 3

MALGANNIS TRAVERSED A STEEP RIDGE, heading west into the setting sun, hoping to reach the opposite side of the mountain before his path was cut off by the encirclement of Moranian soldiers. The last warmth was leaving the day and the temperature was turning from cool to uncomfortably cold. His breath misted as he panted. There were few trees or bushes, which made him feel exposed. He frequently searched the terrain, wary of the men hunting him.

Rounding a corner, he spied a group of uniformed figures below.

As soon as he saw them, he clambered forward to hide behind a cluster of big boulders, shuffling until he could get a better look without risk of being seen. A rock rolled underfoot and he swore as it tumbled down the slope, making a clatter as it fell. He held his breath and waited to see if anyone noticed.

Twenty or more swordsmen in black and crimson stood just a few hundred feet below the ridge. In this case, the soldiers were waiting, guarding the mountain rather than searching its upper reaches. They had evidently been involved in the recent battle: one had his arm in a sling, while another had a bandage wrapped around his head.

Malgannis's gaze moved farther, and he saw something he hadn't noticed before: half a dozen captives a short distance from the larger group. The six men still wore their blue and gold uniforms. All were blindfolded and on their knees with their hands tied behind their backs.

The Moranians were in discussion, until one of their number, an officer from his smart uniform, shining armor, and brisk stride, walked over to the captives with a dagger in his hand. The officer came to a halt directly behind the nearest captive, a young Aranese soldier with curly hair above his blindfold. The officer inspected his shining steel blade, tilting it to make it glint in the afternoon sun.

Then, with a perfunctory, efficient movement, the officer reached down to slash his dagger across his captive's throat. Malgannis's mouth twisted. He saw the officer had positioned himself to avoid the spurt of blood. The officer shoved the man he'd executed, so that he fell to the side, and then moved on to the next captive. Another swipe with the sharp dagger. Another shove. On to the next captive.

Malgannis swallowed. He wanted to look away but he couldn't. All this death. He knew it had been a long time since he had walked the real world. Yet in his bones, he was a man of Aranor. He had been a general. Not just any general, but a man told about in stories even when he had been alive. The soldiers down there could have been his men. What was everyone fighting for? And what did they want with him?

There were too many Moranians down below. There was nothing he could do to help. All he could focus on was trying to find another way off the mountain. This way was blocked. He would have to take a different path altogether.

As he turned away, he ran his eyes over the area one last time and then he saw a moving shape. He started as he recognized the lean frame, unruly black hair, and huntsman's clothing in place of armor. What was the lad's name again? Erik.

Erik was walking with care, but he didn't know about the group of Moranian soldiers he was about to run into. Malgannis couldn't blame him, he hadn't known about them either until he had been about to pass right above them.

He couldn't help remind himself that Erik had saved his life. The lad was stubborn, and didn't know sense when he heard it, but he didn't deserve to die.

He made a swift calculation. It would be close. He was going to have to throw himself down the mountainside if he wanted to reach Erik in time to warn him.

Urgency made his heart beat faster. He didn't have a choice. He had a debt to repay.

✦

Malgannis ran with his feet digging into the dirt, heart burning and chest sucking in ragged breaths. His arms and legs were scratched. A graze had left a red smear on his right shin. Now that he was a little lower on the mountain, he had no idea where the Moranians were. When he saw Erik up ahead, he knew he couldn't call out. He focused on his sprint and scanned the area until he saw a small cluster of trees a stone's throw from Erik's position.

Erik heard him coming at the last moment. The young man turned and his eyes shot wide open when he saw Malgannis charging him. Erik opened his mouth but he was too late, whatever he had been about to say was cut off as Malgannis slammed into him, slapped a hand onto his mouth and wrapped his arms around him to drag them both into the trees.

Malgannis kept his hand over Erik's mouth and pinned him to a tree trunk, even as he tried to control his own heavy breathing. Erik struggled and writhed. Still Malgannis held him in place. Erik scowled, his eyes narrowed and glaring. Malgannis put on a fierce expression and shook his head, jerking his eyes and head meaningfully, until at last he thought he saw something shift in Erik's expression. He raised an eyebrow at Erik, who gave a slight nod. It was only then that Malgannis removed his hand from the lad's mouth.

Malgannis inspected the young man in front of him, who was perhaps in his early twenties. His square jaw was clean-shaven, he had soft brown eyes, and his mop of black hair was tousled, the kind of hair that never combed straight. Most striking about him was the long, finger-width scar on his right cheek. It would have been nasty when it was fresh, but from the pink color, it had healed long ago. He was a good-looking man, but years ago, when he would have been a child, he had been marked for life.

Erik wore a sheathed sword on one hip and a dagger on the other, both obviously expensive—Malgannis had picked up a dead man's sword for himself and the difference was stark. Even Erik's black vest and trousers were well-stitched and made to size, thick and supple.

Wait. Malgannis frowned. Where was the lad's bow?

He moved his head. Through the foliage, he saw Erik's bow, lying on the ground, in the place where Malgannis had crashed into him. He opened his mouth and then closed it, becoming completely still.

He could hear voices.

Looking past Erik's shoulder, he saw several flashes of black and red uniforms. The cluster of trees provided scant protection. Nearby, Erik put a hand on the hilt of his sword as he turned his head to face the same direction as Malgannis.

Malgannis couldn't see much through the leaves and branches, but soon the voices were loud and clear.

"...feels wrong to leave the bodies where they are. I know they're enemies. It's not about final rites or anything like that. It's just... unhygienic."

"Prisoners can always escape. And you heard the captain. He wants us all searching the mountain."

"Searching for what?"

"For anyone. Alive or dead. There's a bounty."

The man made a sound of surprise. "How much?"

"I don't know. Enough to buy an officer's commission."

"Or a soft bed at a fine tavern."

"You fool. It's going to be a lot more than that."

"Wait. What's this?"

"Show me."

"I found it."

"I know that. Just let me look at it."

From Erik's expression, he knew as well as Malgannis what the two men had found.

"Matching quiver. Wonder what that insignia means? Anyway, it's worth good silver. I could help you sell it?"

"I don't need your help."

"Quick. Hide it before the captain sees."

Malgannis heard the voices grow fainter until they were gone altogether. He allowed himself to shuffle. Peering and moving forward, he scanned until he was sure the Moranians had gone, and then he left the trees, with Erik right behind him.

Malgannis checked one last time before rounding on Erik. "Don't they teach boys any sense these days? You were about to walk right into them. Maybe if you spent less time selecting your clothing—"

"Enough," Erik said. "I would have seen them."

Malgannis shook his head. "Believe what you will. You saved my life, I admit it. Now I've saved yours. We're even." He waited for Erik to speak, but the younger man's stony expression was his only reaction. "Now tell me. Do you still think you can get past them to the king?"

"I probably can—"

“Sure, there’s a chance. But trust me, lad, these are odds you shouldn’t take. You’re young. You’ve got your life ahead of you. You’ve yet to make mistakes, to have regrets. This time is precious. You should hold onto it while you can.”

“Fine,” Erik said. “Which way do you think we should go?”

Malgannis nodded toward the setting sun. “We need to go that way.”

“West?”

“Aye. Across the mountains. Then we go south, toward Aranor.”

“It’s the longer route.”

“Trust me, it’s better than death. And it’s the only choice we have.”

Erik kept his gaze on the taller peaks behind Mount Janus. “You really think you can make it?” He glanced at Malgannis. “No offense intended.”

“You said the princess told you to meet me? She described me?”

“She did.”

“Then I’ll make it.”

Thoughts worked across Erik’s face. “She also told me I had to get back to her as quickly as I could.”

“I’m sure she didn’t tell you to get back to her alive, but no doubt she expects that too.”

Erik considered for a moment and then let out a breath. “All right. We’ll do it your way.”

Malgannis gazed up at the mountain they were currently on. The fading light would help. He began to plot a course over the rocky ground, finding places where two clambering men would be well hidden.

He returned his attention to Erik, who spoke slowly. “I know I’m not supposed to ask questions, but if we’re going to travel together, I have to call you something.”

With a start, Malgannis realized once again that time had passed. No one would call him by his true name or recognize his face. He had an opportunity to connect with his past, to Aranor, his homeland, but also to start fresh. His burden, the weight of his sins, was suddenly lightened. He didn’t have to be Malgannis anymore.

“Call me Morgan,” he said. It was close enough. “Ready to go?” He saw that Erik was still having difficulty abandoning the idea of getting to the king. “You want to get back to your princess, don’t you? What was her name again?”

“Coraline.”

“Aye, Coraline. If you want to get back to her, we need to get moving.”

As Erik fell in beside him, Malgannis left unsaid that his curiosity was burning; he wanted answers. At this point, there was only one person who might have them.

Chapter 4

ADIN WAS ONE OF THE WORLD'S GREAT CITIES, the capital of Aranor and the seat of a long line of kings and queens, across multiple dynasties, stretching back across the ages. And, like all great cities, Adin had secrets.

Nothing good was ever said about the catacombs buried beneath the city. The complex of caves and tunnels were dark and sinister. Ancient peoples had built them to house their dead, and countless human-sized recesses were home to sleeping skeletons. Later, the catacombs were extended to provide places for the citizens to hide in when Adin found itself under assault. In more recent times, brigands used some sections near the docks to hide goods being smuggled to and fro. On the whole, children swapped stories of unholy specters and decent folk stayed clear.

The catacombs were the last place anyone would expect to find Coraline Vandryden.

As the king's sister, she was rarely alone, yet here she was, searching in utter darkness, with only a flaming torch for company. The sense of isolation was unsettling. There was no need to be silent, but she kept her breathing quiet and her footsteps soft. The tunnels were irregular, and her wavering torch projected dancing shadows on the walls. The air was dry and the floor was dusty. Her ears were pricked. With every bend and corner, her eyes were constantly peering.

Cora rounded a bend and bit her lip when she saw a row of alcoves, recesses each filled with an occupant, a dusty skeleton that had once been a man, woman, or child. She shouldn't be here. She should leave, immediately. Inside her head, she kept hearing a voice telling her to go. She had to keep making the decision to keep searching.

She forced her legs to move, one in front of the other, and tried to ignore a grinning skull as she passed it by. Her soft boots made swishing sounds on the hard floor. The tunnel ahead forked, and she decided to take the left bend. She always alternated left and right. That way at least she wouldn't get lost. If taking alternate turns meant she ended up exiting the catacombs, she would return and take a different initial turn. She hadn't always employed a system, but then she had become confused, and it wasn't an experience she wished to repeat.

Cora was determined.

Somewhere in the catacombs below Adin was a black temple, a hidden, terrifying place of dark stone and even darker spirits. She had been to the temple before, but she was blindfolded. Now, after taking every possible opportunity to search, she still couldn't find the temple and the man who took her there five days ago.

Five days. Had it already been so many? She was only given sixty. Where was Erik? She knew he wasn't with Patrick. As she held her torch high and navigated the twisting tunnels, she continued to gnaw at her lip in agitation. She didn't even know if Lexen had kept his bargain. They said a black priest never lied. They always took a price, but they never lied. Nonetheless, she needed to know for certain. Was Malgannis again walking this world?

Cora kept circling numbers through her mind. Sixty days to save her brother the king. Sixty days to save Aranor. Five of those days gone.

Gone.

As the word rang inside her ears, her torch flickered and almost went out. She stopped breathing and halted in her tracks. She found herself in a long, craggy tunnel so deep within the catacombs that without light she would never find her way out again. The wavering flame sank low, quivered, and seemed uncertain, before gradually rising up again. She began to breathe once more.

But then she froze.

She wasn't the only one breathing.

The torch shot up before she could think, held high in the tight grip of her slender fingers. The sound of hoarse breath became louder, nearer. Her mind conjured up a vision of a hideous creature, jaws open wide to reveal rows of yellow teeth as it lunged forward out of the darkness. Whatever it was, it was ahead of her. She resisted the urge to turn and flee, and instead held her ground.

A figure appeared out of the darkness.

He was a man in a black hooded robe, with a narrow, pale face visible within his cowl. His robe stretched to the ground, obscuring his feet, but his frame was slender, and although he wasn't tall, his height was greater than hers. His cheekbones were high, and his cheeks were shiny, almost feverish. The dark eyes above his sharp nose were piercing. When he pulled back his hood, his hair was close-cropped and completely gray.

Cora knew her chest was rising and falling far too fast, but she managed to put steel into her voice. "You are a difficult man to find, Lexen Crow."

The black priest was unperturbed. "When I wish to be." His voice was smooth, confident. "Curiosity brought me here. We made our bargain. It is done. What do you want, Princess Coraline?"

Cora felt anger rise within her and fed it; the fire kept her fear at bay. "The Moranians moved their forces toward the Temple of Black Glass." She felt her grip on the torch become even tighter. "No one could have known but you. You told them."

She waited to hear the truth. Lexen had betrayed her to her nation's greatest enemy. He had made a mockery of their bargain.

But surprisingly, he smiled and shrugged.

"I did not. But at any rate, your brother would not let Graven Callow seize Mount Janus uncontested. No doubt you have friends in the region, as well as enemies."

Cora took a step forward, raising her torch high to illuminate Lexen's face. "We had an agreement. Our pact was supposed to remain secret. Answer me. Why now? Why would Graven go for the temple?"

Lexen's eyes narrowed, the torchlight reflecting from his pupils. "As I have already said, I shared nothing. What I can tell you, Princess, is that when a fissure opens between this world and the shadow world, it announces itself to anyone of my order who is listening." He gave a sardonic smile. "As you can imagine, it is not something that happens every day. Your enemies must have wondered who was coming back and why. They would worry that it must be something – someone – come to work against them."

Cora wasn't expecting the black priest's reply. "Graven Callow wants to know who it was?"

"In short, yes. Anyone of my rank could alert him. He would assume it is an enemy returned."

Cora hesitated. Whether or not Lexen was telling the truth, the facts remained. She had done what she had done, and now it might be all for nothing. "What if Malgannis is killed?"

"Then he goes back to where he came from," Lexen said bluntly.

"And our bargain?"

"Remains," he drew out the word, speaking in a soft, sibilant voice. "This is what we do, Princess. The lord of the underworld needs the life force of the living and the souls of the dead. All bargains are honored, and all bargains are freely made, as you yourself know. What happens afterwards is not under our control."

Cora tried to take charge of her whirling thoughts. Her plan wasn't finished yet. She had to do what she could to help the people she cared about.

She realized she might not find Lexen again. While she was here, she needed information.

"How do I know if Malgannis is alive?" she asked.

"I would know if he had left this world." Lexen's eyes lost focus for the briefest instant. "He is alive."

"And Erik?"

"Your childhood companion?" This time, Lexen closed his eyes. "He is also alive."

"I have more questions—"

The black priest raised a warding hand. "We are finished here, Princess. I have nothing more to say."

Cora leveled her gaze on the man in front of her. "If I never see Malgannis face to face, I will do everything I can to make you suffer."

Lexen only smiled. "First, Princess, you will have to find me."

✦

Cora hurried back to the palace. It was a cool, clear evening. She wore simple clothes – leggings and doublet she liked to ride in, all covered in a gray cloak – and few city folk gave her any attention. She walked with long strides as she swept through the narrow streets and past the stone terraced houses, climbing ever upward to reach the high road that led to the grand edifice that dominated the city: Adin Palace.

She again went through what she knew.

When Malgannis was reborn at the Temple of Black Glass, he would have been alone and confused.

She couldn't ask her brother the king for help, not without revealing what she had done, and that was something she could never do. Instead she had sent someone she trusted meet Malgannis and bring him to her: Erik.

She hadn't been counting on the enemy also moving to intercept, and then Patrick hurrying to counter him.

Cora had recently learned that Erik wasn't with Patrick, and nor was anyone matching Malgannis's description. But according to Lexen, Malgannis and Erik were alive.

Her brow was furrowed as she walked. The important thing was that they were alive. She had to assume Erik and Malgannis were together and had evaded the enemy. Graven Callow's forces might have cut them off, in which case Erik would take a different route. Potentially one much longer.

What Erik didn't know was that Cora was running out of time. He didn't know about the sixty days. She couldn't wait for him to reach her.

She had to go to him.

The palace loomed up ahead, growing larger in her vision as she neared. A causeway led from the city to the high stone wall enclosing the palace and the twin gates set into it. The palace was on its own island, connected to the main city, and water splashed on both sides of the thin strip of land. As she crossed, she ignored the drop at both sides, but then, halfway along, she saw something that made her stop.

Downstream, where the Sylvan River opened up and became wide enough for ships to rest at anchor, she saw a cluster of vessels that hadn't been there before. Three warships with graceful prows and streamlined hulls bobbed up and down, and even in the fading light, she recognized the colors of the flags flying from the masts. Blue and red: the ships were from Fastness.

Someone new was in the city. Someone who was going to disrupt all of her plans.

✦

The Baron of Fastness's welcome dinner was hastily arranged. Cora changed into a navy dress that left her shoulders bare. Her handmaidens frantically worked at her dark hair, twining it and twisting it, until she had a loose, complicated braid that spilled down her back between her shoulders. She wore a sparkling necklace, and her index finger displayed her golden ring with a square sapphire, a precious gift from her father. The moment she was ready, she hurried to the grand staircase, where she knew her unexpected guest was waiting.

"Ah, Princess Coraline. You are radiant as ever," said Logan Kane, Baron of Fastness.

He turned to face her, smiling at her from the bottom of the staircase. With him was Lord Byron; no doubt the two men had been sharing gossip.

Taking a steadying breath, Cora regarded Lord Kane as she descended, keeping one hand on the polished rail. He was tall and athletic, with smooth skin the color of ebony and close-cropped salt-and-pepper hair. Despite his conservative clothing in black and gray, the material was supple and perfectly fitted to his frame. He always wore dark colors, ever since the death of his wife by fever, but he was also a man who had never needed to broadcast his status. He was almost a king in his own right, a ruler with an independent streak who always sought more autonomy for his island domain, and he was one of the most powerful lords in the realm.

Cora reached the bottom of the staircase, giving Lord Kane a warm smile as she approached. Despite her inner turmoil, she knew she appeared confident; she might be just twenty-two but she had spent her entire life at the palace. "Lord Kane, you are kind," she said. She held out her arm, and he pressed his lips to the top of her hand. "And Lord Byron." She turned to the second man. "You are well? And your family?"

"They are all well, My Lady. Well, in truth, you know my wife... she worries about this war, and never understands when I tell her I cannot share secrets of the realm," Lord Byron said, spreading his hands.

Lord Byron contrasted with Lord Kane. He was swarthy and heavy-set, with a round face and wide belly. He liked bright colors and had a passion for silk, and tonight he wore a crimson sash like a belt around his waist, over an emerald doublet and yellow leggings. Glittering jewels crowned his fingers. He was a local lord, from Adin, and a good man, Cora's father had always said. But from the way he kept glancing at Lord Kane, Cora knew he would defer to the man beside him.

"Lord Kane, I regret I wasn't here to welcome you," Cora said. "We were not expecting you quite yet."

Cora kept her expression both calm and warm, but she knew that if her handmaidens had been frantic, the palace stewards and maids would have been panicked. Rooms needed to be prepared. The dining hall had to be laid out. The cooks would have been distraught trying to prepare a suitable welcome meal.

"The responsibility is mine," he said with an apologetic smile. "Winter seas are never easy, and when we had a fair breeze and smooth waters, I had to seize the opportunity to bring my visit forward. We in Fastness must stay abreast of events on the mainland, as I am sure you can understand."

"Of course," Cora said. She hid her frustration. She now had two conflicting priorities, to find Erik and Malgannis before her time ran out, and to keep Lord Kane's good will. The last thing her brother needed was a breakaway province in the midst of a war. Instead, what he needed was the Baron of Fastness's silver and his men.

"We are grateful to have you here," Cora said. She inclined her head toward the dining hall. "Shall we?"

"With pleasure."

Soon Cora was seated at the long table with members of the nobility arranged around her. Lord Byron sat at her right hand. Lord Kane was opposite. Lord Phelps, an older noble who was hard of hearing and blind in one eye, was on Cora's other side, while Lady Pike, a gray-haired woman with hawklike features, sat at Phelps's good side. Cora knew she was positioned so that the conversation would mostly be between her and the two lords whose words carried the most weight.

"What news from Fastness?" Cora asked.

"I have little to report, My Lady," Lord Kane said. "The markets are busy. Merchant ships come and go. The silver mines are productive." He hesitated. "Unlike here on the mainland. How goes the war?"

Cora felt a flash of irritation when he directed his words at Lord Byron beside her.

Byron glanced at Cora and then replied. "The king met Graven Callow in battle near Mount Janus."

"And?"

"The battle was indecisive," Byron said.

"But the Moranians held the mountain."

Cora kept her face expressionless. "You are well-informed."

Lord Kane shrugged. "It is hard to knock men off a mountain. Mount Janus brings the enemy one step closer to Vestria's capital Ballina. What do you think, Byron? Is Patrick still too young to have supreme command?" He caught himself and addressed Cora. "Apologies, My Lady. Perhaps we should leave these discussions for later."

"My brother does his best," Cora said calmly.

"Of course," Lord Kane said. "No one doubts his commitment."

Cora stared directly into Lord Kane's eyes. "I am well aware of the challenge he faces. He is a new king in difficult circumstances. I am also aware that he always needs more men."

Now Lord Kane looked uncomfortable. "We in Fastness will always help the realm. Yet we have many concerns that are not shared here in Adin."

"Such as?" Cora asked.

He frowned, and Cora wondered if she had gone too far. "Such as piracy and raiding." He paused, and a sudden silence fell over Cora's section of the long table. Then he gave her a slight smile. "Let me suggest something, Princess Coraline. Spend the day with me tomorrow. Convince me. Tell me why I should send more levies to the front."

For a moment, Cora couldn't reply. She thought about her encounter with the black priest. She had to find Erik. Time was passing. She couldn't wait for him to bring Malgannis to her.

"Lord Kane—"

"Please, call me Logan."

Cora reminded herself. Her brother needed the baron's men.

She kept her face carefully blank. "Of course, Lord Kane," she said, and then smiled. "Logan, I should say. I have no plans for tomorrow. I would be honored to spend the day with you."

Chapter 5

DARKNESS, CRISP AIR, AND SHIMMERING STARS enveloped the Farrion Mountains. The place Malgannis and Erik chose to make their cold camp was like the lowest point in a cupped hand with the fingers spread apart, a valley set snugly within a circle of peaks. The surrounding high ground blocked the wind. A stretch of tough grass would make their beds. It was the best they could do, but it was going to be a chilly night.

Malgannis straddled a rock and chewed a salted strip of meat, relishing the savory taste. He took a swig of fresh mountain water and then followed the meat with a handful of nuts and dried fruit. Last of all, he tilted back a mug and gulped down mouthfuls of oats soaked in water.

Salty. Wet. Crunchy. Sweet. Mushy.

The tastes and textures were so familiar – of course they were – and yet even after a few days he still found himself getting used to the idea of being alive. He was weary to the bone. His muscles ached and his arms and legs were scratched red and raw.

Was it worth it, to have these unpleasant sensations, just so he could experience the occasional surge of pleasure? What was he doing here? If he had thought life's pleasures to be so important, he would have accepted the ghoul's offer. There were more important things. There were sins. And debts. There was redemption.

Only Coraline could give him answers.

Malgannis glanced at Erik, who sat on another rock and was finishing his own mugful of sodden oats.

Malgannis wondered how Erik would react if he told him the truth.

"Wish we could have a fire," Erik said. Setting down his mug, he cupped his hands in front of his mouth and blew on them. "How long can this winter last?" Shaking his head, he reached over to his pack and rummaged inside. One after another, he retrieved two tightly folded packages. "Here." He tossed one bundle to Malgannis, before unwinding the other to reveal a thin blanket. "It's not much, but it's something."

As Malgannis caught his blanket, he realized his earlier instincts had been correct. It was late winter, nearly spring, or perhaps spring had begun but the change wasn't yet noticeable. Little by little, he was understanding the world he had found himself in.

He noticed Erik staring at him. "What?"

"You're lucky I always travel with spare supplies."

Malgannis understood the accusation. Other than the sword he had picked up and the clothing he was in, he had no possessions at all. "Like I said, I lost my things. We're still not out of danger. I can't tell you any more." He was glad that the princess's instructions meant he didn't have to explain; he was tired and in no mood for it.

Erik opened his mouth but then closed it. Instead, when Malgannis stretched his arms above his head and groaned, Erik frowned. "We've got some tough ground to cover tomorrow. Are you sure you're going to be able to keep up?"

Malgannis stopped moving. "I was just asking myself the same thing." He relaxed and gave a wave of his hand. "I'll be fine, lad. This just isn't easy when you're my age."

"And how old is that?"

"Fifty-eight." The age Malgannis was when he died.

Erik made a sound of surprise. "I would have thought you were at least sixty-five."

"Sixty-five?" Malgannis's eyes narrowed. Then, after a moment, he shrugged. "Life is hard when you've had a hard life. How old are you, then, lad?"

"Twenty-four."

"Married?"

"No."

"A man your age should be married by now. Especially a lord, or a lord's son, or whatever you call yourself."

Erik's tone became icy. "I am not a lord's son."

Malgannis guessed he had struck a nerve. "Is that so? There's a story there."

"Not one I'm willing to share."

"Fair enough... Tell me then, why aren't you married? I had a wife and child when I was your age."

"I'm a little busy these days," Erik said sarcastically. "You know. With the war."

"Even with that scar, you're still handsome enough." Malgannis stared directly at the scar below Erik's right eye. "How did you get it, anyway?"

Erik's hand tugged upward, as if he were about to put his hand over his scar but managed to resist. "I was a child. It was a long time ago."

Malgannis placed his hands on his knees and leaned forward as he watched Erik's face, waiting. Before long, he realized that the short response was all he was going to get. "People are going to be curious, lad. You might as well have a story ready."

When Erik kept his lips sealed, Malgannis gazed up at the heavens, watching the stars, and found himself looking directly at the Southern Ring, the circle of stars that always pointed south. He again pondered his situation.

He had died a long time ago. He hadn't even heard of these present-day kings and princesses. What year was it? He wondered if he could find out.

"The king, Patrick..." he said, "how long has he been in power?"

"Only two months." Erik noticed Malgannis's surprise. "King Owen died. That's how Patrick became king..."

Owen.

Malgannis tried not to show his reaction, but he felt a sudden shock. With the single name, he had learned much more than he had expected.

Long ago, Malgannis had a son, a son who became the first Vandryden king of Aranor after Malgannis turned down the throne. Malgannis's son, Alfred, went on to have a son of his own.

Owen.

Malgannis remembered a babe, a chubby boy with a cap of brown hair. He was just eight months old when Malgannis last saw him, crawling, on the cusp of taking his first steps. He had an easy-going nature, always smiling and reaching out to people.

"Owen's father... he was Alfred?" Malgannis asked slowly.

"Of course." Erik's bemused nod confirmed it.

Owen... the same Owen who had died two months ago... was Malgannis's grandson. All of a sudden, this war... everything he was experiencing was brought much closer to Malgannis himself.

"You said Owen died. How old was he?"

"Fifty-five."

"And his father? Alfred?"

Malgannis thought of his charismatic, clever son. Malgannis had raised Alfred the way his own father had raised him, focusing on stewardship and leadership, military strategy and history. Regret was in Malgannis's mind, as it always was when he reflected on his relationship with his son. He had loved Alfred, but in his final years he had been consumed by his quest to hunt down his greatest enemy, until, in his moment of triumph, the quest killed him.

"King Alfred died of old age," Erik said. "Over seventy, I think."

Malgannis felt relief mingle with his sadness. He now had to find out about his grandson. "And Owen? How did he die?"

"In battle."

"Tell me," Malgannis said.

The starlight was bright enough for Malgannis to see Erik's face. "Graven Callow laid siege to Inadris. The king led the army to liberate the city. He was too late. Agents of the enemy were inside the walls and opened the northern gate. When King Owen got there, the Moranians had already burned the city to the ground. There was nothing left to fight over, no one left to save."

Erik looked away before continuing.

"The king battled the Moranians anyway. Graven Callow met him on the field and they fought in single combat." The tension was evident in Erik's posture, in his eyes and jaw. "They say Graven has a gift, or a curse... the lord of the underworld has given him skill beyond that of a normal man. King Owen and Graven Callow fought with swords, and Graven won. He cut the king's head off in front of his men."

Malgannis sucked in a sharp breath. *He killed my grandson. He cut his head off.*

"We took the king's body and left the Moranians in possession of the battlefield," Erik finished.

"You were there?" Malgannis asked softly.

Erik nodded. "My rank is captain."

Malgannis remembered the helmeted warrior on the gray warhorse. Graven Callow... the man who had killed his grandson.

He then had another realization. He pictured a proud figure in silver armor with a blue cloak that snapped in the wind.

"How old is King Patrick?"

"Just twenty-five. Princess Coraline is his younger sister."

Patrick. Coraline.

Malgannis's great-grandchildren.

"You know the princess well?"

"Since we were children."

Malgannis's curiosity about Erik grew. He said he wasn't a lord's son, but he had grown up with a princess, the daughter of a king. Yet Malgannis also knew what Erik's reaction would be if he pressed him further, and he turned his thoughts instead to the war he had found himself in.

"What does Graven Callow fight for?"
"Victory."
Malgannis scowled. "You know what I'm asking, lad. There's always something that binds a force together, even if it's a cloak, a made up fiction."
"You know what the Code of Aranor is?" Erik asked.
Malgannis gave no reaction, but long ago, he had given the code its name. "I think I do, but you tell me."
"After the Great War, nearly, what... seventy years ago, Aranor became powerful. King Alfred brought about peace, and Aranor and the other nations invented a common set of rules. They outlawed slavery, for example. Set a standard for weights and measures."
"The Code of Aranor," Malgannis said.
"There's a movement to end the code, and Graven Callow has taken advantage of it. He says the other nations have lost independence. Had their culture changed. He wants the old laws, the old coins, and if he wants a bigger army, he doesn't want anyone saying otherwise. He calls himself a liberator."
Malgannis had the same people back in his day. "Aye, I've heard it before."
"And now we're at war," Erik said.
"Morania was always strong," Malgannis mused. "Still, they must have allies."
"Nara and Kor fight with them. Some of the things Graven does are popular, and people are paying attention. In Morania, he removed all of the queen's tax collectors—he says it can be the foreign traders who pay the taxes. The one thing he hasn't changed is the ban on slavery. In fact, he's got a new list of what he calls 'crimes of exploitation', all punishable by death."
Malgannis considered. When he had died, he had left Aranor as the greatest nation the world had known. Much had changed.
"And on the field? What is he like as a general?"
"He makes his own rules. No quarter given."
Malgannis remembered another time, and another enemy. During the great war, Malgannis had fought Baelock Fain of Vailand. He also had no time for the rules of war.
Erik continued, "He says he will end the war quickly, but then uses that to justify the things he does. If a town or city doesn't surrender, they destroy everything. Rumandy has fallen. If Patrick can't hold Vestria, and falls back to Aranor, no one thinks we can survive." He focused on Malgannis. "And somehow, you fit into all this. These are strange times, Morgan."
Graven Callow killed my grandson. He cut his head off.

"Morgan?" Erik repeated.

"All we can do is keep moving." Malgannis cleared his throat. "Soon we'll be at the Wormwood. Then, once we're through, we'll find a boat."

"Lake Raynor?"

"Aye." Malgannis nodded. "We'll cross the lake. Over to Grenford."

"Grenford?"

"It's a traveler's town. By the lake."

"Waygather? South edge of the lake?"

"Erm... Yes. Waygather. Then we can provision at Leventhal on our way to Aranor."

When Erik gave Malgannis a strange look, Malgannis suppressed a curse. He had probably said the wrong thing again. "What is it now?"

"Leventhal was abandoned thirty, forty years ago. The river dried up. No water. It's just ruins now." Erik shook his head. "How can you not know?"

"I've been gone for a long time. Across the Sea of Mirrors."

Malgannis was again reminded about how much time had passed. He gazed past Erik at the distant stars, and then his eyes unfocused as a feeling of sadness and regret settled over him.

He remembered blood and battle. He was on the hills outside the stone city of Leventhal, sitting by a fire, when they told him that the Vailanders had murdered his wife and daughter. The raiders traveled by sea and struck the coast of Aranor from the west. He was just the second son of a minor noble back then. A country lord from Rathlee.

"Morgan. Morgan?"

Erik again broke Malgannis out of his reverie. "Eh?"

"Are you still with me?" Erik asked, exasperated. "Where did you go, just now?"

"Just spending some time in the past." Malgannis harrumphed. "Best we get some rest, and then we'll cross the mountains tomorrow."

Chapter 6

MALGANNIS GLANCED OVER AT ERIK as he made a sound of disgust and his boot sank into a pool of mud. Erik yanked out his foot and then brushed a wriggling white creature as thick as his finger from his leg. He scowled at Malgannis, who was watching with amusement.

"Now you know why they call it the Wormwood," Malgannis said.

It was as much a swamp as it was a forest. After the mountains, it had been a relief to descend into gentler terrain, but gradually the trees had changed in nature until they were gnarled and ugly, with roots that were sometimes submerged in sticky liquid. There often wasn't much space between them, so that Malgannis and Erik had to slither between trunks and wade through bogs. Vines hung from above and were far too eager to grab hold of the two men with their snaky arms and prickly thorns. The air smelled foul, strong enough to taste on the tongue, so that the two travelers had to navigate the forest with their lips firmly sealed.

Even as Malgannis trudged through the mud and clambered over fallen tree trunks, he looked at his companion. "Don't worry. It'll get easier when we find a trail."

"Who says we will?"

"Fishermen need boats. Boats are made of wood. Wood comes from trees. Plus, there's hunting in here, if you know where to look."

est. "Hunting?" His gaze rested on a slug the
n, slithering from one hanging vine to another.
k his head. "Well, at least we've lost anyone after us.
n't expect us to travel through.... this."

think." Malgannis cautioned, but then gave a short laugh. "But you've probably got the right of it there." He turned his head, scanning the sky, until he caught sight of the afternoon sun. "We need to head a bit more that way," he said, nodding toward the sun.

There was silence for a time as they reached a flat section with straighter trees and clearings and they were able to pick up their pace, making up for the time spent trudging through the swamp.

"But what if we're nowhere near a fishing town?" Erik asked.

"They're all along the lake."

"Sorry if I can't say I'm filled with faith. You didn't know Leventhal was in ruins. You didn't know anything about the war." Erik gave a short laugh. "Do you even know what year it is?"

Malgannis's eyes narrowed, but he remained silent.

"You don't know?" Erik's smile faded. He waited, but Malgannis didn't answer. "King Alfred began a new calendar, after the Code of Aranor was signed. He started it from the end of the Great War."

"I know that," Malgannis said curtly.

"If you do, then all you have to do is work out how many years it's been since we won the war against Vailand."

Erik paused again, waiting for Malgannis to speak. Malgannis finally muttered, "They use a different calendar across the sea."

"Sixty-six years, Morgan. That's how long it's been."

Malgannis kept his face blank. He had died a decade after the war's conclusion. He had been dead for fifty-six years. His nearest relatives were now his great-grandchildren.

Knowing that Erik was watching him, he thought he should say something. "Sixty-six." He nodded. "I thought as much. You lose track of things when you've been away for a long time."

Dead for more than five decades. Malgannis briefly felt light-headed, out of place, certain in the knowledge that he didn't belong where he was. With an effort, he took hold of himself and decided he didn't want to dwell on it. He would learn more about where he was and what had changed. It would all feel familiar soon enough.

"Look," he said, looking up ahead as he found a chance to change the subject. Through the trees, he saw the clear outline of a trail. Not the hint of an animal track, but a proper path, muddy but wide. "When there's a big lake nearby and a rotting forest, there's only one place this is going. A settlement. You might get to have a bath and wash your hair, lad."

Malgannis looked for a reaction but Erik ignored the comment, pushing past Malgannis to make his way through the foliage, eager to be free of the clawing branches. Malgannis followed behind, and as he emerged from the trees, Erik called out in front of him, his voice low but urgent.

"What is it?" Malgannis hurried forward.

Erik was crouching in the mud. "Tracks," he said. His expression was worried, and Malgannis soon saw what he had noticed. The imprints of horse hooves stretched along the trail, heading in the direction of the lake. The horses were evenly matched in size and their hooves were iron-shod. The imprints were deep; the riders were heavy.

"Soldiers," Erik said. "If they're searching the road for us, we're in danger. We're going to leave our own tracks. We can't help it."

Malgannis gazed along the trail, first in one direction, then the other. He kept his ears pricked, but couldn't hear anything. "It's worth the risk," he finally said. "We'll have to be careful, that's all."

✦

Malgannis waded through the muddy waters by the banks of Lake Raynor. He tried not to think about how much sound he was making. Instead, he kept his eyes on the prize: a wooden fishing boat, tied with a long rope that stretched all the way to the high ground.

The sky was clear, with a hint of yellow on the horizon but the rest a midnight shade of blue. It was early, too early to call dawn, but light enough to see just a little. White mist clouded the great lake's boundary. The mountains that encircled the area were looming silhouettes.

Malgannis reached the boat and grabbed the gunwale. Now standing in waist-deep water, he pushed down. Hard. Water began to pour in, first in a trickle and then a flood. As the wooden fishing boat filled with water, it began to sink, which made his task easier.

He heard a splash and glanced over his shoulder to see Erik in the process of sinking his own boat. Malgannis's eyes continued moving, until he was watching the nearby fishing village. There was little wind, and the pale mist made it difficult to see the row of wooden houses, but still he searched for signs of danger. He was worried, remembering the tracks they had found in the road. Whoever was hunting them was determined.

The idea of sinking the boats had been Erik's. Malgannis had to reluctantly admit, the lad had some cunning. The wooden vessels wouldn't be hurt by some time underwater, and they had a chance to prevent or slow any pursuit.

Malgannis continued to push down until he had completely sunk the boat. He tried to work quietly, but noise was inevitable, and he heard more splashes from Erik behind him.

His work finished, he focused his attention on the last of the fishing boats still bobbing on the lake's surface. Despite his best efforts, he felt anxious as he waded through the chilly water and left swirls in his wake. He reached the boat just as Erik came to join him. With all of the others sunk, this was the vessel they would use to cross the lake. Malgannis first checked inside to see that the boat had oars. He spied them right away, tied with rope to the gunwale. Erik held the boat while Malgannis climbed in, and then it was Erik's turn to tumble over the side.

"Can you row?" Malgannis asked urgently.

"No."

"Then head to the bow."

As Erik and Malgannis both moved, the boat tilted dangerously. Malgannis seated himself in the center and began to plant the oars in their slots, while Erik headed to the front of the boat.

From the direction of the village, a horse gave a loud, startled whinny.

Malgannis shot a fearful glance toward the village. This wasn't the kind of place where people had horses; it made no sense. The locals used boats to get around. There was no road around the lake's edge. There were no fields to give work animals any purpose. Out here, horses meant strangers.

He fumbled with the oars, suddenly clumsy.

"Morgan..."

As soon as he heard Erik's warning tone, Malgannis lifted his gaze, but at first he couldn't see anything in the direction Erik was staring. The muddy bank stretched up to the higher ground. Farther away, heavy mist swirled in the trees.

He continued to look, and then the slightest puff of air cleared the mist away from the trees. A motionless shape gradually appeared. The distant figure was that of a tall man, mounted on a powerful horse. He wore plate armor, along with an angular helmet with a slit for his eyes that gave nothing away.

Graven wanted them. Malgannis knew that he was too far away to make out detail, and yet he also knew that this man's attention was utterly focused on the two men in the boat. He had promised his men a bounty, and yet lost them in the mountains.

Graven Callow turned his head to call something. Malgannis then saw uniformed soldiers running past their leader on both sides to race toward the water's edge. The mist continued to clear and the sky grew lighter. Graven turned his head toward something farther along the lake's edge.

Following with his eyes, Malgannis's dread became sharp and visceral. A second group of fishing boats, three or four of them, lay side by side, high up on the bank. With the low light and mist, he hadn't seen them before.

"We need to get out of here." Erik knew there was no longer any use in keeping quiet. "Now!"

Malgannis took both oars and pulled. At first it felt like they were barely moving, and then the stretch of water separating them from the lake's edge began to get wider. Malgannis faced the muddy bank as he hauled at the oars, churning the water into foam.

Erik was looking in the same direction. "Faster," he warned. His voice grew more urgent. "Pull harder!"

Then Malgannis realized what Erik had seen. A group of archers was hurrying down to the bank, reaching the place where the dry ground began to soften into mud. Even as Malgannis rowed with all his strength, the archers fitted arrows and bent back to point their bows into the sky.

Malgannis felt helpless, unable to change position or shield his body. All he could do was keep rowing as he heard the whistle of arrows and saw black shafts pepper the dawn sky.

"Here it comes!" Erik warned.

An arrow plunged into the water just two feet from the boat. Another struck the hull to lodge quivering in the bottom of the boat, inches from his foot. Meanwhile Graven remained where he was, with only the stirring horse below him the sign of his impatience.

Malgannis kept pulling at the oars, knowing his and Erik's lives depended on it. The distance grew. More dark arrows arced through the sky, but they all struck the water, several feet short of the boat.

Malgannis glanced again at the last few boats. The wooden vessels stayed where they were, and he finally realized that as high up on the bank as they were, they must be boats in need of repair. Even as he felt relief, he kept pulling at the oars. As long as he kept rowing, they would make it.

Graven Callow continued to watch, but soon his figure became tiny, and the village itself vanished from view.

Chapter 7

SOMETIMES, THERE WAS NOTHING more tiring than keeping up a pretense.

Cora had spent another day with Logan Kane, Baron of Fastness. At his request, over the past two days they had gone riding together in the woods near Adin Palace, boating on the Sylvan River, and had toured the palace gardens. As was proper given his rank, they had shared two private luncheons and another dinner with some nobles from the king's council. Cora kept bringing up the war, and her brother's desperate need for additional levies, and Logan kept turning the conversation to her, and to her hopes and aspirations.

Cora was always composed and assured. She laughed and spoke warmly. She never revealed her worry and agitation. Yet she knew that these were days she couldn't afford to lose. She felt like she was trapped inside an hourglass, with the sands of time trickling through her open fingers. While she was riding and boating, Erik would be trying to get to Aranor with Malgannis. She had to find them.

It was late and dinner had at last concluded. Cora swept gracefully past stewards and maids on her way to her personal quarters, which occupied an entire wing of the palace. It wasn't until she entered and heard the heavy wooden door close behind her that she allowed her true feelings to show.

She wiped a hand over her face. Weariness weighed on her shoulders. Despite the fact that her shining dark hair was in an elaborate braid, there were loose curling strands along its length. She thought she was more skinny than slender; she hadn't been eating well, ever since the war. Even the sight of her shining yellow dress and golden jewelry made her angry. What she wanted was to get on a horse, to run, to fight. Instead she was making pleasantries with a man twice her age.

"My Lady, a message."

With a start, Cora turned to see a young woman in uniform. The maid stood uncertainly with a piece of rolled up paper held carefully in both hands. Cora's attention went straight to the unbroken seal. Blue wax, imprinted with a circle of stars. A yellow ribbon.

She knew immediately. The message was from her brother.

"One of the stewards, he gave it to me and said to find you—" the maid began when Cora didn't speak.

Cora couldn't hide her urgent tone. "Give it to me. Please." The maid came forward and handed out the scroll. "Thank you. That will be all."

She waited until the maid had left and then swiftly opened the message.

My sister. I trust you are safe and as well as can be expected. It fills me with relief to know that Erik is there with you. I know he must be eager to get back to the fighting. It is better he stays with you.

This is difficult for me to write. Things do not go well. There are many who resent my command, and perhaps they are right, perhaps I am indeed too inexperienced. We are being pushed back toward Huron Plain and Vestria's capital. We are trying to hold but Graven Callow is always one step ahead of us.

Oh, Cora, I am sorry to share my fears with you, to cast that burden upon your shoulders too. Here, with the men, I must be the strong one. There is no one with whom I can simply be me. There is only you.

I am not sleeping well. The nightmares do not end. I try to maintain a firm grip on hope, but by all the gods, it is difficult. I fear what will happen if the army falls. Our enemy makes no secret of his wish to invade Aranor. We are the cause of every trouble that has ever plagued this world, or so he believes. My utmost dread stems not only from the conquest of our homeland, but our final end. This is an enemy who does not create but only destroys. He will burn our towns and villages. He will tear down our cities. He will enslave our people and salt our fields. You cannot understand the extent to which he hates us.

My sister, if the army falls, if we fail, you must immediately flee. Not to Fastness and not to the free towns of Nara. You must find a ship to take you across the Sea of Mirrors, to where our enemy can never find you...

Cora allowed her hand holding the paper to fall.

But she blinked away her tears as she lifted her chin. There was now resolve in the set of her jaw.

"Silvia!" she called.

When Cora didn't hear a reply, she left the area to head down a hallway. She peeled a curtain aside to enter one of the rooms off to the side.

"Silvia?"

Despite the late hour, the older woman wasn't sleeping. She sat on a chair in the corner, a piece of embroidered cloth on her lap and a needle and thread in her hand. Silva was slim and straight-backed, with flaxen hair and a careworn face. She was a lady of the court and Cora's handmaiden. At times, she also knew Cora better than she knew herself.

Silvia's eyes went straight to the message, still in Cora's hand. "What is it?"

"A message. From Patrick."

Silvia quickly leaned forward. "And?"

Cora didn't reply. She simply shook her head.

"Answer me," Silvia said sternly. "Is he wounded? Has he been defeated?"

Cora felt immediately small, in that way that only Silvia could make her feel. "No." She took a deep breath. "But he says it's just a matter of time."

"Oh, Cora," Silvia said.

She set her needle and cloth down on a side table and pushed her knees to bring herself to her feet. Coming over to Cora, she reached out for an embrace, but Cora instead stepped back.

Without realizing it, Cora had made a decision. It didn't matter what the repercussions were. When she spoke, she could hear the urgency in her own voice. "I need you to find Hailsham. I'm going on a journey."

Curious, Silvia watched Cora's face, but then she simply nodded and headed off. Meanwhile Cora returned to her chambers and began to search for the clothing and possessions she would need. She would leave at first light. The stablehands would have to be alerted so that they could prepare her mare, as well as the other horses heading on the journey...

"My Lady?" A stately male voice asked.

Back at the doorway, Cora saw Hailsham standing with Silvia. Hailsham looked tired, but he was still wearing his crisp blue uniform, and she guessed that he too hadn't been sleeping. He was a lanky, balding, elegant man with a tiny mustache on his upper lip and the rest of his face always smooth. Hailsham was the palace's most senior steward, and like Silvia, Cora had known him her entire life.

"Patrick has asked me to join him," Cora lied. "Needless to say, the request is urgent. Make the appropriate preparations. I will travel light and fast."

A slight widening of Hailsham's eyes was the only sign of his surprise. "At the front? You are traveling to the king and the army?" He frowned and then held out his hand. "May I see the message?"

Cora hated deceiving him, but what she was doing was important, the most important thing she had ever done. "Not this time," she said, meeting his eyes. "This message is... personal. I don't expect to be there for long. Just enough time to quickly see Patrick."

"Ah." Hailsham's hand fell. "I see."

She knew what conclusion he would draw. Cora and Patrick's father had died just two months earlier. The wounds were still raw. Since his death, they had only communicated in writing.

"My lady," Hailsham said. "We must not forget that Lord Kane is here. He may take offense at your sudden departure."

"And that is where I depend upon you, Hailsham. Explain to him that I don't expect to be gone long. If he wants to wait, I will be back soon enough."

Silvia spoke up, "I would recommend Lady Helen to travel with the princess."

Cora picked up the thread. "We will need horses. Supplies. Soldiers for protection..."

As expected, the unspoken suggestion that Hailsham didn't know how to conduct his job rankled. "I am aware of what is needed," he said stiffly. "You will depart at first light?"

Cora nodded. "At dawn."

"Everything will be ready." Hailsham bowed and withdrew.

Silvia waited until he was gone, and then turned to Cora. "Now, Coraline, you can fool others, but as you well know, you cannot fool me. What is this about? Is it something to do with Erik? He also left suddenly."

Cora wondered how much she could reveal. "Erik is in Vestria," she said. "He has someone with him. Someone important. They're heading south together, trying to get back to Aranor."

"And your role is...?" Silvia asked in a stern voice.

"I need to find them." Cora reached out to take Silvia's hand. "That is all I can say."

Silvia's reprimanding manner dissolved. Instead she became pleading as she gripped both of Cora's hands. "Oh, Cora. Why not ask your brother?"

"He has his own troubles," Cora said. "Like fighting a war."

Silvia squeezed Cora's palms. "It's too risky."

"You know I'll have an escort with me and I don't plan to go any farther than the borderlands. In truth, I won't even go as far as the front."

“Be safe, Coraline. Please. Just don’t do anything reckless. Everyone keeps leaving. Your father… Patrick… Erik. I could never lose you too.”

“Patrick is out there fighting, trying to save us all,” Cora said. “I have to do my part, too.”

Chapter 8

THE TOWN OF WAYGATHER sprawled by the lake's edge, hugging the shore and thrusting out multiple piers into the still water. A natural meeting point between the fishing towns of Lake Raynor, Vestria's capital Ballina, and Helmsford in Aranor's north, Malgannis had known it as Grenford, but time changed all things, and he decided that its new name suited it well.

The bustling market was located inside Fort August, a series of defensive structures on a low hill. The fort – more of a stockade – was half a mile from the lake, easily reached by a connecting road, with houses filling the space in between. A wooden palisade surrounded the entire complex, but today the gates were thrown wide open. Malgannis and Erik didn't plan on spending much time in the town, just long enough to get provisions and horses.

Fishy odors, along with the smell of meat, leather, dirt, and freshly baked bread wafted through the market. Spring had finally arrived, and the warm day had brought out locals and newcomers alike, so that the rows between the stalls thronged with townsfolk and farmers, traders and minor gentry. The mingled voices made a constant din.

As Malgannis faced a wooden counter, the vendor on the other side slapped down a package in front of him. "Here you go. Dried figs. Nuts. Salted fish. And oats," he smiled wearily. "Plenty of oats." He held out a hand. "That'll be six copper eagles."

As Malgannis reached into the pouch Erik had given him, he shook his head. Six copper eagles would have bought the man's entire stall back in his day. He counted out the Aranese coins and handed them over.

Hefting the package, he left the stall and scanned the market, looking for the horse traders. Now, he just needed to find Erik. Horses needed a lot more space, and he soon spied the roped off sections at the side of the area enclosed by Fort August's tall wooden walls.

Malgannis navigated the crowds and passed stalls selling everything from ceramics to celestial divination. An imposing man in a black cloak sat at a table next to a sign, offering a conversation with a dead loved one for the mere price of four copper eagles. Malgannis gave the charlatan a dark look. Some things never changed. If there was one thing everyone agreed upon, it was that black priests had no interest in money.

Erik's task was to buy two nags, and Malgannis soon found him with the horse traders. The younger man's unruly hair marked him out as he stood just outside the perimeter of an area fenced with rope, clutching the reins of two horses in his hand, which made Malgannis believe he must be close to the end of his negotiation. The fat trader in front of him, however, had a face that was as pink as the scar on Erik's face. Erik was also scowling. Malgannis heard their raised voices even before he was close.

"—don't know what you're talking about," Erik snapped at the fat trader.

"You're Aranese, that's why you don't understand," the red-faced horse trader growled back, his accent giving him away as a local. "Before your precious code, we Vestrians had our own laws. Same goes for Rumandy. Morania. Kor. Nara... Why should we follow laws made in Adin?"

Erik spoke in a tone of exasperation. "Officials from Vestria help make the laws. Everyone is represented. Your traders, our traders, we're all protected by the same rules."

"But who says what's good for a horse trader in Waygather is the same as for a horse trader in Gila?" The trader lifted a finger to prod it into Erik's chest. Erik glanced down at the thick finger, and then back up again. "It's an empire that's what it is. You're taking away our culture. Our independence. If I were a younger man, I'd join with Graven Callow in a heartbeat."

Erik's eyes narrowed. "He's a Moranian," he said. "If he wins he's not going to give you your independence. He's going to rule you. Then you'll know what an empire looks like. I don't understand how—"

"Wait." The red-faced horse trader interrupted, studying Erik's face. "That scar." He continued to stare at Erik, voicing his thoughts out loud. "They say there's a man with a scar like that at the court in Adin. A commoner, raised to be the king's companion. He's a sneaky one. Controls the nobles from the shadows. What's his name? Wallace, that's it." He smirked. "Erik Wallace. I'm right, aren't it? That's you." He looked Erik contemptuously up and down. "No wonder you're so in love with the code. It buys you such pretty clothing, Lord Erik."

Malgannis picked up his pace, realizing he was going to have to intervene. Erik's face was now blank, and somehow his expression was more frightening than when he been obviously angry.

The fat horse trader's smile spread and he continued without stopping. "What else do they say about you? That's right. You're an orphan, probably a bastard." His grin spread. "And you're secretly in love with the princess, Coraline."

Even as Malgannis lunged, Erik was faster. Erik's movement was a blur as his bunched fist went straight into the red-faced horse trader's mouth. Malgannis grabbed at his other arm just in time to stop a second blow.

The fat horse trader was knocked back and dazed, before he came forward to fight, fists held up. It was only the sight of Malgannis, standing tall and cold-faced, that gave him pause. The horse trader hesitated, before he put a hand on his jaw, which was already turning an ugly color. "Give me those horses back."

Malgannis stepped forward, forcing the horse trader to move back. He took the reins from Erik. "You have your money. I believe our business is done."

The trader opened his mouth to protest, but Malgannis stared him down. "Fine," the horse trader said, throwing up his hands in disgust. He jerked his chin. "Get out of here, both of you."

Erik allowed himself to be led away, and Malgannis remained silent as he dragged both Erik and horses. Erik didn't speak, and even as his expression calmed, he looked straight ahead. The silence continued until they had navigated the market from one end to the other and were on their way out. The crowds thinned, and they found themselves leaving Fort August through the sturdy open gates.

Malgannis halted their new horses outside the fort, by the side of the road. "Erik," he said softly, with a nod toward one of the nags. "You can have that one, lad." He tossed Erik a bundle of supplies. "Here."

Erik caught the bundle, and both he and Malgannis began to unfasten the straps holding the saddlebags closed. As they worked, Malgannis glanced at Erik again, but he remained intently focused on the horse in front of him.

The two horses stirred. Buckles jingled. A soft breeze carried over the occasional loud voice from the nearby market. Malgannis checked his horse's girth and stirrups, while Erik did the same. It was some time before Erik spoke.

"Thank you," he said quietly, without looking up.

"For what?"

"For not asking me any questions."

Malgannis grunted. "If there's one thing I've learned in all my years, it's that sometimes we all need a bit of silence."

Erik tugged hard on a strap and buckle. He met Malgannis's gaze. "Perhaps you do know a thing or two." He gave a slight smile. "As hard as that is to admit."

✦

Nightfall settled on Huron Plain, where a long dusty road climbed a hill and passed by an old inn a day's riding from Waygather. The Red King's Arms wasn't as far as Malgannis would have liked to reach, but at least he would have a hot meal in his belly and a soft bed for sleeping.

The common room was crowded; with the fighting now reaching Vestria itself, many were on the move. The inn's patrons were mostly a desperate bunch, people who had decided that to stay where they were was no longer an option. Uncertainty surrounded the location of Graven Callow and his immense army. Earning good coin no longer seemed so important. Some laborers journeyed to where there was plenty of work. Some traders took risks to find opportunities. Now they all just wanted to go home. And for the people for whom this region was already home... they sharpened swords, checked their fences, and hoped that trouble would pass them by.

Smoke trickled up from multiple pipes and exited mouths in gray clouds before clinging to the low ceiling, and if the beams weren't already black they would have been soon enough. The sweet smell of redleaf mingled with the more savory odors of stew and ale. Voices grew louder as the evening went on. Tonight was a night to rest; tomorrow would come, and it was sure to be a long day. This was a night to forget about the war and to pretend for a time that fears for future and family didn't exist. Distraction was always welcome.

Malgannis and Erik sat at the back of the room, two clay bowls in front of them, both scraped clean, the last juices of the stew mopped up with slabs of black bread. Neither spoke; both were pensive. As one of the serving girls came and whisked their plates away, Malgannis lifted his tankard and took a gulp of strong bitter ale.

Most of the people around him, Erik included, all faced the same direction. A mandolin player sat on a stool by the hearth, a middle-aged woman with curls of blonde hair framing her narrow face. The rise and fall of the glow from the coals lit up her colorful cloak and her fingers moved on the strings like they were dancing. Her style of play was soothing, a climb of notes followed by a descent, with the rhythm never changing.

The mandolin player allowed her melody to slow, and then finished with a series of low notes that hung in the air. Silence greeted her completion as she lifted her instrument and stood, and it was only then that the onlookers became jolted from their reverie. A scatter of applause bounced its way across the room.

Malgannis glanced at Erik. "Time for bed, if you ask me—"

"Wait." Erik held up his hand.

Malgannis followed Erik's eyes to see an old man with a flowing white beard and matching long white hair. The old man crossed the floor to approach the hearth, settling himself on the stool and facing the onlookers. He wore a soft felt hat, gray in color, with a crook in the top. His skin was weathered but his eyes were pale – a Moranian or a Naran, Malgannis would have guessed. As the old man gathered the folds of his ragged gray cloak on his lap, he cleared his throat.

Erik cast a quick look at Malgannis again. "A storyteller," he murmured.

For a time, the storyteller simply sat where he was and roved his eyes over the crowd. He turned his head slowly, meeting one gaze after another, allowing the anticipation to build. During the period when the mandolin player had been filling the common room with soft music, several tables of men and women had continued drinking and speaking, even at volume. Now they all fell silent, one by one.

The storyteller finished sweeping the crowd with his intense stare. He gave the slightest nod. The Red King's Arms was ready for what he had to say.

The old storyteller cleared his throat again. When he spoke, despite his age, his voice was loud and crisp. "He fought Baelock Fain and the nightmare armies of Vailand. He started as a minor lord, a second son from Rathlee, but finished as the greatest general of his age. He was offered the kingdom of Aranor but turned it down in order to pursue his nemesis to the far side of the world." He paused for one breath, two, three. He lowered his voice, but his words were audible to all. "I speak, of course of Malgannis Vandryden, known to both enemies and friends as Ironclaw."

Malgannis's hand squeezed the handle of his tankard tightly. Despite the dim light, his location at the back of the common room, and the wooden table between him and the storyteller, he felt like everyone was watching him.

He wanted to get up and leave. But now no one was moving from their tables. If he were to stand up and cross the floor, all eyes would be on him. He had to stay.

"There are many tales to tell, of as great a man as Malgannis Ironclaw. We could hear about the battles he fought against the Fain, of the time he outmaneuvered his enemy in the Gray Marshes and won the first of his many victories. We could talk about his final victory at Odfeld, whereupon his nemesis fled as his army of barbarians crumbled. We could tell of Malgannis's exploits, and the risks he took, as he pursued Baelock Fain—not for one year, not two, but for ten relentless years, until he finally achieved his goal. We could raise our mugs to heaven as we share the tragic story of the death of Malgannis of Aranor, in his time of greatest triumph."

The storyteller reached down to a metal goblet on the floor at his feet. He took a sip and set the goblet down again. With every pause, he created a sense of expectation and tension.

"What?" Erik asked. "What is it? You've turned gray."

Malgannis didn't trust himself to look at Erik. "It's nothing," he said. "I'm just tired."

The storyteller opened his arms. "Tonight we will talk about our hero's origins. Gather your senses. Open your ears." He brought his palms together. "Let our story begin."

Malgannis scanned the room again, searching for a path to a swift exit. Once again, he forced himself to relax back into his seat. It would soon be over.

He missed the storyteller's opening words.

"...father was a squire, with a sweet manor by the swirling sea in the Aranese town of Rathlee. Lord Vandryden had no castle and only a small force of knight-vassals, but he had a passion for all things military. He read books, histories of the great battles during the Age of Barons and the Age of Barbarians. He was a skilled swordsman, impossible to beat, so the histories tell us. He rarely traveled as far as Adin, but when he did, he never failed to bring home gold from his victories at the royal tourneys."

Enough gold to buy all those books, Malgannis thought, *and all those lessons.*

"When it came to his two sons, Lord Vandryden shared his love of learning, both from texts and from teachers. He enlisted the help of skilled archers, swordsmen, and knights."

Malgannis remembered his father. A tall man with gray hair. Stern but animated. The storyteller forgot to mention his father's love of hunting. Malgannis could still picture the trophies in the Great Hall at Rathlee Manor—stag heads with immense antlers, hairy black wild boar heads with razor sharp tusks, great bear heads with mouths snarling.

"Lord Vandryden's two sons grew to adulthood in a time of peace. Malgannis had children of his own. A daughter and a son. Bronwyn and Alfred."

"Baenwyn," Malgannis whispered, far too low for anyone else to hear. "Not Bronwyn."

The storyteller continued, "Malgannis taught his children the same things his father had taught him. Malgannis's father died and his older brother became Lord Vandryden. Things would have continued as they were." The old man's voice lowered; his tone became grim. "But for the war."

Malgannis noticed the onlookers lean forward. A youth set down his tankard with a thunk, and received a dark look from the older man beside him.

"Before the war, before the Code of Aranor, slavery was rife throughout the Seven Realms. Heartless traders in human flesh, the slavers had to get their wares from somewhere, and most often raided the north. The gentle slaves that attended our lords and ladies, the strong slaves who built our city walls, the laborers who cleared new land for farming, were the sons and daughters of Vailand."

The storyteller slowly shook his head. His next words were bitter. "Evil begets further evil," he said. "Yet it is only in retrospect that our eyes are opened."

Malgannis couldn't help but agree.

"And so, for many years, slavers rode out on their horses and raided the north. Children were stolen from their parents, until one Vailander's younger sister was taken, and he decided he had had enough. His name was Baelock Fain, and he united the disparate tribes of the north as one people: Vailand. He gathered a great army and went on a quest of vengeance."

Malgannis tried to remain calm. *He was a butcher. He cared nothing for human life.*

"At first, the war was distant for Malgannis, his wife, and his two children. But the Vailanders brutally conquered town after town, city after city, until they threatened all of the south."

The storyteller took another sip from his goblet before continuing.

"Malgannis was older than forty, and an unknown figure, when he and his older brother, Lord Vandryden, went to war. They took their sons, now men in their own right. They left their wives and daughters behind."

Malgannis's eyes became unfocused. By all the gods, it felt like a lifetime ago – and it was – but at the same time it felt like yesterday. If he could have his time again, and do things differently, he would. In an instant.

"Malgannis quickly proved himself. When his older brother was killed in battle, he became Lord Vandryden. More lords fell as the civilized nations struggled to push back the assault of the Vailanders. Then the worst happened... the unexpected... the tragic." The storyteller hesitated, as if unwilling himself to continue. "The war reached the quiet seaside town of Rathlee."

This time Malgannis did everything he could not to remember.

"A raiding party struck the manor. The Vailanders came by sea. All the way down the western coast, through the White Sea and the Sea of Aranor. This was Baelock Fain's way. It was what made him so feared, and so victorious. He always struck hard, and fast, and in a way that was unexpected. There was justice in it, or so the Fain likely thought. Let us see how those in the south like to lose their loved ones... The Vailanders burned both the town and the manor. They killed Malgannis's wife and daughter."

"They didn't just kill them," Malgannis spoke with venom.

He realized with a start that he had just spoken out loud. The storyteller had stopped, and was staring at him. Erik was shaking his head, amused but also puzzled. Several heads were turned Malgannis's way.

However the pause was brief, and after a moment the old storyteller smoothly picked up where he had left off. "After his family was killed, for Malgannis Vandryden, everything changed. He no longer sought to hold off the enemy. He wanted the Fain to suffer. Now, the student of war fought back."

A glint came to the old man's eye. He knew he had the crowd.

"Malgannis became consumed with vengeance. When the lords he served were too timid, he knew he had the support and respect of the common soldiers, and overruled them. Bringing all of his knowledge of strategy and tactics to bear, he rose further in the ranks and won battle after battle, until he was the great general, supreme leader of the armies of Vestria, Rumandy, and Aranor." The storyteller became animated, as if ready to leap off his stool and ride to battle. "Malgannis Ironclaw and Baelock Fain faced each other on the battlefield, but were evenly matched, and neither were able to strike down the other. Baelock Fain did terrible things in his pursuit of victory."

So did we, Malgannis thought.

All of a sudden, the storyteller allowed his body to deflate, settling down, until all was calm. "But how the war unfolded is a tale for another day. It is late, dear friends. I will be here again on the morrow. As you go to sleep tonight, remember. There is always a hero ready, but it is only when he or she is most needed that we see them for who they are."

The storyteller bowed and departed, without waiting for applause.

"Morgan. Morgan!"

Malgannis saw that Erik had risen to his feet and stood beside their table, waiting for him impatiently.

"Come on," Erik said. "We need our rest."

On his way out of the common room, Malgannis passed a dark alcove, recessed deep enough that he would have to stop and stare to see who sat at the table only big enough for one.

"Friend," a familiar voice called from the table.

Malgannis let Erik keep walking and stopped at the table. The old man had removed his gray hat and sat smoking a long-stemmed pipe.

"You know a lot about Malgannis?" the storyteller asked. He lowered his voice. "I don't tend to delve into what the Vailanders did to his wife and daughter. Not for all audiences."

Malgannis met the old man's gaze. The storyteller frowned, and then his eyes widened.

"You look..."

"Her name was Baenwyn," Malgannis said. "But I agree. It's good that you don't tell them. Keep it that way."

Chapter 9

"SOMETHING'S WRONG," Malgannis said to Erik.

He scanned the area as they saddled up their horses. It was early morning and they were in the stable yard outside the Red King's Arms. Rain fell in a steady patter, the kind of rain that fell from a solid gray sky and would persist all day. The mingled scent of horses, leather, and mud filled the air. Nags whinnied. Harnesses jangled.

But this wasn't the usual scene of departure after a night at the inn. The stable yard was busy; Malgannis and Erik weren't the only ones departing at first light. Movements were urgent. Faces were drawn. A man barked at a nearby girl, telling her to hurry. A plump woman with gray hair didn't just settle her saddle on her horse's back, she practically threw it on, causing the creature to toss its head and neigh.

"See what you can find out," Malgannis said to Erik. "I'll ready your horse."

Erik headed back into the inn, and as Malgannis tightened straps and gave both their mounts a last drink of water, he overheard some men talking. From their quantity of baggage and fine clothing, he guessed they were merchants, come to conduct business at the market.

"Not just Moranians," a bearded merchant said to his older companion. "Wild men from Nara, as well as mercenaries from Kor."

Even as Malgannis tried to listen, Erik returned. He grabbed Malgannis's arm. "We need to leave. Now."

"What is it?"
"Graven Callow is on Huron Plain, along with his army. Everyone's getting out while they can."
Malgannis swore. "Which way? It's a big plain."
"Some say south. Others east." Erik stared for a moment. "We could be heading right for them." He ran a hand through his mop of hair. "What should we do? Perhaps we should go west..."
Malgannis shook his head. "At some point we have to get past them. We press on."
"But—"
"We'll take the high ground. Come on."

✦

The gray skies and rain continued, making the days blur into one another. The two travelers rode hard, and found themselves alone in the vast expanse of Huron Plain, where hills coated in thick grass rolled on and on. With no sign of any soldiers, they allowed themselves a fire at night. They cared for their horses and became well acquainted with oats themselves; at least the porridge was hot and filling.

On the third day they reached the ruins of Leventhal. Thick woodland had grown toward the crumbling city of stone, so that trees stood tall within four strong walls as if claiming the houses for themselves. Malgannis felt disquiet in his belly as he rode past the place that had once been a grand settlement, almost a rival to Vestria's capital Ballina. In his memory, it had only been a few years since he had walked the streets. Leventhal's metalworkers were renowned, and he had paid twelve golden eagles for a fine two-handed broadsword. He had lodged in the inns and eaten at several of the city's best taverns. During the war, he had given a rousing speech at Century Square, the great gathering place at Leventhal's epicenter.

He realized that as he rode he was trying not to look at the crumbling walls of white stone. He was unsettled because of the reminder of how fleeting it all was—life... memory... civilization. How easy it was to take it all for granted. Structures that took many lifetimes to build could fall so swiftly. The structures that didn't exist in physical form were the most ephemeral of all. Kingdoms felt forever, treaties like they could endure any calamity; the enforcement of law and justice was how things had always been. Until the kingdoms were torn down or absorbed, the treaties broken, the laws ignored...

"It's strange," Erik said, interrupting his reverie.

"Eh?"

Erik glanced his way. "To think that all it took was a river drying up. The people left it all behind, and now... this."

"It's the way of the world," Malgannis said. "Everything is always falling apart. To build it back up again. That's where the effort lies."

✦

The rain became harder, thick droplets of water pummeling from above, soaking the ground and creating shallow pools of muddy water. Despite the fact that it was only late afternoon, darkness fell on the landscape. Erik spied a tall stone wall with part of the roof still remaining, creating some scant but welcome shelter, and they both agreed to make an early camp.

The forest had grown thicker as they traveled south and east, and Malgannis fetched firewood and tinder while Erik hobbled their horses under the outstretched arms of a sturdy oak. They soon had a small fire blazing under the remnants of the beams and tiled roof overhead. Malgannis sat close to the flames with the stone wall behind him. Leaning forward, he held out his hands and allowed the warmth to gradually penetrate his body.

"I miss that inn," Malgannis said.

From across the fire, Erik looked up. "I miss home."

"You'll be there soon enough. Before you know it you'll be having a good long rest."

"No, I won't. As soon as I've delivered you to Princess Coraline, I'm going to where I should be right now. Patrick asked me to stay in Adin and look after Cora. But I shouldn't be in Adin. I should be with the army, at Patrick's side."

Malgannis had his eyes closed but now opened them. "As I understand it, your king gave you an order..."

"He is my friend," Erik said. "And that's the only reason I agreed to go to Adin and stay there. But he's the one risking his life. What if he needs me in battle, and I'm not there for him?"

"It's your life," Malgannis said. "You'll do what you need to do."

The rain continued to patter on the ruined city and the forested landscape nearby. A rumble of thunder sounded in the distance. As time passed, Malgannis wondered if the time was right.

"Erik..." He glanced over at the younger man. "You remember what happened in Waygather?"

Erik stared into the clouded sky. "I remember."

"Is it true?"

"Is what true?"

Malgannis remembered Erik's reaction when he had asked him if he was a lord's son, and then about his scar. "About your parents, for a start."

"I don't like to talk about it."

Malgannis leaned forward to add a stick to the fire. "Fair enough. I understand, lad. As much as anyone can."

After another long pause, Erik sighed. "We'll be in Adin soon enough, so you might as well know. I wouldn't be telling you anything people don't already whisper about." He kept his eyes on the sky, even as he spoke. "After Patrick, King Owen wanted another boy, but he got Coraline. He never let go of the idea, and so one day he was riding past the orphanage at Adin when he saw me... a boy with a fresh wound on his face, and he took me home that very day. I was to be a companion for Patrick. Someone for the heir to the throne to practice on. Someone to balance out his sister and make it so the boys in the household outnumbered the girls." He paused, clearly remembering. "I was six years old, when I went to live at the palace."

As Erik trailed off, Malgannis watched him and wondered what he should say; he was never good at these things. He ended up not saying anything, allowing his companion to continue.

"It was a strange situation, or at least it was for me. The king gave me a life and I suppose I'm grateful. I had my own quarters, and food and clothing, but he never acknowledged me or said a kind word. I don't know if he ever saw me as someone just like his own son. I suppose I'll never know."

Malgannis cleared his throat. "I'm sure..." Unable to find the right words, he trailed off, but was relieved when Erik didn't seem to notice.

"Things got easier," Erik said, "when I was old enough to go to the Academy, and I made myself useful. I keep track of what the nobles are up to. And I'm good at it."

"I have no doubt that's true." Malgannis decided to ask the obvious question. "How did you feel when he died?"

"The king? Strange. I wasn't raised as his child, with Patrick and Coraline. But I still felt something." He looked over at Malgannis. "You asked if I'm a lord. King Owen made me a squire, Lord Wallace of Blythe, but everyone knows it's only for appearances. It wouldn't be right for a commoner to be the heir to the throne's closest companion. To now be protecting the king's sister. Why an orphan? Why me? It doesn't matter what I do. I won't be good enough."

"Some people are fools," Malgannis said, "and jealousy doesn't bring out the best in people." He wondered again how to phrase his words. He knew what he wanted to say. *You're good enough, Erik. Even I can see it.*

But then he was interrupted by something that made him sit bolt upright.

"Wait. What was that?" Malgannis asked.

"I didn't hear any—"

Malgannis held up a hand. He heard it again. A distant beastly sound, harsh and barking.

"That's a wolf," Erik said.

Even as Erik spoke, the sound grew louder. The repeated barking was now unmistakable.

"That's not a wolf," Malgannis said, staring into Erik's eyes. "That's a dog." He leaped toward the fire. "Quick. Put it out!"

Malgannis scraped at the ground and began to throw dirt onto the flames. Erik helped, and in moments they had reduced it to smoke.

Malgannis stopped moving. He exchanged anxious glances with Erik again. He realized he could hear the jangle of armor and tread of heavy boots on the nearby road that passed by the ruins. Men's voices bounced around. The din was something Malgannis knew well; an army was on the move.

Erik stared past Malgannis's shoulder and his face was white. Malgannis turned his head, and saw a handful of figures walking away from the shelter. He only saw their backs, but they were close. Far too close.

More marching men appeared. They wore black and red above their chain mail. Swords dangled from their hips. The Moranian soldiers marched past the shelter in groups ranging from just a few soldiers to entire columns led by officers. Malgannis saw others with them: Narans in loose tunics, with round brown hats like curled up snails, and Kors, dressed in shaggy furs. The range of weapons was vast, from curved swords to javelins, pikes to recurved bows.

Malgannis felt like he was seated with his back to a series of waves. This tide of men rushed past him, eager to move on its way. But soon the water would rush back, someone would turn and see him, and he would be swallowed.

Then he heard a panting and snuffling followed by another bark. A dog with a patchwork pelt rounded the stone wall and saw the two men. With its head low and eyes curious, the animal looked at them both, tilting its head as if puzzled. Resuming its approach, the dog sniffed at the ground as it came nearer.

Malgannis shooed at the dog, but that only made the animal more curious. Both Malgannis and Erik gave more aggressive sweeps of their arms.

The dog stopped. The animal's head dropped but it looked up at Malgannis, fixing him with a dark stare. The lips began to part, slowly but surely, revealing rows of sharp teeth. The dog began to growl. The threatening sound made Malgannis's skin crawl.

Malgannis was no longer sitting; instead he was crouched with his feet poised under his body. The dog's growl dragged out, but when the animal realized Malgannis had stopped trying to scare it away, the snarl faded and lips closed. The dog contented itself to once more sniff with its head low to the ground, getting closer and closer to the two men and their packs.

Malgannis wondered if he should run or stay hidden. He noticed Erik trying to get his attention. Erik cocked his head, clearly asking a question as he jerked his chin toward the trees, where their two horses were hobbled.

The choice wasn't easy. The dog could leave them alone. The army might pass them by. If they tried to run, they would be seen. There was no doubt; it would happen.

Then Malgannis heard someone whistling.

"You stupid mutt. Come here when I call you."

Malgannis looked again at Erik, whose face was still pale, but when he spoke, Erik's voice was steady. "Got any meat?"

Malgannis grabbed his pack and pulled it closer. He rummaged until he found a pouch and took out a piece of dried meat. He waved a rust-colored strip in front of the dog. The creature took immediate focus and began to approach. Malgannis stood.

"Ready?" he asked Erik.

He waited the count of two breaths, and then threw the meat as far as he could, in the opposite direction from the trees. The dog burst into a run.

"Go!"

Malgannis and Erik grabbed their packs, threw them onto their shoulders, and commenced their own sprint. As Malgannis ran with Erik just in front of him, he didn't look back. His legs felt vulnerable. At any moment he expected to hear barking. Teeth would find his lower legs and bite down, holding him fast.

As Malgannis's boots slammed into the ground, he heard raised voices as soldiers saw them. Their horses under the tree now seemed impossibly far away. The shouts behind them grew louder, becoming bellowed orders.

Malgannis knew war. The soldiers would give chase. He and Erik were in grave danger. Where possible, a commander wanted to keep an army's movements a secret. There was a good reason why no one at the Red King's Arms had known where exactly Graven Callow's army was.

If caught, Malgannis and Erik would be stopped from carrying news. If questioned, they might reveal useful information.

Then they would be killed.

Erik reached his horse first. He threw up his saddle and frantically fastened straps and buckles. Malgannis grunted as he lifted his own saddle and settled it onto his mare's broad back. He checked the stirrups, grabbed the pommel, and hauled himself up.

"Into the trees," Malgannis grunted.

He glanced back toward the ruins of Leventhal. Men littered the landscape: Graven Callow's soldiers in black and crimson uniforms as well as his allies and mercenaries. Even as Malgannis watched, a line of riders crested a hill.

Malgannis yanked at his reins and turned his horse to follow Erik. This forest was thin, with gaps between the trees and multiple trails winding back and forth. Erik took a wide path that headed deep into the shadows, and Malgannis followed right behind. Malgannis ducked under a horizontal branch. Dogs barked behind him. Horses whinnied.

Malgannis and Erik kept their bodies low, hugging their horses' necks. Taking advantage of the last of the fading daylight, they plunged deeper into the forest.

Chapter 10

THE RAIN HAD FINALLY STOPPED. Malgannis now led the way, riding his horse at walking speed along a trail that snaked back and forth through the forest, a track thin enough to force them to travel in single file.

"Do you think we lost them?" Erik softly called from behind him.

Malgannis glanced over his shoulder. "It's hard to say, but we need to stay quiet." He nodded toward the path. "It's opening up ahead."

He soon emerged from the path into a clearing. The silver moon was high and lit up the bed of leaves. A thin stream divided the area into two. It was a good place for a camp, but Malgannis knew they shouldn't stop until they had created more distance from any pursuit.

He searched and spied another path, much wider than the one they had been following. He led his mare splashing through the brook, and then approached the broad track he could see through the trees on the clearing's other side.

Eager for a drink of water, Erik's horse snorted.

"Shh." Malgannis frowned over his shoulder.

Erik glared back at him. "You think that was me?"

Then Malgannis heard something. After another glance at Erik to see if he had heard it too, he looked toward the trail he and Erik had been heading for.

Armed soldiers in black and crimson marched into view: first one, then another, and another. The column kept going. Malgannis could only guess at their number.

The officer in front stopped in his tracks. When he saw Malgannis and Erik, his expression shifted, from surprised to determined. His eyes narrowed.

"Halt or be killed!" the officer snapped.

Malgannis was already pulling at the reins to draw his mare deeper into the forest. Sensing Erik right behind him, he dug in his heels until his mount was racing through the trees. He tried not to think about the fact that it was night time, with branches everywhere along with fallen logs, deep holes, wide gullies, and the occasional cliff.

"Spread out! After them!"

The harsh cries made Malgannis put on an extra burst of speed. Spying another thin trail, he skirted a thicket the size of a house to reach it. His horse leaned in to each corner, dashing from one angle to the next. He saw the flash of men's bodies through the brush, even as thin foliage whipped his body. Despite the fact that the soldiers were on foot, there was only so fast he could go. He searched for open ground so he could outrun the pursuit.

He then saw something that gave him hope. Through a break in the trees he spotted a hill covered in grass, an area with only a few trees rather than a forest. The clouds had parted to reveal stars above the hills.

Urging his horse onward, he left the trail and kicked his heels to push his mare the last distance out of the trees. Seeing the improved terrain, the horse gamely threw itself through the saplings and bushes until they were on open ground.

Malgannis and Erik galloped around the base of the hill. But Malgannis's hope shifted to despair when he saw a deep gully with a river at its bottom, forcing him to veer. He and Erik continued to turn, racing along the edge of the gully to find a way past. Malgannis glanced backward to see a large number of soldiers leave the trees to rush the area around the hill. The ravine kept going. The river grew wider. The barrier was impassible.

With no other choice, Malgannis turned his horse and kicked it onward to climb up the hill. Beside him, Erik cast him a fearful look. The two animals lunged upward, climbing hard to reach the hill's grassy summit.

Now Malgannis had a clear view of the surrounding landscape, and saw that the ravine encircled most of their current position. The rest was blocked off by the approaching soldiers.

The soldiers formed a wide line. From horseback on the hill's crest, Malgannis and Erik watched them come. The soldiers all drew their swords. The light of the moon and stars clearly silhouetted everyone below.

One of the soldiers called up. "We want to ask you some questions. Surrender your weapons and come down, or face the consequences."

Malgannis's horse pawed at the ground. He stared grimly down at the approaching soldiers.

"Can we win this?" Erik asked.

"No," Malgannis said. He turned to Erik. By the gods, he was so young. "I'm sorry, lad. Wish I could think of a way through this."

Erik remained determined as he put a hand on his sword hilt. "We can at least try—"

He was interrupted by a new sound. A distant horse whinnied, and then another neigh came right after. None of the soldiers surrounding the hill had horses, which meant that even more enemies were on their way.

"They're going to try to take us alive," Malgannis said. "It's going to be hard to make them kill us. I hope you're up to it."

Malgannis's head moved when he heard the rumble of horse hooves. Trees swished and swayed. Down below, at the line of encircling soldiers, one man turned, then another.

A group of riders burst from the trees.

Erik shot Malgannis a startled look. The riders were knights: tall men on destriers, clad in shining steel armor. Blue cloaks trailed in the air behind each figure as swords held high, they charged the Moranians. One soldier in black and red went down, then another. The Moranians tried to regroup and face up to the new threat, but they were no match for the mounted warriors rushing through their number again and again. Another charge from the knights saw most of the Moranians struck hard with sharp steel and horse hooves the size of dinner plates. Soon only the officer was standing, and then he went down too.

Malgannis and Erik remained in place, beside each other on the top of the hill, as the mounted warriors rode up the slope. Malgannis saw at least a dozen knights, enough to completely surround them. With their faces covered by their helmets, each big man appeared much the same as another. The difference in the size of the horses was pronounced; Malgannis and Erik's nags looked like ponies.

Then the mounted warriors parted, creating a gap to allow another rider to approach. This rider sat astride a beautiful bay mare, a horse larger than most, with a graceful arch to her neck. The night air was still cold, and all Malgannis initially saw was a slender figure in a hooded cloak.

The woman rode closer, controlling her steed with skill to settle to a walking pace. She angled her approach back and forth, taking her time to inspect the two men in front of her. Lifting her head, she stared directly into Malgannis's face.

Malgannis saw something he wasn't expecting. Two piercing eyes looked right into his face. But in contrast to the poise she clearly possessed, the eyes that stared at him for the briefest instant were shocked.

"Coraline?" Erik asked incredulously.

She gave the slightest nudge of her reins to settle her horse in place. Now halted in front of Malgannis and Erik, she raised her hands to pull back the hood of her cloak.

Malgannis saw a young woman – younger than Erik – with long hair, so dark it was nearly black, fashioned in an elegant braid. Her cheekbones were high and her forehead and nose were both strong, creating the impression of intelligence. The silver moonlight sparkled from her eyes, but all he could tell at night was that they matched the color of her hair. The cloak she wore, fastened at the neck with a golden eagle pin, was gray and made from soft wool.

"Erik," she said. The way she said Erik's name conveyed the impression of relief but also impatience. Warmth combined with worry. "You are a difficult man to locate."

"I..." Erik faltered. "It is good to see you looking well, Princess." As if lost for words, he cleared his throat. He glanced at Malgannis. "I found him."

"I can see that," said Coraline Vandryden.

My great-granddaughter.

The princess remained still for a time. She sat astride her horse, staring at Malgannis. Once again, he thought that in spite of her youth, she carried herself with surprising assurance.

Malgannis reminded himself of something. She was the only person who might have the answers he craved.

"Princess..." he began.

"It is not safe here, as you know." She turned to glance down the hillside, and Malgannis found himself admiring her more. She wasn't rattled by what her knights had just done. "Introductions must wait," she said. "I have a camp near here, by the Statue of Palindor. Come. I am sure you are both in need of rest and restoration."

✦

No doubt the Statue of Palindor had decayed like the rest of Leventhal, and with a close inspection the stone would be crumbling and covered with lichen. But in moonlight, the proud warrior appeared unnervingly lifelike as he stood with legs apart and a fist clenched up to the sky.

A cliff fell away near the statue's feet, giving way to a stretch of flat ground where the princess had made her camp. One day, the rains would soften the ground at the cliff's base, the statue would topple and fall, and the greatest of Vestria's kings would sleep, just like his real body in a crypt in Ballina.

Weariness spread throughout Malgannis's body as he approached the camp, passing through a circle of sentries standing guard. His eyes moved from one fire to another. Sturdy tents made him long for bed. Iron pots rested on coals, and the smell of meat made his mouth water.

The group halted and Princess Coraline dismounted. A youth led her horse away, and the knights tended to their own horses. As Malgannis slid off his sturdy mount, another boy came for his mare.

He kept his eyes on Coraline. In the firelight, he noticed a few things about her that he hadn't before. She unfastened her cloak as she approached the largest tent, and he caught sight of the split riding dress she wore underneath, which was embroidered but also practical. Her boots were muddy, but she clearly intended to wear them into the tent without removing them. She was taller than he had first thought. Not that she had his height, but she was only a few inches shorter than Erik. He glimpsed a golden ring with a blue stone on her index finger, the only item she wore that didn't also have a practical purpose.

Malgannis remembered Cora's father. Owen was just a babe. It was all so strange. So much time had passed.

Did she know? Was she aware who he was, and the fact that his blood flowed in her veins?

She paused at the tent's entrance. Her head turned, and she glanced his way. Malgannis wanted to talk to her, but he hesitated. He opened his mouth.

Then from nearby, Erik spoke. "Princess," he said. "I need to speak with you."

"Away from the men," she said.

Malgannis was going to have to wait.

✦

Cora glanced around the tent. A brazier radiated both light and warmth. Incense on the coals masked the scent of smoke. The tent was broken into partitions, and farther inside, thick rugs formed a carpet, along with cushions and chests. She remained near the brazier and fought the urge to bite her lip. Her thoughts were spinning.

"My Lady? You have returned?" Helen poked her head in from the next partition. Plump and prim, with green eyes and her hair in ringlets, the maid was ten years older than Cora but tended to act like she was twice her age. When Helen noticed Erik, her eyes widened. "Lord Wallace?" As soon as Helen said the name she put a hand to her mouth. "Apologies. I was not expecting..."

"All is well," Cora said to Helen. "Please. Leave us." She nodded toward the exit.

"Princess," Helen acknowledged with a bob.

With another curious glance at Erik, Helen threw on a cloak before departing the tent. Cora waited until she and Erik were alone. Then, as soon as Helen had left, she turned toward Erik. He took three big steps toward her.

Cora fell into Erik's arms and buried her head into his chest as he held her tightly. Then, taking hold of herself, she pushed him away.

"I missed you," she said. "I was worried about you."

Erik stared into her eyes, even as she looked into his. He didn't have to say anything. She knew he was happy to see her. But then, something changed, and he glanced back toward the tent's entrance, releasing her at the same time so that they were no longer touching. "She will wonder what we are doing in here alone. Maids love their gossip."

"Father is no longer around, Erik," Cora said with a smile. "We can do what we like."

Erik looked like he was choosing his words carefully. "People speculate."

"Let them," Cora said with a laugh.

He smiled, but the worry never left his eyes, and Cora's smile fell. She had heard the rumors. People said Erik's feelings for her were more than what was appropriate. He was a commoner. An orphan. She was a princess and the heir to the throne. No doubt the idea of a secret dalliance was scandalous enough to get people talking.

Cora wished he wouldn't care so much about what other people thought. She and Erik were close friends, childhood companions. He was handsome and kind and strong. Yet she was old enough to know when a man's eyes lingered on her, and Erik's never had. He cared about her; his face lit up when he saw her, it was true. But ever since she was little, it had been Cora following Erik and Patrick around. She had always been Patrick's younger sister. Erik didn't see her in that way.

Erik was staring toward the wall of the tent, eyes unfocused. "Cora," he said, turning toward her and frowning. "By all the gods, what are you doing out here?"

"I came for you," she said. "And if my senses weren't deceiving me, I believe I just saved your life."

"You didn't just come for me," Erik said. He paused, and glanced again, as if he could see through the fabric of the tent. "You asked me to get him, and that is what I've done. Who is he?"

Cora wished that she could tell him. Erik cared about her, and more than anything, she wanted to share her burden. "I did come for you," she said firmly. "Just as you would come for me if you thought I was in danger." She wondered what she could say. "As for him... I told you before. He is someone important to our cause, even if he doesn't yet know it."

"And that is all you can tell me."

"I simply can't say more." When he opened his mouth, she put strength into her voice. "Erik. This is how it has to be." She softened her tone. "Please."

Frustrated, Erik visibly took hold of himself, smoothing his expression and taking a slow breath. After a few moments had passed, he shook his head. "He is strange. I'll say that."

Cora still couldn't believe who they were discussing, although she was the only one who knew the truth. "What is he like?" she couldn't help herself asking.

"Strong," Erik said. He looked troubled. "A fighter. It's hard to put into words. He's old... a little dark inside."

A gust of wind made the tent shudder. The snap and crackle of the fabric reminded Cora that she was far from home. She shivered, and moved closer to the brazier to hold out her hands to the coals.

"What happened? Why didn't you get back to me like we planned?"

"Graven Callow," Erik said. "He cut us off. We were pursued... hunted. There's a whole army out there..." He turned back toward her. "Does Patrick know you're here?"

"No, and that's how it's going to stay."

Erik opened his mouth but then closed it. "How many men have you got with you?" he finally asked.

"Twenty."

"You have no idea how many enemy soldiers are out there. You should be in Adin."

"I will take that into account." Cora knew her time was running out. She also knew that if Erik remained any longer, they would argue. He had always been protective. "I would like to see him now."

"Morgan?" Erik interrupted himself. "That's not his name. I don't even know his name. Why are we risking our lives for him?"

"Because, Erik, he is the only hope we have. Now, please. Go."

Cora didn't watch Erik leave the tent. Instead she stood beside the brazier and stared into the glowing coals.

She waited for her great-grandfather, Malgannis Vandryden, also known as Ironclaw. As she prepared to meet her ancestor, whom she had brought back from the dead, she forced herself to remember.

Chapter 11

ADIN WAS A CITY ON EDGE. From farmers to city folk, commoners to nobility, war was on every tongue. Winter had been harsh, and yet the bitterness of past months would continue into spring and beyond.

Regardless of the day, Cora prayed at the Temple of White Stone. She knelt, hunched her back, and pressed her forehead into the symbol of the pantheon on her prayer mat. She straightened, and then repeated her obeisance. With each prayer, she named one of the seventy-seven gods in turn—the older gods and then the younger.

Cora was afraid. Her dreams were dark; in her waking moments she was plagued by a gnawing dread. Despite what everyone said, she knew what was coming.

Her father, King Owen of Aranor, was in distant lands, personally leading the army, struggling to achieve victory or at least a truce. Her brother Patrick was with him. Cora's father had always been distant – not like he was with Patrick – but together they were her family, her life. Cora's mother Lilian had died in childbirth. Cora was the young one, and although her father had outdated views about the role of women, she was old enough to understand. People talked.

The war was going badly.

As she wrapped her lips around the wordy names of the gods and asked for their help, she couldn't prevent her terrified thoughts and worst imaginings. Trying to find reason to hope – anything at all – she cast her mind back to the war's beginning.

No one had wanted a war, or at least that was how it had felt, and that was what her father had said, even as events unfolded. Despite Morania's rapid growth and Aranor's relative decline, the Queen of Morania and

Cora's father were on fair terms. Trade continued between nations. Nobles visited one another.

Then along came Graven Callow.

Erik told her how he came to power. He was a captain in the Moranian army, a rancorous man who preached about liberty and despised the Code of Aranor. When Morania had a bad harvest, leading to famine, it wasn't because of rain and blight, it was because of the Code of Aranor. When prisoners took over the dungeon at Gila, it wasn't the fault of Morania, it was because the gaolers were forced to wait for arbiters from Adin, and couldn't administer their own justice.

Graven Callow didn't just hate the code, he openly despised Aranor itself. If Aranor enjoyed wealth, it wasn't due to sound rule, it was because Aranor was bleeding Morania dry. He described his complaints to all who would hear them. Some listened. Many didn't. But what happened next shocked everyone.

The Queen of Morania's palace burned down. The scale of the tragedy was horrific; the palace became a smoking ruin with the queen and her family inside.

Graven Callow took action. Blaming Aranor, he used his own loyal soldiers to seize power before the rest of Morania's nobles could gather strength. He then said that those very nobles were in league with Aranor in their crime against the queen, and soon lords and ladies were losing their heads in Gila's central square.

His suspicions then turned to the rulers of Morania's two smaller neighbors, Kor and Nara. Would they join him in a quest to purge the Code of Aranor from the world, or would they fall to his armies? Impossibly swiftly, Graven Callow absorbed the forces of three nations, and lines were redrawn across the world.

Graven next turned his sights on Rumandy. He led his armies across the mountains and laid siege to Inadris. Aranor, the only nation with Morania's strength, had no choice but to go to war to restore the peace—which meant that Cora's father and brother had now been gone for a month.

Cora bowed and named the next of the younger gods. She prayed, and then straightened.

Everyone said Rumandy was about to fall. They also said Aranor and Vestria couldn't hold against the forces arrayed against them. Cora's desperation meant that prayer was all she had available to her. She would give anything for her nation, for her family – even her own life – if it would make a real difference. She wished she were a man, a strong warrior with a sword and a warhorse, able to fight at Patrick's side and protect her father and her brother from harm. But she had never held a sword in her life. There was nothing she could do to help.

Cora pictured the moment her father, Patrick, and Erik rode out, on their way to war. Her father had given her the same nod he gave the palace staff, along with a quick look and a wave. She forgave him for his lack of affection; it was his way.

In that moment, despite his armor and bright cloak, he had seemed so old. And, at the same time, Patrick and Erik were so young. It was only a few years ago that the three of them had been splashing in the river together. Cora missed them. She was surrounded by people at the palace, but she was all alone.

Cora clasped her hands together. She begged all of the gods. She bargained with them. Please, keep her family safe. Bring Patrick home. Bring Erik home. The men in her life were strong, but they were also facing weapons designed to kill and enemies taught to wield them. They were all she had. She would offer the gods a life of prayer. She would give them anything.

Even as Cora approached the end of her daily ritual, she felt a chill. At the Temple of White Stone, the doors were always open. She turned and looked toward the temple's grand entrance.

The chill took form; it rested cold fingers on her spine and pressed hard.

A slender man stood alone on the landing just outside the temple. He was staring at her, watching her. He wore a black hooded robe. With the hood covering his head, she made out a long narrow face, with sharp features. His eyes were dark and full of intent.

Cora tried to pray some more but when she turned her head there he was again, his attention focused directly on her. The names of the gods fell from her lips. She decided that if she was going to be stared at, she wanted to know why. Climbing to her feet, she headed straight to the temple's entrance.

The slender man in the black robe backed away from the entrance until he was several feet from the doors. Cora took a few steps into the wintry air; there were people praying within the temple, and she didn't want to disturb them. Immediately she shivered and regretted leaving her coat on a peg back inside. It was too late to go back and get it.

Cora crossed her arms in front of her chest and tried to ignore the chill. She stood in front of the slender man. He was older than her by twenty or thirty years. His skin was pale and had a slight sheen, making him look unwell. From what she saw of his hair, it was gray, without any other color.

Cora opened her mouth, but it was the man in black who spoke first. His voice was smoother than she would have expected. From his words, he knew who she was, but he leaned forward, as if he had the superior status.

"Princess, I have seen you pray here every day. I can help you. I know what it is you pray for. I can help your father win this war."

Cora's words of challenge fell from her lips. She didn't know what she had expected, but it wasn't this. "Who are you?" she asked. "What are you talking about?"

"I am a priest, Coraline Vandryden, but I worship just the one god, rather than many." He glanced meaningfully toward the temple before returning his gaze to her. "And unlike the gods you worship here, the lord of the underworld actually does answer prayers."

Dread rose inside Cora's body, bubbling up from her stomach to land an evil taste on her tongue. She realized who the man was, what he was. A black priest. She was standing in front of a black priest, in the flesh. She was protected in the palace, but she knew that they appeared when they might be wanted, ready to make a bargain. Everyone said that the only magic was black magic, the magic of the underworld. Temptation had to be resisted. There was always a terrible price.

Cora had heard the stories. Here was the proof.

She allowed none of what she was feeling to appear on her face. "Please," she said coldly. "Leave me alone."

"Of course." The black priest bowed. "Just remember, Coraline. I can help you."

✦

Cora's father was killed the day before her birthday.

Usually, it was the one day of the year when he appeared to realize she existed. She might get almost as much attention as Patrick. At least he was sure to give her a gift, and she always tried to guess what surprise he had planned for her, but never managed to guess right.

When she thought he was going to give her a horse, he gave her a jeweled ring, a beautiful square sapphire set in gold, with her name written in tiny letters on the ring's inside. When, another year, she caught him speaking with the jeweler, he gave her a beautiful mare—and then a shimmering necklace as well, to wear at balls and banquets.

She was returning from riding in the woods when the news came. It was a beautiful morning, cold and crisp. Frost decorated the lawns outside the palace and her horse's snorts came with puffs of mist. She rode past the dolphin fountain, alongside the gardens, and toward the outbuildings where the stables hid behind a screen of conifers.

She had been upset that her father was going to be away for her birthday. She knew her feelings were selfish – he was away fighting a war, risking his life to keep her safe – and yet the reminder that she shouldn't be thinking of herself somehow only made things worse. Feeling the wind in her face helped to flush away her cares, if only for a time.

A wide road of packed yellow gravel made a lattice-like pattern between the gardens, lawns, fountains, and trees. Her horse traveled at a trot, making a gentle clip clop. Her eyes stung from the cold, and she probably should have worn her heavier coat, but tomorrow was her birthday, and she didn't care.

When she rounded a corner to approach the stables, she knew right away that something was wrong.

Hailsham the steward, bald and lanky but dignified in his crisp blue uniform, stood waiting for her. His expression was often worried, but as Cora approached she saw his face was drawn, the skin tight. He fidgeted with the tiny mustache on his upper lip.

Beside him, Silvia wrung her hands. Cora had never seen Silvia's wheat-colored hair in disarray, but on this morning it was, and where she always made a point of her erect posture, her shoulders were slumped.

Cora tugged on her reins. Her mare came to a stop.

Still on horseback, Cora watched Silvia's face, and then Hailsham's, before returning to Silvia. Cora didn't want to ask. As soon as she did, it would become real, whatever it was they had to say to her.

The silence dragged out. Soon it was the lack of knowing that became unbearable. Cora dismounted. Her movements were sluggish, numb.

Then Cora was standing in front of them. Silvia's eyes were red. Cora knew Silvia well enough to know that she was struggling to keep her emotions in check.

Cora's own breathing was ragged. She didn't want to know. But she had to know. It was going to hurt. If she didn't know, she could delay the pain. Yet it was painful not knowing.

"What..." she tried, but had to lick her lips. "Who...?"

Then she knew.

"Your father," Silvia said, making a choking sound as she spoke. "I'm sorry, Cora. He fell in battle." She cleared her throat. "He was killed."

Cora fell into Silvia's arms.

✦

Later, Cora learned what had happened. Her father went to Inadris to relieve the siege, but was too late. When King Owen discovered what the enemy had done to the city, he forced a battle anyway.

Cora's father met Graven Callow in a one-on-one fight, outside Inadris, while the wider conflict raged around them. Graven Callow thrust his sword through Cora's father's chest. It was a mortal blow, and King Owen of Aranor, Cora's father, died.

But that was not enough for Graven. With the king's body at his feet, Graven cut off his head and displayed it to all to see. The king's men were able to get his body, but Graven kept his head. He put it on a spike above the gate at Inadris.

Cora's brother became king on the battlefield. Rumandy was lost. Patrick retreated with the armies of Vestria and Aranor.

Another message from Patrick arrived. After the loss of their father, Erik was coming home to Adin to be with her.

Cora was desperate to see Erik; life at the palace was lonely, and despite his strained relationship with the king, Erik would also be grieving. Yet at the same time, she wished he wasn't coming home. Erik should be protecting Patrick. That was what he was supposed to do. She knew she couldn't blame Erik. He was too loyal to Patrick to disobey the new king's orders. When Erik arrived, and they embraced for what felt like hours, she knew they were both happy to be together, but also worrying about Patrick.

Patrick was young, just a couple of years older than Cora. He was the jester, the boy who liked everybody, the brother who scared Cora with terrible tales but also took her on his escapades with Erik and earned rebukes from Silvia for getting her dresses covered in mud.

Willem, the Red King of Vestria, was an old, old man, and couldn't leave his capital. Patrick was now in charge of it all, the armies of two nations, fighting a war against a much more powerful enemy.

As Cora's father's bones came home and she buried him in the crypt below Adin Palace, the days passed, becoming weeks. Having Erik by her side gave Cora comfort, and she and Erik shared their grief. And yet she couldn't help herself. She kept waiting for news that her brother was dead too.

She stopped praying at the Temple of White Stone. She was barely eating; food tasted like ash. The news from the front came in fits and starts. Patrick had won a skirmish. He was drawing back to the far side of the Gray Marshes. Some of the Vestrian lords were desperate to sue for peace, even if that meant total surrender. Patrick was dead. No, he was alive, but had lost a battle, and it was Lord Winter of Bolton who was dead.

As one month passed, and then another, Cora had terrible nightmares. In her dreams, she saw the repeated vision of Patrick cut down by a warrior in an angular helmet with just a thin slit for his eyes.

Erik grew increasingly worried about her. Silvia fussed over her. Hailsham bustled about the palace, as if keeping the linen fresh and the bannisters free of dust would make their greater fears melt away.

Then, one night, Cora found herself gasping in her bed, staring at the ceiling. Once again, nightmares had plagued her sleep; her brother had been beheaded in front of her. She couldn't bear it anymore. She had to do something.

Her memory gave her an image. She was outside a stone building facing a man with dark, intense eyes. She remembered the black priest's offer to help her father... an offer she had spurned.

She made a decision.

She went to the Temple of White Stone and sat on the broad stairs outside the main entrance. Clad in a gray hooded cloak, she kept her head down and waited. People climbed up the steps, entered the temple, prayed, and returned the way they had come. No one paid her any attention. Remembering that the black priest had never crossed the threshold, she came day after day and sat in the same place.

Then she looked up, and there he was, standing right in front of her.

Cora looked up at the slender man with his pale face obscured by the hooded black robe. She slowly stood.

Glancing around, she saw that they were alone, a good distance from the temple's entrance. Nonetheless, when she spoke, it was in a low voice, for the black priest's ears alone.

"I have only heard stories," she said. "What can you do? Can you... can you bring him back?" She had to force her next words out. "My father. Can you...?"

The black priest tilted his head forward, staring directly into her eyes. "Return your father from death?"

Cora nodded, not trusting herself to speak.

"Let me explain," he said, still holding her gaze. "The shadow world and this world are close, mirror images of each other." He paused. "Whereas the true afterlife is distant, beyond your imaginings. Yes, those of my order have some power over life and death." When she opened her mouth, he held up a slim-fingered hand. "But I am afraid, Princess Coraline, that I cannot bring your father back from the grave. He has already gone to the next world. Your father has earned the right to be united with your mother."

Cora's feelings were bittersweet. "Then how can you help? What about our enemies? Can you strike them down?"

"Perhaps Graven Callow could die quietly in his sleep, leaving his army leaderless and followers confused?" the black priest asked. He shook his head. "No, Princess. We can only work through people, not directly with them—or against them."

"Then you have nothing to offer."

Ignoring her, the black priest pressed on, "You came here. You want my help, and I do have an offer to make. It is true that I have some power over life and death, however I can only bring back those who inhabit the umbra, the shadow world, neither in the white light of Arcadia nor the fires of Abaddon. I cannot bring back your father, Princess. However there is one there who may give you what you seek."

Cora tilted her head, waiting for him to continue.

"The man I speak of is your ancestor. He is the greatest general of his age, the man who forged your nation into steel and built it into an empire. He defeated the armies of Vailand and brought his mortal enemy Baelock Fain to final justice." The black priest waited for effect; his stare was unrelenting. "I can bring back your great-grandfather, Malgannis, known as Ironclaw."

Cora took a sharp breath. Even hearing the name... Malgannis. People told stories about Malgannis not just in Aranor, but in all the nations of the world.

Her brother was young and inexperienced. With a man like Malgannis by his side...

"How can I believe you?"

"A black priest never lies." He shrugged. "I can show you things that will convince you beyond any doubt as to my abilities. I ask for no gold. We in my order deal in other stores of value."

"What do you want in return?" she asked. "They say you always seek a price."

"Yes, and the price is always high. Very high. But, Princess, I think you knew that before you came here."

Cora's whirling thoughts took focus. Her brother was going to die. Her enemies would destroy everything. They would burn down her city. They would butcher Aranor's people.

Cora spoke solemnly. She knew what she was asking. "What is your price?"

"Your life," the black priest answered. He held up a hand. "Not immediately. I can offer you thirty days. I can bring Malgannis back to this world, and I will not take my price, your body, for thirty days. Your life force is valuable, Princess. You are young and healthy, born to privilege. This bargain can be made. But you must make it willingly."

Part of Cora was screaming at her, telling her to turn around and run and never come back, to hide away and pretend she had never even contemplated doing such a thing.

But Patrick needed her. Aranor needed her. Stuck here in Adin, there was nothing else she could do.

And Malgannis... he was the hero that Aranor needed.

Cora lifted her chin. "Ninety days." She couldn't believe what she was proposing, even as she said the words.

The black priest actually smiled. "You have this one offer, and you would bargain?"

"If I am giving you my life, I need time to set events in motion. Thirty days is too short. I want ninety."

"I can give you ten more days."

"Then we are done here."

The black priest's smile fell, becoming a scowl. "Ninety days is much too long. I proposed thirty." He contemplated, and then finally spoke. "Sixty days is enough to turn this war around or lose it altogether. You have my final offer, and I warn you, do not push me any harder." He stared into her eyes. "Are we agreed? If not, all I have to do is wait until more people die and your desperation grows. And the next time, Princess, the bargain will be worse, I can assure you."

Cora swallowed. "Sixty days. We are agreed." She had one final question, the question she understood to be the most important of all. "What about my soul?"

"Never fear," the black priest said. "Your soul remains your own. When the time comes, you will be free to join your father in the afterlife."

Cora knew what the stories said; she should be specific. "To join my father in Arcadia. Not Abaddon."

The black priest smiled. "That judgment is not mine to make, but yes, I do not expect you to be sucked down into the fires of Abaddon, and our bargain is for your life, not your soul. Your father is in paradise. This is the trade on offer. In sixty days, you lose your life on this world. In return, Malgannis Vandryden, known as Ironclaw, your great-grandfather, will return to life through the Temple of Black Glass."

Cora realized she was holding her breath and let it out. She thought about her life. She had people who would miss her. She immediately pictured Patrick. But also Silvia, Hailsham... Last of all, Erik's face came to her mind.

Cora didn't know much about war, but everyone always said that Malgannis was a military genius. Her mouth was dry and she tried to moisten it.

"What is your name?" she asked the black priest.

"Lexen," he said. He had a gleam in his eyes. "Lexen Crow."

Cora searched for a sign, staring up at the sky. A crow flew past the peaked roof of the white temple. It was a big one. Huge.

"You know what will happen to all this," Lexen murmured. Meanwhile, Cora continued to scan the heavens. "Think of what happened to Rumandy. Aranor is doomed. Bones will litter these streets. Adin will crumble to dust. You have heard the men talk. They say Graven Callow is an expert strategist. A tactical mastermind. The world hasn't seen his like since Baelock Fain, and Malgannis himself. Think, Princess Coraline. It takes fire to fight fire."

Cora had turned away the black priest's previous offer. She could have helped her father but didn't. Patrick was the only family she had left. Her brother was afraid.

Above Cora's head, the huge crow tried to settle onto the temple's roof. But a handful of angry white birds – doves – flew out of some hidden place to frighten the crow away.

Cora focused on Lexen Crow and spoke with steel in her voice. "I will do it."

Lexen glanced around to confirm that they were still alone, and lowered his voice still further.

"Come tonight to the eastern entrance of the catacombs. A rite must be performed. You have a part to play. You will sign our bargain in blood, and you will be marked. It will be frightening, but in three days, Malgannis Vandryden will pass through the Temple of Black Glass and reenter this world."

As soon as he finished speaking, the black priest swept away.

Chapter 12

CORA WAS STILL STARING into the glowing coals held tightly in the brazier's iron grip.

She had performed the rite two weeks ago. That night was the most terrifying of her life. But she played her part and completed it, despite the things she had seen and done.

When it was over, a mark had appeared on her forearm, half way between her wrist and elbow. The blemish was a sickly green, like a gangrenous spiral. Her sixty days began. Now, fourteen of her sixty days were already gone.

She peeled back the fabric of her long-sleeved riding dress to look again at her mark. With every passing day, it became angrier. Now, it had the appearance of a welt surrounded by spidery bruising.

She froze when she heard movement behind her. Hastily she pulled her sleeve back to her wrist. A throat cleared. She turned.

Malgannis stood with legs apart, framed in the tent's entrance.

Cora tried to calm her breathing. The light was low, but bright enough to see him clearly, and now he was made more real.

Malgannis was tall, but she had expected that, with powerful shoulders and a solid torso. He looked strong, even at his age. He had his thumbs hooked in his belt. His hands were huge.

His scraggly hair was long and shifted colors between gray and dark brown. The skin she could see, on his hands and face, was weathered and tanned the color of leather. The dark eyes he rested on her were piercing, and there was fire within them; this wasn't a man she wanted to see angry. He wore high boots with leather laces, black trousers, and a jerkin over a cloth doublet—a slightly archaic costume, but not enough to make him stand out.

He was inspecting her in turn, and she wondered what he was seeing. Erik would have told him enough for him to figure out who she was, and how they were related. Did he see a girl, a child, decorated with jewelry and clearly swimming in waters well out of her depth? Or did he see a determined woman, a princess, who would do anything to ensure the survival of her nation and her brother, the king?

For a long time neither of them spoke. And then Malgannis scowled and walked inside. Given his size, she inadvertently stepped back while he held his hands out over the brazier. He leveled her with a flat stare.

"I have a few questions," he said.

His voice was like a growl, low and rumbling, with the veiled threat of rising to become something much more frightening.

Cora kept her face smooth. "I am sure you do."

"You look pale," he said.

Her brow creased just a little but she ignored the comment. "My name is Coraline, as you no doubt know." She hesitated, wondering what to say next. He rubbed his hands together, eager for the brazier's warmth. She was hoping he could advise her brother. Help them all to win this war. Help Patrick to survive. By the gods, he looked old. "What do you know?"

"Only what I learned from Erik, which was nothing at all."

"I asked him not to—"

"Not to ask who I was? I was dead, and somehow, I'm now alive. I can't figure out myself what is happening, let alone share it with others. I was hoping you would know."

"Perhaps we should start at the beginning," she said.

"You're my great-granddaughter," he interrupted.

She nodded.

"I remember your father," he said. "My grandson. I held him up in the air. He was just a babe." His gave a slight smile. "Strong voice."

Cora glanced at the tent's wall so that she wouldn't have to meet his continued stare. He looked disconcertingly like her father. "This is a strange situation we find ourselves in."

"Why am I here? How is it possible?"

She had thought hard about what she could reveal. "I made a bargain with a black priest."

"For me?"

She nodded.

"Why?" he demanded.

"I need your help. We are losing this war. My brother and I are supposed to protect our people, but Graven Callow wants us gone. Patrick needs you, or he is going to die, as will everyone I care about." She lifted her chin to meet his eyes; he was much taller. "Just like my father died."

Malgannis listened to her speech but revealed nothing. Then his shoulders sank as he sighed. Whatever she had said, it wasn't what he wanted to hear. "Tell me, girl. How am I supposed to help?"

Cora tilted her head, puzzled. "You said it yourself... you're my great-grandfather. You're Malgannis Ironclaw."

"My last name is Vandryden," Malgannis said. "You haven't said how I'm supposed to help."

The furrows in Cora's brow grew deeper. "I've grown up with stories about you. They teach your tactics at the academy. Everyone thought the Vailanders couldn't be beaten, that Baelock Fain was going to rule the world. Instead, it was you. You won. You ruled the world... or at least, you could have."

"I never wanted to be king."

"I know that," Cora said. "You gave the throne to your son. You didn't fight for power, for yourself. You fought for what you believed in. That's why you can help."

"I fought for vengeance," Malgannis said abruptly.

She noticed him looking at the lines on his hands. Battle scars. It truly was him.

But he wasn't a dead hero, a mythical figure told of in stories and praised in speeches by the kings and queens of the world's nations. He was an old, beaten down man, and he was tired. He wasn't the Malgannis who had fought the Vailanders. He was the Malgannis who had died a broken man, having completed his final, successful capture of Baelock Fain, after ten years of trying.

Malgannis cleared his throat, and she wondered what he was going to say. He was wrestling with something, and she felt the kindling of hope. Aranor was his homeland. He was going to tell her what he could do.

"Princess," he said. "I have seen a few things in my time, and I've also listened to what Erik had to say. You've already lost Rumandy. It's a matter of time before Vestria falls. Your brother has an impossible task."

Cora struggled to keep her voice steady. "I know. That's why we need you."

Fire flashed in his eyes. "You aren't listening, girl, or perhaps I'm not being clear enough. You only have one option, and perhaps it's what I should have done all those years ago. If I were you, I would find a ship to take me across the Sea of Mirrors and find a new life somewhere else." His eyes narrowed and his tone became even harsher. "Leave me out of your plans. I don't want any part in them."

As he spoke, Cora couldn't hide her shock. *He isn't going to help*. She kept repeating the phrase, over and over. Of all the outcomes to their meeting, it was the one thing she hadn't been prepared for. For a long time, she found herself unable to reply.

"You built Aranor into what it is today," she whispered.

"It's a shade of what I built. I'm old. I'm tired. I can't do it again."

Moisture began to burn behind her eyes. "They say you loved Aranor. Blue and gold, you would shout, as you led the charge."

"I did..."

"But not anymore? Why not help us?

His eyebrows came together in anger. "Because it's too hard, that's why not."

"Don't you care about what happens to me and my brother? What about your people?"

"I don't owe you anything," he said roughly, "and I don't owe them anything either. When I died, you weren't even born."

"Why, then?" The question was all she had left. "Why did you come here with Erik to see me?"

"Because I was dead and now I'm not. I wanted to know why. I thought there might be something more to it. More than just..." He gestured vaguely. "This."

"Well, you have satisfied your curiosity now." Cora tried to restore her mask, the smooth expression that meant she could keep her emotions protected, but knew she was failing.

"I have," he said. He inspected her for a moment and then softened his tone. "Tell me, Coraline, what did the black priest tell you about me?"

She remembered clearly. "He said you were between worlds."

"And that's where I deserve to be. There is something I want, it's true, and that's why I came here. But it's something you can't offer me. You made a mistake, bringing me back." He shook his head. "You should have known better."

Cora's mouth dropped open as she failed to keep her mask again; she continued to struggle, desperate to hide her feelings from this man, this... stranger.

"Farewell, Coraline," Malgannis said.

"Where are you going?" she asked as he turned to leave.

"I'm heading back to the Temple of Glass to try to get back to where I was." He spoke with heavy irony. "Well, either that or die trying. The outcome is the same anyway."

"Why are you like this? Don't you want to live?"

"I've had my life. I made my mistakes. I don't deserve a second life."

"You have no idea what I did to bring you back."

His face was hard. There was no sympathy in him at all. "Whatever it was, you know I didn't ask you to do it."

✦

Malgannis was again within the forest, on his way back to the north, to Mount Janus and the Temple of Black Glass. He was alone, and preferred it that way, without any other company than his horse, tied up to a tree nearby. He sat with his back against a rock and stared into the flames of his fire. If he wanted a fire, he could have a fire. If someone found him and killed him—well, death was where he was going anyway.

His plan was to get back to the temple. He would dive into the pool with stones in his pockets and his feet tied together. Then it would all be over.

Life was too intense. In front of him, there was warmth from the fire, but if he leaned forward, the heat on his skin would be too hot. At his back was hard stone and chill. He hadn't eaten before riding away from Coraline's camp, and rumbles of hunger felt like they were tearing holes in his stomach. Even if he did eat, the satisfaction would eventually fade, and then he would feel the irritation of hunger again. His legs were sore from riding. Resting them felt good. But tomorrow they would be even sorer. And so it went, on and on.

Life was hard.

He scowled at the flames. He could still see the emotions on the girl's face. In this world, he had people's feelings to deal with. His own feelings. More than anything, he was disappointed. He had thought there was some greater purpose in his rebirth, something more than a girl's mistaken need for an aging general.

At least in the shadow world, everything was numbed.

Chapter 13

CORA SWORE. She could almost hear Silvia admonishing her: ladies didn't swear. But it felt appropriate to the situation.

"This is not good," she muttered to herself.

A gray sky hung like a smothering blanket overhead; it was a gloomy morning, something to match Cora's mood. She was on horseback, heading back to Aranor with Erik riding by her side. Trailing a little way after came Helen, her maid, and then the escort of knights fanned out around them as they followed a muddy path between low grassy hills. They had left early. The Statue of Palindor was already a few hours ride away.

"Halt!" One of the knights called. He looked over at Cora and raised an inquiring eyebrow. "My Lady?"

"Have they seen us?" Cora asked.

She shielded her eyes; despite the lack of sunlight, the pale sky created a painful glare. She focused on a large number of distant figures. They were mounted warriors, side by side on a ridge, where they appeared to be facing the direction of Cora's group. As soon as she had seen their familiar armor and blue cloaks, Cora knew she might be in trouble.

"I would say they have," Erik said. Cora glanced at him but he didn't look her way. "Here they come."

The patrol kicked in. As the riders approached, making their way down the slope in order to meet Cora's group, she sawed at the reins, turning her mare toward the newcomers.

As Cora began to rehearse what she would say, she noticed Helen give her a panicked look. The maid understood little about their purpose here in the borderlands, but knew enough to worry about any repercussions for herself.

Cora maintained her composure and watched her countrymen, resting her gaze in particular on the middle-aged captain at the front. As he rode toward her position, he appeared tired. They all did. These men had been fighting, far from home, for months.

"My Lady," the captain said, reining in. He spent a few moments casting his eyes over Cora, Erik, Helen, the knights, and their baggage horses. She felt her blood rise as he took his time, clearly making a point, but she kept her calm. He finally returned his attention to her. "Your presence here is... unexpected."

"I am sure it is," she said. "Captain...?"

"Harris, My Lady."

"I am sure it is, Captain Harris. But as with many things, it is no concern of yours. Pressing business brought us here and now takes us back to Aranor. We must be on our way—"

"Your brother the king will wish to see you, Princess."

"I appreciate that—"

Captain Harris was firm. "Lady, our enemies are on the move. This area is not safe. I do not relish explaining to the king that I saw his sister so near and did not escort you to his protection."

"You think I would not be safer in Aranor?" Cora gave it one last try.

"In Aranor, yes," he said. "But this is not Aranor."

Cora realized it was no longer worth trying. "Fine," she said. "Lead the way."

✦

Cora and Erik followed Captain Harris as he strode swiftly through the sprawling military encampment. Despite its transitory nature, the camp was huge, the temporary home to the combined armies of Aranor and Vestria, as well as the soldiers who had made it out of Rumandy before the fall.

Rushes laid on the ground helped with the treacherous mud as Cora passed rows of tents with parallel paths between them. Cooking fires occupied larger junctions; hobbled horses stirred at the fringes. The air smelled of smoke, sweat, and stew. The mood from the men was one of resignation to the gray skies, cold, and frequent rains.

Cora wore her gray over-cloak, and even though it wasn't presently raining she kept her hood up to cover her face. Even so, a well-dressed woman drew attention, and curious soldiers glanced her way, eyes widening when they realized who she was. Every reaction was a reminder to Cora that she shouldn't be here. Patrick was going to be angry, to say the least.

And yet, in spite of everything, she was also excited to be seeing him. They had only corresponded in writing since he left for the front, and since then their father had died and he had become king. She knew Patrick would have to be stern for as long as they were being watched by the men, but she was looking forward to a chance to be alone with him. She at least had Erik to share her grief with, as well as Silvia and Hailsham. Who had consoled Patrick? She had been home, in familiar surroundings. He hadn't been able to weep, or to go for long walks and rides and make peace with his regrets. Instead, the leader of a great army, he would have been forced to bury his pain.

Cora left behind the section of Vestrian soldiers in green and silver uniforms. About to enter the greater Aranese section, she walked past some officers meeting under an open pavilion. The officers pored over a table, and although she couldn't see what lay on it, she caught some of their words.

"...all going to come to a head. The question is... where are they now?"

Cora glanced at Erik, wondering how he was feeling. His jaw was clenched, his face filled with resolve. She knew him well enough to know he had come to some decision. She had a feeling what it might be.

"This way," Captain Harris said. He came to a stop at another junction and indicated a tent the size of the dining hall in Adin Palace. "That's the infirmary. You will find the king in there, My Lady."

"Thank you, Captain."

With Erik at her side, Cora approached the open-sided tent. She didn't need to wonder where her brother was, there was only one corner where a large group of onlookers stood in a circle facing something. Heading over, she made her way forward until she saw that the group encircled one of the infirmary's many beds.

Cora saw Patrick.

She almost cried out loud, just to see his face. Everything was driven home, how much she had missed him, how alone she had felt these past months. Without thinking, she grabbed hold of Erik's hand and squeezed tightly. But she didn't approach right away.

Patrick was busy.

The closest to the infirmary bed, Patrick remained crouched on one knee and held the hand of a groaning, wounded soldier. Cora couldn't stop herself from inspecting Patrick's face. He always had a sunny manner, but at the moment, he looked worn, like he had aged a decade or more. His brown hair was lighter than hers, chestnut to her ebony, and matched the color of his short beard and mustache. They both shared the high cheekbones that were an inheritance from their mother.

As Cora stood with Erik, she continued to watch her brother. Patrick didn't have her habit of keeping his face expressionless. He allowed his emotion to show for all to see, as he held the wounded man's hand and gazed into his pained, contorted visage.

Cora blanched when she saw the blood welling around the wounded soldier's torso. The man's breath wheezed in his chest. His eyes darted from one place to another.

"You are dying," a solemn voice said nearby. Cora followed the sound until she saw a robed white priest, a man with a snowy beard, standing on the other side of the infirmary bed. "I can ease your pain with a potion and give you final rites. I am here. Give me your agreement."

Cora waited for the wounded man to nod. White priests were healers and confessors. They gave blessings to new babes and eased the suffering of those at the end of their lives. Their temples filled every city and their kindness was legendary. And they did it all without magic, for as they constantly preached and Cora knew herself, the only magic was black magic.

"No," the soldier panted. He coughed and sputtered blood across his lips and chin. "Bring me a black priest."

The crowd of onlookers stirred. The soldiers near Cora and Erik exchanged glances.

Patrick spoke in a soft, but grim voice. "Are you sure, Tomas?"

"I..." The wounded man, Tomas, coughed again; it took some time for him to get out the words. "I am certain, Sire. It is what I want."

Patrick nodded to someone. A few moments passed, and, surprisingly swiftly, a newcomer came to the edge of the group. The black-robed figure didn't need to ask the onlookers to draw apart.

Cora turned and watched, holding her breath as she stared at the face within the black hood. But when the newcomer removed her hood, rather than the slender frame and intense stare of Lexen Crow, she found herself looking at green eyes and an olive complexion, framed by curling honey-colored hair. The black priestess was a woman, and she was surprisingly pretty.

The wounded soldier on the bed watched the woman in black come to his bedside. "I want to make a bargain," he said hoarsely. "For my life, but not my soul."

"I first must see your wounds," the black priestess said. Coming in closer, she inclined her head at Patrick. He was the king, but he released the man's hand he was holding so she could come in.

As the black priestess inspected Tomas's wounds, the white priest made a sound of disgust and withdrew. The black priestess ignored him and without hesitation tugged the linen bandages away from the soldier's torso. Cora's jaw tightened. Her mouth tasted strangely metallic. She saw deep, slashing wounds and blood that kept rising up. The black priestess bent down to make her assessment.

"You may last the night. It is possible," the black priestess concluded. She gently but firmly replaced the bandages to where they were before. "Give me your remaining time on this world and I will grant you a small boon."

"I..." Tomas blinked, and all of a sudden he wasn't a man, he was a small boy, alone and frightened. "I want to speak with my wife."

"Say these words," the black priestess said. She bent down and spoke into the soldier's ear.

Tomas began to murmur. His voice rose at the end. "I agree to this with my eyes open."

Cora remembered saying the same words, although her own rite had been much more elaborate.

And she had given the black priest much more.

"Sire..." Tomas turned his head to gaze up at Patrick. "This is what I want. Leave me now."

Patrick opened his mouth but then his lips closed. He nodded. Reaching in again, he gaze the soldier's hand a final squeeze. "Farewell, my friend."

"Farewell, Sire."

Patrick opened his arms and addressed the group of onlookers to move them away. "Let us leave."

Cora couldn't help but watch for a moment longer. She saw the black priestess grab the soldier on the bed by the elbow. Even as Cora looked on, a spiral-shaped welt, an ugly green blemish like a bruise, appeared on his forearm. The black priestess's eyes glazed.

"What is it?" the priestess asked in the voice of another woman. Her tone was confused. "What is happening?"

Tears flowed down the wounded soldier's cheeks. "My love... it's me. I'm dying."

The green blemish on the soldier's forearm began to grow. It traveled up and down his arm, continuing up to the exposed skin on his neck. Cora shivered. The black priestess's mark traveled up toward his face. Clearly, he didn't have long, but hopefully the priestess had granted him enough time to give him the solace he sought.

Then Cora felt a strong hand take her forearm and guide her, hauling her out of the infirmary. Patrick's eyes were fiery, but he didn't say anything until he had led her away from his men.

Cora found herself back in the open air, under the gray sky, standing in front of her brother. She had forgotten how powerful he could seem. He had the athletic build of a natural warrior, and was taller than both her and Erik.

"Cora?" Patrick demanded. He glanced at the man beside her. "Erik? What in the names of all the gods are you doing here?"

Erik remained silent. Cora knew that she was the one who had to reply, but for a moment she was speechless.

"I wanted to help you," she said.

Her words were foolish even to her own ears. She knew she sounded like a little girl, recklessly putting herself in harm's way to be with her older brother, when she had never held a sword, knew nothing of warfare, and would only give Patrick another thing to worry about.

Yet she couldn't say anything more. She had wanted so badly to do something for him.

Malgannis was a mistake.

As Patrick glared at her, she fought to keep her eyes from welling up. She had made a bargain, a bargain for her life, and it had come to nothing.

"You were helping me by staying in Adin," Patrick snapped. His attention shifted. "Erik. I gave you one order—"

"It's not his fault," Cora began.

"Sire!" called a parade-ground voice, making the three of them turn. Cora saw a barrel-chested officer with his helmet under his arm. "Our scouts just returned. We have sighted the enemy."

Patrick started. "How near?"

"We are readying for battle."

Cora was watching Patrick's face. He didn't appear anxious or frightened; he looked eager. "Finally," he said.

"Patrick..." Cora began.

He reached out to take both her arms. "We will speak later." He saw something in her expression. "Don't worry," he said with a smile. "We have been chasing each other all over Huron Plain. This will likely be another skirmish." He pulled her in for a hug, and she held him tightly. "I love you," he said into her ear.

"I love you too."

He pushed her away. "Now, stay here until I get back. I'll get a proper escort ready to take you to Adin."

"Patrick... We need a proper chance to talk. There is something I have to tell you."

"We'll talk later, I promise." Patrick began to get distracted, glancing away from Cora to look at the preparations in the camp. He returned his attention to her, but she knew her brother. He had the poise of a cat about to pounce. "Have courage, Cora. Now, I must go."

Patrick gave her hand a final squeeze, and strode away to meet the barrel-chested officer. Words between them were swift and hurried as they traveled the camp, calling out orders as they went.

As she watched her brother's back, Cora couldn't help remembering some of the words he had written to her. *There are many who resent my command, and perhaps they are right, perhaps I am indeed too inexperienced.* She remembered Logan Kane, Baron of Fastness, expressing the same concern.

Patrick would be fine, she told herself.

"Cora."

She saw Erik standing in front of her. His eyes were filled with sympathy, but the familiar resolve was still in his jaw. "He is right. Have courage." He cleared his throat. "Now, I must leave you. You know that I have to fight with them. I am a captain in the army. I need to take my place."

"I know," Cora said. It was all she could say.

"We'll speak afterwards," Erik said.

Cora nodded, and watched as Erik rushed away to catch up with Patrick. Soon Cora was standing alone, in the midst of a storm that somehow left her completely untouched. As officers roared and soldiers raced to their bidding, she looked toward the open-sided tent, wondering about the wounded man in the infirmary.

There were no onlookers now. There was no black priestess.

Instead, a sheet of white linen covered a motionless lump on the bed.

Chapter 14

CORA COULDN'T REMAIN STILL. There was a strange atmosphere in Patrick's camp, both tense and expectant. The life that had filled the place had evaporated. Not long ago it had been bustling, the scene of purpose and activity. Now, it was a ball after the guests had left, a dinner of half-empty plates and chairs in disarray. She couldn't help but ask herself the question: would the people come back?

She found herself searching, moving about the place, poking her head into empty tents and receiving curious glances from cooks and camp followers. It took her some time to find the woman, but there she was, a figure in a hooded black robe. The priestess was walking with a long stride, taking the main path that bisected the camp.

Cora stopped. "Priestess," she called.

The black priestess paused and glanced over her shoulder. She slowly turned. "Yes?"

Cora walked up to the woman in black. A few strands of hair the shade of honey poked out from the woman's hood. Cora met her green eyes. "I need to speak with you."

The black priestess's expression remained cold. "Your needs and mine are not the same."

Cora softened her tone. "Please."

"What is it?"

Cora glanced around. "Not here."

She indicated the black priestess to follow, and the woman sighed and fell in behind her. Cora led her to a narrow passage between two tall tents where no-one would see them.

Cora hesitated, and then peeled back her right sleeve. The ugly green blemish had grown. The mark was yet to reach her wrist or elbow, but the tendrils were beginning to wrap all the way around her arm.

"I want to know if I can reverse this."

The black priestess's eyes were wide with surprise. There was something else too: mingled sympathy and sorrow. She spoke in a low voice. "You must know, Princess. A bargain once struck can never be reversed."

Cora had expected as much, but her heart still sank. She wished she had never heard the name Malgannis. "Never?"

"The only one who could ever remove that mark is the priest or priestess who put it on you. And that is something they would never do." The black priestess reached out and unrolled Cora's long sleeve back to its original position. "Never fear, Princess. I will never tell. This mark is for you to bear alone."

The black priestess turned and strode away, leaving Cora to watch her go.

✦

The sun peeked between the clouds, showing its face before returning once more to hiding. The gray sky had shifted to white, and the lack of rain still held, but the day was just as gloomy.

Malgannis reined in. He was on high ground, half way along a trail that traversed a long slope. A line of trees was on one side, while on the other, the hillside descended, falling away toward the plain where the ruins of Leventhal littered the landscape.

A moment ago trees had framed the trail on both sides. It was only now that the hillside had opened up, giving him a clear view of the broken city below, and the rolling terrain surrounding the crumbling walls and stone structures. He had been thinking about the Temple of Black Glass. He was determined to go there, taking the shortest route possible.

Yet he had stopped. Despite everything, he had to watch. Two armies were about to collide on the plain, outside the remnant of Leventhal's outer wall.

Malgannis's roving gaze moved from one place to another. He saw two hills, one on either side of the plain. Each hill looked like a strange, colorful forest. The hill on the right, farthest from the ruins, was home to a swath of small figures, one a mass of blue and gold, another green and silver, horses in a cluster, archers in rows. The other hill, at Malgannis's left, thronged with the darker colors of Morania, Nara, and Kor.

Malgannis couldn't help it. He assessed the different forces and the way they were deployed; he read the terrain, searching for anything that might reveal the outcome of the battle. The Aranese and Vestrians had chosen their ground well. An abutment gave their archers somewhere to move to once the battle began, a place where they had coverage of the plain but enough height to make them difficult to dislodge. The commander – Patrick, Malgannis couldn't help reminding himself – had the steeper hill. His knights would gather momentum and strike the enemy position with terrible force. The enemy possessed a far greater number of infantry, but fewer bowmen and mounted warriors.

Malgannis's eyes didn't stop moving. He took his vision farther, to places unexpected, and that was when he saw them.

Broad dark shapes with long spindly legs stirred in the trees a few miles uphill—the same hill where Malgannis had reined in. He saw the flashes of movement, knowing he was looking at a number of horses; it didn't matter how many, because the fact that a battle was about to begin told him that he wouldn't find a small force gathered up here where no one would expect them to be.

Returning his attention to the scene below, he noticed something else in the ruins. A few long, thin sticks poked up from behind a series of low stone walls. All he saw were the tops of the bows, but he knew he was looking at archers. As with the horses, it didn't matter how many he could see now, Graven Callow would have deployed the numbers needed to make all the difference when battle was joined.

As he experienced a rising dread, Malgannis fitted the pieces together, working it out in his mind.

The Moranians couldn't have prepared for this battle at the last minute. Instead, Callow had left these units here days ago. Meanwhile, he had moved his army around, pretending to fall back and choose the battleground at the last minute.

Genius.

Even in his reluctant admiration, Malgannis's nostrils flared, and as his horse sensed his tension, the creature stirred underneath his body. He realized his hands holding the reins were tight, the knuckles white.

A long, low horn blast shook the trees and filled the air with a rumbling that Malgannis knew all too well; tactics may shift and change, but the horns always sounded the same. An answering horn pealed from the direction of the Aranese forces.

The army of Morania began to move.

The charge began slowly, gathering speed, like ants spilling down a hill. The figures grew larger in Malgannis's vision as they raced toward the plain, becoming individual soldiers. A thin line of horsemen drew away from the larger host of Moranian infantry, and one warrior on a gray warhorse wore plate armor with an angular helmet, right at the front as he held his sword high.

The first blast from Aranor signaled the archers, who stepped forward and bent their bows and bodies to launch a volley of arrows sailing into the air. The black shafts arced across the sky, reaching their apex, before the sharp metal head dragged them down. Holes appeared in the ranks of the enemy infantry as they ran.

Aranor and Vestria charged too, even as the archers commenced another volley into the midst of the enemy infantry heading toward them. A force of knights remained on the hillside, ready to turn the tide where they could make the greatest difference.

Both sides now had mounted warriors outdistancing the soldiers on foot. There was still some time before the two armies collided...

Malgannis spied Patrick at the lead of a group of knights, greater in number than the force gathered around Graven. Malgannis remembered when he had first seen Patrick, a dashing figure in his silver armor and blue cloak, leading his men at Mount Janus. Back then Malgannis hadn't known who he was.

He didn't like what his mind was telling him. Patrick was his great-grandson. He was Cora's brother. Cora had wanted Malgannis to help him.

Malgannis started. Was that Erik? The man's frame was too familiar, along with his hair and the way he sat his horse. Erik was part of the group of knights charging on horseback, close by Patrick's side.

Malgannis wiped his hand over his face. He found himself wanting to take command and make changes to what was happening below. He leaned forward, knowing he was too late to do anything but also fighting the urge to snap his reins and roar at his horse. Part of him didn't want to watch.

Out in front of his infantry, Graven was too tempting a target for Patrick, who deftly turned his knights at the gallop so that they were lined up perfectly to charge into the smaller group of Moranian horsemen.

Here it came. Malgannis knew what would happen next.

The archers rose from hiding. As they straightened, they leveled their bows and pulled their bowstrings to their ears. The line of Aranese knights was right in front of them. Each knight had his back to the archers.

Strings thrummed. Malgannis could almost hear the sharp snaps from his position. This time, the arrows didn't arc through the air. The shafts shot straight ahead, and sharp iron peppered the knights from behind.

Men and horses screamed. Knights tumbled from their saddles.

Seeing the threat, Patrick had no choice. He wheeled his knights again, to turn them toward the ruins. He couldn't leave the archers where they were.

With their speed and heavy armor, the knights would cut through the weaker archers. But as they navigated between the remnants of the city wall, they were inevitably slowed. Swords rose and fell. Patrick's knights were swift and efficient. But by the time they had cleared the area, the two great forces heading straight for each other across the plain were about to smash together. And with no opposing knights to slow him down, Graven led his powerful horsemen punching into the Aranese infantry.

This time the crunch was audible even from Malgannis's height. Patrick regathered his knights and they raced toward the conflict. Graven was in the middle of the plain, a helmeted figure with his sword arm slashing left and right.

Malgannis had never felt so powerless. If he were Graven, this was when he would make the decisive blow.

On cue, the horses in the trees farther up began to leave their hiding place. The hill was steep, and they had to be careful, but a great number of them descended the slope to circle around the ruins.

Back on the battlefield, Patrick's reserve force had already joined in. The two armies surged back and forth. Horsemen mingled with swordsmen but also spearmen and archers. Large patches of black and crimson moved left and then right. A section of green and silver became enveloped.

Graven's hidden knights formed up. As a long line, they began to trot, then canter, and holding together in a row, they moved into a gallop. Malgannis searched for Erik but couldn't find him. Patrick was more readily made out in his silver armor and crown etched into his helmet. Soldiers fought and died. They milled back and forth. Graven and Patrick were each moving closer to the other.

The new force of knights striking the army of Aranor was like the crack that broke a mighty tree in half. Patrick's army began to crumble. Malgannis knew it was over when, at the rear, soldiers began to flee.

Graven and Patrick continued to draw near each other. The battle shifted. They were far apart, but then the horde of fighting men surged again.

The two leaders clashed together, one in a silver helmet with a blue crown, the other with steel facets obscuring his face.

Time slowed. Malgannis's vision became utterly focused on the engagement between the two men. He forget where he was, consumed by the sight of his great-grandson as he clashed swords with his enemy.

Patrick blocked an overhead blow and countered with a thrust. Graven knocked Patrick's sword to the side. Patrick tilted his body to evade Graven's blow. The two swords smashed together again.

Then Graven did something unexpected. He butted his gray warhorse into Patrick's white courser. Patrick was thrown off balance.

"Get up," Malgannis muttered. All of his attention was completely focused. "Get up!"

Patrick's body was low, his head down near his saddle as he struggled to right himself against the weight of his armor dragging him down. Both of Graven's arms went high, bringing his blade above his head. Malgannis didn't want it to happen... it couldn't be happening.

Graven's arms came sweeping down. With terrible force, he crashed his sharp steel blade onto Patrick's neck. When Patrick's armor prevented a clean strike, Graven pulled his weapon back. He lined up his sword and then thrust the point into Patrick's throat. He knew what he was doing and found the gap between helmet and armor. Patrick dropped his own blade. His hands went to his neck.

Seeing their king in trouble, the Aranese knights charged into the fray. Graven was pushed back, farther, until the maelstrom of battle carried him away. Patrick's companions caught him as he toppled.

Malgannis was utterly still. He didn't blink. He was no longer breathing. He knew he had just watched his great-grandson killed in front of him.

Coraline. Poor Coraline.

Wait.

Malgannis had last seen Coraline and Erik together. If Erik was with Patrick... then she must be too.

All of a sudden, time began to move once more. Malgannis gasped. His eyes burned like fire.

But there was also another fire inside him, a rage that built up and fed him. This was a sensation he hadn't experienced in a long time. Urgency was like lightning throughout his body; searing heat burned his blood. He made a decision, not with his head, but with his heart.

He yanked at the reins to turn his horse. He cried out and slammed his heels into the animal's flanks. Below Malgannis, the army of Aranor and Vestria continued to fall apart, breaking into small groups of soldiers that fled for their lives.

Malgannis put his head down and spurred his horse onward.

Chapter 15

CORA PACED THE INTERIOR of the sparsely furnished tent her maid Helen had somehow claimed. She glared at Helen, who sat by a table with a book in front of her. The fact that Helen didn't appear to be aware of her pacing made her even more tense and irritable.

"I can't handle this," Cora said. "I'm taking a horse..."

Helen shut her book with a snap and set it down. She stood and walked toward Cora until she was directly in front of her. "No, Lady, you are not. Not this time. Lady Silvia told me not to let you do anything foolish. And I am more afraid of her than I am of you."

Cora lifted her chin. She opened her mouth to retort when she heard a series of sounds that made her body go rigid.

Hooves thundered on the ground. Horses whinnied with the panicked shriek Cora had only heard a few times in her life. Men's voices were just as frantic.

Cora stared at Helen as her maid looked right back at her, showing the whites of her eyes. The cries and screams grew louder.

Cora reached out, grabbed Helen's hand, and pulled them both from the tent. She immediately fell back, nearly run down as an Aranese horseman galloped through the camp. Blood spattered the knight's face; his expression was terrified.

More riders raced heedlessly along the path through the camp. Men pulled up, jumped off their mounts, and entered tents. They grabbed packs, threw themselves back onto horseback, dug in their heels, and fled.

The mounted warriors came in ones and twos, and then a steady trickle. Their eyes were wild. None of them stopped to talk.

"What's happening?" Cora cried to a knight whose face looked like a wine stain.

He ignored her and nursed his right arm, holding the reins in his left. His two companions both carried sacks of grain on the saddles in front of them. They were cantering, and soon picked up pace to follow the other riders racing away from the camp.

Everyone was taking the same route: away from the direction they had taken to reach the battle.

A bald soldier with a salt and pepper beard emerged from the tent just opposite Cora's, on the other side of the main path. With his pack heavy on his back, he reached his horse and began to stuff additional bundles into his saddle bags.

"What's happening?" Cora shouted at him.

The bald man climbed up onto his horse's back. He glanced at Cora. His expression was something she knew she would never forget: despair mingled with desperation along with fear and grief.

"The king is dead," he said. "We lost the battle. Get out of here. While you can!"

Without another word he roared at his horse and galloped away, following the other riders all with the same plan. Cora doubted he knew who she was. Just a woman in camp, standing open-mouthed, so shocked she was numb.

The sounds of panicked horses and men began to fade away from her consciousness. Her vision became black at the edges, with the visible portion shrinking smaller and smaller. She felt like she was underwater, at the bottom of a deep dark well. The water surrounding her was cold, so cold she couldn't feel a thing. Her mind wasn't connected to her body; it was somewhere else, and she didn't know if she wanted it back. The water made her sway. The only light she could see was rippling. Shapes became blurred. Sounds were muffled.

Cora was dimly aware of foot soldiers swarming the camp, grabbing anything they thought they needed as they ran. Helen was yanking at her arm, over and over again, screaming at her.

"Coraline. Coraline! If that's true then you're now the queen. We have to leave. Now!"

It wasn't true. Cora knew it wasn't true. Patrick couldn't be dead. She had just seen him. They had embraced. They had made plans to talk.

"It isn't true," she realized she was saying it out loud.

Then someone was standing in front of her: a tall man with a powerful frame and long graying hair past his shoulders. His eyes were dark and fierce.

"It is true," Malgannis said. He reached out and took Cora's shoulders. He didn't shake her; he simply stared directly into her eyes. "I saw it, Coraline. I am sorry."

Cora felt like her body had drained of all blood. "Erik?"

"As far as I know he is alive.

"Why are you here?" she whispered.

"I've come to help."

She shook her head. Her voice was hoarse. "Then you are too late."

"That may or may not be the case," Malgannis said. "Either way, right now, you need to get out of here. Your brother is dead, but you must survive."

Cora yanked herself free of his grip. "I don't need you." She faced her maid. "Helen, get the horses."

Helen didn't move; she was staring past Cora's shoulder. Cora whirled and realized what her maid was looking at.

She saw a Moranian knight ride down a young soldier, slashing him across the back. More enemy horsemen rushed into the camp, cutting down anyone they found. Cora realized that the attackers were rushing the area; in moments they outnumbered anyone else, and they only kept coming.

A mounted warrior in black uniform drew her attention. The rider had scars on his face and the feverish look of a man in the midst of battle rage. He held a naked blade, red with blood. Scanning the camp, he spied Cora standing with Helen and Malgannis. He kicked his powerful warhorse forward and raised his sword into the air.

Malgannis hadn't seen the scar-faced Moranian. "Coraline, you need my help. What would Patrick want?"

When she couldn't tear her eyes away from the frenzied Moranian, Malgannis noticed what had fixed her and Helen's attention.

"Here," he snapped at Helen. "Take this."

Cora watched Malgannis hand a length of reins to her maid, and realized he had a horse with him, a sturdy mare with a broad back.

Helen took the reins. Malgannis drew his sword. The Moranian spurred his horse onward as he came in to attack.

Malgannis smoothly stepped to the side and thrust. The Moranian gasped. His startled horse screamed and reared, kicking its legs. The animal was huge, but Malgannis grabbed hold of the reins with one hand and shoved the scar-faced warrior off the saddle with his other. He put a hand on the horse's flank to calm the creature.

When the horse at last settled, Malgannis pulled himself up onto its back. "Here." He held out a hand to Cora. "Trust me." She shook her head, and he raised his voice. "You brought me here for a reason. I'm all you have left."

Cora remained where she was, and he turned to Helen.
"Get up onto the horse. Hurry!"
Helen nodded; her face was white. She turned toward Malgannis's mare.
But then a rider brought his horse crashing against Helen. He brought his sword slashing down across Helen's body. She screamed and her back convulsed.
Cora felt a strong hand reach out to grab her. The hand pulled her hard, lifting her and throwing her onto horseback.
As soon as Cora was settled in front of him, Malgannis spurred the warhorse on. The rider who had cut down Helen charged after him, and he whirled to thrust his sword into the warrior's chest. He then whipped at the reins and dug in his heels to shift into a gallop.
Together, Cora and Malgannis raced past the tents and bodies, until they had left the camp behind.

✦

From a high knoll with a sweeping view of the plain, Graven Callow surveyed the battlefield.
Time had passed. Where before, men had surged and fought, screamed and died, all was now calm. Soldiers' corpses lay scattered across the grass, dirt, and mud. Most wore the green and silver of Vestria, or the blue and gold of Aranor. The larger lumps were horses. Ruined flesh filled the area between two hills, beside the sprawling ruins of stone.
On his orders, soldiers in black and crimson moved across the battlefield. Their heads turned, eyes roving, gaze alighting from one prone figure to another. Their attitude was one of searching. When they found a wounded enemy, they crouched down. A hand on a forehead yanked back a man's skull to expose the neck. A dagger whipped across a throat.
At another place, long lines of kneeling captives were those who had surrendered. Rather than die in battle, when the tide had turned against them, they had become surrounded and thrown down their weapons. Graven watched as more of his soldiers moved behind the line of prisoners., traveling from one captive to the next, slicing and knocking aside, slicing and knocking aside. He was indifferent to the captives in green and silver, other than to remind himself that every dead enemy was a potential gain for his own side. On the other hand, whenever it was a soldier in blue and gold, a man from Aranor, he felt a surge of triumph. The balance of power had shifted. The exploiters were learning what it

felt like to be dominated by another.

Seated on his dappled gray warhorse, Graven watched the aftermath of his victory. His plate armor encased his body and his helmet covered his head, but the slit for his eyes meant he could easily watch everything from his position on the hill. He was pleased to be liberating the world. Here he was, a commoner, poised to become ruler of it all. Under him, there would be no multitude of lawmakers, arbiters, and tax collectors. He would make sure of it. And Aranor... Aranor would suffer.

"It was a decisive victory," a baritone voice said beside him.

Graven glanced at Halvar, mounted beside him on his draft horse. The huge Vailander with short black hair had red spattered on his face. His wide-spaced eyes were cold, and never looked any different, even when he was caught up in the fighting.

"Indeed," Graven said. "Aranor's end is now in sight."

Graven saw a Moranian captain riding up toward him, along with a dozen horsemen in black and crimson trailing behind. With a wave of his hand, Graven impatiently beckoned for the captain to approach and make his report.

"Well?" Graven demanded. "What of the king's body?"

The captain shook his head. "They got it out, along with what's left of Aranor's army. We had to choose between taking their camp and pursuing their knights. The good news is we have the camp. Our forces have seized weapons and taken prisoners."

Graven knew that with his face obscured by the helmet, the captain couldn't see his expression. Even as Graven's eyes narrowed, the man had continued digging his own grave.

Graven considered his options. Whatever people thought, he wasn't rash. He made calculations and thought hard about consequences. He was going to have to alter what the fool of a captain had done, and order his men to do everything they could to seize Patrick's body. There were witnesses, and there had to be consequences, or he would lose authority.

"Halvar." Graven turned to his second. "The captain made the wrong choice." He allowed his wrath to enter his voice. "Surely he should know that a king's head on a pike is worth more than some pots and pans."

Halvar's gigantic draught horse plodded forward to nudge against the captain's smaller mount. The captain shook his head frantically from side to side. His skin was gray. He turned to look at the men behind him, but they were all staring in any other direction.

Halvar reached to the mace by his saddle – a huge iron ball on a thick steel handle – and lifted it high. The captain yanked at his reins and tried to turn his horse but too late. Halvar brought his mace down in a blow that made the sound of a splitting log as it crushed the captain's skull. The next sound was a thud as the captain's body toppled from the saddle.

“These prisoners the captain mentioned,” Graven said to the other riders. “My orders have not changed. You know what to do?”

“Yes, General.”

“And if you do not understand why, then you are also a fool. Fear is our ally. Fear travels ahead of us like smoke before a wildfire. It is fear that will bring a swift end to this war, an end that finds us victorious. Understood?”

“Yes, General.”

“Any other orders?” Halvar asked.

Graven knew that with this victory, Vestria was lost. The conquest of Aranor would come next, and then it would be done; he would be ruler of the entire world.

“Restore order to our men. Then, we have some small tidying up to do. Let us remove Vestria from the war, so that Aranor stands alone.”

Chapter 16

“THIS TIME, PERHAPS THINK about aiming at the target, rather than the tree,” Patrick said with a grin.

Erik glanced at Patrick, who sat on a log, chewing on a blade of grass and watching Erik sight along the arrow. It was a warm summer’s afternoon, and sunlight glowed from Patrick’s chestnut hair. Golden rays also struck the fuzz on Patrick’s chin and above his lip; he was trying to grow a beard, but so far he wasn’t having much luck. His brown eyes twinkled.

Patrick grinned again, but he also nodded encouragement. “Go on, Erik. I’m only jesting.”

Erik’s arm tensed as he held the string at his ear, his hand clutching the bow making incremental movements up and down. He stared directly at the target to focus on the concentric rings of red and white. The target wasn’t that far away, but it always felt much farther when he tried to strike it with an arrow.

He was well aware that Patrick was watching him. As always, Erik was keen to show himself well. Patrick’s last two arrows had both come within inches of the bullseye. Erik’s first had gone wide, landing deep in the tree trunk so that his shame was visible for all to see.

Erik opened his fingertips and loosed.

The string quivered and the arrow flew from his bow. Erik saw a flash and then anxiously checked to see where his arrow had struck.

The arrow's shaft quivered from the tree trunk, even farther than Erik's previous arrow. Erik lowered the bow and tried not to look at Patrick.

"Erik," Patrick said. He got up from his log and walked over. As Erik turned toward him, Patrick laid a hand on his shoulder. "Remember. We only have to practice until we get it right."

"I know," Erik said. He glared at the target. "Let me try again."

"We take turns, us Vandrydens," Patrick said with a smile. "Even if you are now a lord, you will have to wait for me."

Erik wondered if he had heard Patrick correctly. He knew he had a confused expression his face, while Patrick's smile broadened.

"It's true," Patrick said. "Father has made you a lord. You are now the squire of Blythe."

Erik turned to look toward Adin Palace. "I don't understand. What does it mean?"

"It means you're now just like anyone else who comes to the palace. You'll have your own lands. You'll even have your own income. Not much, but it's something."

Erik had a sudden worry. "Do I have to leave?"

"No, of course not. It's more about how you fit in here at the court. You're only a year younger than me. Soon you'll start to have responsibilities."

Erik's gaze was still focused on the palace. "When did he do it? Did he ask you to tell me?"

Patrick's smile became slightly strained. "Father is always busy, Erik. You know that." He gave Erik a clap on the back. "Now, there is only one thing for us all to work out. What name will you take? You're a lord now. You can't just be Erik Son of Adin."

As Erik stood stunned, Patrick held out his hand and, with a start, Erik gave him the longbow. Patrick grabbed himself another arrow, and soon stood with legs apart facing the same target that Erik had tried to strike a moment ago.

Patrick pulled the bowstring until it was tight, his arm straining with effort, and glanced at Erik. "I know," he said. "Erik Stormcloud."

Patrick laughed. He released his arrow and even with his body shaking, he struck the third ring from the center. His enthusiasm at last broke through Erik's pensiveness, as it always did.

"Erik Sharpsight," Erik said, grinning as Patrick walked over to the target to yank out his arrow.

"Erik the Strong," Patrick replied quickly. He walked up to Erik to hand him the longbow.

"Erik the Wise," a new female voice called from behind them.

Erik turned to see Cora. Without him being aware, she had sat herself down on the log where her brother had been a moment earlier. Her long hair was loose and spilled down her shoulders, and today she wore a yellow summer dress that contrasted with her shining dark locks.

"It's true," she said with a smile. "You have always been wise."

Patrick gave her a worried look. "Be careful, Cora. Father doesn't like to see you here with us. Not while we're at practice."

"Father is always busy," Cora said. She stood up and came over to stand near Erik. She must have had a scent in her hair, for he breathed in a floral aroma. "Can I try?" She indicated the longbow in Erik's hands.

"It takes a long time to learn," Patrick said. "We could be here all day."

"What else are we doing?" Cora asked. "We have all day, don't we?"

"She has a point," Erik said. "Come on, Patrick. Let her try."

"If Father catches us..."

"You can blame it on me," Cora said.

"Or me," said Erik.

Patrick glanced from Cora to Erik and then shook his head ruefully. "You both know I'll be the one blamed, but why not." He glanced at Erik. "Erik? Show her how to stand."

Coraline gave Erik a hopeful expression, opening her arms to indicate he should move her about as he needed. Erik tilted her body, placing one foot forward, the other back. He put the longbow into her hands, and maneuvered her fingers to have the correct grip.

"Ready?" he asked.

"I think so," she said hesitantly.

She tried to draw the string back, but it was meant for someone stronger, and in the end, she was only able to get it halfway to where it needed to be. The string thrummed, and her arrow at least went in the right direction.

"Oh," she said.

"It was a good first try," Erik said. He remembered what Patrick had said. "You only have to practice until you get it right."

Cora smiled, and it lit up her face. "Then let me go again."

"It's Erik's turn next," Patrick said.

Cora held out the bow, but Erik didn't immediately take it. Instead, he looked into the distance and spoke clearly and loudly.

"Wallace," Erik said.

Both Patrick and Cora looked confused.

"What's that, Erik?" Patrick asked.

"Wallace," Erik repeated. "That can be my name. It was my mother's last name..."

Erik stared at the ground, rather than at either Patrick or Cora. They knew it... he knew it... he never spoke about his childhood.

"I didn't know you knew your mother," Patrick said softly.

Cora spoke softly. "Anytime you want to tell us anything, Erik, we're here."

Erik nodded, but he didn't say anything. He wondered if he regretted what he had revealed. But when he looked up, he saw both Patrick and Cora smiling at him.

"Lord Erik Wallace," Patrick said.

"Erik Wallace, Lord of Blythe," Cora said. "I think that sounds better."

"We'll have a celebration ball," Patrick said, "in your honor. You're old enough now for balls."

"Can't we have a dinner?" asked Cora. "Then I can attend."

"Erik?" Patrick raised an eyebrow.

"A dinner," Erik said. He smiled.

"A dinner it is," Patrick said, reaching out to squeeze both Erik and Cora's shoulders. "We will welcome you Erik, as one of us. Father will come. I'm sure of it."

One of us. Erik knew he never would be.

But he continued to smile. "We have something to celebrate. Now let us try to strike this target."

✦

Erik wiped water from his face and concentrated on keeping his horse to the muddy track he was following. Rain dripped down from the foliage overhead, to strike the carpet of leaves and pine needles with a patter. The heavy droplets of water made pinging sounds as they struck soldiers' helmets, shields, and armor. Deep puddles and trenches in the path made for difficult passage. Horses snorted and men panted as they all plodded together through the forest. Conversations were murmured. Everyone was cold and wet.

Erik rode with a companion at his side, a young lieutenant named Norris. Not only did she serve under him, they had trained together at the academy in Adin and fought side by side in the war until King Owen's death sent Erik back to Aranor. Norris was slender but athletic, with a strong jaw and blonde hair she wore tied behind her head in a ponytail. She also had a dry sense of humor. Today, however, no one was smiling.

"They prepared the field," Norris muttered. "It wasn't a last minute choice at all. Those archers... I'm still having nightmares." She glanced at Erik. "How many did we lose?"

"Too many," Erik said.

"Remember Evans? He always kept a flask under his pillow at the academy. He did the same thing in the war. I saw them open up his neck. And Stone... He fell with half a dozen arrows in him. And then, when Graven Callow fought the king..." She trailed off. "I'm sorry, Erik."

"It's fine," he said. Despite the fact that he considered Norris a friend, he was nonetheless aware that he was the captain, and she was his lieutenant. "Erik?"

"Sorry." She ventured a shaky smile. "Cap'n."

Erik realized that he was so used to thinking of her as Norris that he had to search his memory to retrieve her first name... What was it again? It finally came to him: Rosie. Glancing her way, he decided that Norris suited her better. In her armor, weary after a difficult battle, her pretty first name seemed vaguely absurd.

"We just have to focus on our task," Erik said. "It's on us to get the king's body back to Adin and lead these men to safety."

Erik turned when a mounted soldier came riding up to him, an old warrior with a face full of prickly hair.

"Captain," the rider said in a growling voice, heavy with the accent of Aranor's south. "The general wants to see you."

Erik nodded, and sawed at the reins to turn his horse around. He moved into a canter, following the old soldier past the long column of trudging soldiers. Some of the men glanced up at him as he rode past, but most of them kept their heads down and simply concentrated on placing one foot in front of the other, thoughts of their homeland no doubt on their minds.

The litter bearing Patrick's body drew Erik's attention. Draped in Aranor's blue and gold flag, it was still clear to all what lumpy load the six burly men were carrying on poles. They were going to have to burn the body, Erik knew, in order to take Patrick's bones home to Adin. He just hadn't been able to bring himself to give the order. Erik's eyes were red but they were dry. He had wept all he could for the man who had been like his brother.

As Erik rode, he spied a thin older man with gold stripes on the breast of his uniform and a thick blue cloak draping his shoulders. General Baden was wincing with every step his horse took on the muddy ground. His face was white and his teeth were bared; a sheen of sweat coated his forehead. Only one hand held the reins of his horse, the other was pressed against a bandage wrapped around his torso.

"General," Erik said as he neared.

"Wallace," General Baden wheezed. "Well? Any news? Any other officers of rank?"

"We have six captains, including me," Erik said. "Other than that, you're still in charge."

"The gods are cruel," Baden said. "I'm a dead man, and there's no one else to take command." He peered to both sides, as if searching for hope in the trees. "No doubt there are more of us out there. We might pick up some bigger units, heading for Aranor like we are. They'll keep to the forest too... it makes sense." He gave Erik an appraising look. "They say you're strong under pressure, Wallace. Not just clever in court but a competent fighter. Until we find someone else who ranks above you, you are my second. Understood?"

Erik kept his voice steady. "Understood, General."

"Good. Now help me out with some information. How many do you think we are?"

Erik scanned up to the head of the group, and back down to take in its length. "Perhaps a third of the number we had on the battlefield."

"That many?" Baden sounded surprised. "I wish I could look for myself."

"I've made a count," Erik said.

"Yes, yes. No need to be prickly, Wallace. What's the mood of the men?"

Erik knew that morale was on knife edge. They were a sad, grieving group, after the terrible defeat and the death of their king. Fear was ever-present. Erik knew that Graven would be hunting them. Getting the men to safety would be a struggle.

"As well as can be expected," he said.

"Yes, I know what that means. The best thing we can do is cross the border. That, and pray for an end to this godforsaken rain. Our route is clear enough. What else?"

"We need to prepare the king's body so we can take his bones to Adin."

"Yes, we must do what we must. We will do it tonight. You will speak some words?"

"I will," Erik said.

"Good. He was a good king. Brave. None of us saw that trap."

"He was a good man," Erik said. He didn't trust himself to say more.

"Wait. Look," Baden said, glancing at Erik. "Scout."

The scout, a lightly-armored woman with long auburn hair, weaved her horse through the trees to reach their position in the ragged column.

"General. Captain," the scout said, bringing her mount near.

"Any word on the queen?" Erik asked immediately.

"Not a sign of her."

"Keep searching," Erik said. As the scout nodded, he felt Baden's eyes on him. "General?"

"Coraline was at camp, wasn't she? She had horses?"

"Yes." Erik nodded.

"Then we have to hope she kept her wits about her and fled."

“General, another thing,” the scout said. Worry filled her eyes. “We’re being pursued. They know where we are.”

Erik had known Graven would be hunting them. Now the real trial would come. “How near?”

“Half a day behind us.”

“Too close,” General Baden said. He focused his attention Erik. “We don’t have a choice. We need to leave archers in ambush positions. See to it, right away.”

“Ambush?” Erik asked. “But how will our men catch up with us?” When Baden didn’t immediately reply, realization dawned. “Oh.”

“You know what I am saying,” Baden said.

“We’ll doom them.”

“And save thousands,” Baden said. “We’ll ask for volunteers, which is a task I’ll leave to you.” He grimaced and clutched his chest, before nodding at Erik. “Quickly. Get to it, Wallace.”

Chapter 17

THE SUN CLIMBED ABOVE the Aran Mountains, a thin, spiky range that curved like the spine of some gigantic, long-dead creature. Yellow rays lit up white peaks and bathed the conifers below the snow line. Crackles and thuds bounced across the valleys as the evergreens released the weight of all the frozen water that clung to their branches.

Just below the mountain range's eastern perimeter, a high trail followed the ridge. The Skyway was an ancient road, put to use long before the draining of the Gray Marshes, when there was no other way to get from Huron Plain to the northern reaches of Aranor. So high up, the air was thin and crisp, while the sun somehow felt both closer and warmer. The Skyway was the best route to take in order to reach Adin, Aranor's capital, without detection or fear of pursuit.

Malgannis nonetheless never stopped scanning, both ahead and behind. As he kept his mount moving, with the weight of two people on its back, he had the overriding impression that he and Cora were utterly alone. But, when carrying something precious, it always paid to be careful.

The horse's hooves clip clopped on the hard ground. Malgannis and Cora traversed the high trail along the slope of a wide valley. On the opposite slope, Malgannis saw where a recent avalanche had torn a swath of snow and dirt through the landscape. In the distance a wolf howled.

Cora sat in front of Malgannis, so that he had his arms protectively around her. Sometimes she slept, and other times her eyes were unfocussed. Throughout the journey, she had barely spoken unless it was truly necessary for them to communicate, perhaps about gathering firewood or leading the horse to water. Malgannis never pushed her.

Instead he commented on small things. As he held her close, the same way he had once held his own daughter, he talked about the coming of spring. They rode past a waterfall, where snowmelt had carved a path down a cleft until it shot through the gap between two rocks and arced through the sky, tumbling down to strike somewhere shrouded in spray far below.

"My mother used to say that clouds are born in waterfalls," Malgannis said, glancing down as they rode past the torrent from above. "Water is sucked into the mist, which is carried up on rainbows high into the sky."

"Clouds come from the sea," Cora said. "The sun heats the water, which becomes vapor as it warms."

"Ah," Malgannis said with a slight smile. "Of course clouds come from the sea, but that is because at the edge of the sea is a giant waterfall."

"The world is round," Cora said woodenly. "You know that."

Malgannis frowned, even though she couldn't see his face. "Round? Don't be a fool. We would fall off. It is clearly flat, girl. Unless something has drastically changed in the fifty or so years since I died."

"Malgannis," Cora said irritably. "I may not know much about warfare, but I did study history and geography. The world is round, and you know it."

"I suppose you must be right," Malgannis said. At least he had her talking. "Tell me, Cora, how did you study history without studying war?"

"Stop it," she interrupted. "I don't want to talk about war."

Malgannis suppressed a curse. He had been doing so well. Silence ensued, broken up only by the clapping rhythm of the horse's footsteps. They rounded a cliff wall, and Malgannis saw the vista open up. The current valley would soon terminate, but a pass appeared to lead into the next. A few clouds hovered around the taller peaks, but the fair weather was holding.

"We'll take the Skyway until we join the King's Road," Malgannis said. "Then, once you're safe, we can talk about winning this war."

This time, as expected, Cora didn't reply. Malgannis's heart reached out to her. She had lost her father and now her brother.

He felt a great weight upon his shoulders.

✦

Time passed. Nights were spent with the two travelers wrapped in blankets, huddled side by side. By day, the horse plodded onward with two weights on its back, one heavy and the other light. The Skyway stretched on and on. Aranor, and the palace at Adin, felt impossibly distant.

Cora rode enclosed between Malgannis's arms and body. Her eyes were on the dramatic landscape, where forbidding mountains shot high into the sky as if each were trying to impress the heavens above. The emerald trees mimicked the peaks, thrusting up their own green spears. Pale blue water sped along a wide river that followed the valley floor. Yellow spring flowers decorated the grassy slopes between the forest fringes. Birds filled the air with chirping music as they flitted from one tree to the next, dancing and circling one another, carrying twigs and leaves, forming nests, getting ready for the next generation.

Cora had many things to focus on, but her gaze was blank, and her mind's eye was seeing something else altogether.

Malgannis had told her, simply and matter-of-factly, how her brother had died. A slash onto the neck. Followed by a stab in the throat. Her brother toppling from the saddle. His knights closing in. Malgannis had been certain of that.

She knew she should be thinking about the implications of her brother's death. She shouldn't spend so much time worrying about what his last thoughts had been, whether he had been afraid, or in terrible pain. Instead, she should be thinking about the future.

There was only one thought that gave her hope. Malgannis had been certain that the king's companions in battle had managed to get away with Patrick's body. Erik was alive. She was going to see him again.

It had been a while since Malgannis had tried pointing out features of the landscape. Or sharing memories of his own youth, growing up in Rathlee on Aranor's western coast. She found herself missing his light comments.

As soon as she had the thought, Malgannis cleared his throat. "I know this is hard," he said. "But you are queen now."

Cora remained silent. How could it all have gone so wrong? She had never wanted to be queen. What kind of queen was she, if she wasn't present for her people in their time of need? In just over six weeks, the black priest would have his price, and she would be dead.

"I will help you, Coraline," Malgannis said. "In return, I must ask some things of you. I expect your honesty and your trust. I need you to be strong."

Cora bristled. "I have never lied to you."

"Then tell me about how I came to be here. You said you made a bargain. What was the price you paid?"

She shook her head. "You can ask me anything but that."

"Why not?"

Cora sat straighter and turned to look into the weathered face of her great-grandfather. "Let me ask you a question. Why did you spend all these years in the shadow world? Why not go to Arcadia, to heaven? Surely you earned a place. Why remain as a shade? Why haunt the world you came from?"

The slightest sign of pain struck his eyes, and coming from him, she knew she had struck him in the heart. For a time, he remained cold-faced and stared straight ahead.

"I am not a hero," he finally said. "I have made many mistakes. That is why."

"That is all you'll tell me?" Cora asked, facing ahead once more. "Then it seems we both have secrets to keep."

Malgannis grunted, but he no longer pressed her. A wind came up from the pass they were approaching, and Cora shivered. Instinctively, his arms closed in to keep her warm.

"What now?" she asked.

"We need to keep moving," Malgannis said, "and make plans as we travel. I think we're ready to do that now. Do you?"

She tried not to bite her lip. "I'm ready."

"Good," he said. "Our situation is bad, Cora."

"I know," she said.

As the Skyway plunged into the gap between two mountains, a verdant region of plains and fields revealed itself. The path would soon wind back and forth, tilting downward to reach a new land: Aranor.

"And if there's one thing I've learned..." Malgannis's tone was sober, "before things get better, they always get worse."

✦

Where the journey had been one of silence and solitude, of quiet comfort and the processing of raw emotions, it gradually began to change.

Cora and Malgannis picked up pace. Cora asked questions and Malgannis answered them. He queried her in turn, learning about Aranor's defenses and how many men had been called up to fight, and how many might still be available to join the struggle.

Meanwhile, their strong horse was evidently pleased to be descending to gentler terrain, and soon had his fill of green grass and sweet mountain water. Aranor was a lush land of wide open spaces and empty regions, but they also saw pastures and farmland. Spring had arrived. Cora had returned to her homeland.

Malgannis had just finished explaining to Cora how Graven Callow had prepared the battlefield in advance and then lured in Patrick's army.

"How do you prevent something like that?" Cora asked.

"It sounds easy in retrospect but in the moment it never is. Patrick's scouts would have rushed to tell him that they had tracked down Graven's army. If Patrick and his generals were cautious, the scouts could have returned to the area with three, four times the number and cast in wide circles, checking for any hidden forces." Malgannis's voice was pensive. "Also, they could have kept count of the enemy's numbers. Graven had hidden some of his knights and archers. If they had compared the count from their last battle to the count at the next, they might have discovered the trap."

Cora frowned, trying to understand. "Does that mean our generals didn't do their job properly?"

"No," Malgannis said. "Because for every argument, there is always a balancing counterargument. Your brother could have spent a lot more time assessing the enemy, but that would have given Graven more time to prepare. The enemy could use that time to dig ditches and build fortifications. Trust me, good fortifications make a bigger difference than almost anything else. Then, as far as counting, there are a lot of reasons for numbers to go up and down. New divisions arrive and old ones leave. Mercenaries come for good pay and depart when the fight no longer seems worthwhile. Armies are havens for illness."

Cora's head was spinning. "Then how do you know what to do?"

She felt Malgannis shrug. "You make your best judgment with the information you have. Where possible, you contrive events so that you're the one making the first move. You make your enemy react to you. And you already know what that reaction is going to be, and you've already planned for that too. And on it goes."

"We lost though," Cora said. "Our army is broken."

"Broken, yes," Malgannis said. "But what is broken can be fixed. It's not to say that we're not in a difficult position, but if there is a way forward, I will find it."

Cora waited as he paused, gathering his thoughts.

"Battles are lost when one side runs," he said. "You have to put yourself into the mindset of a common soldier. Not a knight – knights are almost invulnerable on the battlefield unless they're facing other knights – but an infantryman who might have had some basic training and now prepares to face a huge number of men trying to kill him. He fights for his comrades, his country, and his king—most times in that order. He stands side by side with hundreds, thousands of men just like him. Battle is joined. He and his companions begin to run and then collide into the enemy. Everything is confusion. He has no idea whether victory is imminent, or if he is surrounded and he and his companions are the last of his countrymen left on the field. There is screaming and grunting, slashing and blood in all directions. He sees soldiers in enemy uniforms. There seem like quite a lot of them. Someone cries his name in panic. The fear spreads. One soldier in the same colors he is wearing flees, running past. Then another. What does he do? He bolts also. It is very rare in a battle for an entire army to be wiped out. I don't mean to trivialize so much death. Just that the victorious force is the one that holds the ground. That is the objective."

"So there is hope?" Cora asked.

"Some. There will be a lot of Aranese soldiers rushing back to the border. And not just Aranese, but also soldiers of Vestria and Rumandy still willing to fight."

Cora slowly nodded. She then hesitated, eager to learn but worried he might lose patience with her. "There is something you should know. I told you that my father didn't teach me the same things he taught Patrick. I don't think I'll make a good queen."

She had another unspoken thought. *Even with the limited time I have.*

Malgannis smiled, or at least, she heard a smile in his reply. "No decent king or queen ever thinks they're good enough. The only ones who do are the bad ones."

"If we can rebuild the army, what then?"

Malgannis didn't immediately answer. When he did speak, it was to return the question. "What do you think?"

Cora realized then how weak her voice was sounding. She had a choice to make. She had grown up without an expectation of such great responsibility. Yet the fates had thrust responsibility upon her. Her choice was to continue to play the princess, or to become the queen.

This time, she spoke more forcefully. "We have to abandon Vestria and retreat to the border forts."

"True," Malgannis agreed.

"Any of the Red King's soldiers who still want to fight will have to accept Vestria's fall. They have the smaller numbers. For now, Vestria is lost. We need to retreat and rebuild our strength. Vestria isn't strong enough to face Graven alone."

"Many of your generals won't like it," Malgannis said.

"They'll see we have no other choice," Cora said firmly. "You'll explain it to them."

He chuckled. "I like this side of you. Keep going."

Cora thought hard. "But you can't just go to the border forts and start giving orders. You will need the support of the lords in Adin." She stared straight ahead. "And Adin is where we're going."

Malgannis dug in his heels. With an open road ahead of them, a wide flat road with a river on one side and grassland on the other, they picked up speed. "I'll get you safely there," he said. "I promise."

Chapter 18

CORA WAS WORRIED. She and Malgannis were at a place where all southbound roads converged at a chokepoint, the Bridge of Willows, the only way to get from Aranor's north to Adin. Skipping the bridge wasn't an option, not without adding several days to their journey.

The landscape had taken on a more settled quality as they left behind the sparsely-populated forests and farmland of Aranor's northern reaches. The bridge was huge, spanning the breadth of a wide ravine, and Cora first saw it at the limits of vision. As the dusty track climbed up ridges and wound between tall hills, the wide wooden bridge gained the appearance of a lattice of brown sticks.

The distance was deceiving. Soon the track merged with a much wider road, the King's Road, which was the far more common route to take between Aranor and the neighboring nations. The road climbed; the Bridge of Willows then revealed itself in all its spindly glory. The individual beams weren't massive; it was supported by the ingenious interlacing between the supports and horizontal planks. Every one of Cora's senses told her that it shouldn't stay up, that the failure of any individual beam would see the whole edifice come crashing down. But that wasn't the source of her concern.

Malgannis was leading their horse by the halter. Cora and Malgannis both walked, giving the animal some respite. The King's Road led straight ahead, to where two stone columns framed the road and opened straight onto the bridge itself.

Malgannis glanced at Cora. It appeared he had been having the same thoughts she had. "In my day wayfarers would look for travelers on the bridge to rob."

She kept her gaze fixed straight ahead and continued walking. "Some things never change."

Malgannis had the halter in his left hand, allowing his right hand to rest on the hilt of the sword he wore on his hip. "Keep your wits about you," he said. He glanced at the ring with the blue sapphire that Cora wore on her finger. "I would remove that ring, if I were you. It looks expensive."

Cora looked down at her finger, and then tugged at her golden ring until she had pulled it off completely. Her ring was more than expensive; it was special, a gift from her father. She slipped the ring into a pocket in her cloak and then put her hand on her pocket to keep it safe.

Meanwhile, up ahead, she began to hear the sound of beams creaking and groaning. The horse snorted nervously as they passed between the tall stone columns and took their first clattering steps onto the bridge. The wind made a howling sound.

Cora stayed alert and kept her eyes and ears open. The bridge was wide, the breadth of a medium-sized sailing vessel. Its span was inordinately long. The farther Cora and Malgannis ventured, the more the wind gusted around them until they could barely hear the clip clopping of their horse's hooves, let alone their own footsteps. The Bridge of Willows began to sway. Cora reminded herself that it had been here for a long time.

Yet she couldn't help look over the side rail. The gorge that the bridge spanned was deep, walled with steep rock faces. She felt giddy and tore her eyes away from the drop.

"Cora," Malgannis said in a low voice.

Cora and Malgannis were most of the way across., but Malgannis had brought them to a halt. Looking straight ahead, Cora saw some men, three of them at least, at the end of the bridge, barring their way.

Cora turned. More men blocked the other end of the bridge. She glanced at Malgannis's face. Was he afraid? His lips were thin and his eyes looked angry. But it wasn't much different from his usual expression. He certainly didn't give much away.

The attention Cora now gave the drop at her side was entirely different in nature. Jumping was out of the question. They were directly over the gorge, where the black rock came together in a series of depressions far below. Her father had once told her there was a river down there. Climbing the lattice of wooden struts and beams underneath them was unthinkable.

"What do we do?" Cora asked quietly.

“We hope they don’t have bows,” Malgannis said, hand on the hilt of his sword.

The three brigands in front of them began to move, walking toward them. Cora saw them more clearly: they were surprisingly well-dressed, with leather boots, sturdy trousers, and jerkins that actually fit. She also made out the weapons in their hands. One gripped a sword, but the other two held contraptions with broad arms and tight strings, pointed in their direction.

Malgannis swore. “Crossbows.”

Cora turned to scan over her shoulder. The other group remained where they were for the time being. “I have an idea,” she said. She cast a quick look at Malgannis. “Let me handle this. I just need you to look tough.”

Tall and solid, he gave her a flat stare. “What?”

“It doesn’t matter,” Cora replied, returning her attention to the three approaching men. “Just draw your sword and stay with me.”

Rather than remain in place, Cora headed toward the three men, while Malgannis readied his sword and came with her. She decided the one in the middle must be the leader. He was taller than his companions and looked older, with stubble on his cheeks and a felt hat worn at a rakish angle. The leader with the hat was one of the men with crossbows, and moved his weapon from Malgannis to Cora, before settling back on Malgannis.

Cora was the first to speak. “Well?” she challenged the leader. She didn’t allow any of her fear to show. If there was one skill she had, it was hiding her emotions. “The toll... what is it?”

The leader frowned. “Who said anything about tolls?” He moved his crossbow to point once more at Cora.

Cora put on an air of impatience. “I am carrying an important message for the king’s council in Adin. A message that cannot wait. You are in the business of earning tolls, and I now expect us to agree a sum of money. You will allow my guard and I past, and I will then leave your toll at the end of the bridge.”

The leader looked Cora up and down. “You talk like a lady.” He spoke curtly. “Let’s see what you’re carrying. You,” he glanced at Malgannis, “hand me those reins.”

“Listen to me,” Cora said sharply. “Our message cannot wait. The king is dead but his sister, Coraline, is alive. She now makes her way back to Adin, but she is in danger. The palace must know, and so must the people.”

“I don’t believe you,” said the grizzled leader in the felt hat. “And even if I did, I don’t really care.”

Cora realized with a sinking feeling that her attempt at bravado was failing. Malgannis's eyes were anxious, which for him spoke volumes; they would be lucky to get off the bridge alive.

Her mind worked furiously. She didn't have a choice. With terrible reluctance, she reached into her pocket and withdrew her ring. As she held it up, displaying the blue stone, all of a sudden, she had the attention of the three men.

"Do you know how I know she is alive?" Cora demanded. She was aware of Malgannis frowning at her, shaking his head slightly. "I know because I am Coraline Vandryden." She turned the ring to show the letters of her name. "You can read my name, written on the inside of this ring. I must get back to Adin."

The leader in the felt hat didn't even pretend to squint. He simply held out his hand. "Give it here." He smiled. "I'll be able to look at it better."

Cora's frustration brought color to her cheeks. She took a step back, even as she held the ring in the air. The blue sapphire reflected the sun's rays. The gold was shining. "This is worth more than I would warrant you see in a decade. Or perhaps a lifetime."

"All the more reason to give it over."

Cora knew she was going to have to give the ring up, even though it went against every fiber of her being. "First, let us agree. I think it is an appropriate toll." She stared into the leader's eyes. "Do you?"

"Maybe you've got more."

"I don't," Cora said. Her eyes moved meaningfully toward Malgannis. "All I have is my big friend here."

"We have crossbows," said the leader with the felt hat.

Malgannis spoke for the first time. "I never liked crossbows," he said. "Too hard to maintain. They malfunction half the time, and that's if you oil them and clean out the gears." He glanced at each crossbow in turn. "I can see you don't know what I mean."

"We know what we're about," the leader said with a scowl.

"And I can have my sword on you in the blink of an eye," Malgannis said.

"Wait," Cora said quickly. When everyone looked at her, all of a sudden, she thrust out her arm so that her hand was well above the drop. The ring was held between her fingertips. "Make your choice. You keep the ring. You know what it's worth. Or someone is going to get hurt."

"Wait!" the leader barked.

Cora hated what she was doing, even as she opened her hand and let go.

The golden ring plummeted. The brigands all cried out.

"Someone once told me there's a river down there," Cora called over the howling wind. "You had best hurry. How long will it take you to get down there? An hour? Half a day?"

The three men exchanged swift glances. The leader put both hands on the rail to stare down into the ravine, and then whirled and waved an arm.

"Go!" he cried.

He hurried along his companions, until they were sprinting, pushing past Malgannis and Cora to join their fellows on the bridge's northern side. As the three men raced away, Cora was aware of Malgannis's attention on her.

"That was brave of you," he said.

"They won't find it."

"You know they might."

Cora knew he was right. "At least I didn't just give it over. And I'm going to be queen. If I want to, I can send a hundred men to look for it, and for anyone trying to sell it." She nodded toward the far end of the Bridge of Willows. "Let's get across, while the way is clear."

Chapter 19

THE CITY OF ADIN lay ahead.

The King's Road now thronged with traffic. Farmers with carts full of root vegetables jostled with herders leading pigs and cattle in single file. Merchants with dozens of horses as well as trains of carts filled with barrels traveled past Malgannis and Cora, heading north toward Helmsford, where the nearby border forts were Aranor's final defense. But the road was wide and there was space for all, whether laborers heading in for a day's work or soldiers in blue and gold riding out on patrol.

As the horse carrying Malgannis and Cora crested a hill, no one else took particular notice of the walled city that dominated the vista ahead. But for a moment they stopped, and neither of them spoke.

Adin, a city of crimson roofs and gray stone, was entwined with the Sylvan River, a broad, slow-moving watercourse that formed a tight loop before straightening out again. Adin had been built on the dry land enclosed by the loop, and a canal had then been cut so that the river became a moat. There was only one bridge connecting the King's Road to the city's main gates, and it was a drawbridge, able to be lifted up to the towers near the water's edge, hauled up in dire need with pulleys and chain.

The Sylvan River didn't just fulfill the purpose of a defensive moat; it was a major artery for Aranor's trade. The river was deep, and when both banks opened up it formed lakes large enough to house dozens of ships at anchor. One trade route connected Adin with the Sea of Mirrors in the east, where bold merchants sailed with cargos of exotic goods. The other route followed the King's Road overland to Helmsford and then to Vestria's capital Ballina and Harven in Rumandy—or at least that was where the traders used to travel, before the war.

Towers stood at regular intervals along the city's perimeter, following the gray outer wall that enclosed the entire settlement. Within the tall stone wall, streets and avenues, shops and houses, gave physical form to Adin's sizable population. Farther away, Adin Palace straddled an island separate from the city, with its own wall of cleaner white stone. Malgannis had never lived at the palace; it was his son who had become king; but he knew there were extensive lawns and gardens, as well as a private wood reserved for riding and hunting. A causeway connected the city and palace, joining Adin's two portions, one large and one small.

Malgannis remained where he was for a time, gazing at the grand city as he experienced a mixture of strange emotions: the warmth of homecoming, the sadness of time passing, and regret that he had died so far away.

Here he was. And yet Adin had never truly been home. His home, where he had met his wife, and married and raised his children, was Rathlee, and the small manor that bore the same name, before the Vailanders burned it all to the ground.

He felt Cora's attention. "Has it changed much?"

"It's bigger," he said. He pointed to a section enclosed within the tall wall. "In the east, there, around that hill... that was farmland. Mostly cattle."

Cora's voice was puzzled. "Inside the city?"

He smiled wryly. "Yes. Inside the city." He continued his inspection. "Is that temple new? The one not far from the causeway to the palace."

"The Temple of White Stone," Cora said. "I suppose you could call it new," she smiled, "but I'm not sure if I can. It was built before I was born."

"The outer wall is new," Malgannis said. "We just had the river."

"What do your military senses say? A hard city to conquer?" Cora asked seriously.

Malgannis's took some time to reply. "They say that in my day we didn't need an outer wall. Our strength was out there." He nodded in the direction of the King's Road, the way they had come, toward the wider world. "Our power was in our wealth. In our armies and our allies."

"Times change," Cora said.

"They do."

Malgannis glanced at Cora; there was an obvious question he could ask, about how she was feeling to be coming home, the sole survivor of her family's dynasty.

But he knew how she felt from her eyes, and he held his tongue.

"We made it, Cora," he said instead. "I'm not your protector anymore. There are plenty here able to do that better than me. Just like you, I'm going to need a good wash and some very good clothing." He nodded toward their destination. "That's what's going to matter in there."

✦

Adin was much more imposing up close.

Instead of tiny buildings and walls viewed from a lofty distance, the same features were now life-sized, the walls transformed to the mighty fortifications they were, manned by soldiers patrolling back and forth along the battlements.

Not everyone could simply cross over the drawbridge. Malgannis and Cora reached the mainland side and joined a queue, where half a dozen guards moved between the various groups trying to get into the city. Malgannis watched as the guards warded away vagrants, inspected cargos, looked for weapons, and asked questions in their search for spies. Meanwhile, the horse snorted and stirred, startled by so many surrounding people, forcing him to hold the creature close.

Then it was their turn. The guard who challenged them had a patch over one eye and a surly manner. Malgannis could almost guess the guard's story: he had been given drawbridge duty after being caught in some infraction.

The guard with the eye-patch stared at Malgannis first, inspecting him up and down. He spent a lot of time looking into Malgannis's eyes.

Malgannis forced himself to restrain his irritation. The guard then moved on to Cora. Despite the warmer weather, Cora wore her gray cloak, which was as muddy as the riding clothes she had underneath. The way the guard leered at her made Malgannis's blood rise, but rather than say or do anything, he simply cleared his throat.

"Eh?" the guard grunted and scowled. "Slow down, old man." He gave Cora one last appraisal and then nodded toward Malgannis. "What's your business in the city?"

Malgannis opened his mouth but it was Cora who spoke first. When Malgannis saw her face, he realized she had twin red flushes on her cheeks. Her eyes and forehead were blank, but her voice was tight.

"I am Coraline Vandryden," she said. "Step aside, if you know what is good for you."

For a brief moment the guard's mouth dropped open. Hearing Cora's stern voice, another gray-haired guard was staring their way.

Then the guard with the eye-patch burst out laughing. "Did you hear that Toby?" He grinned at his older friend. "It's the lady, come to claim her throne."

"It sure is. Can't believe we didn't realize it sooner." The gray-haired guard gave a theatrical bow. "Welcome, Queen Coraline."

"We are at your service." The guard standing in front of Malgannis and Cora was still snorting. He put his hands on his cheeks, as if suddenly shocked. "But where is your ring with a blue stone?"

"I lost it," Cora said flatly.

Malgannis scowled. "Quiet girl," he growled at Cora. She was so surprised her mouth snapped close. He addressed the guard and stared into his one eye. "I'm looking to enlist."

"Aren't you a bit old?"

"I was once a captain," Malgannis said.

Seeing Malgannis's expression, the guard decided not to press the issue. "What about her?"

"She's my daughter. Wants to get herself work at the playhouse, but you'll probably see her pouring ales next time you're at the tavern."

The guard's brow furrowed as he thought but then he nodded. "Fair enough." He indicated for them to pass. "In you go."

The queue thinned out as the new arrivals were allowed to pass across the drawbridge in small groups. Malgannis and Cora kept to the left side of the bridge, while people heading in the opposite direction stayed to the right. As soon as they were alone, with the horse's hooves clattering on the bridge's wooden planks, Cora glanced at Malgannis.

"You're the new queen," Malgannis murmured swiftly, before she could speak. "The people can't see you like this. A ruler has to have an entire structure behind her. It's not just being king or queen by birth and blood. It's the palace staff, the council of lords, the palace itself, the city, the economy, the army, soldiers, ceremonies, priests..." he trailed off.

Cora was quiet for a time and then she nodded. "I will remember that."

"It's one of the most important lessons there is."

There were no further obstacles as they passed through the city's main gates, which were open wide, and entered through a vast opening in the surrounding walls of stone.

The city assaulted them immediately.

Malgannis hadn't seen so many people in one place since the battle at the ruins of Leventhal. They walked up ahead and hurried past his vision; some followed the main avenue that led from the gates, others plunged down one of the intersecting streets. He saw laborers in smocks, dusty masons, and smiths with black smudges on their faces and hands. Merchants in fine clothing rode on horseback. Women chatted at street corners, ignoring the bawling babes in their arms other than to bob them up and down.

Both Malgannis and Cora knew that to reach the palace they had to go straight ahead along the broad avenue. Trees bright with pink spring flowers lined the boulevard on both sides, providing some welcome shade from the sun that shone from directly overhead. The city's smell began to grow. Woodsmoke mingled with refuse and the floral aroma from the trees. Food odors wafted from somewhere up ahead.

Malgannis glanced at Cora. No doubt this was all familiar to her. Adin was her home. This was where she had grown up. And yet there was one thing that he hadn't been expecting, and perhaps she hadn't either.

The color black was everywhere. Many of the city folk, particularly the older men and women, wore sober clothing without any other hue. Alcoves along the stone walls contained figurines; they were shrines dedicated to both the younger gods and older. Candles burned in the alcoves, and no doubt their tenders kept them lit night and day. Black flags flew from steeples and towers. Black bunting decorated the bigger trees.

The news had traveled ahead of them. Adin was a city in mourning.

Malgannis's gaze frequently returned to Cora, but whenever he looked her way, her face was carefully blank.

After leaving behind the frantic scene at the gates, they saw another crowd up ahead and soon passed through a section of market stalls. No one gave Malgannis or Cora a second look. They were just another two people passing through, a young woman with a man old enough to be her father, leading a big horse by the halter.

Malgannis kept his ears open. He overheard a few snippets of conversation.

An old laborer was chatting to a companion at a stall selling ale. "...next the border forts will fall. They say Logan Kane, the Baron of Fastness, might be king. Someone has to be."

"I hear the princess is alive," his companion replied.

"I'll believe it when I see it."

Malgannis and Cora then passed a pair of pretty young women buying vegetables.

"Father says we should leave while we can. I don't think he means it but it's hard to know for sure."

"You know what they say happened at Inadris."

"Don't even talk about it. Please. It's hard enough..."

When they were in a new, quieter section of the city and would soon be approaching the palace, Malgannis heard Cora say his name.

"Malgannis?

"Aye?"

"Do you promise? Do you give your word that you will help me?"

Malgannis stared into her worried eyes. "I said I would," he said seriously.

"We have to save Aranor."

"I know."

Cora nodded but didn't say more.

The streets and houses changed in nature, becoming quieter and more elegant. The quarter that brushed up against the causeway to the palace had been home to the city's wealthy even in Malgannis's time. In the distance, a bell tolled, and following the sound, Malgannis saw a tall spire and guessed he must be looking at the new Temple of White Stone he had seen from outside the city.

Malgannis slowly tilted his head back when the vista opened up ahead. He found himself looking at the tall edifice that was their destination, a grand, graceful structure with multiple wings, a central hall, terraces, balconies, towers and turrets. A wall enclosed it all, and the only approach was via the causeway, a section of land like a bridge connecting the town and palace.

"Here we are," Malgannis said.

A promenade followed the river, a path bound by a low stone wall, where city folk could walk and look across the water at the palace. The palace guards were on the far side of the thin swath of water. They paced around the palace and stood at the twin gates, bearing long pole arms, prepared to lower their weapons to bar the way. Because they were palace guards, the imprint of an eagle decorated their blue and gold uniforms.

"Now you can announce yourself. The palace is yours." Malgannis stopped at the end of the paved strip of land and gazed toward the gates on the other side. "You are the queen."

Cora drew in a deep breath. Lifting her chin, she walked onto the causeway.

Malgannis gave her time, letting her set her own pace a stone's throw in front of him, until at last he followed behind.

Chapter 20

CORA HAD BEEN CROWNED.

She stood alone, on display on the viewing balcony of Adin Palace. She raised an arm to wave, and a loud cheer rose up to her from below. Meanwhile, the roar from the direction of the town was mightier still. She turned slowly, hand in the air, gazing down to where a select group of the city's residents massed on the lawns in front of her. Women in embroidered dresses and men in elegant doublets filled the space between the palace and the surrounding wall. Across the causeway, where the new queen must look tiny to the onlookers, any citizen who wanted to see her thronged the promenade on the river's other side.

The fair weather had persisted, the season shifting from cool to warm. A day of feasting had been declared. Queen Coraline Vandryden had been blessed at the Temple of White Stone. The people had welcomed their new monarch. The palace staff had distributed barrels of ale throughout the city, along with fresh bread, salted beef, and pickled pork. Hope was in the air.

The great iron bell at the Temple of White Stone began to peal. The day's ceremonies had been planned in detail, and Cora knew to remain on the balcony until she heard seventy-seven peals, one for each of the elder and younger gods. Then the people below her began to disperse, as they were invited into the palace's great hall for music and feasting, and Cora withdrew.

Two faces greeted her, both stern in their own way. Malgannis stood and inspected her. This was a different Malgannis: for a start his face was clean, and he wore black and dark blue clothing he had chosen himself. However his graying hair, flowing to his shoulders, hadn't changed much other than to receive the slightest trim.

The other person in the room was Silvia. She was as grave-faced and straight-backed as ever, and her flaxen hair was tightly bound in a bun. Although she wore a festive dress, her expression didn't match.

The dress Cora wore looked like beaten gold, and it felt just as stiff. It had so much embroidery that she felt like she were covered in yellow spiderweb, and the waist was cinched so tightly she could barely breathe. A crown rested on her head, a delicate spiked circlet decorated with blue sapphires at regular intervals. Her shoulders were draped in a blue silk mantle interwoven with glittering stones.

"You did well," Malgannis said.

Silvia cast him a scornful look. "She said fourteen words. I would not even call this her first test." She leveled her gaze at Cora. "I know you think you were shouting, dear. But next time speak even louder."

Cora's eyes moved from face to face. Malgannis and Silvia were so different, yet they both wanted what was best for her. As soon as they met, they had taken an instant disliking to one another.

Malgannis wasn't someone to back down. He returned Silvia's scowl. "Getting into the water is the first step in learning how to swim."

"I will be in charge of the proverbs around here, Lord Morgan," Silvia said.

Silvia was interrupted when someone shouted from outside and the sound rose up to the balcony. "For queen and country! Long live the queen!"

More voices took up the call. It grew in volume, until it became a powerful cry. "Long live the queen!"

Cora's heart was still racing. Just a moment ago, thousands of people had been looking at her, wondering if she had the strength to lead Aranor through the trials ahead. She wished more than anything that this burden hadn't been thrust upon her.

She missed her brother. She missed her father.

Glancing down at herself, she suddenly felt hot and uncomfortable. The dress was too constrictive. She wanted it off. All of it. The mantle. The dress. The crown.

Cora began to tug at the fastenings keeping the blue mantle held in place. Her fingers fumbled, and with a sigh, Silvia hurried up to her.

"Let me help," Silvia said.

Malgannis looked apprehensive. "I will make my exit. Cora... I mean Your Majesty. We will speak later."

Cora nodded vaguely in his direction, focused on the sudden sensation of being smothered. "Get it off," she muttered, wriggling her arms out of the long sleeves.

"Yes, yes," Silvia muttered. "Turn a bit more..." She sighed and shook her head. "If you'd only let me help you put this on in the first place..."

Malgannis bowed and backed away. Cora watched for a moment as he headed straight for the doorway.

But then Cora heard something change in Silvia's voice. The woman who was the closest thing she had to a mother trailed off. The shuffling of fabric ceased altogether.

And Cora remembered why she had insisted she put the golden dress on herself.

"What is that?" Silvia asked softly.

Malgannis stopped moving toward the exit. Cora became still. She realized where Silvia was looking.

Part of Cora's forearm was exposed, and the green, spiral-shaped welt had grown, traveling nearer to her wrist and elbow. Silvia turned Cora's arm and peeled back more of the golden fabric, to reveal a larger portion of the black priest's mark.

Cora tried to jerk her arm away but Silvia was strong, and held her in place.

"Coraline?" Silvia demanded, staring into Cora's eyes.

Cora finally managed to free her arm. She reached out and grabbed a shawl, throwing it over her shoulders to cover herself. A few tugs returned her dress to its former position so at least her arms were covered.

But it was too late.

Cora hugged the shawl to herself. She knew she was under scrutiny.

"I have had a full life," Silvia said seriously. "I know what that mark means." She shook her head, and a wretched tone entered her voice. "You are the queen, Coraline. You were just given blessings at the Temple of White Stone. Desperate wretches may deal with the black arts, but you? By the gods, what bargain have you made?"

Cora wouldn't meet Silvia's eyes. "We are all desperate, at one time or another."

Malgannis still stood with his back to them. But as Cora watched, he slowly turned, until he was facing them both once more.

Silvia tilted her head. She focused on Malgannis as if seeing him for the first time.

He glared back at her. "What are you staring at?"

"It's something to do with him," Silvia said, "this stranger in our midst." She began to think out loud. "You disappear to find Erik." She glanced at Cora. "Who you say has someone with him... someone important." As she pondered, she returned her attention to Malgannis.

For a time Silvia stared into Malgannis's face. Something entered Silvia's expression, and her eyes widened.

"Dear gods. It's just like in the painting downstairs. You're—"

"Don't say his name," Cora said quickly.

Malgannis shrugged his shoulders and returned to his former position, taking a seat on a cloth-covered stool. He spread his knees and leaned forward to address Silvia. "About what she did... I don't know either."

Silvia's manner had changed completely. "Are you here to help us?" she asked, clearly awestruck.

"I am," Malgannis said.

"Please. You must know something about the bargain she made."

"Nothing. She won't tell me a thing."

Silvia shook her head as she appraised Cora. "You foolish girl. The price..."

"It is done now," Cora said.

Silvia gave a long, drawn out sigh. "This is one for the tales."

"No tales," Malgannis said. "No need for her to suffer the same fate as me."

"Oh, Cora. What did they want? Did they want your first born? Do you have to marry someone?"

"I told you not to ask," Cora snapped.

Silvia pursed her lips. "A black priest always takes a price."

"Both of you." Cora decided she had to take control of the conversation. "We are at war. Our survival is at stake."

"But what about him?" Silvia asked, indicating Malgannis. "What are you going to tell them?"

"Tell whom?"

"Why, the lords in the palace. The generals in the army." Silvia glanced toward the window. "The people out there."

"He is my new advisor," Cora stated.

"Hmmm," Silvia said. She cocked her head and spoke with familiar sarcasm. "So you will tell them all that you have a new advisor, Lord Morgan, a man they have never heard of. This man has come to advise their queen – also new – in her time of need. They shouldn't ask questions, however they will be seeing the two of you spending a lot of time together. Oh, and by the way, they are to take his orders as if they are your own."

Cora and Malgannis exchanged glances.

"Oh," Cora said.

"The one you have to watch out for is Logan Kane," Silvia said. "You know it as well as I do. The baron is quick. And powerful. If he weren't here in Adin, your task might be easier. But here he is."

Cora's anxious eyes went from Silvia to Malgannis and back again. "What do we do?"

For once Malgannis was without an answer. "I'm the stranger here."

"Let me think," Silvia said.

"You'll have to think quickly," Malgannis said. "People will wonder who is spending so much time with the queen."

A new voice interrupted them. One of the stewards entered the chamber and bowed, keeping his eyes lowered.

"Your Majesty. A message for you. They say it is important."

✦

Adin Palace had never been Malgannis's home. It was his son's home, his son Alfred, the king, who became the first of the Vandryden dynasty. And yet Malgannis knew the palace well, which made him feel a strange out-of-body sensation to once again be walking the corridors and to know his way around. Some things had changed: a few doorways had shifted; decorative patterned paper now covered surfaces that had once been painted. He passed a doorway and glanced inside. The music room was now a drawing room. Another opening drew his gaze. The portrait room was now a trophy room, with heads of boars, bears, and stags decorating the walls.

He tried to banish the memories and bring himself forcefully into the present. He was walking with long strides, but knew to maintain the appearance that he was trailing Cora, and it was she who was in front. The queen had changed into a more comfortable blue dress that displayed her shoulders and complemented her hair color.

She drew every gaze. As they navigated the palace, courtiers and palace staff peeled away, bowing as they gave the queen space. Malgannis glanced at Cora again. She was beautiful, he realized. Her jewelry sparkled and the blue dress clung to her slender frame. She had a commanding, elegant presence that Malgannis had rarely seen in others. Perhaps he didn't need to worry about drawing attention.

He had the thought too soon.

Of course they all wanted to see the queen. The young woman many of them had seen grow from a child was reborn, to inherit a position no one thought she would have. Something in her had changed. How could it not? She had been marred by the tragedy of her father's death, and then her brother's. Responsibility was now etched into her face and in the way she held her chin high. Things were no longer the same, and she knew it as well as they did.

They all wanted to see the queen, but once they had, their curious attention moved onto the tall man with long graying hair following at her side.

Malgannis became conscious of the stares of everyone he passed. Who was this stranger to the palace? How did he fit into the wider ranks and hierarchies and circles of power? Did his obvious favor affect them?

Malgannis needed a good story, and soon.

Cora swept through a grand archway and into an immense room with walls of polished wooden paneling. Chairs rested at regular intervals along the room's perimeter. Paintings of Aranor's forested landscapes, horses sipping at the river, and placid ships at anchor added color to the space. A number of nobles in bright costumes milled in a small crowd; evidently they had come straight from the festivities downstairs.

Malgannis scanned the room and the people within it, learning what he could. One young man with a dirty face wore plain dark clothing and practical riding boots. Cora evidently came to the same conclusion that Malgannis did, and went straight to the messenger.

"Who is it from?" she asked, holding out a hand.

The messenger gave a bow and then held out a scroll. "From Lord Wallace, My Queen."

Cora took the scroll and glanced at Malgannis. Her eyes sparkled. "Erik."

She eagerly broke the wax seal, with a second red circle beside it to indicate the importance of the contents. Malgannis watched her face. Color had come to her cheeks where before they were pale. Some of the suffering eased, and softened the tightness that had been in her eyes since her brother's death. Malgannis was even surprised at his own pleasure to learn that Erik had definitely made it out of the battle alive. Cora may have lost her brother, but she still had Erik.

Cora scanned the message quickly and then looked up. "It is addressed to the palace council. Erik doesn't know I'm here." She continued to read. "He says he has gathered our men and retreated to the border forts. Many of the officers fell in the battle. He and the other captains are making decisions together. The wardens of the forts want to know who is in charge."

One of the nobles in the room spoke up. He was swarthy and heavy set, with thick jowls and garish clothing. His baritone voice was both curt and commanding. "What reply shall we give him, Majesty?"

"Lord Byron," Cora said, and Malgannis filed the name away. "We will tell him I am here and well. We will be sending someone to help him soon."

“Who?” an older man with a hooked nose challenged. Perhaps he was blind in one eye, for he tilted his head in an odd way as he stared at the queen.

A lady with gray hair and a patrician nose frowned at the blunt question. “Know your place, Lord Phelps.”

Cora didn’t respond to Lord Phelps. Instead, the old man mumbled something as he bowed.

“Today is an important day for Aranor,” Cora said. She ran her gaze across the room as she spoke, to take in all the milling lords. “It is a day of hope. Please. Return to the feast. I will join you there. Soon we will meet and we will discuss important matters. But for now, let us celebrate our nation. For there is no doubt in my mind. Aranor will survive.”

Lord Byron snapped his heels together, although his girth made the movement clumsier than it might otherwise have been. “Long live the queen!” he called.

The other lords echoed his words, and Cora remained still and expressionless.

Then she left the room, and Malgannis followed her out. The lords filed off in the other direction, and when Malgannis glanced over his shoulder, he saw them walking away and whispering into each other’s ears.

Chapter 21

TWO DAYS HAD PASSED since Cora's coronation. She again wore the blue mantle studded with shining prisms on her shoulders. Her golden crown rested on her head. A blue dress flowed down far enough to cover her feet. She sat in a chair that had been elaborately carved with fanciful swirls and painted gold. The chair wasn't small, it was huge, with a high back and arms that swallowed Cora's real arms resting upon them. She was on a raised podium, so that everyone else had to look up to meet her eyes.

Cora hoped that if she kept thinking of it as a chair, she wouldn't worry so much about how the day would go. But it wasn't working. She was seated upon a throne, the seat of the kings and queens of Aranor. Malgannis stood beside the podium, also facing the assembled group of nobles in front of them, a careful selection of the most powerful lords and ladies of the realm, or at least those who had remained at court in Adin rather than join the fight at the front. Many had sons who were away fighting. Many of those sons would never return.

Together, Cora and Malgannis needed to convince the nobles that the stranger beside the queen deserved his place at her right hand.

Cora knew she was on display, but at least the audience chamber wasn't as big as some of the halls—it had to be intimate in order to fulfill its purpose. She was allowing her nobles to argue in front of her, letting them expose their hopes and fears without interruption. She wondered if the idea came from watching her father.

"To abandon our ally—" Lord Phelps was saying in a voice filled with worry.

Hawk-faced Lady Pike spoke in a scornful tone. "Vestria is lost. We have to think of ourselves."

"What will I say to Lord Dalton? He dines tonight at my house!"

"Tell him the truth," Lady Pike snapped.

Cora raised a hand; the lords and ladies fell silent. "Let us have agreement. Vestria has fallen. If we wish to aid our ally, the best thing we can do is defeat our enemy." She swept her gaze across the room. "Now. I have summoned you all here because our army needs leadership. We need someone to lead our forces. A general."

From the circle of onlookers, Lord Byron stepped forward to give a short bow. "My Queen. I would be most grateful to—"

He broke off when Cora again held up her hand, but she smiled slightly to soften any sting. "Thank you, Lord Byron, your offer is noted."

Even as Cora spoke, she was watching the faces arrayed around the room, however there was one man who drew her attention more than any other. Lord Logan Kane, Baron of Fastness stood with a cluster of companions arrayed around him. When Cora had left Adin to find Erik, she and Logan had been sharing company while she tried to convince him to send more levies to the front. She didn't know if she had offended him with her sudden departure, but no one could have known that when they saw each other again, she would be the queen.

As always, Logan's black trousers and gray doublet looked expensive despite their lack of embellishment, and his ebony skin was smooth, with only a few creases around his eyes. Malgannis beside her was just as aware—whatever Logan decided, others would follow.

"There is a candidate for commander of our armies I wish to present," Cora said. "Now, you all know Lord Wallace of Blythe and the history he shares with my family. You also may know that some weeks ago, Lord Wallace disappeared on a secret quest. When important news came to my attention, something that could change the outcome of this terrible war, there was no one else I could entrust to act upon this information. I can now reveal where Lord Wallace went and why."

The nobles leaned forward, captivated. Cora had thought hard about what she would say. Everyone liked a good story, especially one with a mystery.

"I was recently contacted by a man from Aranor who had been living for decades in the land of Tor Gaeron. This man had sent a missive to the palace, and with my brother at the front, I was the one who received it. He introduced himself and said he wanted to come home to Aranor. Eventually, he wished to retire to a quiet manor in the south, to spend his years raising horses and growing wine, and he sought favor and assistance with his homecoming. In return, he offered his services, for he was a student of war, and was aware of our struggle."

Cora's eyes inadvertently moved to Logan. The baron was focused, paying attention to every word she said.

She continued, "What this man offered was beyond value, and I immediately sent Lord Wallace to escort him here. He and Lord Wallace met, and they journeyed together. Meanwhile, I also traveled to the borderlands, to the front. An audience was arranged with my late brother the king, but that is when disaster struck," Cora glanced at Malgannis, "and amidst the chaos, it was this man who helped me to get safely home."

Malgannis remained stone-faced, even as he was under the scrutiny of all the nobles.

"Why would I risk so much?" Cora asked. "Why would Lord Wallace? The reason is that this man is not any son of Aranor." She lowered her voice. "He is also the Stone General."

From her delivery, the assembled nobles were expected to react, and that was what they did. A few gasped. Others exchanged glances filled with wonder. However, as Cora and Malgannis were both well aware, none of them knew who the Stone General was.

Cora elaborated, "My father shared tales of the Stone General. He was famed even when I was a girl. I have no doubt that many of you are familiar with his exploits. For those of you who entered the academy, you will have studied his battles and tactics."

Many of the lords surreptitiously scanned their own number, looking to see if they were the only ignorant one in the group. No one spoke up. Cora knew what they were thinking. She had come up with the idea. It wouldn't pay to reveal that they should know who their queen was speaking of but didn't. She also knew that with the younger men away, the only lords present who had studied to enter military service had done so a very long time ago.

"Morgan is his name, Lord Morgan, although he was not born to privilege. As a young man, he was a soldier of Aranor, before the lure of distant lands took him across the White Sea. Soon, Lord Morgan found himself in Tor Gaeron, where he earned a place at the king of Tor Gaeron's side. You all know of the war against the Ravagers. He was instrumental in winning that war. He is a leader, a strategist, and a great warrior. He also knows the hearts and minds of men."

Cora saw Malgannis again under the inspection of the crowd. She didn't sense outright hostility, but there was definitely some confusion.

Logan spoke up. His voice was deep and projected inner confidence. "My Queen," he said. "If it please you... If this man is to lead our forces, we wish to hear from him directly. To us, he is a stranger."

"Of course, Lord Kane," Cora said. She turned to Malgannis. "Lord Morgan?"

Malgannis took a step forward. He lifted his chin and moved his head to meet the eyes of every man in turn. He didn't smile or put on a pleasant expression.

"You need to hear some hard truths," he said. "But before you do, let me clarify a few things about myself. I am not begging to be here. I am here to help the queen, because she asked me to, and because there is no one else to do it. If you don't want me here, I will go. Although I don't think you would be doing your queen a service."

Murmurs came from the group of nobles, but their voices fell silent when Malgannis spoke over them.

"I am a military man. War is all I know. I don't know much about how to organize a nation's wealth or how to host balls and banquets. I don't dance. I can't play an instrument. My father raised me to fight with a sword, ride a horse, aim an arrow, and win a battle. I have been tested in the field," he paused, remembering, "you don't know how I've been tested. And no matter where I have fought, no matter how many times I have claimed the battlefield, or retreated in the face of bad odds, or dealt with unruly allies, some things never change. You see patterns. You learn that powerful forces generally defeat weak ones. Home terrain is a disadvantage, compared with an enemy who can pillage and plunder and live off the land. The fact is, for Aranor, I don't know if this war can be won."

One by one, the nobles paled. There were a few notable exceptions. Portly and swarthy, Lord Byron stood with determination in his jaw. Logan Kane's nostrils flared; as Cora's father had always said, the man had steel in him.

"As our queen rightly said, Vestria is lost," Malgannis said. "Our forces have retreated to the border forts. If I leave this palace, and this city, as commander of Aranor's armies, I plan to go to the border immediately. I have seen enough to know that our enemy is a skilled strategist, ready to find our weaknesses and exploit them without hesitation. I spent time as a soldier, here in Aranor. I know the border forts – all three of them: Martenhal, Balgaven, and Claregantry – like I know the face of my long-dead wife. If the three fortresses fall, then Aranor falls. There aren't many who can win this war for you, but if anyone has a chance, it is me. I make no false promises. But war is what I know."

His speech completed, Malgannis stood with his thumbs hooked into his belt.

One by one, the nobles turned to Logan Kane, and in that moment, the baron's true power was revealed. His brow furrowed as he pondered.

Cora held her breath as she waited. She had spent a few days with Logan, just the two of them, and had come to know him to a degree, but despite his request for her to use his first name, their relationship had remained somewhat formal. She assumed that was just his manner; after all, he was much older than her. Her status had also changed; she was now the queen. She had no idea whether she could count upon him now.

At last, Logan spoke slowly, "I have outstanding queries... reservations if you will. However I will not question our queen in her own hall." He bowed in Cora's direction. "I must confer with the other senior members of the chamber. In private. We have a queen, but we also have a council."

Even as he finished, disappointment sank into Cora's chest. She had seen her father in similar situations, and had enough experience to know that despite his gracious words, he was planning to deny her his support. He didn't know the man standing beside Cora, and he certainly didn't know that in truth he was looking at Malgannis Ironclaw, a general to save their nation in its time of peril.

Perhaps Logan wanted to take charge himself. He was ambitious, so Cora's father always said. Cora fought the urge to bite her lip. She knew that if she lost the nobles now, the chance would be gone forever. Without power, Malgannis wouldn't be able to do anything at all.

Something occurred to her.

The idea was shocking, but then she had to remind herself how much she had already committed; there could be no turning back. She had given everything. She was destined to die.

Cora leaned forward on the throne "Lord Kane," she said. "May I speak with you briefly?"

"Of course, Majesty."

"Please." She beckoned. "Approach."

He stepped forward, and she continued to beckon until he had climbed up onto the podium. She motioned for him to bring his head close to hers, and then she whispered into his ear.

"I promise you, Logan, this man is the general we need. He must go to the front. Meanwhile, here in the palace, I will need your help." As she spoke, she knew he was listening. "I propose an alliance, a unification, of your house and mine, of Fastness and Aranor." She knew she had to make herself clear, but every dream for her future that she had ever had disappeared as soon as she said the words. Her life was gone. This was the final act that brought it home. "I propose marriage."

Logan was more than surprised. But if he was as ambitious as Cora's father said he was, he wouldn't balk at having even more influence than he already had. His wife had been dead for many years. He had been eager to spend time with her. Even as he stood by the throne, he paused a moment to reflect.

Then he descended back to his previous position. All eyes were on him. No one was looking at Cora, and so she was able to grip the arms of the throne to steady herself.

Logan allowed the tension to build and then spoke with confidence. "The queen must have our full support if Aranor is to stay strong. She is our queen. We must trust her judgement. The general we need is standing by her side."

The nobles all exchanged glances, but any murmurs were silenced by Lord Byron's stentorian voice.

"Then let us welcome our new commander," Lord Byron proclaimed loudly. He bowed toward Malgannis. "May the gods guide your decisions. Lord..."

"Morgan," Malgannis said flatly.

"Lord Morgan of...?"

"Of Aranor."

As Cora felt relief mingle with her sadness, Lord Byron clapped his hands together. His jowls shook as he raised his arms high. "Lord Morgan of Aranor, may you lead our armies to victory against the gravest threat Aranor has ever faced. And may our glorious queen's reign be a long one. Long live the queen!"

"Long live the queen!" the nobles echoed.

A new voice called loudly, an echo of the group.

"Long live the queen!"

Following the sound, Cora shot straight to her feet. Someone new had entered the council chamber. If she hadn't been where she was, she would have already been running, arms wide open.

Erik was approaching with long strides. The familiar look of pleasure was on his face as his eyes remained fixed on her.

The nobles immediately recognized him, parting to let Erik approach the throne. A sword dangled from Erik's hip, and he still wore his blue and gold uniform; evidently he had hastily come straight to the palace. A few smudges of grime were on his cheeks and his hair was tousled.

"You have made a wise decision," Erik repeated. Coming to a halt in front of the throne, he nodded at Malgannis. Erik didn't know much, but Cora knew he would always support her. "Lord Morgan is the general we need."

Voices rose in a din. "Lord Wallace!"

"What news?"

"Did you just arrive?"

"Do the border forts still stand?"

As Cora sat herself down again, she raised a hand. "Silence!"

Immediately the lords all fell silent. Muttering apologies, several bowed in her direction. Everyone turned toward Cora to hear what she had to say.

"Lord Wallace?" she asked gently.

Erik gave a bow, made awkward by his armor. "My Queen. I... Words cannot describe how I feel to see you safe and well." He looked like he would continue but caught himself. "The border forts stand," he said in a loud voice. Relieved murmurs greeted his words, but Erik shook his head. "Yet Vestria has fallen. Our enemy now occupies Ballina and holds the Red King prisoner. The sway of the Moranians holds throughout that great nation, as it does in Rumandy. Graven Callow's forces have the scent of final victory. His numbers grow day by day. Aranor stands alone."

Cora couldn't blame the lords for the despair they obviously felt. Malgannis had said that Vestria's fall was inevitable, but it was one thing to hear it as a potential outcome, and another to know it for certain.

"We need to make decisions," Erik said. "I came here as fast as I could to have them made. It appears that perhaps my concern was unnecessary." He gave Malgannis a nod. "We need a general, and a general has been named."

Cora's joy and relief had been so strong that she had forgotten what she had just done. With Erik's words, she was now reminded. She glanced toward Logan and then back to Erik.

She had tried hard to never allow herself to hope that one day, she might marry for love. But as for Erik, he cared about her, and wanted what was best for her. He didn't know about the sixty days. He didn't know that what she had done, she had done out of necessity.

In her heart, she knew he would never understand.

✦

Erik lingered by the rose gardens, out near the dolphin fountain where he knew that Cora would see him. He glanced at the grand palace that loomed over the lawns and gardens. By the gods, it felt good to be home. Soon he would return to the border, but he had missed being here with Cora.

He used the time to plan. While he was in Adin, he needed to speak with some of the nobles. There were still a few holding out some of their fighting men to keep order in their own lands. He would ask them some quiet but direct questions, and impress upon them how grave the struggle was. If need be, he would threaten to expose their secret mistresses, hidden wealth, and their hunts in royal forests that rightfully belonged to the queen.

He had no reservations. Nothing was more important than Aranor's survival.

As he waited, he swept his gaze over the palace and its grounds and reminded himself that it was all Cora's now. He was still getting used to the idea—she was the queen. Perhaps she was right. Perhaps he shouldn't worry so much about what other people thought. They were no longer children. He and Cora bore terrible responsibility, but they no longer had to do as they were told.

He saw her approaching.

With the help of her maids, Cora had always taken care with her appearance, but she was also someone who liked to ride horses and run under the open sky. Now, there wasn't a strand of hair or curl of fabric out of place. Her braid was in so many coils it must have taken an eternity to fashion. Her blue dress hugged her slender figure so that her waist looked too thin to hold up her torso. So much had changed. The circumstances were tragic, and their future was fraught with peril, but Cora was now the ruler of a great kingdom.

Erik smiled at her as she neared, but strangely, she didn't return his smile. Instead, her face was carefully blank. He knew her well though, and a tightness around her eyes gave away her anxiety. Something had her worried. His smile fell.

"Cora? What is it?"

"Erik," she said. She managed a smile, but didn't hold it for long. "I'm so happy to see you well. We haven't had a chance to speak since..."

"Since the battle. I'm sorry," he said, meeting her eyes. He wanted to reach out and take her hands, but they were in the gardens, rather than somewhere private.

"You loved him too," she said.

"But he was your brother."

"You know he thought of you that way. As a brother. Thank you for bringing him home."

Erik frowned. She was still being strangely formal. "I was so worried about you... I couldn't stop thinking about the things that could have happened." He remembered his surprise at seeing Morgan standing at Cora's right hand. "He went back for you?"

"He did. I wouldn't be here without him."

Erik's arms twitched. She seemed so aloof, so alone. He wanted to embrace her. "It's cold out here. Shall we head inside?"

"Here is better."

Erik noticed something on her finger, a golden band set with diamonds. "You have a new ring," he said in surprise. "What happened to your other one, the one your father gave you?"

"I lost it." She looked sad for a moment. "Erik..."

Puzzled at her tone, he searched her face. Her careful expression was anything but reassuring. "What is it?"

"There is no easy way to say this." As Cora hesitated again, Erik grew increasingly anxious. She wasn't acting like herself. "You know that people marry for different reasons. When you are a prince or a princess, a king or a queen, it is rare to marry for love." He saw that she had one hand tightly clasping the other. "Long ago, the baron of Fastness gave my father a proposal, a proposal my father refused." She stared directly into his eyes and after another steadying breath, she spoke clearly. "A proposal of marriage."

Erik frowned, confused.

"Back then, my father thought a more important alliance could be forged. But, as you know, circumstances have changed."

Erik realized that he was hearing her correctly. Slowly, he began to understand the direction she was taking. "I don't understand," he said. "There are no alliances to make. You were a princess and now you are the queen..."

"Circumstances have changed," Cora repeated. "Aranor stands alone. My rule must be strong."

Erik glanced toward the palace. In his mind's eye, he again saw the nobles arrayed in front of the throne, with the baron surrounded by his powerful faction. He remembered Cora, up in front of everyone, beautiful, fragile, and isolated.

He returned his attention to Cora. "Cora... You haven't seriously..."

"Logan Kane and I are to be married," she said. "His wife has been dead for fifteen years. His son and daughter are no longer children. He can help me. I need him."

Erik couldn't help himself. He imagined Cora embracing the much older man... kissing him... sharing his bed. He tried to thrust aside the images that kept appearing. "But Cora... of all people... him?"

"You will address me correctly," she said.

His eyes widened. He wanted her to tell him that it had been forced upon her, that she had no other choice. Instead she wasn't even trying to soften it. She was reminding him of his place. She would make her own decisions, and he had no right to question them.

"Very well. My Queen," he said. Despite trying, he was unable to keep an icy tone from his voice. "If you choose to marry a man well over twice your age, that is your right. You are correct. A queen must produce heirs. There is no other suitor with his rank and power."

"I am not doing this for heirs," she said.

He waited for her to continue, but when she didn't, he gave a sharp nod. "You have your reasons, and it is not for me to concern myself with your affairs." He shook his head. "There was a time when we shared our hopes and fears but it is gone now, in the past. I only want what is best for you. And yet, it is you who won't trust me." He saw pain in her eyes. "Evidently it is time for me to go then, to return to the border under the command of Lord Morgan, a man whose true identity still remains unclear. I will fight our enemies. And we will see if he is able to do what your brother and father could not."

"Erik..." Cora said as he turned away. "Don't go like this."

He paused again, but that was all she said. "We've known each other for a long time. How else do you expect me to leave?"

When she didn't say any more, he strode away, leaving her standing by the dolphin fountain.

"Erik. Wait," she called.

He stopped, but kept his back to her, and didn't turn.

"Perhaps I should go with you..."

"To the border?" He spoke in a tone of condescension, even though he knew it would rankle her. "Stay here, Your Majesty. You are far too important to fall to a stray arrow."

He resumed his swift stride, leaving her standing alone.

Chapter 22

CORA CAUGHT HER BREATH, her flickering torch held high. A row of four grinning skulls stared back at her. On a shelf, below the alcove with the skulls, arm and leg bones had been arranged like kindling prepared for a fire. The rib bones and other parts were nowhere to be seen.

She had reached a dead end. With no other option, she had to go back.

With an effort, she turned her body around. For some reason, having the skulls stare at her back was even worse. She forced herself to walk, one step at a time. Eventually she reached the place where the low-ceilinged tunnel forked, and this time she took another passage she had yet to travel.

Despite her fear, her thoughts kept returning to Erik. She had only been given a few weeks of life, and she had used the time to hurt someone she truly cared about. Erik knew she was hiding important things from him. He could probably sense that the prospect of her marriage to Logan Kane didn't bring her any joy at all. Worst of all, he thought she no longer trusted him, when she knew that of anyone, he would always be there for her.

She didn't know what to do. When her curse came to final fruition, she didn't want Erik's last memories of her to ones that brought him pain. She wanted him to remember the bond they shared. Erik and Malgannis would both soon depart for the border. The struggle might be protracted. Nearly half of her sixty days was gone. She might never see Erik again.

She needed more time.

As she explored the catacombs, part of her wished she could hear sounds other than those she made herself. Her breathing was as soft as she could make it, but it was still too loud; the fear she was trying to bury made her chest rise and fall too swiftly. Her torch gave an occasional crackle. With every step forward, her boots crunched on the fine, powdery gravel that lined the floor in this section of the catacombs.

A squeaking sound made her freeze in place. The high-pitched squeal came from somewhere up ahead. Rats, she guessed, as her mouth twisted.

She told herself she had to keep going. One foot at a time, she followed the tunnel as the ceiling became low and she was forced to duck under a particularly tight section. Her torchlight made the shadows dance. Another branch in the tunnel lay ahead of her. This time she would take the right-hand turn, which would make her explorations easier to remember.

She whispered it out loud. "Left Right. Left. Right. Left. Right. Left left. Left right."

Surely, at some point she would find the black temple where she had signed her bargain in blood. Even if she didn't, this was her only way to find the black priest who had blindfolded her and taken her there, when she had agreed to his price near the end of winter. Lexen Crow came and went as he pleased. But if she wanted to locate him, she didn't know where else to go.

She stopped in place when she heard something that sent a spike of fear along her back.

This time it came from behind her. She was certain she had heard a tripping sound, like a big man taking a footstep and then making a sudden halt. For what felt like an eternity she stood in place, listening. She turned and held her torch high, but the passage became entirely black just a stone's throw from where she was standing.

There was nothing else she could do. She had to keep going.

The long tunnel continued. It began to twist, turning slightly in one direction, then another. Cora's rounded a corner and saw a shadow standing directly in front of her.

Cora gave a startled cry. Even when she saw the slender frame and black robe, and realized that Lexen Crow was the man waiting for her, she still had to wait a few moments to speak.

His skin was even yellower then she remembered. As he drew back his hood to expose his face, there was redness in his eyes, and rather than slender, he now looked thin. From his appearance, he was seriously ill. He was also angry, tilting his head forward to stare at her.

"You are taking a great risk in coming here," Lexen said, almost hissing. "You are the queen. Your movements are observed."

Cora raised her torch high to reveal his face. "I need more time."

The black priest shrugged. "I gave you sixty days. That is the agreement we made."

"I want to change it."

He gave a short sardonic laugh. "And why would I agree to that?"

Cora had thought about this for a long time as she explored the catacombs, searching for this one man. The mark on her arm had grown angrier; it had started to hurt, especially at night, with a constant sting as if the skin were rubbed raw. She was prepared to give the black priest whatever he asked for.

"There must be something I can give you," she said. She stared directly into his eyes and made her meaning clear. "Anything."

Lexen slowly looked her up and down. Cora's stomach felt tight. But then he gave her a mocking smile. "My passions do not lie in that area." His smile fell. "There is nothing you can offer me, Your Majesty." He glanced at her arm. "On your final day, that mark will spread until it covers your entire body. When it does, the end will be quick. Your death will come in thirty-seven days."

A shuffling sound, like moving grit, made Lexen lift his head to look past Cora's shoulder. She had heard it too. More rats.

Cora tried again. "Lexen, please," she said. "You're the only one who can help me. There must be a way. It's not enough time. I want to change our bargain."

"You have what you wanted. He has returned and he is helping your people. I have stayed true to my word. The question is, will you stay true to yours?"

Cora frowned. "What do you mean?"

"I heard a rumor, that you were considering going to the border."

"My actions are no concern of yours."

"Ah, but they are, Queen Coraline," he emphasized her title. "You must keep yourself safe. When we made our bargain, I gave you sixty days. If you die before that time, by some other manner, then the bargain is void." He fixed her with his eerie stare. "Let me make myself clear. If our bargain is void, then Malgannis goes back to where he came from."

Cora felt a chill. Without meaning to, she absently touched her forearm.

"You must say here, Coraline. Close to home, where you will be safe. If you risk yourself, you risk the man you gave so much to bring back. I hope I make myself understood. When the time comes, I will collect my price, and then, Coraline, you may rest easy. These matters that so concern you will have no hold on you at all."

✦

Thirty-seven days.

Malgannis had stopped breathing. He told his limbs to move but instead his thoughts kept crashing into one another, colliding with the force of a storm. He knew he needed to move, to clear the tunnel before Cora turned back and ran straight into him. But he could barely process what he had just seen and heard.

When Malgannis had found Silvia, and explained that he was looking for Cora before he left for the border, she told him that Cora had just left the palace a short time ago. Where had she gone? Malgannis asked.

Silvia was worried, she told him. This wasn't the first time Cora had snuck out of the palace, taking no protection with her at all. She had left wearing a hooded gray cloak, obviously to keep her identity hidden.

Malgannis left swiftly. Using Silvia's description, he managed to find the slender woman in the gray cloak, walking purposefully with the hood covering her hair. Cora left the palace via a side gate. She crossed the causeway to enter the town. Now and then she glanced around, checking that she wasn't being followed.

Malgannis kept a safe distance. Rather than challenge Cora, he couldn't help wonder where she was going. He followed her as she crossed streets, turned down alleys, and headed deeper into the city. Eventually, in an ancient part of the town where the streets were at different levels, she reached a low cliff, and a rusty iron gate set against a dark hole. Pulling the gate open, she glanced around, and then retrieved a torch from the floor just inside the passage. Using a tinderbox she pulled from her cloak, she struck flame to the torch, and then plunged inside the shadowed interior.

As he watched her vanish inside the tunnel, Malgannis had to know.

He waited a few moments, and then opened the gate, wincing when it groaned. He counted for three breaths, and then made his way into the passage.

For a long time he followed the young woman as she held her torch in the air and navigated the catacombs. Twice he was nearly caught as she reached dead ends and turned back to follow a different branch. She heard him trip, and peered back at him, but he was in darkness, and her stare was unfocused.

He heard every word of her discussion with the black priest.

Many things now made sense. He remembered what had happened when he was presented to the nobles. Cora had said something to Logan Kane, and the baron had changed in an instant, lending his strong support to the notion of Malgannis as general. Cora and the baron were now engaged to be married. It was after discovering what she had done that Malgannis had sought her out. Surely there must be another way.

Now he understood. Cora would be wed to Logan Kane for just a short time. And then, she would die. In one swift move, she had gained the baron's support and also arranged her own succession.

The black priest would take what was left of her life force. Not just a few hours or a day. All of her remaining years would be gone, and she was young, with her life ahead of her.

She did it for him. For Malgannis. He had been reborn at the Temple of Black Glass. She gave her life for him.

The foolish girl. The brave, innocent, foolish girl. He wished, more than anything, that she hadn't done it.

How could he do what she expected of him? How could he not?

As the black priest turned to depart, Malgannis memorized the man's features. Long, narrow face. Black hair. Thin frame. Wan skin. And something else: a tattoo on the back of his neck, close to his scalp, a crescent with a horizontal arrow piercing it. The symbol was vaguely familiar.

Malgannis knew he needed to go before Cora saw him.

And he needed time to think.

✦

Malgannis and Cora walked side by side, following the paths between the manicured gardens. They passed the roses, and a fountain fashioned of multiple basins that each flowed into the other. Dark green hedges surrounded them. Malgannis kept glancing back until he could no longer see the palace, and he was certain that they had complete privacy.

"Well," Cora slowly said. "If you aren't going to begin, then I will. We might not see each other for some time." She paused. "How is Erik? I haven't seen him. I heard he's been at the barracks–"

"Cora," Malgannis said. He stopped walking. As she also came to a halt, he met her gaze. His voice was deadly serious. "I know."

She frowned at him, as if she didn't know what he was talking about. "About what?"

"About your bargain. I followed you into the catacombs."

Her eyes widened. "You dared to..."

"Don't try," he interrupted. "Who else knows? About the price you paid?"

Cora's mouth worked for a moment; her face was suddenly pale. "No one knows. Not about that part..."

Malgannis didn't know what to say, and so his words came out on their own. "I'm not worth it, girl."

"That may be," Cora said. "But I made my bargain, and you are what I have got."

Malgannis glanced at her arm, presently covered by the yellow sleeve of her dress. "Can I see it?"

"No—"

"Please," Malgannis said. "You need to share this burden."

Cora took a deep breath. Glancing around, she gradually began to roll up her sleeve. She exposed the smooth skin below her wrist. It was unblemished, without a mark on it. She continued to peel back the material. Then Malgannis saw what looked like a blue-green bruise, if bruises had the form of curling claws. His eyes widened when she kept going, and he saw mottled purple and red, as if her skin were terribly burned.

"By all the gods," he said. "Does it hurt?"

"It's nothing," she said. She swiftly tugged her sleeve back into place.

"Look," Malgannis said. "I've been thinking hard. You can't kill a black priest, that's what everyone says. That mark is with you, no matter what happens to that man, Lucius."

"Lexen," Cora corrected. "Lexen Crow."

"Lexen," Malgannis repeated. He cast his mind back. "I met a black priest once who described seeing the first stones put down at Adin. They are not of this world."

For the first time, Malgannis saw Cora allow her tension to show on her face. "At least I have someone to take my place."

"Did you know what it would do to Erik? Your marriage?"

Cora nodded.

As Malgannis stood facing her, he saw her youth, and also the fear and worry she was burdened with. At the same time, she had such spirit, to somehow be finding the resolve to keep fighting. He realized his eyes were becoming moist. When his vision shimmered, he wiped his eyes.

"Cora," he said softly. "Why did you have to do this to me? To yourself?" He trailed off. He didn't expect an answer.

Words were failing him. He did the only thing he could. He opened his arms.

"Come here," he said. "Cora, Cora... You should tell someone. Tell Silvia. She loves you. Don't face this alone."

She entered his arms, and he wrapped them around her, burying her face into his chest.

"Child of my child of my child," he murmured. "I am sorry."

Chapter 23

"THIS IS MADNESS," Erik said. "Let someone lighter do it."

Malgannis tilted his head back to gaze up the cliff. He fought the impression that it looked sheer, without foot or handholds. Instead he took his time to inspect the surface, his gaze moving from tiny ledges to protruding knobs, thin chimneys to gouges where he might wedge a foot or fist.

"Someone lighter?" Malgannis asked. He didn't stop his inspection to glance at Erik. "Someone younger, you mean."

"Why you?" Erik challenged.

"Because I've had a full life," Malgannis replied. While he planned his ascent, he stretched his body, side to side. "A very full life. I'm not going to let some young soldier, even if he's a volunteer, die on this cliff. And because if I can make the climb, so can the men. That's why me."

"You're a fool," Erik said. Taken aback, Malgannis finally looked at his companion. Erik's expression was fierce. Dressed in the uniform of a captain, he pointed at one of the metal stars on Malgannis's black jerkin. "You're the general, the supreme commander. Do you want to die, here in the mountains, before we even reach the border forts? You aren't supposed to take risks like this."

Malgannis pulled his arm across his body and counted for three breaths. He then stretched the other arm. He tried to touch the ground without bending his knees, and held the position, pleased when his fingertips were only a foot above the dirt. Wobbling, he stood on one foot, holding the other behind his buttock. When he almost fell he swapped to the other leg.

When he was done, he looked down at himself. He decided to keep his boots on. A coil of rope lay on the ground, and he now picked it up to throw it over his shoulder. He then cracked his knuckles and returned to looking up the cliff.

"You don't win wars by doing what everyone expects of you," Malgannis said.

He reached up to the first of the handholds he had plotted and then bent his leg to wedge his foot into a cleft. Pushing with his leg, he searched with his other leg and found his second foothold.

"The legs," he muttered. "Climb with the legs."

He tried to keep his movements smooth. A brief pause to rest. Then shift to the next hold. Another pause. Body ascending higher. Don't look down.

He knew not to look down, but that didn't stop his mind from working. How high was the cliff? Sixty feet? Eighty? Was he doing this because he felt that he had something to prove to Erik? Or perhaps to himself? He wasn't even sure himself.

Coming to a chimney, he was able to wedge his foot in and then bring the other higher still, while his arms kept his overall movement upward. He grunted and heaved. Another foothold. The chimney was going to come to an end, and he didn't want it to.

He reached the end of the easy stretch. Panting, he peered up to see a ledge right above his head. He decided to remain in place while he rested his aching muscles.

"Morgan!" Erik called. "Everything all right?"

Erik's voice sounded distant, which meant that Malgannis was high. The wind began to pick up, whipping his clothes around his frame. He managed to avoid looking at the ground.

"Fine. Just resting," he called without looking down.

How was he supposed to get over the ledge? He scanned the surrounding area. There. A knob where he could put his foot was just a couple of feet from another protrusion. Once up, he would be able to climb over to the ledge.

He knew he couldn't wait any longer. Just remaining in position would drain his energy. He gritted his teeth and leaned over to grab hold of the knob. His foot scrabbled until it rested on a thin shelf. Time to throw his body forward and reach out.

Malgannis's right foot slipped.

For a moment both of his legs were unsupported. All that was holding him up were his hands gripping the cliff face. His right foot frantically searched to find purchase once more. His left foot dangled uselessly.

Time slowed.

"Malgannis! I told you not to climb so high!"

The stern voice was that of his mother. A vision came to him of her standing far below, her face drawn with anxiety as she watched him on the high branches of a mighty oak.

"Lad, get back up, and climb back on again."

The stentorian voice belonged to his father. Malgannis lay on the ground and stars sparkled in front his vision. The back of his head had struck the ground hard as he fell off his horse. The creature snorted, as if laughing at the boy it had bucked off.

"My love, please come back to me. Don't die up there."

This time he heard the sweet voice of his wife. She was gazing up at him as he sat on horseback, saying goodbye as he prepared to travel north, heading to war. He would never forget how beautiful she looked that day, with her chestnut hair in tresses and love in her eyes. It was the last time he would see her.

Malgannis's arms screamed at him. His hands wanted to let go, but he made his muscles give one last effort. At last his foot found the little shelf once more. His other leg planted itself down on the bulge he had seen earlier. The pressure was now relieved from his arms.

He found himself covered in sweat, his chest heaving. Someone was shouting at him. Glancing down, he saw Erik watching him with a panicked expression his face.

Don't look down.

Malgannis remembered too late. His head swam as he realized he must be near the top of the cliff, for the ground looked impossibly distant. He knew in his heart that to fall would be to die. His head would split like a round fruit. Legs and arms would break; his spine would be crushed.

"I'm... fine..." he called down, returning his attention upward. But his voice was hoarse and he had to repeat himself. "I'm fine!"

He knew he needed the climb to be done with. Without allowing himself any more time to think, he reached over to the ledge, which was now close to his present position. He pulled himself over and up. As soon as he was on top of the ledge, the idea of sitting and taking a rest was tempting, but instead he straightened until he was standing. He inspected the next stretch of cliff.

With a rising sense of relief, he realized the climb was over. The top of the cliff was just above him.

He reached up, and pulled himself up and over. He had made it.

For a short time he lay on his back and stared up at the blue sky. A few clouds drifted past, pushed along by the stiff wind. His breath began to even out. His heart rate returned to something approaching normal.

At last, he stood.

He now walked away from the drop, toward the narrow pass that was the reason he had gone to the effort to get here. A mountainous landscape stretched out at both sides. In front of him, two sharp peaks formed a juncture, and as he approached the place where the steep rocky walls met, he felt a different kind of rising tension.

He climbed over the rock, and gradually the vista opened up.

Malgannis soon found himself on top of another cliff, this one much gentler, not much more than a steep slope. He gazed down at a valley, well protected, with mountains on all sides and just a single flat stretch of the valley floor to get in or out. A winding river drained out through the same exit. He saw the trickling columns of smoke that rose from campfires. Tents filled the valley from end to end. Men in uniform moved about. Flags colored black and crimson fluttered in the breeze, the red 'V' catching his eye.

Malgannis knew that the Moranians felt safe where they were. Their guard would be down.

He was pleased as he returned to the cliff he had climbed. Slipping the rope from his shoulder, he tied it around a pillar of rock and threw the other end down until it stretched all the way to the ground.

He watched the activity below.

Erik had left the cliff as soon as he saw Malgannis had made it up. In his role of captain, he was now giving orders, making sense of the five hundred new recruits they had brought from Adin.

After Malgannis's confirmation as commander, Malgannis had known he didn't want to leave the nation's capital empty handed. The border forts had to hold. With the assistance of Lord Byron, who was surprisingly helpful, he had put out the call, and these recruits had answered. Malgannis had swiftly led his small force over the King's Road to Helmsford. He had then taken his group sharply away from Helmsford to plunge into the Stony Mountains, circling around toward the border forts from the side. Now, all of his scouting from high points had paid off. They had found the enemy camp in the valley, and this difficult but secret approach,

When Malgannis arrived at the border forts, he wanted to already have proven himself. And when these fresh soldiers arrived, he wanted them to have the confidence that only victory could bring.

A young soldier began to climb the rope. He grunted and used his legs to good effect, completing the ascent much more quickly than Malgannis had. Malgannis reached down to grab the man's hand and help him up. Together, they assisted the next recruit. Once several of them were up to the top of the cliff, Malgannis left them to it.

He returned to the pass, waiting and watching at a point where he could see into the valley. He scanned the area, counting the number of tents, planning his attack.

Hearing shuffling and scraping, he turned to see Erik climb over to join him.

"We'll rest here tonight," Malgannis said. "Then we'll hit them before dawn."

Erik spent a few moments gazing down at the valley. "Morgan?"

"Eh?"

"This is just one division. We have an entire army to defeat. What then?"

"One step at a time, lad," Malgannis said. "It only takes a snowflake to start an avalanche."

Chapter 24

CORA SAT ON A FOLDING STOOL and stared at herself in the mirror.

It was an oval-shaped bronze mirror, resting on a stand, and was smaller than what she was used to in the palace. Yet the maids and stewards knew what they were doing, and despite the fact that she was in a tent, her surroundings were sumptuous.

The tent – or perhaps pavilion might be a better word – had seven compartments. Thick rugs lined every floor. Silk curtains divided one section from another. There were chests filled with linen, chests packed with clothing, and more chests just for hairpieces and jewelry. Expensive incense burned in a brazier, dispersing the mingled scent of sandalwood, musk, and rose.

Cora's crown rested on the table by the mirror. She watched her reflection and saw a dignified young woman with glossy dark brown hair wearing an embroidered red dress. She wore a necklace made of bands of gold each as thick as her little finger. Her cheekbones were high and her lips were red and full.

And yet, she gazed into her own eyes and saw frustration and fear. More than anything, she saw uncertainty. Instead, what she wanted to see was resolve.

Behind her, Lord Byron was talking, and her eyes moved to watch him in the reflection. Today he wore a tunic of crimson and blue, clothing that was tight on his stout frame and contrasted with his swarthy skin. He waved his hands as he spoke, and the jewels on his fingers sparkled, even as his chin wobbled.

"...which makes nine hundred in total. Well done, My Queen. Another four hundred also signed up from Eastern Penstone. Tomorrow when we visit Fort Penstone itself..."

"Lord Byron," Cora interrupted. She turned to face him directly.

"Majesty?"

"I want to do more. More than offer stirring words and entreat our men to help with the struggle."

Lord Byron's tone became gentle. "My Queen... This is the best thing you can do. The people love you. When they see you in person, they realize how important it is for their sons to join the war."

Cora heard movement, and a moment later the curtain was pulled aside as a newcomer entered the room. Logan Kane's gray hair matched his tight-fitting vest, and he wore a black doublet and black trousers over leather boots. With his fine clothing and ebony skin, he was a handsome man, despite his age.

"That will be all, Lord Byron," Cora said.

Lord Byron bowed. "Until tomorrow, My Queen."

Cora slowly stood, waiting until Lord Byron had completely left. Whatever Logan wanted, he looked impatient. As he stood in front of her, she realized that although he was much taller, his shoulders were slightly stooped in a way she hadn't noticed before.

"Coraline..." he said. He hesitated, as if unsure how she would react to his words. "The announcement of our engagement has the people feeling hope, even as they send their sons to the border forts. I wish to discuss the wedding. Perhaps..."

Cora held up her hand. "As soon as we have returned to Adin."

His eyes widened slightly, but then he looked pleased. "Then we are in agreement."

"Is there anything else?" Cora asked.

"No, that is all." He bent to lift her hand, and pressed his lips against it. "I bid you goodnight." He smiled. "Until the morning, Coraline."

As Logan left, Cora sank back down to the stool, finally alone. Or at least she felt alone. When a different curtain stirred, and Silvia entered the room, Cora knew her handmaiden had listened to every word.

Silvia had a steaming mug in her hands, which made Cora smile. The older woman set the mug down near the mirror. Seeing her own face, Silvia made a sound of mock astonishment and patted down her flaxen hair, before smoothing her tight gray dress. Cora's smile grew wider.

"Hot tea," Silvia said. "Just the way you like it." Putting her hands on her hips, she watched Cora for a moment and made a sound. "Now what's wrong, dear?"

Cora glanced at the mirror. Again she saw it: frustration, fear, uncertainty. "I think I'm just tired."

Silvia pursed her lips. "There has been a lot of banqueting and speeches. A lot of travel in a bumpy carriage. Tonight is your first early night in a long time."

"I suppose it is," Cora said.

Silvia paused. She glanced toward the corner of the tent. "I suggest you look in the wooden chest over there. The one next to the big clothing chest."

"Why?"

"Trust me."

Silvia departed without another word. Her curiosity aroused, Cora headed to the chest and knelt in front of it to unhook the fastenings. Opening the lid, she saw familiar books, tomes that usually rested on the shelf in the library at Adin Palace. There were books about the geography of Aranor and the histories of the different towns and regions. More books described the noble houses, the great families, and the lineages and alliances connecting one house to another. She felt initial disappointment; Silvia seemed to think that what she needed was more study.

Cora continued to move each book aside, until she came to something different.

She lifted up a leather wrapped bundle tied with string. Wondering if it might be what Silvia had been speaking about, she pulled the tie, unfurled the leather, and discovered a scroll inside.

She held up the scroll to read it.

Coraline.

I was never able to raise my own daughter to adulthood. There are things I wish I could have told her. Since our arrival in Adin, I have been working to share what little wisdom I have.

I hope it is of use.

M.

Cora then discovered line upon line of short sentences and paragraphs. The words were direct. Very much like the man who had written them.

They will try to take your freedom, and you will have to fight to keep it.

Never be timid, not in public nor in private.

Try to ask the questions that everyone else is afraid to ask.

Never stop reading. Never stop learning.

Always challenge the wisdom of the herd.

There is nothing wrong with revealing ignorance, if true knowledge is the result.

You learn by doing.

Become a thief. Learn others' skills and make them your own.

Keep your capabilities secret from your enemies.

Cora put the scroll down, even though she had much more to read before she finished it.

"Silvia," she called.

Silvia soon poked her head into the room. "Yes?"

"Fetch me Lord Byron."

"At once."

Silvia's head vanished, and Cora wrapped the scroll back in its leather covering. She bit her lip, thinking, as she returned the bundle to the chest and closed the lid. While she waited, she began to pace the length of the tent.

"My Queen?" Lord Byron looked into the room and then entered when he saw her beckon. "How may I be of assistance?"

"Lord Byron," Cora said. *Never be timid.* She put strength into her voice. "Where are the new recruits going first?"

"Times are desperate. We are sending them straight to the border forts, to the front. They must be trained on the journey and learn in the field from their officers and their fellows."

Keep your capabilities secret from your enemies. "Will our enemies know about the reinforcements?" she asked.

"They may learn."

"Is there anything we can do about it?"

Lord Byron's round face creased as he pondered. "Perhaps they could arrive in the night... and travel in smaller groups." He rubbed his chin. "It would add a small delay..."

"But it could be worth it? We may gain an advantage if our enemies do not know about the extra numbers."

"It would be worth it, yes." He nodded. "Yes," he repeated. "I think it is the right thing to do. I will see to it right away."

"Thank you, Lord Byron. Well done."

Cora found herself becoming more confident. The feelings of frustration were melting away.

Another idea occurred to her.

"Lord Byron." She stopped him on his way to leaving. "One more thing. What is the speech for tomorrow?"

He frowned. "Well, the same as today."

"Who wrote it?"

"I believe it was Lady Trent."

Become a thief. Learn others' skills and make them your own. "Please send her to me. I want to find out how she crafts her words, and perhaps we can create something together."

Lord Byron opened his mouth. She knew what he was going to say: something about getting her rest or allowing those in her service to share her burdens.

But as he lingered, Cora smiled. “I will be waiting, Lord Byron.”

His mouth snapped shut. He bowed. “Of course, My Queen.”

When Lord Byron was gone, Silvia came to the doorway. She didn’t say anything, but simply looked at Cora’s face.

“What?” Cora asked, as Silvia continued to watch her.

“Nothing, Your Majesty,” Silvia said. “Nothing at all.”

Chapter 25

THREE GREAT FORTRESSES guarded Aranor's northern border.

Martenhal, Balgaven, and Claregantry, known as the border forts, defended a region between the Aran Mountains in the west and the Stony Mountains in the east, where the low ground between mountain ranges would usually grant an army easy access. The border forts barred access to the town of Helmsford, the King's Road, and the direct route to the capital, Adin.

Aranor's key defenses were well-located. The border forts took advantage of a natural break in the terrain, where the Hills of Harr sheared off in a long cliff that towered over the flat plain. Each fortress sat within eyesight of the other but in the center of its own half circle, like three people standing side by side with their arms wide apart. Rocky paths and trails connected the high ground with the plain, as well as a wide curling road, allowing the flow of people and trade in and out of Aranor.

Any large enemy force traveling into Aranor had to deal with the border forts first.

Malgannis and Erik led their five hundred soldiers along the high road toward the border forts. A forbidding landscape surrounded them, with forests above and stretches of barren rock below. As Malgannis rode on horseback with Erik beside him, he turned to look at the column of soldiers behind him. Not recruits anymore; he made sure they knew that he no longer called them that. He had now led them on three raids, two at dawn and one at night. They had been tested, and now they were soldiers. Fresh soldiers, with much still to learn, but soldiers all the same.

Malgannis faced forward once again and fixed his eyes on the largest of the fortresses and the first in the line of three. Martenhal loomed ahead, gray and hulking, made of dark stone hewn from the nearby mountains. Even the slanted afternoon light couldn't make the stronghold glow, and in the distance, Balgaven and Claregantry were also silhouetted. Malgannis had thought of the strongholds as old even in his time. Together, they were among the most massive structures he had seen.

Memories flooded back as Martenhal grew larger in his vision, until it dominated the sky, and he was only seeing the top section, with more stretching down to the plain. He remembered cold corridors and hearths that did nothing to warm the surrounding stone. Tense conversations had filled the place as officers discussed the advance of Baelock Fain and his army of Vailanders.

And yet Malgannis had never had to defend the border forts, and despite the impression of strength and solidarity, he was worried. Some of the walls and beams had been crumbling even then, more than fifty years ago, and he doubted they had been replaced.

At least he was reassured by the blue and gold flags flying from the towers and battlements. Martenhal was now close enough that the men could travel the rest of the way on their own. Malgannis nodded at Erik. "Let's ride ahead. Have the officers take them in."

Erik passed the instruction down, and then followed Malgannis as he spurred his horse onward, to approach Martenhal's tall gates.

✦

Martenhal's interior was glum and brooding, just like the man who had been tasked with its defense. Lord Barrington, Warden of Martenhal, had a lanky frame, sad eyes, and a downturned mouth that rarely smiled.

Malgannis and Erik were alone with Barrington in the workroom where he clearly spent most of his time. A few items decorated the sparsely furnished space: a sturdy desk with a high-backed wooden chair, an ancient table, a handful of other chairs. Maps lay spread out on the table. There was no hearth, and all three men wore thick clothing. A patterned rug was the only item of color.

No one was seated. Malgannis watched as Lord Barrington walked toward the window – little more than a square hole in the stone – and stopped to gaze out, his arms behind his back. He looked at the view for a moment before dragging himself away.

Malgannis knew what kept drawing Barrington's attention. The enemy camp dominated the back of the plain until it disappeared behind the hills. The number of tents was frightening.

"You made an impression before you arrived, General," Barrington said. "We were exhausted. Barely holding on." His drooping eyes developed a far away stare. "Ever since the defeat at the ruins of Leventhal it is as if some doom has clouded our struggle. There was some respite as the enemy captured Ballina, but it wasn't long enough." He stared up at the ceiling and scanned the stone. "We had barely begun to patch these fortresses up before the attacks began." He returned his attention to Malgannis. "Your raids have given us some much needed time. There hasn't been an assault in six days. Now, we can make plans to fight back."

"I'm afraid it won't last," Malgannis said. "They have numbers."

"The new recruits—"

"Require training," Malgannis interjected. "We need to think outside of what we have here at the border." He nodded toward Erik. "The captain here has given me an idea, but I first want to make sure we haven't missed anything." He headed toward one of the maps on the table and Barrington and Erik joined him. Soon they were all leaning over the map as Malgannis prodded a particular place with his finger. "Tell me about Rumandy."

"The enemy holds the Gray Marshes. Rumandy is cut off and the Moranians hold Harven. You will have heard about what happened at Inadris."

Malgannis followed the map to places farther still. "How reliably does Nara follow Morania?"

"If there was any hesitation at the beginning, it is now gone. Graven Callow is winning this war. Already the leaders of the other nations are wondering about the new order he will establish, and maneuver themselves for optimal position."

"It's the same in Kor," Erik said.

"Indeed," Barrington said. "And Vestria has fallen, the Red King now a prisoner."

Malgannis continued to scan the map, looking closer to Aranor's border. His attention moved to the broad swath of peaks that made up the Stony Mountains. The region containing the three fortresses had an interesting name: the Hills of Harr. Once, a people had lived in these lowlands, until, long before Malgannis's time, King Dargan of Aranor drove them away to find new homes deeper in the mountains. Seeing the strategic value in the location, Dargan then tore down their cities and used the stone to build Martenhal, Balgaven, and Claregantry.

"What of the Harrmen?" Malgannis asked.

Barrington was puzzled. "The mountain men? The Harrmen are not friends of Aranor. When we hear of them, it is only when they have robbed our traders and raided our villages."

"I hear they are tough fighters," Erik said. He didn't continue, allowing Malgannis to lead the conversation.

"Tough fighters who don't like outsiders," Barrington said. "I'm sure they are just as eager to see our end as our present enemy. You wouldn't know, lad, but they consider the ground we're standing on to be their land, not ours."

"Tough doesn't come close," Malgannis said. "But you're right about these hills. The Harrmen have long memories, and they want nothing more than their lands back." He was pensive for a moment, remembering. "They even asked us to abandon these fortresses, and at the time, we agreed."

Barrington frowned. "That was years ago, during the Great War. I am surprised you knew." He harrumphed. "Then it is settled. Enough about the Harrmen."

"Warden, please," Erik said quickly. "Hear us out. Perhaps there's an opportunity here."

"I need not remind you," Malgannis said. "Our situation is desperate." Barrington opened his mouth but then snapped it shut when he remembered: Malgannis outranked him, even in his own fortress. "If I were confident of holding the line here at the border – which I am not – you still do not win a war by digging in. We need strength, which means allies, and there is an entire nation of Harrmen buried away in the mountains."

"But listen to what you are saying," Barrington persisted. "Why would the Harrmen ally themselves with us? You know about the agreement to abandon these fortresses. Therefore you also know—they think we betrayed them."

"Obviously they have good cause to feel wronged, because here we are. However no enemy has reached this region in living memory. The gold mines in the Stony Mountains are legendary. If Graven Callow is allowed past this border, the Harrmen stand to suffer as much as we do." Malgannis thought about the immense difficulty of the task ahead. Yet Cora was depending on him. He had to make a difference. Erik had given him the idea, and updated his knowledge, but he was the one who believed he could make allies of the Harrmen. "We have a narrow window here. The border forts aren't presently under attack. We have taught the men we brought with us to conduct raids, which will keep our enemy worried. The queen has promised me there will be more recruits on their way. We need time to train them. If I can find us some allies, we can think about fighting back."

Barrington shook his head, but he knew he had to relent. "The decision is yours, although I believe it will be a waste of time." His gaze took in both Malgannis and Erik. "I assume you have agreed a next step?"

Malgannis knew that his next words were going to surprise Erik as much as Barrington. "I have a plan, but it is something only I can do. I intend to leave immediately."

Barrington's eyes widened. "Wait just a moment, Lord Morgan," he protested. "You are in command here—"

"I have to agree," Erik said. "I assumed I would be the one—"

"No," Malgannis said, forestalling further debate. "It has to be me. They have to know they are dealing with someone who can make decisions. Someone at the top." He held up his hand. "This is my decision. I can promise you, however, that I'll return as quickly as possible." He waited, but no one challenged him further. "Now.... one more thing. Warden, I will require your signet ring."

Barrington hesitated and then gave a sharp nod. "Fine." He yanked off his signet ring and handed it over. "But you will at least take young Wallace with you."

"I need to go alone."

"Lord Morgan... you cannot go out into the mountains on your own."

"I can take care of myself."

"I must insist."

"No," Malgannis said. He knew that Erik was unaware of his true identity, and it could become a problem for his planned encounter.

"General," Barrington said with a stubborn set to his jaw. "You may have the support of the queen and the council of lords, but you need us border wardens too, and we can be difficult. Erik is known to us. We do not know you. If you are going to take my signet ring into the mountains and deal with the mountain men, he is going."

As Malgannis considered, he saw the resolve in Barrington's face. He also saw Erik looking perplexed. If Erik had to come, he supposed he wouldn't mind the company. He could worry about the rest later. "Fine, then. I agree. While we're gone, train the recruits. Otherwise, don't make major moves." He raised a warning finger. "Most importantly. Our enemy is clever. Don't let your guard down, not for a second."

Chapter 26

GRAVEN CALLOW stood framed by the entrance of one of his largest tents. His narrowed gaze was on the decrepit fortress that was Martenhal and the other two strongholds in the line, all guarding the high ground above the plain. Wind whipped his hair. He was on a hill, with the rest of his immense military camp laid around him.

He considered as he watched the three hulking stone structures. The blue and gold flags flying from the towers and battlements fluttered merrily, mocking him.

Something had changed.

He could sense it. There was new leadership among the Aranese forces. He was being issued with a challenge.

He had thought it too easy before. Rumandy had been swiftly conquered. King Owen was useless, both as a military leader and a warrior on the battlefield. His son Patrick was little better and had easily fallen to his blade. Willem, the Red King of Vestria, was locked in a dungeon. In his dotage, he had wept when he first saw Graven's face.

Now... now he was being tested for the first time. The raids had forced him to look to his sentries and defenses, for nothing affected a soldier's morale like poor sleep with a sword by the pillow. He had thought the encircling mountains were protection enough, and they were, but that was from the enemy he had been fighting before. It took courage to climb over difficult ground in darkness, and to attack a far greater number. The soldiers of Aranor were never bold before.

Someone new was leading them. And in order to answer the challenge, it was time for him to try some new tricks.

He tore his attention from the three border forts and turned toward the tent's wide entrance. As he walked, he passed two armed guards, solid men made of muscle, carefully selected Moranians who had the stomach for the kind of work that went on in this place. "It is time," he instructed. Without a reply, they turned and set off.

Continuing toward the tent's innermost compartment, he glanced at a brazier with a pair of iron tongs resting in the coals. Tools covered a bench: pincers for removing finger and toe nails, cutters for removing appendages, long needles for poking, curved blades for slow disemboweling. A bucket full of clear water sat on a table, beside a wad of perfectly white linen cloths.

He ducked his head to enter the next section, where the candlelight was low and shadows danced. As he approached, his attention went to his prisoner.

The long-haired man lay on his back on a wooden frame. When he saw Graven approaching, his eyes shot wide open with fright. With a typical Aranese nose, he was handsome, perhaps in his early thirties. Trousers covered his lower half, but his muscular torso was bare, as were his feet.

Although the prisoner was tied down and spread-eagled, there wasn't a mark on him. He would have seen the tools, however, when he came in. Often that was enough. As Graven neared, his prisoner's chest rose and fell furiously, as fast as a horse after a long gallop.

Graven came to a halt and stared down at his captive.

"Hello, Darin," he said. "Do you know who I am?"

"I... I think so," the prisoner said in a hoarse voice.

"You would know me as Graven Callow. You have been here for a long time... several hours. Would you like to go home?"

"Y... Yes."

"Of course," Graven said softly. "I understand. This is not a comfortable position to be in. For you to leave, I must ask something of you. Are you ready, Darin? Do you want to know what it is?" He continued without waiting for a reply. "Here is what you are going to do. You are going to return to Martenhal. And at a time of your choosing, when circumstances are most favorable – but no longer than five days hence – you are going to set the fortress on fire."

The Aranese soldier nodded. His eyes were showing their whites. "Yes, My Lord."

"I am not a lord," Graven said. "I have never been a lord, and I am never going to be." He smoothed his expression and smiled. "Now. Your thoughts are written on your face. You think you can tell me what I want to hear and then I will let you go. Once you are back with your comrades, safe at last, the idea of starting a fire that will burn your countrymen alive, and weaken your defenses at the same time, will seem absurd."

Graven leaned down over the wooden frame and the terrified man stared up at him.

"However there is something you do not yet know. You are not the only soldier of Aranor I have spoken with. Before you, I captured several of your fellows. And I asked them a simple question under torture: who, among their number, hails from nearby? This was a simple question. Perhaps even an innocent question. I received an answer."

Graven put his face right in front of his prisoner's.

"I found out that you, Darin, are from the small village of Kinley, not far from the three fortresses I can see outside. I sent some men to sneak past the lines to get your village. They brought back two prisoners. I went to a lot of effort, yes, but, then, taking a fortress is a lot of effort."

Graven called over his shoulder. "Bring me the wife and child."

The two guards appeared a moment later. The woman was bound, gagged, and blindfolded, her head jerking one way and another as she was hauled in. All Graven saw of her features was grubby skin, hair the color of wheat, and the drab clothes of a farmer. The child was a sturdy boy, a lad of twelve or thirteen, also tied and blinded in the same way as his mother.

"Please!" Darin cried.

"Silence," Graven snapped. "You will set fire to the fortress. And I must be impressed. Or in five days, they die." He paused for effect, and drew out his next word. "Horrifically. This war has gone on for long enough. Aranor must fall, and then order can be restored. By doing this, you will be sacrificing the few, but saving the many."

"Please..."

"You will do it."

Darin nodded frantically. "Please, don't hurt them. I will do it. Please."

Graven waited, inspecting the man's face, allowing the moment to linger. He nodded. "Good."

After waving at the guards to leave, taking the woman and boy with them, he gave a final long stare at the man on the wooden frame, reading his face, before nodding once again. Satisfied, he left the darkened room to follow the burly guards out, past the tools and implements, until he was once again in the open air.

"What do we do with them?" one of the guards asked in a low murmur, indicating the woman and child.

"Take them away. Kill them so they can't talk. Then release our prisoner and we will see what happens next."

Graven again watched the three fortresses as the guards departed.

Something had changed. It might even be linked to what had happened at Mount Janus and the Temple of Black Glass. He had never tracked down the two men who had fled across the lake.

There was a new leader out there, he was sure of it. He needed to find out who it was.

✦

Cora stood wrapped in cloth, unable to move, with pins at various locations close to her body.

The dressmaker, a matronly woman who never stopped frowning, pursed her lips. "Don't move," she said. "I will be back in a moment."

Before Cora could protest, the dressmaker vanished, leaving her standing in an awkward position with nothing to hold her attention. She scowled and remembered Malgannis's advice.

They will try to take your freedom, and you will have to fight to keep it.

As she stood in place, unable to move, she wondered whether Malgannis had known how true his words would be.

Cora had returned to Adin and soon it would be time for her wedding. Festive bunting decorated the streets. The palace was the scene of constant activity. Barrels kept arriving. Painters brightened the halls. Poor Hailsham would have been tearing out his hair, if he hadn't already lost it all.

Cora didn't like to think about the expense, despite the fact she had tried to keep the cost as low as possible. She was going to be married, and yet she viewed it all from a distance, her feelings about it dispassionate. What she was doing was important. Her duty was to her people. Aranor had lost one king, and then another, but now, at least if something happened to their queen, someone – Lord Kane – would be ready to take over.

What no one except Cora knew was that her future husband was destined to be king in just four weeks, twenty-eight days. Logan was a clever man with strong allies in the council. She felt he would make a good king.

Despite all the cloth draped over her, Cora shivered. She turned her head to see an open window, with a yellow curtain fluttering in a chill breeze. A shuffling sound from farther back drew her attention. She couldn't see an obvious source. She turned her head even more. Nothing. Then the whisper of footsteps came from the other side. Her head whipped around.

The black priest stood directly in front of her.

Cora managed to resist crying out. As soon as she had recovered, her eyes narrowed. "What do you want?"

"Greetings, My Queen." Lexen Crow had a crooked smile on his face as he gave her a little bow. When he moved, she saw something she hadn't seen before: a tattoo of something on the back of his neck. He moved too swiftly for her to see what it was. "I come to again remind you about what is going to happen..." he trailed off. "In truth, to satisfy my curiosity. Why get married?"

"You're no fool. Why do you think? To strengthen my rule when we need strength more than ever before."

"For the succession?"

"Of course. You of all people should know. I'm not giving up much. A few weeks of my life, yes..."

Lexen raised an eyebrow as he interjected. "But is it so little, when they are the last weeks of your life?"

"All I care about is the survival of my homeland."

Lexen paused, studying her. As he did, she wondered at the feverish cast to his skin; if he was ill, he appeared to have grown worse. Eventually, he nodded to himself. "You are noble, as well as beautiful. It is almost a shame..."

Cora snatched at his words. "A shame?"

"Nothing," he said with a wave of his hand. "What is done is done. A bargain, once made, can never be undone."

"Except by the one who made it," Cora said, remembering what she had learned at Patrick's camp.

He gave her a look that was almost sympathetic. "And that is something I would never do." Hearing a sound, he glanced past Cora's shoulder. "Until we meet again, Coraline Vandryden."

Cora turned to see the dressmaker returning with rolls of shining white satin on her arms.

And the black priest was gone.

Chapter 27

MALGANNIS BLOCKED AND PARRIED, facing a skilled opponent who was both younger and stronger. Meanwhile Erik fought in a frenzy, taking on two swordsmen at a time.

Even as Malgannis gritted his teeth, raising his sword again and again, he worried about Erik. The ferocious struggle was taking place on a steep hillside beside a collection of wooden huts and penned sheep, and a drinking trough was in his way as he tried to circle round and get closer. Erik needed his help.

They had been fools. Malgannis wished he had properly scouted the area.

They had been heading deep into the Stony Mountains, climbing from one valley to the next, with the next section of level ground always higher than before. Malgannis's memories had solidified on the journey. He had a reasonable idea where he was going: to where the tallest mountains looked like jagged teeth gnashing at the sky.

At first, the rugged landscape had been barren, the valleys dry and rocky, with just a few gnarled trees clinging to the upper slopes. Then, as they reached areas touched by snowmelt, isolated homesteads began to appear in the distance. Out here, there was no question: the farms belonged to Harrmen.

It had been Malgannis's idea to approach the homestead that lay directly in their path. They might be able to get some information that would lead them to the heart of the Harr nation. It had also been Malgannis's idea to show themselves from a distance; he didn't want to frighten the farmer and his family away.

He should have been more cautious. The signs were there: recently dug graves, blackened sheep bones tossed in a pile beside the main house. The three deserters – Moranians – had discovered the Harrmen homestead. After killing the family and burying them, they evidently planned to wait out the war. When Malgannis called out, they had come running with swords drawn.

Even as Malgannis fought, he saw Erik dart inside one of his opponent's defenses, opening himself up to attack from behind, but the lad was lucky enough to make his thrust with the briefest moment to spare. Desperate to come to the younger man's aid, Malgannis at last found an opening and cut down the man in front of him.

His attention immediately went to Erik, whose next blow struck home, finishing his nearest enemy. Erik then whirled and blocked a steel blade, crossing his sword in front of his face. Metal scraped against metal. Erik took a step back. Another side step made his opponent turn to face him. Erik launched into another attack, grim-faced as he hacked back and forth, cutting and advancing, until the second opponent fell to his slice across the torso.

The fight was over. After all the fury, comparative quiet ensued.

Malgannis stood panting. Sweat coated his forehead and dripped down his face. He heard the cries of wheeling birds overhead, come to watch from a safe distance. He lowered his weapon and then felt rising anger as he turned to Erik. "What was that about?" he demanded. He held up his sword meaningfully. "I was about to come to your aid."

Erik didn't immediately reply. He blinked, as if confused, and then scowled. "I didn't need your help."

As Malgannis noticed something strange in Erik's face, he shook his head and went over to one of the dead men to crouch and wipe his blade clean. While he did, he thought hard. The look was something he had seen before, after too many battles and sword fights, when friends and companions had fallen around him. Erik gave off the impression of someone who didn't care if he lived or died.

Malgannis had first noticed it in the dawn raid before their arrival at Martenhal. But surrounded by men for them both to lead, Erik hadn't always been close by, and Malgannis hadn't been sure enough to say anything. After one of the night raids, Malgannis had been aware that some of the men were treating Erik with newfound respect. He could certainly fight, they said.

But what Malgannis had just witnessed was something else altogether.

"We should get away from here," he said. "There may be more of them."

"I'm not afraid."

"Then you are a fool," Malgannis growled. "Come on."

Malgannis waited impatiently for Erik, but didn't open a conversation until they had left the homestead far behind. Soon the wooden buildings were a distant cluster at their backs as they climbed up to a gap between the mountains to approach the next valley. A forest of evergreens swallowed them, providing shade from the blazing sun, which shone from the midpoint of the clear blue sky. As they walked on a carpet of pine needles, Malgannis cleared his throat.

"Like to talk about it?" he asked, watching Erik's face.

The younger man stared straight ahead. "What is it you want to know?"

"What was that about?"

"I don't know what you mean."

"Lad, I was watching. You left yourself open. A better swordsman would have killed you. And you're good enough to know that."

"I don't know what you want to hear."

"You're angry."

There was color in Erik's cheeks. "I was fighting an enemy. And you're wondering why I was angry?"

"That's not what I mean and you know it. You've barely been talking since we left Martenhal." Malgannis reflected. "Something happened, just before we left." He continued to think out loud. "We spoke to Norris, gave her some orders. Reviewed the men. Inspected Balgaven and Claregantry. Talked to the engineers. There was that proclamation from the palace..."

He finally realized.

"Cora's marriage. You knew about it when we left Adin. But then that message came. Remind me. When is the wedding?"

"Today," Erik muttered.

Malgannis was silent for a moment. "You love her?"

"I've known her since I was little."

"That's not what I asked."

"She's the queen. I'm a commoner."

"That's not quite true," Malgannis said. "Lord Wallace, I believe I heard them call you. You're not the first man to become a lord rather than be born to it. And you still haven't answered me."

"She shouldn't be marrying him," Erik said. "She doesn't love him."

"Kings and queens often don't get a say in who they marry."

"But she did. She made the choice."

"Aye, she did make the choice," Malgannis said. "Tell me, lad, do you think she found it easy to do or hard?"

Erik didn't reply.

"She made the hard choice," Malgannis said. "And that makes her strong. Perhaps you're upset because you wish she had chosen from love, not duty. Or, perhaps you're lying to yourself, as much as anyone else, and although you tell me you and Cora could never be together, part of you wishes otherwise. She is going to be married. That's hard for you to bear. I understand. You don't have to be happy about it. I was young once, as strange as that may seem."

Erik said nothing. He stared straight ahead. Malgannis wasn't sure what he was thinking, but some of the tension left his face.

Meanwhile, Malgannis left unsaid that Cora's decision was one that wouldn't affect her for long. As he glanced at Erik's face, he felt guilt for the secret he was carrying, along with even more sympathy for the man beside him. Erik thought he had lost Cora forever, now that she would be married to another man. And yet Malgannis knew, although he tried his best not to think about it—in just a few weeks, Erik was going to lose Cora completely.

"Morgan?" Erik asked, after some time had passed. "You know I know barely anything about you." He glanced at Malgannis as they walked. "Do you have a woman?"

"Aye, lad. Not now, but I had one once. A long time ago."

"Who was she? How did you meet?"

"I was a little younger than you. I'd seen her before, once or twice, but she was from the next town along. She was the daughter of a farmer." He smiled. "Well, a farmer with a vineyard, stable yard, and a manor bigger than my father's. We had a few vines of our own, and I pretended to consult her expertise. In truth, I knew little about wine and cared even less. My parents caught wind of my visits and brokered the marriage, but I was the second son, so it wasn't too complicated. She was beautiful. I loved her, and still do."

"What happened?"

"We had children, a boy and a girl. Some twenty years the gods gave us, twenty happy years. We trained horses and looked after the harvest. We raised our children and built upon our home."

"And then?"

"And then, when I was no longer a young man, my son and I were called to war."

Erik frowned, calculating. "What war?"

"A distant war, lad. A faraway war. I worried about my son and if I was doing the right thing, but I also knew I couldn't stop him from taking his place. I thought my wife and daughter were safe back home. Said goodbye with a wave and a kiss. But then raiders came. They..." Malgannis trailed off.

Erik watched Malgannis for a time. "I'm sorry."

“We all need a reason to fight,” Malgannis said. “I won’t lie. That was mine. The gods know I fought for my country. But more than anything else, I fought for revenge. I’m no saint. I know it, better than anyone.”

Malgannis shook himself, banishing old memories, dragging himself back to the present.

He glanced at Erik. “If you want to do something for her, fight for the same thing she’s fighting for. Keep your head. Help your nation. Stay alive.”

Chapter 28

CORA WAS A MARRIED WOMAN.

She had always thought she would feel different, complete in a way she had never been before. As a young girl she had watched weddings from a distance, seeing the smiling bride, happy and resplendent in her beautiful white dress. Cora was a princess: one day that bride would be her, and her own wedding would be ten times as grand.

In adolescence she had become more interested in romantic love, as she watched the young men among the palace guards from her bedroom window, judging them, deciding on favorites, with nothing more than a handsome face to go by. She peeked in at her father's balls in the grand hall, mesmerized by the dances, and the women in whirling dresses and men in elegant costume.

She became keenly aware that the physical games she used to play with Erik – the throwing around and climbing up onto shoulders – were suddenly not appropriate anymore. Her body changed, filling out in new places. And so did Erik's, as he studied at the academy and learned to fight with a sword. When they swam in the river, she wore a special costume, and then they stopped swimming together at all.

As a young woman she began to appreciate the endurance of love. When she saw an old couple strolling along the promenade, she smiled at the way they leaned in to each other and held hands. At the markets, several stalls had husbands and wives working side by side, and there was something sweet in their casual familiarity. Cora's mother had died giving birth to her. Yet every Harper's Day her father had lit a candle in her mother's memory.

Now Cora was married, but in her case, marriage and love weren't related at all. She hadn't met someone who fascinated her, someone she wanted more than anything to be close to. She wasn't even preparing herself to get to know her new husband over many years.

Cora would be Logan's wife for just a few weeks. The ceremony was just that, a rite in the eyes of the gods, and a treaty under law. Love never entered her thoughts at all. What she had done was purely rational. Strategic.

And yet some parts of the ceremony were intimate, behind doors, between two people on their wedding day. This part of a marriage couldn't be denied.

Cora sat on her bedside, and Logan, her new husband was beside her. She wore a special nightdress fashioned specially for this occasion, if that was what it was. The long-sleeved garment was embroidered in some places, frilly in others, and exposed the bare skin of her legs. She had always imagined someone else in front of her now. She found herself thinking about Erik. Would he ever understand?

Logan reached out to touch her knee, his hand traveling upward. He was so focused on her body that he barely paid attention to her face. His breathing was different, labored. He continued the movement until his hand was about to slide under the nightdress. His breath came faster still.

Cora saw the top of his gray head. He had been such a regular fixture at the palace that she remembered when she was a girl and he had seemed like an old man to her, even then. Her father had always been a little angry with the baron of Fastness, who always wanted special rights for his island, and often seemed on the verge of breaking away completely.

When Logan's hand moved under the fabric, Cora couldn't help it.

She flinched.

Immediately she bit her lip. She was the one who had approached him about the marriage. Complex emotions welled up from her body, twisting her stomach: regret, guilt, worry.

Logan became still. Slowly, he straightened, until he was staring into her face. She expected to see anger there, or even worse, shame; evidently the attraction he felt for her wasn't reciprocated. What would she do if he spoke out? He could call the marriage off. In the eyes of the gods, it would be nullified, as if it had never been. He would rightfully seek redress. Her support among the lords would crumble. Aranor would be bickering, at war with itself, as Malgannis was stripped of his rank.

Cora knew her soul was bared. Logan was staring into her eyes. But she didn't see anger or shame. She was relieved to see compassion.

He sighed. "Coraline... I see fear in your eyes," he gave a slight smile, "and more than a little steel. Relax."

Logan leaned in to kiss her, the first private kiss they had shared. Cora was unprepared; her lips were dry. He let his face press against hers for a moment, and then withdrew. Then he reached up to stroke the side of her face.

Cora gathered herself. She forced a smile, hoping it wouldn't appear as a grimace. This time she was the one to bring herself close to Logan, tilting her head and parting her lips, to kiss him on the mouth.

He was initially surprised, but then his arms went around her. His breathing began to sound like panting. They both tumbled over, onto the soft linen of the bed. Soon she was on her back and he was lying over her, the palms of his hands pressed down on either side of her head. He kissed the inside of her neck.

Then he reached down, fumbling to move the nightdress upward.

And for the second time, Cora involuntarily tried to pull away.

Logan stopped what he was doing. He kept his head down and eyes hidden from her, and then he looked up. Shuffling along the bed, he moved until he was lying beside her. He propped his head up on his elbow so that they were facing each other on their sides.

"Coraline, your father and I were not friends, but I respected him. I am not going to force myself upon you. However, you know as well as I do that you need a child. We need a child." He paused to make his meaning clear. "Aranor needs a child."

Cora gave a slight shake of her head. "There is no time for me to bear a child."

"You don't know that."

"It doesn't matter what happens between us," Cora said. "I will fall. And soon, sooner than you might imagine, you will be king."

Logan was clearly perplexed. "Ah, Coraline, I am left wondering what tales your father told of me. I never wanted to be king. In truth, I wanted you. But willingly, not like this."

With a series of shuffles, he took himself off the bed until he stood beside it. Cora sat up, and he reached out to take her hand. When he squeezed it, she squeezed back. She knew he was going to depart.

"Come to me when you are ready," Logan said. His voice was sad. "Until then, I will continue to wear the colors of mourning, for my beloved wife is dead."

✦

Malgannis and Erik huddled close to the ground, hidden by the boulders around them.

"What are they doing?" Erik whispered.

Below them, a wide plateau faced a breathtaking view of the mountains. Chanting drifted up from the area, where at least a hundred mountain men and women worked at some shared activity.

One group assembled logs, each on top of the other, laying them until they worked at a structure the size of a small house. Another group surrounded a round pool with a low wall of stone. The surface of the pool was black as they danced in slow circles around it. One thing common among the Harrmen was that their faces had been powdered with white ash.

"Ancient rites," Malgannis murmured. "Older than the black and white priests and their temples. The Harrmen are an old people. They call themselves the First People." He turned to meet Erik's eyes. "Our ancestors."

Erik's head moved as he noticed something, and Malgannis followed his gaze. Six big Harrmen rounded a corner to come into view. They were big, hairy men with clothing of pelts and furs, and carried a litter on their shoulders. Black circles of soot lined their eyes; their faces were as white as the snow on the tallest peaks.

Malgannis saw a body on the litter: a burly black-haired man with eyes staring sightlessly up at the sky.

The dead man had his hands composed on his chest, seemingly at peace, although the impression was marred by the blood on his limbs and torso. Some of his clothing was torn, but he wore a vest that left his shoulders and arms bare, along with hairy trousers. From his naked wounds, he had died violently.

The litter bearers headed directly toward the pile of logs, which Malgannis realized was a funeral pyre. The chanting from the Harrmen dancing around the black pool grew in volume. The six men settled the litter directly onto of the wooden pile.

A tall, lanky Harrman with wild eyes and white furs draped around his body appeared with a flaming torch in his hand. He lifted his torch high and chanted in a gravelly voice, calling up at the sky. Then he knelt at the pyre and thrust his arm deep underneath the body on the litter. He lit one place, then another, before tossing in the torch. Soon flames were rising ever higher. Some Harrmen stopped to watch, signing a stirring dirge. Their sonorous melody mingled with the chants from the dancers at the pool.

Malgannis gripped Erik's upper arm. "Watch."

Smoke rose from the body. Gray clouds rose up to obscure it completely, and then the flames were so high, fed by the gusts of mountain wind, that Malgannis could almost imagine feeling the heat from his position.

At some unspoken signal, the Harrmen by the pool ceased their circling motion. As one, they stopped to face the water. Their chant fell to silence. The singers by the fire turned away from the flames, also becoming focused on the pool. The scene was suddenly quiet.

The wild-eyed man who had carried the torch approached the circle of water. His expression was concentrated as he leaned over the surface. He slapped his hands together in a loud clap.

Nothing happened.

"What—?" Erik began.

"Watch," Malgannis said sternly

Another clap split the air, echoing from the hills. The wild-eyed man stared down at the black water. He gave a third and final clap.

The pool began to bubble. Malgannis shot a quick glance at Erik, whose eyebrows had shot up. The bubbling became more vigorous. All of the Harrmen arrayed around the pool were tense and expectant.

The water in the pool now boiled like a pot resting on the coals. Yet there was no accompanying steam.

Erik gave a low cry. Something broke the surface. A domed object appeared, black as the surrounding water. The object rose up, and it was connected to something. There was hair clinging to the dome, dripping with water. A man's neck appeared, then the curvature of his back as he straightened. It was as if he had been crouched under the water, and was slowly, gradually, returning to his feet.

He wore dark clothing: hairy trousers and a vest that left his arms and shoulders bare. His hair was black and long, and as wet as his costume. He stretched, raising his arms over his head, and his eyes were wide and triumphant as he gave a mighty roar.

The onlookers bellowed back, just as loudly.

Malgannis shot another look at Erik. Even Malgannis was shaken, and he had been expecting it. The man in the pool was the exact same man as the person whose body was even now enveloped in smoke and flame.

"How is that possible?" Erik asked in awe.

"You think I know?"

"Wait." Erik tilted his head, puzzled. "What's happening now?"

The wild-eyed man disappeared from view, and when he reappeared he had a bundle in his arms. At first, it was unclear what the contents of the bundle were. Then the high-pitched sound of a bawling babe came gusting up to Malgannis and Erik's hiding place.

Malgannis swallowed. He had forgotten this part.

Erik knew instinctively what was about to happen. "No." Forgetting about his concealment, he made to stand. "They can't—"

Malgannis grabbed Erik's arm to yank him back down. "Don't you move."

The wild-eyed man held the bundle high and carried it to the edge of the plateau, where the cliff sheared and dropped away. He gathered himself, and threw.

Erik's face was gray. Malgannis knew he must appear much the same. He tried to speak but his mouth was dry. He had to swallow again.

"We just saw a man come back to life," Malgannis said. "You know what they say. There is always a price."

Erik shook his head. "I cannot ally myself with these people."

"You can."

Erik tried to stand again, shaking Malgannis away. Malgannis lunged to stop his companion, although he wasn't sure where the lad was going.

Then he heard a challenging voice. He turned. Erik spun around at the same time.

Four Harrmen stood facing them with spears leveled, ready to thrust and kill.

Chapter 29

THE GROUP OF HARRMEN marched through the mountain pass, which became a tunnel as the walls of rock closed in overhead. They herded along Malgannis and Erik, forcing them to march with them, guarding them at all times.

The Harrmen had cleaned the white ash from their faces and the black from around their eyes, but with their furs and beards and gruff tones the change didn't make them appear any friendlier. Malgannis often noticed Erik's eyes drifting to the front of the column, where the dead man who had come back to life was one of the leaders. The man ate and slept; he laughed and joked with his companions. If he was bothered by the fact that he had recently been dead, he didn't show it.

The pass opened up onto a broad valley, an immense lowland nestled within a framing ring of sharp mountains. Along the valley's wall, Malgannis saw tall, arched openings: entrances into the city that was carved into the rock. He and Erik were taken along a path toward the largest of the openings, where columns supported the ceiling and torches lit the interior. As they neared the grand tunnel, Malgannis glanced at Erik to see the younger man scanning the landscape.

"So many," Erik murmured.

Malgannis knew that to count the openings would be a waste of time; each entrance would lead somewhere different. The city of the Harrmen wasn't dug deep into the mountainside, but what it lacked for in depth, it more than made up for in its sheer sprawl.

Down below, green grass carpeted the lower slopes. Multiple thin rivers looked like veins criss-crossing the valley floor. Crops in neat rectangles were divided with paths between them, where distant Harrmen looked tiny as they worked at the land.

"Now you know why we're here."

"Silence!" One of the Harrmen, a warrior with an axe at his belt and a beard like a bird's nest, glanced over his shoulder. A moment later, Malgannis heard someone up front. The warrior scowled at them again and held up a hand. "Wait."

"Where are you taking us?" Malgannis asked.

"To the mountain king."

Some of the group departed, leaving Malgannis and Erik with an escort of a dozen burly warriors, all armed with hammers, axes, and two-handed swords. Malgannis wasn't sure why they were waiting, but then the warrior who had called back gave a nod and began to walk, and he felt himself prodded from behind.

As they were about to enter through the columned opening in the mountain, the bearded warrior turned again to glare directly at Malgannis. "From this point, only speak when you are spoken to, outlander."

Malgannis kept his mouth shut and nodded.

Comparative darkness soon swallowed them. Some light from the outside crept in, but it was the glow of firelight and torchlight that enabled Malgannis to see. He guessed that someone had gone ahead to alert the king to their arrival, for they were marched directly to a high-ceilinged hall.

Three hearths lined one stone wall, with a matching trio on the other. The fires within them burned brightly. At the very end of the hall, an imposing throne had been carved from the surrounding rock.

Malgannis was curious as he and Erik approached, still surrounded by their escort. The throne's occupant became clearer. The mountain king wasn't a tall man, in fact, he was short enough to need the height given to him by his throne. But what he lacked for in stature, he made for in breadth, for he was thick and stocky, with a neck like a bull. His face was round, and his beard was in multiple braids, each decorated with golden rings. He wore the pelt of a mountain cat on his shoulders and a leather jerkin. A matching leather skirt covered his legs, while his calves were bare and hairy.

The escort stopped moving. Someone called out.

"Bow before Cedric Nine Lives!"

Malgannis and Erik were both shoved until they fell onto their hands and knees. Malgannis bowed his head, staring at the ground, before climbing back his feet.

The warrior with the bird's nest beard stepped forward to approach the king. "They say they come from the border forts of Aranor." He passed the king the signet ring that Malgannis had procured from Barrington and then withdrew.

Cedric Nine Lives turned the ring in his fingers, and then leaned forward. He first inspected Malgannis, looking him up and down, and then gave Erik an appraisal. When he returned his attention to Malgannis, he cocked his head, puzzled.

"You came here with a purpose. What do you want?"

Malgannis stood with legs apart. "I bring an alliance..."

Cedric snorted. "With Aranor?" The Harrmen in the hall chuckled. The mountain king's stare was cold. "You have lost your war. You have nothing to offer."

Malgannis spoke loudly, "We have not lost. We share the same enemies, and they are in your lands. We came across deserters living in one of your homesteads. They slaughtered the family and made the house their own. No doubt they are not the only trespassers you have encountered." He paused to let his words sink in. "Rumandy is occupied. Vestria has fallen. Morania wishes to control the entire world. The only nation who still fights – your neighbor, and your only potential ally – is Aranor. We are strong, but we need help. If Aranor falls, it is only a matter of time before these lands are conquered too. Your gold mines are well known." He clearly enunciated each of his next words. "Our mutual enemy, Graven Callow, will come here."

Cedric's tone became scathing. His lip curled. "Leave, fool, or I will cast you down the mountain."

Malgannis tried to keep a scowl from his face, and the moments passed as he considered his options. There was only one thing he could do. He had thought it might come to this, but he had hoped otherwise.

When he turned, it was to focus on Erik. There was a reason he hadn't wanted Erik to come on the journey.

"Take him away," he said, indicating his companion.

"Why?" Cedric Nine Lives demanded.

Erik was obviously confused.

"I have words to say without him present."

Cedric tugged on his braided beard. He considered for a time and then made his judgment. "I give the orders here. He stays."

Malgannis tried again. "It is best if he—"

"I have made my judgement," Cedric said. "Now, say what you have to say and then go, before I change my mind and have you killed after all."

"I need him gone—"

Cedric called to his warriors, who stood on either side of the hall and watched the proceedings. "Throw them off the mountain."

The warriors came forward.

"Wait!" Malgannis bellowed, causing everyone present to freeze.

Malgannis squared his shoulders and stared directly into the mountain king's eyes. As he spoke, he tried not to think about Erik standing beside him. "This is not our first encounter, Cedric," he smiled darkly, "although when we last met you were Five Lives... It must be risky, being king of the Harrmen." His smile fell. "I am without my black gloves, and I am older than when we last saw each other, many years ago. But you know me."

Cedric combed his fingers through the braids of his beard and then beckoned. "Come closer." When Malgannis approached the throne until he was just a short distance away, Cedric screwed up his face. "You look familiar." He cocked his head and then his eyes widened. "Ironclaw?"

Malgannis couldn't think about Erik now. "Many years have passed and yet here we stand, old allies, reunited when again the world is faced with peril. We faced the Vailanders on the battlefield. We fought together and won. I ask that you fight with us once more."

Cedric's obvious shock shifted to a glare. "If it is truly you, Ironclaw—"

"It is," Malgannis said.

Cedric raised his voice. "If it is you, your son did not honor the bargain we made. Four hundred and twelve years ago, you drove us off our lands. And then, when we fought with you against the Vailanders, you said that when the fighting was done you would return us the hills we once called home. Instead, you betrayed us. The Hills of Hair were never relinquished. Your fortresses are filled with your soldiers."

"My son was worried about Morania's growing strength. It appears he was right to worry."

"The facts remain. We had a deal. Why would I trust anything from you?"

"You had a deal with me, which my son did not honor. He is now gone from this world, as is his son, and his son's son, fallen in battle at our enemy's blade. Once again, you are dealing with me." Malgannis lifted his chin. "I am returned. My name is Malgannis Vandryden and my word is iron. This is my second life. Fight with me, and when victory is ours, I will see to it that your lands are returned and the border forts are reduced to rubble."

In his peripheral vision, Malgannis was keenly aware of Erik staring at him open-mouthed.

✦

Malgannis and Erik sat across from each other with a flickering fire between them. As Erik pondered, staring right at him, Malgannis lifted the flask in his hand to take another sip of the fiery Harrman liquor Cedric had given him, feeling the liquid burn the back of his throat and slide down his chest.

"They say that only the cursed can come back to life," Erik said, watching Malgannis through the flames.

Malgannis remained silent, other than to lift the flask again.

"What is the afterlife like?" Erik asked.

Malgannis swallowed and stifled a grimace. "I don't know. You would have to ask Cora's father and brother."

"How could you not know?"

"I never made it that far." Malgannis was irritated at Erik's puzzlement. "It is a long story, lad."

"King Owen was your grandson. Which means Patrick was your..." Erik's voice was incredulous, "your great-grandson?"

Malgannis nodded.

"And Cora is your great-granddaughter."

Malgannis nodded again. "Aye, lad. That she is."

"She knew you were coming back," Erik said slowly. "She sent me to get you." His eyes widened as he came to a conclusion. "By all the gods... don't tell me she—"

"She knew," Malgannis interrupted, but he didn't say any more.

Erik waited, clearly expecting Malgannis to continue, but when he didn't, color came to Erik's cheeks. "I deserve to know."

"She is her own person. As am I. Her secrets are hers to share."

After some more time passed, Erik gazed in awe across the fire. "You really are him?"

Malgannis took another swig from the flask. "Aye, lad," he said. "I am."

Erik stared at the ground, thinking the implications through. "If they knew... the men... the people..." He shook his head. "But we can't tell them."

"No, we can't."

Erik looked up. "You won the war against Vailand."

"I did."

"What do you think our chances are?"

"All I'll say is that our position is worse now than it was then."

"Oh," Erik said.

Malgannis was eager to change the subject. He turned his head to look down the long rocky slope. A multitude of campfires twinkled back at him. After a long conversation with Cedric Nine Lives, he and Erik would be returning to the border with allies.

"Do you think they'll make a difference?" Malgannis asked.

"They're tough," Erik said. "Of course they will."

Now Malgannis spoke for himself alone. "But will it be enough?"

Chapter 30

MALGANNIS REACHED THE TOP of the crest and stopped in his tracks.

He found himself staring at Martenhal. But in his vision it was no longer a fortress. Instead he was looking at a charred ruin, too big and forbidding to be a house and too ugly to be a manor. The convent had four towers, but one was burned nearly to the ground. The gate was at an angle, half fallen away.

Fire. Licking up the walls. Blackening the wood. Burning the people inside. Smoke pouring through the corridors. Fire, scorching flesh, turning it to ash, until nothing remained but bones.

A hand took Malgannis by the arm. Someone was shaking him.

"Malgannis? Malgannis!"

Malgannis shook himself. The past was gone; he brought himself back to the present. The imagined facade melted away, until he knew that what he was seeing was truly in front of him.

Fire had scorched half of Martenhal.

"Come on," Erik cried.

Malgannis and Erik burst into a run, racing toward the stronghold. Following the road that led directly to the gates, Malgannis scanned the fortress, trying to understand what had happened. He saw arrows sticking out from the wooden beams at the roofs and in the seams between the stones. The shafts pointed out toward the plain below the fortress. Much of the gray stone was black and even the tall wooden gates had been scorched at the bottom. Blue and gold flags still fluttered from a couple of the towers. More pennants flew proudly from the poles on the battlements. But the fortress had been sorely wounded.

Malgannis smelled the sour tang of burned wood and the moldy scent of the water used to douse the flames. The fire had happened in the past, at least a few days ago, for there was no longer any smoke. He slowed and then stopped altogether, realizing there was no longer a need to run. Without a word between them, he and Erik approached the gates at a slower pace, while he continued to learn what he could.

There were places where the flames couldn't have leapt to travel from one area to another; someone inside Martenhal had started the fire in multiple locations. Flames had crept up from the bottom of the gates until the defenders put them out. And while the fire raged, the enemy had attacked.

Graven Callow's forces had advanced toward the fortress while Martenhal's defenders were too busy with the fire to rain arrows down on their number. Once in position, enemy archers had launched volley after volley at the soldiers manning the walls above. Scaling ladders had slammed against the battlements. The assault had eventually been repelled, and the fire had been extinguished, but only after heavy losses. Malgannis could see them now: rows of fresh graves, located near the trees half a mile from the fortress.

"Ironclaw." Malgannis heard a gruff call from behind him.

Turning, Malgannis realized that he had almost forgotten about Cedric Nine Lines and his long column of Harrmen.

"We will remain on the high ground," Cedric said.

Malgannis frowned. "I need you on the walls. We have an agreement."

"Listen to my words," Cedric said. "We will remain on the high ground," he repeated. He nodded toward the hills, a short distance from the road that led to Helmsford. "Up there." He waved at his men. "Come on." As he led his warriors away, he called back. "We will speak on this."

Worried about his new allies, Malgannis watched the Harrmen go, and then resumed his approach to the gates. He heard a shout and the gates began to open.

Two figures exited, both in the uniforms of officers. Malgannis recognized Norris, the blonde lieutenant with the square jaw and her hair in a pony tail. The other soldier was younger, almost a boy, with sandy hair, a wispy beard, and freckles on either side of his nose. Their eyes were shadowed; they both looked tired.

"General, Captain," Norris said. "Thank the gods you're back."

"Where's Barrington?" Erik asked.

"Killed in the attack," Norris said. "A Vailander fights with them, a huge man with an iron mace. Smashed the warden's head in." She nodded at the young officer. "This is Finlay. He's one of the reasons we still hold Martenhal."

"The lower gates?"

Finlay nervously cleared his throat. "Strong as ever, General. They went straight for the battlements."

Malgannis glanced inside the open gates to see a set of burned stairs, a collapsed roof, and more bodies covered in white linen. "What happened?"

"One of our men," Norris answered. "Finlay? You can tell it best."

Finlay scratched at his thin beard. "We thought he'd been captured. Went out on patrol and none of them came back. But then he appeared a week later. I asked, but he said he knew nothing about what happened to the patrol—he snuck off to head home. Wife and child in a nearby village. Not the first time he's done it. Usually his friends would cover for him, but not this time... he seemed genuinely shocked when I told him they'd all disappeared."

"Go on," Erik said.

"Whatever happened, he was hiding it well," Finlay said. "He's been with us for years. I knew him pretty well." He wiped a hand over his freckled face. "He set fire to the cellars, the kitchens, the stables, and finally the gates. We had to fill him full of arrows."

"And that's when they attacked," Malgannis finished.

Both Norris and Finlay nodded.

"We have to be one step ahead of them." Malgannis couldn't hide his frustration. "I told you to watch out for tricks."

"General," Erik said quietly. "You told Barrington, and he's no longer with us. Don't get angry. They held."

Malgannis knew that Erik was right. He was more frustrated with himself than anyone else. There was no one else who could have made his bargain with Cedric Nine Lives. Yet he was needed here. If Martenhal had fallen, Balgaven and Claregantry wouldn't have been able to stand, not with the enemy having a foothold on the higher ground.

Remembering his last exchange with the mountain king, Malgannis glanced at Erik. "Go and ask Nine Lines to join us." As Erik headed off, Malgannis frowned at Norris, whose mouth was working soundlessly. "What is it?"

"Who is to become warden of Martenhal, General?"

"You want the position?"

"By all the gods, no."

“Then you might be suitable,” Malgannis said with a humorless smile. “I’ll let you know by the end of the day.”

“We have more recruits, sir,” Finlay said. “I was just settling them in.”

“How many?”

“Six hundred. Mostly from Penstone. They arrived in the night. There’s a good chance the enemy doesn’t know about them.”

“Thank the gods. At least there’s some better news.” Watching the battlements, Malgannis muttered, “If we keep fighting to hold these fortresses they will fall. We have to counter.”

“Is that possible?” Norris asked seriously.

“It has to be.”

Malgannis continued to scan the old fortress when he heard a voice calling.

“General!”

Malgannis turned and saw Erik hurrying toward him. He scowled when he saw that Erik was alone. “Where’s Nine Lives?”

Erik didn’t look pleased. “He wants to speak with you.”

✦

The Harrmen were already making camp and settling in. Tents crackled and snapped as they went up and fabric was drawn tight by the supporting poles. Pots rested beside fires. Several bowmen settled quivers of arrows on their shoulders as they prepared to go hunting. Harrmen warriors tested their skills on one another, lunging and slashing with wooden practice swords.

Malgannis found Cedric seated on a log by a fire. The mountain king was gnawing on the bones of some bird, tossing each to the side once he had stripped the meat with his teeth. As short and stocky as he was, with his hair and round face, he looked like anything but a king.

“Nine Lives, what is it?” Malgannis called as he approached. He came to a halt and hooked his thumbs in his belt, staring down.

Cedric sucked a bone clean, threw it onto the ground, and then glanced up. “We passed a village on the way here, you will remember. I had my men ask some questions, and I have learned some things, Ironclaw. The situation is not like it was when Aranor’s king was dead and you were all that was left. Aranor has a queen. A woman named Coraline. Some relation of yours, I expect, for she has your last name.”

“Yes, we have a queen. What of it?”

“I’ve learned my lesson. You could fall in battle, and this queen could deny any knowledge of a pact between us. I want to meet her.”

"The queen is in Adin."

Cedric shrugged. Finishing his bird, he wiped his hands on his trousers. "Then take me to Adin."

Malgannis's nostrils flared, but Cedric was unperturbed. "We need your men here."

"No one is going to fight for you, General, or whatever your title is. Not unless I give the order, and that is something I will not currently do. That fortress over there," Cedric nodded toward Martenhal, "is on our lands. Queen Coraline must acknowledge our pact."

Malgannis saw the stubborn line in Cedric's jaw. "The queen will honor our bargain. Let me send a message, and she will give a clear reply. In the meantime, I need your men to fight with us."

Cedric pondered. "No. We remain where we are until I have the queen's agreement in writing."

Chapter 31

CORA WAS IN HER QUARTERS in Adin Palace, where she was thought to be preparing herself for dinner. She was ready, and knew that her new husband was on the terrace with Lord Byron and Lady Pike, but rather than join them, a quill was in her hands as she made swift marks on the paper spread out on the desk in front of her.

She wore a yellow dress, cut square at the neck, with long sleeves to her wrists. She always wore long sleeves. Even as the middle of spring approached, and the days grew warmer, she never exposed the skin of her arms.

That mark will spread to cover your entire body.

She surreptitiously rubbed at her forearm and then stopped as soon as she realized what she was doing. A soft tread and the sound of opening and closing chests reminded her that she wasn't alone. Silvia had just placed hot tea on the desk, and was now bustling about, tutting as she corrected the work of the maids. The older woman rarely stopped moving. Even when she was seated her hands were busy, sewing, knitting, and embroidering.

Cora still hadn't acted on Malgannis's advice to tell Silvia the whole truth about what she had done. She knew that Silvia loved her, but at the moment she could pretend that things were a little like they were before—before she became queen, and before she ever met the black priest. Clearing her throat, she checked that her sleeve was in place, and gave a few tugs on the folds of dress. When she turned, her expression was composed.

"Silva... what do you think about this?" Cora read aloud from the paper in front of her. "'If we do not stand together, our children will never know hope.'"

Silvia glanced up from her kneeling position in front of an open chest. "You know this is not my area, dear."

"Is it too dark?"

"I suppose it might be. People also need the promise of something better."

Cora wrote some fresh words and then considered. "How about this?" She paused as she spoke to give effect to each phrase. "'One bright day... we will all say to our children... that when it was required... and hope was all we had... the people of Aranor stood together.'"

"That's better." Silvia's expression changed and her eyes shifted as she noticed something. "Hold on. Someone's here."

Silvia pushed herself to her feet and left the room, and then Cora heard a youthful male voice. "A message for Her Majesty. Marked urgent."

"Thank you," Silvia said.

Silvia returned, holding a rolled up piece of paper, and Cora immediately looked at the seal.

At first, she didn't understand the meaning behind the menacing eagle's talon, but then it became clear. The eagle: one of the symbols of Aranor, appearing on everything from coins to jewelry. A claw. Ironclaw. Cora knew what was meant, but no one else would think anything of it.

"It's from... him," Silvia said, hesitant to say Malgannis's real name aloud as she passed Cora the message.

As Cora broke the seal, she glanced up. "Are you going to stand there and watch me?"

"Yes," Silvia said. "I am."

Cora began to read. Characteristically, Malgannis didn't ask how she was or wish her good health, or even offer his congratulations on her marriage.

My Queen,

I have important news. I have a potential ally with me here at the border. He is the king of a nation with reason to hate our enemy as much as we do.

A king? Cora couldn't make sense of it. All of the world's nations had fallen. But then as she continued, her eyes widened. Malgannis was talking about the Harrmen, the mountain men.

I have been to their city. They are a strong, hardy people, and are the allies we need. Without them, the enemy will grind us down here at the border until these fortresses fall. Graven Callow can afford mistakes, but we cannot. We must change the direction of this war. To do so, we need power. We need allies.

I need you to draw up a treaty, between you as Queen of Aranor and King Cedric of the Harrmen. Once, centuries ago, the Harrmen lived in the Hills of Harr, which still bear their name today. Aranor drove them off their lands, and built the border forts, using the stone of their towns and cities. The Harrmen want their lands back, and I have promised to return them. In exchange, they will fight with us. Without them, we cannot win this war. With them, as soon as the war is over, we must tear down our strongest defenses, for that is the deal I have made.

Cora's mouth opened in horror.

"He has asked you to do something, hasn't he?" Silvia asked.

Cora stared at the paper for a long time. "He has no idea what he is asking."

"Coraline... He is your father's grandfather. You have given him the task of winning this war. He probably does know what he is asking."

"He wants me to promise to give up part of the kingdom. Perhaps the most important part."

"And in return?"

"He says he has potential allies." Cora looked at Silvia. "What do I do?"

"You do what he says," Silvia said simply.

"But how?" Cora asked. "Erik isn't here. He's smart. He knows the nobles. He—"

Silvia interrupted her. "Do you know who else is smart? And who also knows the nobles? Your new husband. The man you married to strengthen your rule. This is why you did it, Coraline. Get him to prove his worth."

Cora knew that Logan was still wearing the colors of mourning. He was giving her time. They were supposedly married, but had never completed their union. Logan wanted her to come to him.

Her new husband was hoping she would approach him in his bedchamber, not with a problem even he would struggle to solve.

✦

Night fell on the city of Adin, and the palace that was the city's most prominent feature. Cora paced back and forth on one of the palace's highest balconies. She gazed out at the city lights and occasionally stared up at the stars. She had to do something to relieve her tension.

She turned as approaching boot heels made clapping sounds on the balcony. She saw Logan's tall frame as he joined her at the rail and faced her in the darkness.

"It is done," he said without preamble. "It was difficult, but the treaty you ask for will be drawn up and ready to send by tomorrow."

"Thank you," Cora said sincerely.

"However I will not be signing it, and neither will any other member of the council."

Cora turned to face her husband directly. Initially shocked, she now spoke coldly. "I do not understand, husband."

"I will not be signing until I receive an explanation, one that I find satisfying."

"For what?"

Cora wondered if he was talking about their marriage, but it made no sense. She tried to read Logan's expression, but it was difficult without much light. All she could really see was his tall silhouette, now made intimidating by his tone.

"I have something to discuss... something I am bringing to you in the first instance, in order to give you a chance to explain. Today has been a long day, with much argument between the members of your council. I found myself thinking, and before delivering the news about the treaty I decided to do some reading."

"And?" Cora asked warily.

"I have just now been reading about the king of Tor Gaeron's war against the Ravagers. I know the truth, Coraline. Our general, Morgan, is not who he says he is." He watched her face. She didn't speak. "At no point is a Stone General mentioned in the written accounts. I have read about victories and defeats. I discovered two completely different treatises on the strategy and tactics that won the war for the king. He would have been discussed. At the very least there would be a note about him. No man from Aranor led Tor Gaeron soldiers into battle. He is not the Stone General. In fact, there is no Stone General. I have no doubt in my mind."

Behind Cora's back, she pressed her fingertips into her palms. Meanwhile, Logan stared at her, waiting for her response.

It was some time before she replied. "You are correct," she finally said. "He is a great general, but the wars he fought in are nothing you would have heard of. I couldn't tell you the truth before. I didn't know you. I didn't know if I could trust you."

"Go on," Logan said.

"The fact is, he has a secret, and it is a secret that I share too. I will confide in you, but please, it must stay between us." Cora hesitated, drawing the moment out. "Lord Morgan is my uncle."

Logan tilted his head, surprised.

“He is my father’s older brother... well, half-brother. Grandfather met a woman before he married. Lord Morgan is the result. He doesn’t want anyone to know, and I’m sure you can understand why. I am a new queen—young, and a woman. There might be those who prefer an older set of hands, a male set of hands, to be in charge of the realm. Lord Morgan wants to protect me from all of that. Believe me, he will give everything he can to see that we survive this war. I trust him completely.”

Logan’s eyebrows went up as her words sank in. “By all the gods,” he said incredulously. “He is almost a king himself.” He put a hand to his mouth. “I always thought something wasn’t quite right.” He looked away. “I must apologize, Coraline.”

“That isn’t necessary,” Cora said. She reached out and took her husband’s hands. “Please, Logan. This must stay between us.”

As he gazed out at the stars, his face filled with astonishment, Cora wondered how long he would be able to keep the secret. The nobles loved their gossip. Word would spread, although no one could ever say anything out loud.

“It is late. I must bid you goodnight,” Logan said. Still holding her hands, he titled his head, inquiring.

Cora raised his fingers to her cheek. “Good night, husband. I will see you in the morning.”

Chapter 32

FLOWERS COVERED THE HILLSIDES. Birds sang from the treetops. Days became longer.

Hope was in the air.

Malgannis walked the battlements of Martenhal. The smell of new mortar was everywhere; even now he found himself passing two laborers working with bucket and trowel. He took long determined strides. A message had come from Cora, and after reading it, he found himself more committed than ever, more impassioned. A treaty had been concluded. Cedric was now a firm ally. Malgannis was going to lead Aranor to victory.

Malgannis's high position meant he had a sweeping view of the plain. As he walked, he gazed out at the enemy camp and considered his options. He was making final preparations. Soon he would no longer be forced to defend. He would be ready to fight back.

Someone – perhaps Lord Byron – had directed the new recruits to arrive secretly, in the night. Malgannis wished he had remembered to ask who it was; he wanted to thank them—the quiet addition to his numbers meant he had greater options to surprise his enemy.

He now had three main groups at his disposal.

There were the soldiers – mainly from Aranor, but also men of Vestria and Rumandy – veterans like Erik and those under his command. At the ruins of Leventhal they had suffered a terrible defeat, but time had passed and events had moved on. The raids had taught them a new way of fighting. They had a new general, the mysterious Lord Morgan, who was rumored to have developed his skills fighting wars for distant kings. They had a new queen, the beautiful Coraline Vandryden, who was eager for them to avenge the deaths of her father and brother.

A second group was made up of the recruits, youths from the regions of Aranor, some with hunting skills but others who had never held a sword. They were strong and well-fed. They were also inexperienced.

Finally there was the Harrmen, tough warriors, able to navigate difficult terrain and fight well no matter where they found themselves. They had gone to war to drive away a conquering enemy, for the alternative was for Aranor to fall and their mountain kingdom to be next in line for conquest. They fought because if they were victorious against Morania, Aranor would return the borderlands that had once been theirs.

Malgannis stopped to stand at the edge of the battlements and stare at the enemy camp. The grassy plain stretched on and on below him, flanked by tall cliffs. The camp was huge. The distant tents blurred together; the black and crimson flags were tiny dots.

He then looked in the other direction, scanning the fortress. He would keep all the new recruits in the three strongholds. The veterans he would lead onto the field. Before battle was joined, he would get the recruits to stay hidden. It would look like the fortresses were empty, which would present the enemy with an irresistible target when they saw the force on the open ground. Graven Callow's numbers were much greater than Malgannis's. All he would have to do was crush the smaller army on the plain and he would win the war.

Malgannis narrowed his eyes at the landscape that would soon become a battlefield. He had put everything he could into thinking like his enemy. After all his conversations with Erik and the other commanders, and everything Malgannis had seen himself, he knew that Graven was tactically clever—very clever. When Graven saw that Martenhal, Balgaven, and Claregantry had all emptied out, he would make a swift decision. He would send bands of fast warriors to the fortresses to try to capture them.

Graven's capturing parties would encounter Malgannis's first surprise. The three fortresses would be far from empty. The recruits were inexperienced, but Malgannis had developed his plan so that they would be fighting from a strong position, behind stout walls of stone. Anyone Graven sent to the fortresses would be tied up, which meant fewer soldiers to face on the plain.

Even so, Graven would know that he should concentrate on Malgannis's army on the open ground. Unlike in the last large-scale battle, there were no steep hills to give momentum to a group of charging men and horses. There were no ruins for archers to hide in. There was no forest for screening secrets. The two groups would face each other on level ground. Size, strength, and tactical skill would win the day.

However, the mountainous terrain was deceptive. When the time was right, Malgannis would reveal his second surprise. The Harrmen would head out in the night, to hide in the hills and cliffs that bordered both sides of the plain. In the morning they would huddle among the rocks, their furs and drab colors enabling them to blend in with their surrounds.

In the heat of battle, when the two opposing forces were embroiled, the Harrmen would emerge from hiding. Pouring down from the cliffs, they would smash into Graven's army, to squeeze from both sides. Last of all, the recruits would pour out of the fortresses and add their numbers to the veterans, until the enemy was overwhelmed.

As Malgannis rehearsed his plan in his mind, an irregular clapping sound caught his attention. He saw two youths in uniform, sitting cross-legged on the stone as they faced each other. One had his hands pressed together as he held them out; another did the same thing and tried to slap his companion before he could yank his hands away. Whenever they made a strike, they both laughed uproariously.

Malgannis watched them for a moment. One was brown-haired while the other's hair was blonde. Both were fresh-faced and bright-eyed. Neither had whiskers, or even fuzz on his chin. Another slap, and both laughed. Here they were, about to be facing enemies with sharp swords who were trying to kill them, and they were playing a childhood game.

As Malgannis frowned, he saw a familiar figure with sandy hair, blue eyes, and a freckled face. Captain Finlay hurried over to the two new recruits. He hissed something at them and grabbed them by the armpits to yank them to their feet. They were all young, but the difference in their ages was apparent. Compared to Finlay, the two youths looked like they shouldn't have been out of their mother's clutches.

Commander Finlay, Malgannis reminded himself, not captain. Malgannis was tasking him with holding Martenhal, in charge of the entire fortress and all of those within it. He was a brave man and a good leader. He would hold fast.

Scanning the battlements, Malgannis saw that the pair he had seen weren't the only ones who looked so young. The veterans had left the walls and were readying their armor and weapons, which meant that already the soldiers manning the battlements were the youngest and newest to the border.

Malgannis had to remind himself that they fought to protect their loved ones. But still he felt disquieted.

There was so much at stake.

✦

"Did you have to tell me?" The man in front of Erik had a narrow face and thin frame that barely filled his fine clothing, and was clearly upset as they stood outside Martenhal's tall gates. His name was Wesley, and his father was a minor lord from south of Penstone. The hundred armed fighters he had brought with him were already inside the fortress, which meant that they were alone, where no one could hear them speak.

Erik kept his face impassive. "Your father didn't give me a choice."

"I was happy to come and fight, I will have you know."

"I don't doubt that," Erik said. "But your father, on the other hand, was not happy for you to come."

"And so you sent me a message, to tell me that he has been sharing a bed with a woman who is not my mother. I have had the entire journey to wonder. Who is she?"

Erik spoke bluntly, "If I told you who she was, there might be consequences. My plan was simple, and I make no apologies. I knew that if I told you, you would confront your father. He would then know that I know, and that I was giving him a final warning before further steps are taken. He had fighters needed here at the border. We do what we must."

"Your reputation is well-deserved." Wesley said, shaking his head. "Still, you can't tell me half the truth. I ask you again, who is she? Is she one of the maids? A village girl?"

"I do not destroy," Erik said, "I merely move things along. You made it here, that's the important thing. Any further questions should be directed at your father."

Wesley glanced at the fortress nearby. "That is if I survive long enough to get the truth out of him."

"I thought you said you were happy to come and fight?" When Wesley didn't answer, Erik decided to let him be. "If you need help settling in, see my lieutenant, Norris. She's the one with the blonde hair."

Wesley sighed, accepting the inevitable. "I remember her. Pretty girl."

"I suppose she is, but I wouldn't make any advances if you value all your limbs attached."

Wesley made a sound of surprise. "You and her...?"

"No," Erik said flatly.

"A friend of yours?"

"No."

"Then what? She doesn't like men?"

"Of course she does. She's friends with half the division."

"Ah," Wesley said. "I think I understand."

"Off you go." Erik jerked his chin toward Martenhal's gates.

Shoulders slumped, Wesley left Erik to join his men within the fortress. Meanwhile Erik remained, looking toward the south, in the direction the newcomers had come from. Another hundred men. Every new fighter would make a difference.

In the coming days, he would learn how his other messages had fared.

✦

Cora sat on her throne and tried not to wriggle. The high, hard back made for an uncomfortable perch, particularly when she remained in place for hour after hour. If kings and queens were intended to conduct much of their business from a chair, someone should have thought to make it comfortable.

Her tension made it even harder to sit still. The palace was too quiet for the momentous events taking place elsewhere. As she rested her wrists on the arms of the throne, she realized she was rapping her fingertips on the wood and forced herself to stop.

With a final flourish, the man standing in front of her concluded his speech. "And so, Majesty, the price of iron continues to escalate. Never fear, however, for our next voyage shall bring more essential goods to your great city, and to those who need them most." The merchant trader bowed. With his sun-streaked hair and bronzed skin, he had the look of a man of the sea. His fine clothing also described him as a successful trader.

"Thank you, Captain, for your time and your words," Cora said. "That will be all."

"Your Majesty."

As soon as the sea captain turned away Cora glanced at the back of the audience chamber, where a steward held aside a curtain for him to depart through. She gnawed at her lip, wondering if there was any news, but everyone in the palace knew to alert her to anything that came from the border.

Cora wondered. Would it be today? Was this the day when the fate of her nation would be decided? Why should she bother with what she was doing now? She should be there.

Frustration coursed through her. The last message from Malgannis had said he was preparing his great challenge, his attempt to push Graven Callow back from the border and turn the tide of the war. He wasn't sure of success, but his bold move was the only chance to dramatically alter the balance of power. Cora needed to hope for the best, but prepare for the worst.

The guard standing near the steward bumped the base of his halberd on the floor. A newcomer entered; he was a tall man, Cora saw, not as well-dressed as the last sea captain and twice as weathered.

"Captain Dewar of the ship Neveren," the steward announced.

Dewar came up to the throne and gave a clumsy bow. The stiff overcoat he wore on top of his sailor's whites looked ill-fitting; Cora guessed he had thrown it on just for this occasion. He was clean-shaven, with green eyes and long shaggy brown hair.

"Your Majesty, you asked to see me?" he asked in a rasping voice.

Malgannis's teachings were still clear in Cora's mind. *Knowledge is power.*

"I wish to know what transpires in the world, Captain," Cora said. "I want to know about the places you have visited and the things you have seen." She regarded Dewar with a level stare. "Where have your travels taken you before Adin?"

Dewar pursed his lips as his brow furrowed. "From the port of Penstone, Majesty," he said hesitantly.

Cora kept her face smooth and managed to stop herself from once again rapping her fingers on the arm of her throne. Penstone was part of Aranor. News between the two towns was frequent. "And before that?"

"Before Penstone there was a storm. We sought harbor in the Jagged Gulf." His eyes grew shadowed. "'Twas a bad storm, Queen Coraline. We were there for a week before it blew over, and even then the seas in the gulf were among the worst I have sailed. We saw some others floundering. Never found out if they made it. Before that, we were in the port at Kiora—"

Cora held up a hand. She knew that if she was going to make the effort to talk to the sea captains, she should be thorough. "Others, Captain?"

"Strange ships. Black with high prows."

"Strange?" Cora pressed.

Dewar cleared his throat. "I haven't seen many in the seas I sail. They were big galleys. Like they have in Vailand."

"How many?"

"Seven? Eight? Enough to stay clear of them."

Cora leaned forward, suddenly interested. She stared intently into the captain's green eyes. "Why would Vailand ships be in the Jagged Gulf?"

"Seeking shelter," Dewar said with a shrug.

"Is that what they were doing?"

He screwed up his face, visibly thinking and remembering. "No," he finally said. "Now that you mention it... they were heading higher into the gulf."

Cora's instincts told her she was hearing something that might be important. As one thought led to another, her mind worked at speed.

People said a man fought by Graven Callow's side, a huge Vailander who rode a draught horse, for no other creature could support his weight. It was odd enough for people to remark on it; Morania and Vailand were separated by the Sea of Kor, and the people of the two regions had little to do with each other.

"What day did you see them? You said you were there for a week."

Dewar began to look frightened. Cora knew there was color in her cheeks as she glared down at him. As Dewar licked his lips, at the back of the audience chamber, Cora saw the stout, swarthy figure of Lord Byron. He was watching the proceedings and anxiously twining his hands.

"The third day," Dewar said.

"And did you see them again?"

"No. That is why I thought they might have hit trouble."

Cora glanced at Byron and they met eyes. She knew that she and Byron would be making the same conclusions. Vailand was an old enemy of Aranor. Since the Great War – the war Malgannis won – Vailand had disintegrated into tribalism once more. But there were still powerful groups in the north, warriors and their forefathers who would have been plotting revenge for decades.

Vailand was far away. The locus of the war was now the three fortresses on Aranor's border. But the Jagged Gulf carved a deep furrow toward the Stony Mountains. From its end, a force of hardy men could make it through the mountains to Martenhal, Balgaven, and Claregantry.

And no one was hardier than the Vailanders.

Cora's heart began to race.

Graven Callow was planning a surprise.

Chapter 33

THEY TRIED TO STOP HER, but in the end, they couldn't.

Cora knew that Malgannis had to learn the news about the Vailanders heading his way. She had barely finished talking to the sea captain, Dewar, when she cleared the audience chamber and grabbed Lord Byron by the arm to haul him out onto the terrace.

"I'll summon a messenger from the city," Byron said quickly. "One of our fastest riders." Even as he spoke, he became agitated when he saw the look on her face.

Cora's mind was working at a frantic pace. All she could think about was the travel time to the border. "How long will it take to summon a rider? There's no time."

"Just a short while..." the portly lord began, before trailing off.

Cora knew that the messengers were always men. She was slight and slender; she had never seen a messenger who weighed as little as her. She also possessed two of the costliest horses in Aranor. One of them had won the Royal Championship three years in a row. The other was younger and stronger and was being trained for next year's race. Cora had been riding since she could walk. It would take too long to find a messenger, let alone the best man for the journey.

No. She knew it in her heart. No one would be able to get to the border as swiftly as her.

When the grooms at the stables saw Cora come charging in, asking some of them to saddle her horses, and ordering others to prepare saddlebags with trail mix and water, Lord Byron's protests fell on deaf ears.

Cora threw on her riding cloak, and within minutes of learning the news, she was on her way through the palace grounds, across the causeway, and into the city on her way to the gates. People jumped out of the way when they saw her coming. She rode one horse and the second, her spare mount, came clattering along behind her.

She traveled the King's Road in a fury. It took her just a day to reach the Bridge of Willows. No one was there to block her way or challenge her as she raced across the bridge's span.

She was finally doing something. But she was also desperate. Malgannis needed to know what was coming. Erik was in terrible danger.

She could only hope she would be in time.

✦

A dry, dusty wind gusted over the plain, tugging at the grass, sucking any moisture from the landscape. A few wispy clouds obscured the sun but then pulled apart to reveal the fiery yellow circle. As it traveled, the wind brought the combined scent of leather, metal, and sweat.

Everything was ready.

Malgannis rode along the front of the line. He waved as he galloped, and heard the thunderous din of thousands of voices bellowing together. With Erik riding beside him, he reached the end of the row of soldiers and his horse reared. He pulled at his reins to turn sharply. His eyes never stopped moving as he inspected the scene. Glancing at Erik, he saw his companion nod, and then they both rode back in the other direction.

Malgannis wore chain mail on his torso and a hardened skirt of metal strips above matching greaves on his shins. Metal bracers covered his arms but his head was bare, so that his long graying hair was divided in the middle to hang to his shoulders. By now, everyone knew his face, from his dark eyes, to his skin like old leather.

If Malgannis was the stern commander, Erik was the bold young warrior. With his square jaw, and his serious brown eyes, he was handsome, and his scar on his cheek only served to make his face distinctive. Malgannis was pleased to see that Erik's new armor fit him well; Malgannis had personally ordered it for Erik from Helmsford.

As Malgannis and Erik rode past, the archers shook their bows and the infantry raised their swords in the air. Someone started to smack his sword onto his shield, and another followed, until it was taken up by all, making a clatter that would easily be heard by the enemy at the other end of the plain.

But Malgannis wasn't just getting his men's blood up, readying them to fight. He was using the opportunity to check that all the deployments were crisp, the lines were straight, and everything was as it should be.

He scanned the lines and columns and the spaces between them. The rectangular mass of men was on flat ground, a few miles in front of Martenhal's walls. Archers stood side by side at the front and on the flanks, ready to unleash their hail of sharp arrows and then pull apart when the charge began. The infantry formed the bulk of the army, and those who would lead the advance were the strongest and most experienced among them.

Malgannis pulled up in the middle of the line, where everyone could see him. He drew his sword and held it high.

He heard a cheer rise up, time and again. "General! General!"

Erik reached down to pat the flank of his horse. He met Malgannis's gaze. "If they only knew who you really are."

"It's enough that they follow Lord Morgan," Malgannis said. "And as for you, Captain... Raise your sword. They are going to follow you today. Let them call your name."

Erik hesitated and then reached down to grab the hilt of his sword. He drew it slowly and then arched his back to thrust his blade, pointing it into the sky.

"Wallace!" the cheer went up. "Wallace!"

Malgannis smiled at Erik's surprise. He then lifted his gaze to look up at the walls of Martenhal. From his position, he could continue turning his head to inspect the other two fortresses, Balgaven and Claregantry. Each stronghold guarded its own section of the high ground. The three looked apparently indomitable as they gazed down on the plain. Malgannis's vision settled on the battlements of Martenhal, where a solitary figure stood on top of the tower with the best view of them all. Finlay was still standing exactly where Malgannis had last seen him.

Malgannis now turned away from the fortresses to face the direction the enemy would come from. He nudged his horse forward to climb a slight rise, the highest terrain in the immediate area. Erik came to join him, and they watched and waited together.

As Malgannis rehearsed his strategy, he thought about Cora. He had sent her another message. She would know that this was the day when it was all going to be decided. Everything came down to this one battle.

He heard the sound of marching.

Even he found the regular thud of heavy footsteps and metallic crunching intimidating. He turned back toward the men. Making sure they could all see him, he lifted up his sword. He slapped the blade against the metal gauntlet on his forearm. After a pause, he did it again.

Taking up their cue, the swordsmen again began to clash their swords against their shields. Archers holding the first arrows they planned to unleash began to clatter the wood against the stocks of their bows. When the new sounds rose up to mask the heavy marching, Malgannis was satisfied.

"You've done this before," Erik said, glancing at him.

"No two battles are ever alike," Malgannis replied.

The first enemy soldiers came into view.

Malgannis saw that Graven had deployed his archers in a similar fashion, at the front and on the flanks, with his infantry surrounding the bowmen in a wider line. The first soldiers came a halt, then the next behind them, and on and on it went. The sound of marching could no longer be masked by Malgannis's clatter, even though the enemy soldiers were still tiny figures. The black and crimson flags grew larger as the Moranian soldiers neared. At last, the enemy came to a halt. The two groups stood facing each other with a long distance between them.

From his position on the hill's crest, Malgannis scanned the enemy deployment and nodded to himself. There were no hiding places for knights: Graven's mounted warriors made up a couple of rows near the back of his formation. And there was Graven himself, seated on his dappled gray warhorse among them. He again wore his plate armor and his angular helmet covered his head. He was too far away for Malgannis to see much more of him.

The main focus of Malgannis's attention was the enemy's two flanks. He glanced at one side, and then the other. He saw only soft groups close to where the plain bordered the cliffs: archers, spearmen, and light infantry. If Graven knew about the Harrmen hiding in the mountainous high ground, he would never have arranged his forces the way they were.

As Malgannis began to feel hope, he addressed Erik. "Any flag from the enemy?"

Erik shaded his eyes and scanned the host of Moranians and their smaller number of allies. "None."

"Then there will be no discussion today," Malgannis said. He spoke to himself as much as Erik. "All of this about some rules made in Aranor. All of this death."

Malgannis knew what would happen next. Someone would sound a horn. Then one of the two armies would start to run. The other force would fill the sky with arrows. But soon they would have to run too, or there would be no momentum in the charge. And so the battlefield would be filled with running men, threatened by arrows falling from the sky, until the two groups crunched together.

Knights would look for soft parts in the infantry to charge. The other knights would try to counter them. Chaos would ensue.

Malgannis turned to call down to the standard bearer and the barrel-chested man in blue and gold beside him clutching a curling bronze horn. "Let the enemy come first," he instructed.

He had barely finished speaking when a sonorous blast came from the direction of the opposing force, filling the plain, bouncing from cliff to cliff. The blast went on and on.

Then the enemy began to stir. The line in front began to move, from a jog into a run, and the soldiers behind followed right after them. In moments, Graven Callow's army was streaming directly toward Malgannis's position as he watched them come.

Malgannis called back. "Archers! Ready!"

Creaking sounds came from behind him as the bowmen fitted their arrows and pulled their strings back to their ears.

"Loose!" Malgannis bellowed.

Multiple snaps accompanied the whoosh and whistle of a multitude of arrows being propelled into the air at high speed. Malgannis watched straight ahead as the black shafts arced through the sky in front of him. The enemy kept running. The arrows lost height and began to fall.

Malgannis judged the enemy advance. This was the moment when he had to make rapid decisions, all of which could cost him the battle. He wasn't sure if he would have time for another volley before ordering the charge. He had to choose now.

"Second volley!" He roared. "Archers. Ready. Loose!"

The first set of arrows slammed into the charging enemy, creating holes as men fell down. The second volley filled the sky. Even as the sharp arrowheads plunged into the enemy ranks, Malgannis turned to the horn player.

He drew his sword to make his meaning clear. Meeting eyes with Erik, he then leveled his sword to point it at the enemy.

"Charge!"

✦

Victory didn't taste quite right.

Bodies lay strewn across the terrain. In the end, when it was over, Malgannis held the battlefield.

He stood panting and realized he had lost his horse and had no idea where it was. In the great collision, after everything slowed, a Moranian swordsman had tried to pull him from the saddle. Malgannis had fought his opponent off, but his boot had become dislodged from the stirrup. Enemies surged all around him. He could barely move against so many men on both sides. He knew it was safer to throw himself off.

Of course, losing his horse meant that he was one of the men thrusting, stabbing, gritting teeth and keeping close to the soldiers of his own side. Malgannis was a skilled warrior, but by now the enemy knew who he was and kept coming at him. Erik charged back and forth, scattering foot soldiers as he swept his sword arm left and right. The soldiers in blue and gold gathered around Malgannis and held firm. But it wasn't until Malgannis saw warriors in furs, and saw Cedric Nine Lives leading his Harrmen into the fray, that he realized he might have a chance of winning the day.

He now stood surrounded by bodies, with the dusty wind in his face.

It was a strange moment, the immediate aftermath of a battle. Some of the nearby soldiers simply sat on the ground, staring at nothing and speaking to no one. Others grimaced as they gripped wounds on their limbs or torsos and tried to hold in their own blood. Harrmen laughed and hugged each other. The most common expression was relief.

Hearing a mighty cheer, Malgannis turned to see some young men who were wild with jubilation, shaking their weapons into the sky as if in defiance of the gods above. Then, spying movement out of the corner of his eye, he turned to see Erik approaching on horseback, grimy, but blessedly unharmed.

Erik brought his horse all the way up to Malgannis. He frowned and tilted his head. "What is it? You should be happy."

"Where is he?" Malgannis asked, scanning the battlefield. "And his knights?"

Erik faced away from the fortresses, toward the direction the enemy had come from. "The knights... They were behind the army, and then they were gone." He squinted, as if trying to spy out Graven in the distance. "They probably fled." He returned his attention to Malgannis. "There will be time to hunt them down. I know it isn't ideal, but once everyone knows Graven is defeated, the war will change."

"Fled..." Malgannis said slowly. He still didn't feel comforted. "Probably." He turned toward the three border forts, scanning each of them, although he couldn't see much from his distance. The blue and gold flags were still flying. Men stood watching from the battlements. But something wasn't right. Making a decision, he rested his gaze on the horn by Erik's saddle. "Call up the knights. I'm taking them to Martenhal."

"Let me do it."

"Lad—"

Erik held up a hand. "You're done in, old man." He gave a slight smile. "Let me do it." He spurred on his horse and called back over his shoulder. "I'll see you back there."

As Erik rode away, Malgannis tried to understand the flow of events. Both he and Graven would have known that the battle was going to be decisive. And yet Graven hadn't charged with his knights, enabling Malgannis's own knights and the Harrmen to combine their strength and swiftly gain the upper hand.

Every sense was telling him that he should be worried. He turned to scan the battlefield and waved at a nearby mounted warrior in the colors of Aranor.

"Soldier!" Malgannis called. "I need your horse."

The mounted soldier came over. "Of course, General," he said. He dismounted and held the horse by the reins. Malgannis adjusted the stirrups and then climbed up.

"Thank you," Malgannis said crisply.

He kicked the horse's flanks and navigated the milling soldiers and the dead and wounded on the battlefield. The victory meant that he had captured a large number of prisoners, and they were all lined up on their knees, at least a few hundred of them.

As he rode toward Martenhal, he stared up at the battlements. As he came closer and closer to the walls, he raised a hand to the soldiers watching him from above.

A chill ran up his spine. He allowed his arm to fall. No one waved back.

The churning in his stomach grew stronger. Before long, he was close enough to rein in.

The soldiers left to defend the fortress, recruits most of them, were held up by poles and spikes. Their eyes stared without seeing.

Martenhal was lost. The fortress had fallen.

Malgannis forced himself to keep looking. His gaze traveled up to the tower. A young soldier with sandy hair and freckles was exactly where Malgannis had left him, from where Finlay had an all-encompassing view of the plain below. And yet, Finlay's eyes would be seeing nothing, nothing at all.

An arrow flew from Martenhal and sank into the ground a dozen feet from Malgannis's position. A second arrow forced him to withdraw.

Malgannis spurred his horse into a gallop. He took himself as close as he could to Balgaven and then Claregantry, until he knew. The scene was the same. The figures on the battlements, dressed in blue and gold, were all propped up, held in place to maintain the appearance of standing. All three fortresses had fallen to the enemy.

Malgannis could only think of the poor boys who had been placed in his care.

As he returned to his men, he knew then, even as he felt rage dominate every other emotion: Graven Callow wasn't as cunning as Baelock Fain, the man Malgannis had believed would never have an equal, who had nearly conquered the world with smaller numbers and inferior weaponry.

Graven Callow was more formidable still.

As Malgannis rode back to the battlefield, the repercussions of what he had learned were still sinking in.

He had won the battle but lost the war.

Chapter 34

THE MOOD WAS ONE OF SHOCK and disbelief. Everyone soon knew what had happened.

For once in his life – both his lives – Malgannis was indecisive. He nudged his horse one way and then another, turning his attention to the three fortresses, and then the direction that the enemy had come from when battle was first joined.

He waited for Erik to return with the group of knights he had taken with him, but as time passed, there was still no sign of him. He wondered what might have happened. Erik was surely too clever to run afoul of an ambush. He had a group of skilled, armored knights with him. He would be fine.

But where was he?

How could Graven have captured the fortresses, when Malgannis blocked the only access? If there was a force approaching from the mountains – a large enough, strong enough force to capture the three border forts – Malgannis should have known about it. He had gone through all the potential allies and enemies in detail. The only nation who hadn't joined the fray was Vailand – if it could be called a nation – but the local kings were fiercely independent, and there was no way they would follow a man from Morania.

"Ironclaw."

Malgannis's head jerked around. There was only one man who would call him that, but at least Cedric Nine Lives spoke the name when only Malgannis could hear. The short mountain king with the thick neck and braided beard was on horseback, which was unusual; the Harrmen preferred to fight on foot, and only used horses for farm-work and travel.

“Look,” Cedric said. He rode up to Malgannis and indicated something away from the three fortresses. “Someone coming. Thought you might like to know.”

Malgannis shielded his eyes. He saw a solitary rider approaching, a thin man in the black and crimson colors of Morania. One hand held the reins, the other displayed an unfurled length of white cloth.

As Malgannis watched the newcomer approach, the Moranian envoy ignored all the eyes on him. He came closer, and obviously knew who he was riding to meet, as he pulled up in front of Malgannis.

The thin Moranian spoke plainly. “You have prisoners of ours. We have prisoners of yours.” He glanced meaningfully at the three fortresses. “You are invited to discuss terms.”

Cedric spoke in a low voice. “It’s a trap. You know it is.”

Malgannis glanced back at Martenhal, before returning his attention to the envoy. He couldn’t help thinking about all the boys he had abandoned, left to die, when his enemy somehow outmaneuvered him and seized the three fortresses.

“How do I know you haven’t killed them all?” Malgannis asked.

The envoy looked up at Martenhal. He lifted his white flag above his head and began to wave it back and forth.

As Malgannis watched, a long line of uniformed figures stepped forward until they were on the edge of the battlements. Where before, there had been a thin screen of displayed bodies, there was now a multitude. The uniforms were blue and gold.

Malgannis wondered: was Erik among them? He scanned the soldiers – his soldiers, his men – but didn’t know. Either way, he owed it to them, to himself, to try to save them.

He stared directly into the envoy’s eyes. “I want to meet Graven himself.”

“Agreed,” the envoy said. “You will approach unarmed. As will he. You will both have a second waiting on a horse nearby. There will be no others.” The envoy turned to point at the summit of a hill, a crest that was part of the rugged terrain near the cliffs. “You will arrive together. On that hilltop.”

“Don’t do this,” Cedric Nine Lives warned.

Malgannis interrupted the mountain king. “I need a second, Nine Lives. Will you come with me?”

“Aye, I will,” Cedric said, shaking his head. “Fool that I am.”

✦

For the first time, Malgannis was about to come face to face with his enemy, the man who had killed Cora's father and brother.

Malgannis had heard the stories from Erik, but then he had seen the butchery first hand. Finlay should have been home with his family, not a young corpse put on display, up on the tower at Martenhal. Those boys... they all should be home with their families.

The hilltop lay just ahead. As his horse gained height, climbing toward the crest, Malgannis took another look at the walls of Martenhal. He then turned his gaze toward Balgaven and Claregantry, where the same sight greeted him. From his new vantage, he could take in the sheer number of soldiers, the youth of Aranor, lined up on the battlements. He could also see the enemy archers arrayed behind them, bows bent back, arrows lined up on their targets.

The hill's summit was as large as a farmer's field. Reaching the top, Malgannis reined in, and Cedric pulled up beside him.

Two other riders also sat astride their mounts, a few hundred yards away. Malgannis's gaze first went to Graven, seeing a man of about his own size, seated on a gray warhorse that pawed at the ground. Graven still wore his plate armor, the interlocking steel covering his legs, his waist, his torso, and his arms. Chain mail gloves enclosed his hands as they held the reins of his horse. The angular helmet left just a thin slit for his eyes. Malgannis could see nothing of his face, not even a hint of his skin.

Malgannis tore his eyes from Graven Callow to inspect the man he had brought to be his second. He had heard about the huge Vailander – Halvar; they said his name was – but it was something else to see the man in the flesh. The draft horse he rode would be useless in battle, but Vailanders weren't known as horsemen. His white skin and deep-set eyes gave him the characteristic look of his people, along with the black hair he wore close-cropped. He openly carried a mace on his lap, a thick steel pole with an iron ball fixed to the end.

"By the gods, take a look at that man," Cedric breathed. He raised an eyebrow at Malgannis. "Still want to do this? If I have to intervene, I don't like my chances with him."

"I have to," Malgannis said. "And your horse is twice as fast as his. Strange as it may be, I trust you, Nine Lives."

Cedric's eyes betrayed his anxiety. "I've already said this, but you're a fool."

While he was still on horseback, Malgannis turned one more time to take a look at Graven's prisoners, the boys he was trying to save. Malgannis had his own prisoners, perhaps not quite as many, but the men from Morania he held were valuable, skilled soldiers, worth much more in battle. If Graven had sense, he would negotiate. Even if he was cold-hearted and cold-blooded, a fair exchange – boys for veterans – would see him gain the bigger advantage.

Malgannis dismounted.

He drew his sword from the scabbard at his side and handed it to Cedric. Malgannis then waited for Graven to slide off his own horse. The man who styled himself a liberator slid a sword from his own scabbard. The huge man on the draft horse accepted the hilt.

"He could still have a hidden knife," Cedric muttered.

"He's wearing full plate," Malgannis said, keeping his eyes on his enemy. "He has to wear any weapons on the outside."

Cedric spurred his horse a few paces toward the man walking toward them. Graven was approaching with his arms spread wide, and now stopped. Cedric opened his mouth to call out. "Turn around. Show me your back."

Graven Callow slowly turned, displaying his armor from the other side, continuing the movement until he had completed a full rotation.

"No weapon," Cedric reluctantly admitted.

The meeting had been carefully orchestrated. Malgannis knew that even if he had a knife, Graven had the armor to stop or slow any attack until his second arrived.

"It's time," Malgannis said.

Like Graven Callow, he kept his hands visible, at his sides as he walked slowly forward. However, unlike his enemy, Malgannis wore just his chain mail, skirt of steel strips, greaves, and bracers, leaving his head bare. It had been a long, wearying day. Sweat had dried on Malgannis's face. The graying hair that fell to his shoulders was lank and matted.

Malgannis kept his gaze fixed on the man he was approaching. His jaw began to clench, tightening and relaxing, tightening and relaxing. His vision closed in, until all he could see was the thin slit in Graven's helmet.

Graven Callow stopped walking. He maintained his posture, with his mailed hands still spread to show he was without a weapon.

Malgannis saw that Graven was tall, as tall as he was. He was leaner, with wide shoulders but less thickness in the torso. Physically, they both looked evenly matched. And still Malgannis could not see his enemy's face.

Malgannis came to a halt. He lifted his chin. "What is your proposal?" he asked without preamble. He waited. The seconds dragged out. "Well?"

Graven said nothing. There was clearly life in him. Unlike a suit of armor in a hall somewhere, he was breathing. But Malgannis had yet to hear his enemy's voice.

"I have five, maybe six hundred of your men," Malgannis said in a growl. He turned to nod toward the border forts, and then faced Graven again. "Now let those boys go."

The moments passed. Cedric sat on horseback at one end of the field, while the huge Vailander, Halvar, watched from the other. Malgannis and Graven faced each other with a short distance between them.

Malgannis felt himself becoming angry. "Well?" he demanded. "What do you want?"

Slowly, Graven placed his hands on either side of his helmet. His arms tensed. He began to pull upwards to remove the helmet from his head.

The first thing Malgannis saw was long, straight hair, as black as night, darker even than the midnight shade of his armor. Then Malgannis saw a chin, sharp as a dagger, with skin so white it was almost translucent. Thin, red lips formed a wide mouth like a horizontal gash. As the helmet came completely off and the man it had been hiding regarded Malgannis with a deadly stare, Malgannis recognized the high cheekbones and deep-set eyes.

Blood roared in Malgannis's ears. As his heart gave loud, jagged beats, he was transported back, to the darkest time in his life, the reason it all came to a terrible end.

"What I want," said Baelock Fain, "is to make you suffer. Just as you made me suffer, Ironclaw."

Malgannis couldn't breathe. It was all the same.

His Vailander accent was softer, but it was still there, in the incisive, rasping nature of his voice. His pale, narrow face was no different. He was the exact same age he had been when Malgannis last saw him.

Malgannis had spent a decade searching for Baelock Fain, tracking him across the kingdoms, following rumors, doing whatever it took to hunt him down. He had turned down the kingship of Aranor in his quest for revenge. He had done unspeakable things in his pursuit of his nemesis, the man who had stolen his life, taking away any love he had, robbing him of his wife and daughter. Baelock Fain had unleashed savagery upon the world. Countless men, women, and children had died at his hands, and the hands of his warriors.

Now history was repeating itself. But this time, Baelock Fain was going to win.

"Graven Callow," said Baelock Fain slowly, as if tasting the different syllables on his lips. "I like the name. A typical Moranian name, but also... somewhat unique. Graven Callow," he said again. "I chose it myself." He smiled. "Ah, Ironclaw. You are slowly catching up. I can see you had no idea."

Malgannis tried to speak, but it was an effort. "How?" he whispered.

The man Malgannis knew as both Baelock Fain and Graven Callow spoke grimly. "I unleashed a war among the demons and escaped the seventh circle of hell. I found myself in the shadow world, where it seemed that I was doomed to spend eternity." His lip curled. "By the gods, the umbra is a boring place. I almost wished I was back in Abaddon." He smiled. "Almost, but not quite."

Malgannis realized. "The ghouls."

"They wanted me to return to hell, but there was only one way I was going back. We made a bargain. If they wanted me back in Abaddon, they first had to give me life. I came back through the pool, just like you did, Ironclaw."

"But you're a Vailander."

"This is my second life, as it is yours. Why must I be doomed to suffer the same failures? When I came back I looked at the shape of the world. Vailand has again fallen to tribalism. But Morania... Morania was well placed to throw off the yoke of Aranor." Baelock Fain paused. "Look at us," he said with another thin-lipped smile. "Two dead men, reunited. This is a merry dance indeed."

"How could they give you power?"

Baelock Fain shrugged. "Long ago, Vailand was exploited, our children stolen by slavers from the south. Then, after our war, you and your sons found another way to take advantage of the weak, with your laws and taxes, all controlled from Aranor. The people wanted to hear what I had to say. There was no hiding my hatred... of you and everything you touched, the shackles you built, the stamp you put on the world. I enlisted in the army. A man of Morania with a Vailand accent. Stranger things have happened." He glanced toward the border forts. "I now have the strength of two identities to draw on. It was men of Vailand who took Martenhal, and the other two. You never even saw it coming."

The face. The black, narrow eyes. Baelock Fain. The reason Malgannis was cursed to haunt the shadow world. Graven Callow was Baelock Fain reborn.

"You killed my wife and child," Malgannis said.

"Not personally," Baelock said. "I sent the raiders, and they had their instructions, but as you know I was not even there. Come, Malgannis. That was long ago."

"You killed my grandson."

"King Owen?" Baelock sounded surprised. "Ah yes, him. I barely remember him. He was no fighter. Not like you."

"And his son."

"Patrick." Baelock rubbed his knife-like chin. "A better swordsman. But still far from an even match. Ah, Ironclaw. I always wondered who would have been the victor, if we were to duel." He appraised Malgannis, looking him up and down. "But you were always older than me, and your last years were not kind, not kind at all."

"I could have been king of Aranor. I spent my nights in the best taverns, even as I hunted you down. And where did you sleep? Under hedges. On ships. Always with one eye open."

Malgannis knew he had struck a nerve when Baelock snapped back at him. "And yet you died before me. I stayed true to myself, but did you?"

Malgannis stepped forward, ready to fight. But then he glanced past Baelock Fain's shoulder at the huge Vailander, seeing him watching closely. Malgannis knew he had the captives at the border forts to think about.

Baelock Fain noticed his frustration and smiled. "I have to say, I am reveling in this." He gave a dry laugh. "Two dead men, here again. I still fight for freedom, but this time it is not just Vailand I serve but the entire world. Your beloved Aranor is doomed. Meanwhile, the name I have chosen – the name Graven Callow – will resound throughout history. My second life will be the greatest a man can live. I will even find out the secret of the black priests' immortality, and make it my own. Who needs the afterlife when I can live forever here. Eh, Malgannis?"

Malgannis's nostrils flared. The prisoners, he reminded himself. He had to free the prisoners.

"And now," said Graven Callow, the second incarnation of Baelock Fain. "As for you." He sneered as he cast his eyes over Malgannis's frame. "When someone came back, I was desperate to find out who it was. The black priests demand a high price. I thought to myself, whoever it is must be important indeed. I lost you in Vestria. But then, after I killed Patrick, a new commander emerged. I knew, I hoped, that it would be you."

With a terrible, sinking dread, Malgannis began to realize something. He hadn't known Graven Callow, or at least he had believed him to be a stranger. He wasn't sure what price Graven would demand for his captives, the youth of Aranor.

But he did know Baelock Fain, the butcher of Vailand.

"We have been here before," Baelock said. "This isn't our first dance. You won't kill my men, Ironclaw, slicing their throats, butchering them like animals, disarmed and frightened as they are. We are different sides of the same coin. Both men of war. Yet you are weak and I am strong."

Baelock raised his arm. He held it up for the duration of a long breath and then dropped it. Malgannis couldn't help himself; he turned to watch.

He didn't hear the arrows, but he saw the impact they made. The soldiers in blue and gold, lined up on the battlements, crumpled one after the other. The same scene unfolded at all three of the fortresses. The archers again drew their bows. The captive soldiers fell down.

Malgannis roared and lunged at Baelock, who took several swift steps backward to take himself out of the way. The huge Vailander spurred his draft horse forward and at the same time raised his mace.

"I have your fortresses, Malgannis," Baelock said, still taking footsteps backward. "Let us see you strategize your way through this one. You won, once. Now you will be the one watching as I have the final victory."

Baelock's second, Halvar, brought the black warhorse with him. Baelock Fain, butcher of Vailand, grabbed the pommel of his saddle, pulled himself up, and rode away.

✦

"Just kill them," Cedric said.

Malgannis felt dozens of sets of eyes on him. As he regarded his prisoners, hundreds of them, lined up on their knees close to the site of the recent battle, he knew his men felt the same way as Cedric. They had all seen what had happened at Martenhal, Balgaven, and Claregantry. The eyes that stared up at Malgannis were red. Pain and anger filled every face.

Malgannis forced his own thoughts to turn away from the grisly memory. That was what he wanted... Baelock Fain... the man who had plagued his life and death. For Malgannis to react emotionally. He had to instead think about survival.

He glanced at the sky. The sun would soon be level with the cliffs. The core of his army had been victorious, and held the plain with only light losses. But he had to form them up and get them moving. If he stayed any longer, he knew he risked attack.

Malgannis watched his prisoners for a moment and then shook his head. He raised his voice so that all his men could hear him. "There won't be any more killing today. We have this one night to get onto the road to Adin." He focused on Cedric. "You should prepare your men. The next days won't be easy. Moving an army in retreat, while being pursued..."

"And them?" Cedric nodded toward the prisoners. "You know you can't take them with you."

"I'll leave them tied up," Malgannis said. "They might slow the enemy down." When he saw Cedric's bemused expression, he scowled. "What else would you have me do? This is a waste of our time. We need to get onto the King's Road, while we still can."

Cedric Nine Lives tugged on the golden rings he wore around the braids of his beard. "Listen, Malgannis... We won't be going with you."

Malgannis's mouth opened. It took him a moment to reply. "We have a deal."

Cedric turned toward the battlefield, and rested his gaze on a fur-clad warrior's body. He was a big, burly, grizzled man, with blond hair and three parallel scars on his face. The mountain king's eyes continued to move, to another body, and then another. "We lost many. We now need to bring them back. The Rite of Rebirth is something we can only perform at home."

"Losses were to be expected. You signed a treaty."

Cedric shrugged. "As did you, Ironclaw. And then what happened?" He nudged his horse forward, and reached out to grip Malgannis's arm. "Aranor is lost. I'm sorry. You can't win." He turned toward the hilltop where he had watched Malgannis's confrontation. Dropping his voice, he spoke for Malgannis alone. "Is he truly Baelock Fain?"

"He is."

Cedric nodded to himself. "Then I pity you the coming days."

Chapter 35

CORA REINED IN SO HARD her mare's hooves skidded on the graveled road. The sky was clear behind her, but up ahead, something altogether different filled her vision.

At first she had thought the dark haze past the distant hills was the beginning of a storm. Now, as she watched from the crest of a hill, with the King's Road below her, she was gripping her reins so tightly her hands were hurting.

The plume of smoke was the color of coal and turbulent, coiling around itself as it rose ever higher. The swathe of black sky was thick, so wide from one end to the other that it could only mean one thing.

The city of Helmsford was burning.

Cora remained in place. She was too late. Erik. Malgannis. All of those youths she had sent to the front. The people of Helmsford... they would have suffered like the citizens of Inadris her father had gone to help. Back then, her father had failed. Later, Patrick had failed.

Now she had failed.

And her failure was the greatest of all, for her enemy was now on Aranese soil, and Aranor's sons and daughters would fall like wheat under a scythe.

She could see them now. Small groups of people dotted the faraway hills. The tiny figures moved with speed, fleeing the city's destruction.

Helmsford itself was hidden behind another crest, taller than the rise that marked Cora's current position. She wondered what she would see if she continued just a little farther. Helmsford was a large, walled settlement, with a beautiful white temple and a river that flowed directly though the city's heart. The colorful houses looked like children's sweets.

The citizens were miners, farmers, and craftsmen. Goat and mutton from Helmsford graced the tables at countless houses in Adin. At every market in the capital, Helmsford wool commanded the highest prices. Traders came and went from across the nations; if Adin was Aranor's heart, Helmsford was its hands, reaching out to the rest of the world.

Cora had been to Helmsford more times than she could count. And now the city was burning. If she looked upon it, she would see...

She couldn't dwell on the horror of it all. She was the queen; she had to be strong. The border forts must have fallen. Any of Aranor's soldiers left would take the King's Road. Events would now move swiftly. With such turmoil, the decisions she and others made would have rapid and rippling repercussions.

She steeled herself and tried to think of the things Malgannis had taught her. He had instructed her to read, and read she had. He had told her she should talk to others, and receive their wisdom, and she had asked questions not just of lords, but of common soldiers, officers, and librarians at the academy in Adin.

Graven Callow had conquered the border forts. There was no other explanation for what she was seeing now. Helmsford was burning. What would Graven do next? He would be sensing victory, close to completing his conquest of the world. Now was the time to move fast.

He would immediately pursue Aranor's soldiers, leading his army all the way to Adin. He wouldn't give the capital time to prepare. Despite its impressive walls, Cora knew that the city wasn't as well fortified as the border. Even as her thoughts spun, she saw the map of Aranor in her mind.

She had no choice. Tearing her gaze away from the horizon, she turned back the way she had come.

✦

West of Helmsford, a thick patch of forest clung to the low ground between two sharp hills. A few caves peppered the area, deep, dark places that only a few people knew about. One of those people was Erik.

Erik stood at a high point, under a tree, but in a position where he could see far into the distance. The night sky was moody, purple rather than black, and completely devoid of stars. Erik's gaze was fixed on a reddened, glowing area. He knew exactly what he was looking at.

He kept imagining the same thing happening to Adin. Cora was there. And yet Erik was stranded, cut off from the route to the capital.

A shape moved in the darkness. He heard a scuffle as someone climbed up to him. The slender form of Norris appeared silhouetted, with her pony tail behind her head and fires of Helmsford at her back.

"I don't know how you can watch." She glanced over her shoulder and even though Erik could barely see her face, he knew how she felt from her posture.

"Imagine if that were Adin," Erik said. "It soon will be. He's doing it, Norris. He's destroying us. One day, that will be our homes."

His thoughts were dark. After the battle, he had encountered resistance on the ride up to Martenhal, and had been stunned to find himself battling scores of Vailanders. He and his strong knights survived the ambush, and had charged uphill, until he was close enough to see Martenhal's walls through a gap in the trees. He would never forget his shock at what he had seen. More Vailanders, along with soldiers of Morania, moved about the fortress, keeping themselves hidden from below.

Erik had pressed on: perhaps the other two strongholds still held; they might even need his help. But then, farther up, he had spied a great number of pale-skinned northerners on the high ground. He tried to find a way around them, taking a thin trail through the trees that climbed onto a steep slope.

His new vantage meant he discovered more enemy forces on the battlements of Balgaven and Claregantry. Erik knew then that all of the border forts had fallen. He also knew he couldn't go on any farther.

And yet, he couldn't return to Malgannis either. After learning that the three strongholds had been captured, he had inspected the landscape below, to see that Malgannis had led the army away and Moranian soldiers now commanded the terrain. There were few options available, and Erik had to think about the knights under his command. He had led his men through the forests and deep ravines, heading in the only safe direction: west.

"There must be something we can do," Norris said.

Erik kept his eyes on the red horizon. "The border forts are occupied. Helmsford is burning. Graven Callow will already be on the King's Road, in pursuit of our forces."

"Captain..." Norris persisted. "We are behind enemy lines. We have to take advantage of it. I suggest we harass them on the road. We might be able to prevent them forcing a battle with the general. We can at least try to slow them."

"We can't," Erik said soberly. "Not with sixty men."

"Sixty knights," Norris said firmly.

"We just fought a battle. We have no food for our horses. We don't even have provisions for ourselves. We are in no position to ride out and take on thousands of enemies."

Norris remained silent. Erik wished he didn't have to give her the naked truth. He wished he wasn't right.

As he watched the fires of Helmsford, he knew he had to banish his despair. The past had already happened. He had to think about the future.

What would Malgannis do?

Erik had read the histories. He had studied at the academy. And he had met the man.

Malgannis would do something unexpected. Something surprising. Something with implications that could alter the outcome of the war.

"Turn our horses loose," Erik ordered. "Hide our armor in the caves. We travel light."

"Where to?" Norris asked.

"West. And North."

Norris couldn't hide her surprise. "To Vestria?"

"Aye," Erik said. "To Vestria."

There was silence for a time as Norris processed the implications of Erik's order. "I'll tell the men," was all she said.

As she left, Erik stared straight ahead, allowing his anger to fill him with determination.

And yet he couldn't help himself thinking... Gods help Malgannis. Because Erik knew he couldn't.

✦

Malgannis glanced over his shoulder to check on the long column of soldiers he was leading. The King's Road was wide enough for two wagons to pass each other, but uniformed figures filled its breadth, and the column of walking men followed the road over hills and around corners, until it disappeared behind a bend. Malgannis rested his eyes on the wounded, where the group slowed, thinning in the middle. The stronger soldiers he had positioned at the front and back.

"Come on," he muttered. "Hurry up."

The King's Road was firm and well-maintained. Malgannis was able to make good time, but the same thing applied to the enemy. There had already been skirmishes. Enemy riders appeared at the top of nearby hills, launching arrows down at the army of Aranor, disappearing before Malgannis's own bowmen could take them out. The constant worry was wearing at everyone's nerves.

The landscape so far had been gentle, but the terrain was now climbing, slowing the column still further. Malgannis's brow furrowed as he looked to the right, seeing tall peaks with snowy white caps. He remembered traveling the Skyway with Cora. When the mountainous region brushed against the King's Road, and the two paths merged, the ascent would become steeper still.

"General!"

He turned to see a mounted archer riding toward him, a red-faced man in a captain's uniform. Half a dozen men followed behind, also on horseback, and like their leader they carried bows on their shoulders along with quivers of arrows.

"Captain?" Malgannis replied.

The red-faced rider pulled up, breathing so hard it took him a few moments to speak. His name was Lewin, and he was a veteran, with stubble on his cheeks and bristling hair that stuck out in all directions. Lewin wasn't slender, but despite his paunch, he could fight equally well with sword or bow.

"We've sighted some enemy knights," Lewin said, still catching his breath. "A hundred, maybe more." He nodded toward the closest rocky peak. "They're out in the hills, trying to come abreast of us."

Malgannis looked toward the peak, even though he couldn't see anything. If a hundred enemy knights charged his column, everything would fall apart. Then, when the main host caught up, there would be a massacre.

"How long?" he asked.

Lewin tried to speak, but broke off in a cough. "See those trees, past the top of the hill?"

Malgannis scanned farther up the King's Road. His column of soldiers would soon head up to a crest, then plunge through a small wood, before climbing higher still. "I see them."

"The enemy knights will have to ride through the trees to get to us," Lewin said. "Good site for an ambush."

Malgannis nodded. "Good man."

Lewin touched two fingers to his forehead and then spun his horse, leading his group away. He gathered more mounted archers as he went. The enemy knights would be turned back before they could attempt a charge.

The army of Aranor kept moving. Anxious soldiers' eyes remained on the road. There would be no rest. None at all. They would only stop if their pursuers halted first.

Time passed in strange ways. Malgannis was desperate to get his men to safety, which meant that distant landmarks took forever to reach. At the same time, he felt that the passage of seconds, minutes, and hours was far too swift. As the ground continued to climb, he kept turning his head to look back. He could now see all the way to the end of his long column.

And there, just a few miles farther, he saw the enemy.

Baelock Fain's force was larger than Malgannis's ragtag army. Unlike Malgannis's column, they marched in a crisp formation, with scouts and riders on the flanks and knights up front. Moranians made up by far the largest number. Their black and crimson uniforms clashed with the green and brown colors of Aranor's countryside.

Shielding his eyes, Malgannis searched. One of those warriors on horseback was Baelock Fain. Malgannis's enemy had a face now, and it was a face he knew well. He no longer pictured a tall man in an angular helmet. He saw snow white skin, thin red lips, and long coal-black hair. He saw a chin as sharp as a razor and high cheekbones. And deep-set eyes that had no compassion at all.

Malgannis knew that Baelock would be enjoying the chase. He and his gigantic Vailander no longer needed the scent of their quarry; they had Malgannis's defeated army in sight.

As Malgannis returned his attention to the road, he was keenly aware of how many lives he was responsible for. His mind was constantly working, but this time he couldn't think of a plan. At the rate his men could travel, Adin was still days away. Along the way, there was nowhere with fortifications, nor anywhere to mount a defense, until the capital itself.

Baelock's army would easily catch up before then.

And Malgannis knew that he would lose any conflict. His men were short on supplies. They were fleeing, taking their wounded, desperate to reach safety. They needed to rest and regroup. Surviving an open battle was unthinkable.

Could he defend a hill? No, he would be surrounded, and then what?

His worried pondering moved on. Could he expect any help, perhaps from Adin? No, the palace would only now be learning about the defeat at the border and the destruction of Helmsford.

Malgannis's only hope was to go faster, much faster. But there was only one way to do that.

Spying movement, Malgannis watched as Lewin led his group back down the road. A few horses trailed after them; the saddles were empty.

The captain had performed wonders, and yet when he rode up to Malgannis, worry filled his face as he stared down the hill toward the enemy.

"We turned them back," Lewin said gruffly. He paused and shook his head, before meeting Malgannis's eyes. "We both know that we aren't slowing them enough."

"We do."

"Any ideas?" Lewin asked, scrubbing at his stubble.

There was no benefit in hiding the truth. "No."

"Me either." Lewin glanced from side to side. He spoke even more quietly than they already were. "We could leave the wounded."

Malgannis knew as well as Lewin that it was the only chance they had to outrun the enemy. "No."

"It's the last thing we can try."

"No," Malgannis repeated. "In another world, with another adversary, perhaps we could count on our enemy's mercy. But with this enemy, that is something we can't do. I will not leave the wounded."

Lewin nodded soberly. "Then all we can do now is pray."

Chapter 36

THE CLATTER OF FOOTSTEPS was deafening. In a continuous rattle, boots rang out against the wooden planks of the Bridge of Willows, making a sound like hail on a tiled roof.

Cora tilted her head back, staring upward. She was watching the crossing from far below the bridge, almost underneath it. Steep walls of black rock surrounded her. Father down, the ravine's sides became close to vertical and formed a deep depression.

As the crossing progressed, Cora continued to hear footsteps while she watched through the bridge's timbers. Malgannis and Erik would be up there—if they still lived. There were so many of her countrymen, of all ages, clad in blue and gold uniforms. As the soldiers of Aranor walked over the wooden bridge, shoulders slumped and eyes downcast, they crowded the entire edifice. It would take a long time for them all to pass.

From underneath, Cora had a different perspective of the bridge's construction. The Bridge of Willows looked spindly from a distance, but the timbers were ancient, and despite how thin they were, its builders had found a way to make it last. The sound of water in the deepest part of ravine was a trickle rather than a torrent. The beams that supported the Bridge of Willows were dry. It didn't rain often in these parts.

And yet, when she turned toward the far side of the sky, she saw dark clouds gathering, pushed by the wind to head her way. For a moment, a rumble of thunder was louder than the clatter of soldiers' boots on the wooden planks.

Cora peered downstream. The ravine was too wide and steep to cross at any point other than the bridge. As the terrain fell, the rocky walls eventually drew apart to form a gorge, and then a wide river with tall banks.

The river could be crossed. It wasn't an impossible prospect. Cora knew because she had done it while assessing the merits of her crazed plan. She had raced her horses to the nearest village to gather the supplies she would need, and then come back. She had made certain of the different elements of her idea. The river could be passed, but not by an army of soldiers, clad in armor, with horses and supplies, tents and spare clothing.

If there was no bridge, an army would be forced to go the long way around.

Cora returned to watching her countrymen cross the Bridge of Willows. As soon as the last soldier was over, she turned her attention away from the bridge, and onto something else altogether.

She had built the fire in a sheltered place. The alcove she had chosen protected it from the wind, which was picking up pace as the storm gathered in the sky. Her fire was big, almost the size of a funeral pyre, and made of thick planks. Even the handcart she had used to move the timber sat on top of the raging flames. A loud snap sent sparks scattering over the surrounding rock.

Additional long timbers lay halfway into the flames, their ends bright with fire. Cora bent to pick one up. A wave of heat rolled over her; sweat coated her forehead. Now that she was close, the crackle of flames was the loudest thing she could hear. She couldn't believe what she was contemplating.

For a moment she stared at the blazing end of her plank, and then at the bridge's nearest supporting beam, and then back to the flame again. She didn't feel confident. Even if she saved the fleeing soldiers, she would be dooming an entire region of Aranor. Graven Callow might not be able to go straight to the capital, but he would be able to ravage a great part of the north. She was making a conscious choice that would see towns and villages burned and people killed.

Something appeared, out of the corner of her eye.

Her attention moved swiftly. She looked toward the far side of the bridge, and the curling road that climbed up to reach it. A portion of the road was visible, and despite the distance, she knew exactly what it was she was seeing.

Soldiers of Morania came into view, so many that they looked like colorful insects. They would soon be at the bridge, perhaps even too soon for her plan to work.

There was no time. She had to act now. With her flaming plank in hand she ran toward the first beam she had selected. She carefully set the plank down at the base of the wooden support. Hurrying now, she sped back to the fire. She grabbed another fiery timber, raced over to the bridge, and put it down nearby.

When she seized the next plank, a sharp stinging sensation traveled from her arm as she burned herself. She ignored the pain and hurried back over to the bridge. This time, she laid her timber underneath a horizontal support.

But even as she worked, frustration mingled with her desperation. Her plan was working, but it was all happening too slowly. She kept going, returning to the fire time and time again. It wasn't that her fire wasn't big enough, or that she didn't have enough wood. She had thought her idea through, and all she had to do was transport sections of her fire from one place to another. The problem was that in waiting for her countrymen to cross, she now didn't have enough time.

Even as she darted back and forth, her eyes kept returning to the individual fires she had already placed under the bridge. At several sections, flames were licking up the beams, catching one onto the other, blazes growing larger by the second as the ancient wood, dried out by decades of exposure, caught fire. She placed more burning planks. Time and again she came back for more.

"By all the gods, Lady, what are you doing?"

The strong male voice made her look sharply over her shoulder. Three men stood watching her as she worked, bemused expressions on their faces. Despite their presence and her own surprise, Cora knew she couldn't falter. She set down another length of flaming timber. The gusting wind was now doing some of her work for her, sending flames racing from one support to the next.

"It's her, the one with the ring," said one of the men.

"The ring we never found," said another.

Cora recognized the three brigands, dressed in tight-fitting brown clothing, and in particular the tallest of the group, an older man with stubble on his cheeks and a felt hat worn at an angle.

"I asked you a question," the brigand with the hat asked. "I must be mad. From here it looks like you're setting fire to the bridge."

"That's our bridge," said one of his companions. "It's how we make money."

Cora stopped what she was doing and stood near her fire, panting as she regarded the three men. "Help me now, and I'll make you rich."

The leader tilted his head. "How rich?"

One of Malgannis's maxims came to Cora. *Sometimes you just do what it takes to survive another day.*

"Six hundred gold pieces each," Cora said. "And a full pardon from the queen for any crimes you may have committed."

The three men exchanged glances. "How can you speak for the queen?"

Cora spoke matter-of-factly. "Because, as I already told you, my name is Coraline Vandryden, and I am the queen of Aranor." She didn't have time to try to convince the three brigands as she pointed toward the enemy soldiers heading for the bridge. "Graven Callow killed my father and my brother. You saw our soldiers cross. Our enemies will be next. We have to destroy the Bridge of Willows before they can make it to the other side."

The three men stared at each other, and then back at Cora. They took in her dark, braided hair, her high cheekbones, her leather riding boots and muddy but expensive cloak.

The leader of the brigands finally spoke up. "If you are an actor, or a madwoman, you have me fooled." He considered. "We want a thousand gold pieces. Each. And a full pardon for sixteen of us."

"Done," Cora said. "Now help me with this fire. Let's show our enemies what happens if they don't pay the toll."

The four of them set about their task. As they brought flaming planks to where they were needed, they each cast frequent glances to check on the advance of the Moranians toward the Bridge of Willows. The wind blew harder as they worked together, setting fires at multiple places, until the lower quarter of the bridge was burning and they could only look up to see what happened next.

Then, all of a sudden, thunder pealed again, and it began to rain.

✦

"What's that?" someone asked.

Malgannis turned to look back. His brow furrowed, and gradually his eyes widened as he stared at the Bridge of Willows. He saw the enemy soldiers climbing the road. They were almost at the towers that opened up onto the bridge, about to commence their crossing.

"By all the gods," another soldier breathed.

"Is that smoke?"

The gray plumes came from below, rising up to cloud the bridge until the whole structure looked like it was floating rather than supported by timber beams. A thicker, darker pillar of smoke rolled as it climbed into the air. The wind gusted, blowing Malgannis's hair around his face. From where he stood, he didn't know whether the bridge was burning or there was something on fire beneath it.

Then something stung his face. Another splash against his cheek was a heavy droplet of water. He glanced overhead to see black clouds gathering together. A rumble of thunder sounded directly above him. More droplets landed on the rocky ground and on soldiers' heads. It started to rain with force.

The enemy soldiers kept marching.

Malgannis knew he should keep his group moving, but everyone was exhausted, and they all remained where they were, watching the events unfolding at the Bridge of Willows. The men carrying the wounded set their stretchers down. Soldiers shrugged off their packs to drop them at their feet. Everyone stood wearily. A lot of lips were moving; Malgannis found himself praying along with them.

Rain streamed down from the sky. Thunder boomed. Smoke billowed up from underneath the bridge. Malgannis had to believe his own eyes; someone was trying to save him and all of the men he was leading. The Bridge of Willows had been old even in his time. Now someone was trying to destroy it, to burn it to the ground.

Malgannis heard a new sound: the clatter of a multitude of boots. The enemy had started their crossing. He didn't want to meet the eyes of any of his men. It hadn't worked. The heavy rain continued. He watched through the rain and smoke, seeing the colored uniforms of soldiers on the far side of the bridge.

Gradually, the torrent of rain became a steady patter as it eased. The droplets falling from the sky became sparse, and then the sun peeked through a gap between the clouds.

Malgannis's mouth dropped open.

There wasn't just a fire underneath the bridge, the entire structure was raging. The inferno had now reached the planks that made up the level path. Flames licked up one of the wooden rails. He didn't hear the shouted order, but he saw the soldiers flee as they raced back off the bridge and onto solid land.

The rain had now stopped altogether. The fire grew even as the soldiers that had pursued Malgannis all the way from the border pushed past each other in their haste to get off.

A loud groaning became a series of snaps like the sound of countless trees being felled. As one beam crashed down, another felt its own support weakened, and threw its weight on top of the next in line.

In front of Malgannis's eyes, the Bridge of Willows came crashing down in slow motion. The roar the timbers made as they fell was deafening. With all the smoke and dust, everything became a clouded confusion. The bridge that connected Aranor's north with the rest of the country was ruined forever.

Malgannis turned to see Captain Lewin staring at him, a stunned expression on his face.

"I can't believe it," Lewin said. "What just happened?"

Malgannis didn't know himself. But he took a deep breath and opened his mouth to bellow, he wanted as many men to hear him as possible. "We keep moving! Slower now, men. Take care of your comrades." He allowed himself to smile, for the first time in a long while. "Thank the gods, we're going to make it."

Chapter 37

ERIK SAT AT A SMALL TABLE in a dark corner, with just a tiny candle for light. He was waiting for someone, but he was early. He kept his head down, his ears pricked, and his face buried in his tankard. Now and then, he took a swallow of brown ale. His only companion, Norris, did the same. Neither of them spoke.

The Red King's Arms was a more somber place than when Erik had last been here with Malgannis. The crowd was smaller; there was no musician or storyteller. Instead the faces Erik saw were worried and suspicious. The men and women at the tables talked in low tones.

Erik had already learned a few things. Willem, the Red King – who was an old man when Erik was a boy – was still alive, but held prisoner in Ballina, Vestria's capital. All of Vestria was occupied, and the conquered people could only grieve the sons who would never come home. In the towns and cities, like Waygather nearby, they fearfully paid their taxes to Moranian officials and followed the curfew that meant they couldn't be out at night.

Someone moved past Erik's table. He and Norris both watched as two newcomers, both older laborers in dusty clothing, settled themselves at the table opposite. Whatever they were discussing, one of them was shaking his head in disbelief.

"Someone out there is looking out for Aranor, that's for certain," one round-faced man said to his skinnier companion.

Erik started. Before he knew what he was doing, he had left his table and leaned down to put his head close to the two laborers. "What news?" he asked urgently, keeping his voice low.

The round-faced man glanced from side to side. "Your accent. Aranese?"

Erik nodded.

"They say the Bridge of Willows burned down. Aranor gave up the north but their army made it back to Adin."

"It's inevitable though," said the skinnier man. "Sorry." He shrugged at Erik. "Soon enough, once Graven is done with the north, he'll lay siege to the capital. Then they win."

"Shh." The round-faced man frowned at his companion.

"And the queen?" Erik asked.

"In Adin. She gave a stirring speech, they say. The army's been saved. Still, you have to feel sorry for her."

Erik fought to control his reaction, steadying his breathing rather than show his joy and relief. Cora was alive and well. At the moment, she was safe. He thanked the two men and quietly returned to Norris. Seating himself back down, he relayed what he had learned.

Norris's strong jaw tightened as she clenched her fists on the table. "There is hope."

"There's hope," Erik agreed. "And that's why we're here."

"Something to eat?" A pretty curly-haired bar girl paused to lay a hand on their table.

"Maybe later," Norris said with a smile for the girl.

"Kitchen closes in an hour," she said, shrugging as she moved onto the next table.

Erik noticed Norris following the young woman with her eyes. "She's a little young for you."

"I know," Norris said with a theatrical sigh.

"Why the sigh?" Erik raised an eyebrow.

"It's been a while. There was someone, back at the border... nice woman... but she had two missing front teeth."

Erik's lips curved upward. "She did not."

"She did," Norris said seriously. Erik never knew when she was joking. "And thighs the size of smoked hams."

Erik's smile broadened "Why smoked?" he asked. "Why not just ordinary hams?"

Norris allowed her own smile to creep up on her face. "I don't know. Just sounded better. In truth she was a beauty. I have no idea if she's still alive." She glanced over at Erik. "And you? Who do you think about at night? There was this rumor... but in truth I've never had the courage to ask you about it."

Cora's face immediately came to Erik's mind. "Perhaps you should keep it that way."

"If it's true—"

"There's no one." Erik cut her off.

"Sorry, cap'n, a sensitive issue," Norris said. She turned her head and lowered her voice. "Careful."

Two soldiers in black and crimson entered the inn, one of them slamming the door behind them. The bigger of the pair, a stocky man with a thick matted beard, gave the occupants of the common room a sweeping, challenging stare. Erik made a swift appraisal, noting their leather armor and swords in scabbards at their waists. He knew he didn't want trouble. Not yet, at any rate.

The bearded soldier called to someone at the back of the room. "We're looking for someone. A runaway slave."

The innkeeper came forward, holding a towel in front of his body like a shield. "There's no one here like that."

"We'd like to take a look for ourselves."

"Of course, of course," the innkeeper said, bobbing his head.

Glancing at the two laborers at the next table, Erik saw them scowl. But Norris was keeping her face in her tankard, and Erik made sure to do the same. As the two soldiers passed Erik's table, the bearded man spoke up.

"You. Lift your head."

Erik raised his head. He tried not to think about all of the things he had seen. While the soldier stared at him, he kept his expression carefully blank.

"Too old," the smaller of the pair said. "The boy we're looking for is sixteen."

"A sixteen year old slave?" the skinny laborer at the next table spoke up.

"What's that, old man?"

"Shh." The round-faced man grabbed his friend's wrist. "It's nothing."

"Tell your friend to watch his tongue."

"I will."

Erik felt his tension remain even when the two soldiers moved on. He heard the innkeeper ask if they were finished but they said they wanted to see the kitchens and the lodgings upstairs. The common room remained silent as the two soldiers went upstairs, and was still ghostly still until the innkeeper and soldiers returned. After another scan across the room, the two men opened the door and it crashed closed behind them, until at last, they were gone.

Norris spoke in a soft murmur. "After that, do you think he's still going to come?"

"I don't know," Erik said. "Thorne isn't a real name. He's cautious."

Erik took another sip of ale, but remained pensive, unsure if he should keep waiting. He decided to give it another hour.

"I think this is him," Norris suddenly said. "Oh, no, mustn't be. It's a woman."

Erik heard footsteps and then looked up as a woman came over to their table. She was tall, with skin the color of Erik's brown ale. She also looked strong, with a frame that filled her blouse and loose trousers on her muscular legs. Her lips were full and curls crowned her head.

"Move along," she said to Norris, whose eyebrows shot up, but she shuffled along the bench. The woman then sat down. Spying the innkeeper, she waved at him and pointed at Erik's tankard.

"Thorne?" Erik asked quietly.

"That's me," the woman, Thorne, said in a low, gruff voice. "Erik?"

Erik nodded. "This is Norris." He indicated his companion.

"You were there?" Thorne asked. "At the border? When it happened?"

"We were," Erik said.

"I thought my brother was dead," she said. "I even started making a wreath to throw in the lake. When he showed up at my house..." She shook her head in disbelief. "He said you've got sixty men?"

Norris spoke up. "Sixty plus me and the captain here."

Thorne glanced around and then leaned forward to speak in an even quieter voice. "I know where there's a bunch more. Vestrian soldiers, hidden near the ruins of Leventhal." She looked at Erik and Norris in turn. "What about that one? Were you there? At that battle?"

"We both were," Erik said.

"One defeat after another." Thorne's full lips twisted as if she had a bad taste in her mouth. "You're truly prepared to help us?"

"I am," Erik said, "or I wouldn't be here. Tell me about the garrison in Waygather."

"You've seen the stockade?"

"I've been there," Erik replied. "Norris hasn't."

"There's a lot of them in there. Two hundred Moranians, maybe three. How do you plan to get in?"

"Is the market still operating?"

"Not in Fort August, not anymore. They moved it down to the docks."

Erik swore. "That was my main plan."

"I've got a few ideas of my own," Thorne said. "But first, we need to work a few things out. After Waygather, we go to Ballina. We keep going until we've freed all of Vestria."

"That's your price?" Erik asked.

"Aye," she said.

"Then we have an alliance."

Norris frowned at both Thorne and Erik. "Aren't we moving a bit too fast? Even if we can free Waygather, it's just a small victory. All of Vestria? That's a lot to expect."

"I don't do half-measures," Thorne said. "This is happening, whether you're with us or not."

Erik thought about Malgannis and his climb, when they first got to the border, and the words he had said. "It only takes a snowflake to start an avalanche."

✦

Malgannis stood on the palace balcony. He rested his arms on the stone rail, stared up at the heavens, and felt weary to the bone.

He had promised Cora victory, and instead he had lost all of northern Aranor. If some heroic person hadn't destroyed the Bridge of Willows, he would probably now be dead, and the city around him would be a smoking ruin.

Baelock Fain's army was now free to ravage and plunder. And Malgannis knew the nature of his enemy; he didn't want to conquer and occupy, he wanted to see Aranor humbled and make his old enemy suffer. It was Aranor who stood up to him and brought his advance to a halt when he first came down from Vailand. It was Malgannis who broke him on the battlefield, and Malgannis who tracked him down and captured him, leading to his execution on the hills just outside Adin.

Malgannis didn't like to think about what was taking place in the north. And what would happen after: soon enough, he would learn about his enemy's approach to the city. It would take Baelock time to get around the multiple rivers in the north and through the Witherglen in the east. But he would come.

Malgannis was now engaged in the frantic building of defenses. The Sylvan River that enclosed the city, with its multiple wide sections and powerful fleet, would help. The enemy would find Adin difficult to conquer, with the river on three sides and the canal on the fourth. The bridge would be raised. The city was defensible.

But Malgannis knew, with the heavy weight of experience, that this enemy was simply too powerful.

He remembered when he advised Cora to get onto a ship and travel to somewhere across the Sea of Mirrors, to seek safety rather than suffer a terrible fate. He could get onto that ship with her. Perhaps he could seek out someone wise, someone who might know how to reverse her curse.

It was a foolish idea. There wasn't another option. He had to stay and fight.

He drew in a slow, steadying breath. He gazed up at the stars and saw a comet streak across the night sky. His fists bunched up as they rested on the stone rail.

He knew this enemy. They had already fought a war before this one. And Malgannis wasn't as strong as he was before.

He had to change tactics. He had to learn from his mistakes if he wanted to fight back.

Squaring his shoulders, he stared grimly up at the comet, and vowed to all the gods that he would do better. He had to think. To plan. To seize the initiative.

He had to prove to Cora that her sacrifice wasn't in vain.

Chapter 38

CORA'S SLEEP WAS FITFUL.

She rolled back and forth, her eyes pinched and tendons tight in her jaw. Little moaning sounds came from her lips. The mark on her arm was increasingly painful, but was far from the only reason for poor sleep. She kept remembering the things Lord Byron had told her, despite wanting only to forget.

In Aranor's north, everywhere was burning. Bodies lay in the streets, unburied, for there was no one left to tend to the dead. Corpses floated on the rivers; more than one had flowed down to Adin on the Sylvan River. Farmer's fields had been salted so that nothing would ever grow again. Dead dogs and horses had been thrown into village wells to poison them.

Cora's nightmares were filled with soldiers in black and crimson destroying everything in their path. She heard the screams of men, women, and children. The people of Aranor were suffering. They were her people. She was supposed to protect them.

Her dreams became more personal. A helmeted warrior was standing right in front of her, his shoulders shaking with laughter. Adin Palace was burning with her in it. Erik was a forgotten corpse on a battlefield. Silvia's eyes were filled with blood.

Cora's head shuffled to the side. There was a dark force in her bedchamber, a smothering, tapered shadow, looming over her.

Her head moved back to the other side. The shadow was shifting, stretching, becoming longer. Starlight shone through the open curtains. She tried to open her eyes, but fatigue kept dragging her down again. The shadow was a figure, holding something long and pointed. She needed to wake. Her life depended on it. Slumber kept hold of her, clutching her with a relentless grip. The pointed object was raised above her chest.

She was so tired. She needed to rest.

Something wasn't right.

Her eyes flicked opened.

The bald man leaned over her, eyes glinting, lips parted, dagger held in his hand. Cora rolled and cried out. The dagger plunged into the bed.

She kept rolling to take herself off the bed. Slamming into the ground, she wriggled, until she had shifted into a crouch. She stared at the assassin and banished the last cobwebs of sleep.

He was a thin man, so lean he was almost skeletal, with a completely bald head and the pale skin of a northerner. With Cora on the far side of the bed, he lunged over the top of it, scrabbling on hands and knees to reach her, like a cat making the final dash for a bird.

Cora screamed. The assassin reached her and slashed at the air. She dodged and felt the whisper of the blade past her torso. As he prepared to make another swipe, she threw herself past him to reach the foot of the bed.

A statue rested on a tall stand, not far from the window. The size of her head, it was heavy. Without a thought she grabbed it and turned and threw.

The thin, bald assassin grunted as the hard object impacted his abdomen. But he was far from down, and he raced around the bed to reach her.

She spied something by the cold hearth – an iron poker – and sped over to the fireplace to grab the handle. Whirling she brought the length of metal up just in time to fend the assassin off. He snarled and tried to thrust his dagger toward her eyes, but she brought the iron poker between them, slashing back and forth.

She knew she couldn't fend him off for long.

"Help!" she cried.

Even as she cut the air with her poker, she cast swift looks at the door. Surely someone must hear her. The assassin made another lunge at her. She weaved to get around him, keeping her poker between them at all times. But the movement took her farther from the door.

The door burst open. Events moved so quickly that initially she didn't know what she was seeing in the darkened room. The figure in the doorway was black. Something flew from it, a small metal object.

The assassin's eyes shot wide open. He dropped his dagger and clutched his throat. Blood welled between his fingers, where a triangular throwing knife had penetrated his neck and still stuck out from his skin. The throwing knife fell from his neck to the floor. The assassin tried to stem the flow of blood and staggered over to the open window, but then tumbled past the curtains. Cora heard the thud his body made when he hit the ground.

The shadowed man in the doorway hurried over to her. "Are you hurt?" he asked urgently.

The iron poker fell from Cora's hand. She was struggling to catch up with what was happening. She saw a black hooded robe, clad around a slender figure. The man had a pale narrow face with a sheen to his skin, and dark, intense eyes.

"Lexen?"

Lexen Crow reached Cora and patted her arms, turning her around, and then back again. "You're not hurt," he said, sounding relieved.

"I don't understand."

The black priest went over to the window. He peeled back the curtain to look down at the ground below, and nodded to himself. He then crouched to retrieve his knife, returning it to somewhere inside his robe. "I came as soon as I learned of his existence. It appears I was almost too late."

"Who...?"

"Who sent him? Graven Callow, of course. Or Baelock Fain, you may also call him. I am sure Malgannis made you aware of his... former identity."

Malgannis had told Cora about everything that had happened at the border. Well... almost everything. She knew he was leaving out the worst parts, but what she had learned was bad enough. For all of his conquering, what Baelock Fain truly wanted was to see the end of Aranor. He wanted Malgannis to suffer, and by extension Cora. Erik was gone, presumed dead.

It was after Cora learned about Erik that her nightmares began. Malgannis said he had last seen Erik with his knights. But if he was alive, wouldn't he have tried to rejoin the other soldiers fleeing the border? She worried about him constantly, imagining him on the wrong side of the Bridge of Willows, desperately calling her name.

Lexen's last words slowly sank in. The fact that he had named their enemy meant he had known. All along, he had known.

"You knew," she said. "About Graven Callow."

"I did."

"Why didn't you tell me?"

Lexen looked like he was carefully choosing his words. "Would it have changed anything? It is hard to say. It might have made you realize how desperate your struggle was, which may have made you more likely to commit to our bargain. Alternatively, knowing about his rebirth might have made you wonder why. Why him, of all people? Surely of anyone, Baelock Fain should be in the seventh circle of hell. You would have become frightened, just when I was trying to earn your faith, if not your trust."

Cora persisted, knowing she might not see him again. "But why choose me? Why were you so eager?"

"There are wider events taking place in worlds outside this one. Baelock Fain was... instrumental... in causing some trouble in Abaddon. He made it out, and the only way we could get him back where he belongs was to first bring him here, to the real world." The black priest lowered his head, his tone deadly serious. "Yes, he is returned, but death is a part of life, and if he causes misery in this world, that is not my concern. Also, you must remind yourself, someone else is returned, someone who might stop him."

"Malgannis," Cora said.

"Yes," Lexen said with a nod. "Malgannis." He paused for a moment, as if wondering if he should say more. "Unfortunately for you, Malgannis is not living up to his promise."

As Cora heard loud footsteps and voices calling out, Lexen glanced over his shoulder. "I must go." He took a few swift steps to the window and the material of the curtain billowed around him, hiding his body. When the fabric stopped shifting, he was gone.

✦

Cora was in darkness, watching as the door to her bedchamber – her new one – opened a crack, revealing a vertical slit of light. She saw a silhouetted figure, moving slowly, silently. A hand pushed the door open wider. She heard breathing.

In the wider pool of light, she recognized Silvia's careworn face.

"Silvia," Cora said aloud. She realized her voice was shaking. "Tonight is not the night to creep into my room."

Silvia pushed the door open all the way, revealing a shuttered lantern in her hand. She was in bedclothes, and pursed her lips as she entered the room, placed her lantern on a high table, and opened more of her lantern's panels to allow light into the room.

Silvia then came and sat on Cora's bedside. "I am sorry, Coraline." It wasn't often Silvia apologized. "I doubted you would be sleeping, not after what happened. Sometimes it helps to talk."

The palace guards had found the assassin's body below the window, but Cora hadn't mentioned anything about the black priest, letting them assume that quick wits, luck, and an iron poker had saved her life. New quarters were found for her, and a guard was outside her door.

Nonetheless, when Silvia came to her room, Cora had been lying on her back, tensed and staring up at the ceiling. She had almost been killed in her sleep, with a dagger thrust into her chest. If she went to her usual bedchamber, she would still see the gouge the blade had made in the bed.

She couldn't stop thinking about how close the assassin had come to succeeding. At the same time, she remembered what the black priest had told her. If she died before her time came, before the end of the sixty days, Malgannis would go back to where he came from.

As Silvia shuffled closer on the bed, she tilted her head, frowning, and then pulled back the bedsheets to reveal Cora's body. She immediately revealed that Cora was fully clothed, with a sharp knife held tightly in her right hand.

"Oh, Cora," Silvia said. "My poor Cora. I wish we found ourselves in better times." She disentangled the knife from Cora's hand to place it gently on the bedside table. But as she took the weapon, and Cora sat up at the same time, she inadvertently brushed against Cora's forearm.

Cora winced, stifling a cry of pain at the same time.

"What is it?" Silvia asked. She looked at Cora's arm, and then made a sound as she remembered. "Oh." She shifted position on the bed, so that there was no chance she would accidentally repeat the same movement. "It hurts?"

Fabric covered Cora's skin, but the green and blue welt had grown until it wrapped completely around her arm, like a constrictive snake. "Not much," she lied. "It's fine."

Silvia met Cora's eyes, her face filled with compassion. "My love, you know you don't have to hide your problems from me."

Cora knew that it was true, and after the eventful night, she felt frightened and alone. Her mark was a constant reminder of her curse. Malgannis had said she should tell Silvia her full story, but she was afraid.

"You fought off an assassin," Silvia said. "Is sharing your problems so hard?"

Cora made her decision, but even so, when she spoke, it was in a soft voice. "In truth, someone saved me... The black priest who gave me my mark."

"Truly?" Silvia's eyes widened. "He came here, to the palace?"

"He is a black priest. He comes and goes as he pleases."

"Why would he save you?"

"Because, in less than two weeks, my life is his to claim." Cora knew she had to keep going. "There is something I have to tell you... about the bargain I made..."

✦

Malgannis fumed.

He was outside Adin, across the river from the city's wall of gray stone. It was early, and the rising sun cast his broad shadow in front of him. From his present position, the crenelated battlements looked like a long row of teeth. His plan was to travel around the city's perimeter and locate any sections in need of upgrade or repair, vulnerable to an attacking force.

But all he could think about was the assassination attempt from the previous night.

He walked with an angry stride, finding it hard to focus on what he was doing. The next tower he scanned was in fair condition. The wall between it and the next tower was fine. He saw a few soldiers pacing the top of the battlements, holding bows or tall spears, but one day soon, a far greater number of defenders would wait atop those very walls and prepare to fight for their homes and families.

Malgannis thoughts were as turbulent as the Sylvan River flowing by his side. Baelock Fain had tried to kill Cora. What if the black priest hadn't come to save her? This enemy was vicious; if anyone knew that, it was Malgannis. At the border forts, when Malgannis had made a surprise attack with new allies, Baelock made a shock move that was even bolder. While Malgannis was busy with defenses and supplies, Baelock attempted to assassinate the queen. Malgannis could do better. He had to do better.

Even as he inspected the city's fortifications, he knew that his problem didn't lie with the stoutness of the walls. He wasn't going to have enough men to properly defend its length. The new recruits were even younger than those who had died at the border.

He continued his tour anyway. As he walked, he thought about himself, his origins, and the skills he could bring to bear. His father had raised him with a sword in his hand and a book by his bedside. The books were always about the same topics: ancient military conflicts and the tides of history. That was why, when they offered him the kingship of Aranor, he had turned it down. He knew too much about fighting, and not enough about governing.

Well, it was part of the reason. If he was to be honest with himself, he allowed his son to take the role instead because Baelock Fain had gone into hiding after the war and someone had to track him down.

As was often the case when he thought about his pursuit of Baelock Fain, unpleasant thoughts came to the surface... thoughts he shied away from.

He returned to the younger version of himself, to nights reading by candlelight and firelight, straining his eyes and educating his mind. One of the books he remembered was about the ancient civilization of Hai-Kor, before it fell and in a later age became the much smaller nation of Kor. The empire of Hai-Kor once dominated both the east and the west. Their armies were feared throughout the land. And the core of their army was the Fire Clan.

During his war against Vailand, Malgannis had formed his own version of the Fire Clan. He had built a distinct, elite unit he had named the Iron Fist, made up of the strongest, most skilled warriors picked from across his army of allied nations. The Vailanders came to fear Malgannis Vandryden and the Iron Fist. It was around then that Malgannis had taken to wearing black gauntlets. He had consciously grown his legend.

Malgannis stopped walking and gazed at the city as he pondered. His thoughts were dark, but also fierce.

He cast his mind back to when he first realized that he had returned to life. He had been eager to throw off the shackles of his fame and reputation, to start again with a new name. Since then, nothing he had tried had gone to plan.

Perhaps it was time to bring back some more of the man who had lived and died decades ago. He didn't have to finish up in darkness again, not this time, and not in this life. As he considered, he had an idea about where he could start.

What if he made a new Iron Fist? Something faster, because what he required was speed. He needed a special force, as nimble as it was strong, something to anchor his army in battle, but also to harass the enemy as they rampaged through Aranor's north.

He told himself that he could do this. There was a way he could embrace parts of what he had done and who he had been.

If he wanted to defeat his enemy, he was going to have to.

Chapter 39

THE PARADE GROUND beside the soldier's barracks was probably the safest place in Adin. Cora sat in the gallery, on a long wooden bench outside the waist-high fence. It was a hot day, and without shade, she found herself sweating, particularly in her long-sleeved dress. The strong sun meant she was squinting, and she was already tired enough to have bags under her eyes. She still wasn't sleeping well; the mark on her arm continued to grow, and there was no news about Erik. For some reason Malgannis thought that attending today would be good for her.

She watched him now, focusing on the tall and aging general with the shoulder-length hair. Malgannis was taking quick strides on the yellow sand as he moved from one place to another. Several hundred soldiers milled about. Malgannis had assembled them at one end of the parade ground, while at the other, ten separate warriors stood and waited.

Cora appraised the ten warriors, who were evenly spaced as they watched the proceedings. She knew that Malgannis had personally selected the nine men and one woman. They were all huge, even the woman, at least a head taller than the average soldier, with the muscular frames that came from a lifetime of training and hard work. Their faces were hard and deadly serious. They wore leather armor, to reveal only a few patches of skin, and held wooden practice swords, polished clubs, or bows and arrows.

Between the ten warriors and the mass of regular soldiers, four colored flags flew from poles stuck into the sand. Each pole was about a long stone's throw from the other, and stood beside a big metal basket. Cora was curious about both flags and the contents of the baskets, but she tore her gaze away when Malgannis finished forming up the soldiers into orderly ranks and files.

He walked until he was standing in front of the mass of soldiers. He opened his voice to bellow; he could make himself heard when he wanted.

"I am forming a band, a special force of the best fighters. Not good fighters. Not fair swordsmen. Not decent shots with a bow. The best. That is why there are so many of you," he turned, "and just ten of them." He nodded toward the ten warriors. "They are here to test you."

Cora again glanced at the nine men and one woman. She wondered about the bravery it must take to take on one of those huge fighters. And the confidence to have any expectation of victory.

"There are some others here too, in case they are needed." Malgannis indicated the nearby buildings on the other side of the fence. For the first time Cora saw half a dozen men and women in white robes, watching the proceedings like her. Each of them carried a satchel that was no doubt filled with the tools of his or her trade: linen bandages, needle and thread, and for the most dire situations, milk of the poppy.

Cora found herself leaning forward.

"Today will be the hardest day of your life," Malgannis continued, pacing in front of the group. "You are here to prove yourself to your queen." Heads turned as soldiers looked toward Cora. "No man likes to be embarrassed in front of a woman." He gave a grim smile. "Especially when that woman is the sovereign of your homeland. Know this. She is watching." He waited to let his words sink in. "You are also here to prove yourself to your comrades, and to me." He stopped his pacing. "But most importantly, you are here to prove something to yourself."

Cora realized that she no longer felt tired, or uncomfortably hot, or plagued by the mark on her arm. If her countrymen could do what they were doing, she could be here to give them her support.

"Today, you are putting your lives on the line," Malgannis said. "But the hundred who make it, who prove themselves the best among you, will be paid ten times the rate of a common soldier. More importantly, you will know that when times are difficult on the battlefield, it is you who will turn back the tide of the enemy. And tomorrow, when I go to the north, to fight back against the horrors taking place up there, it is you who will be going with me."

With a start, Cora realized what she had just heard. Malgannis wasn't going to stand by any longer. He was planning to locate the enemy and fight back.

"Long ago, Aranor had the Iron Fist, who fought like lions against the Vailanders. What we need now is more than an Iron Fist. We need something fast as well as strong. The best hundred among you will become the Iron Spear!"

A gruff roar came from the assembled soldiers in response to Malgannis's words.

"Now here is what you will do," he instructed. "Archers: move to the red flag. Swords to the blue flag. Maces, axes, and hammers to the gold flag. Spears and javelins to the green flag." As the soldiers began to break apart, he continued to call out. "In the baskets you will find bows and rounded arrows—the arrowheads are blunted, but that doesn't mean they won't hurt. You will find wooden practice swords. The blades aren't steel, but the wood still has an edge. You will find clubs and hammers and the like. The spears are in that basket by the green flag."

The soldiers were all different in the way they responded. Some were hesitant and waited to see what their companions were doing. A few looked anxious. There were many, however, who wore fierce expressions as they decisively went to a flag, searched a bucket, grabbed a weapon, and hefted it while waiting for the next instruction.

As the soldiers divided into four crowds, Malgannis watched with legs apart. "You will have already realized that you won't be fighting like you do in the army. With numbers, it makes sense to use the same weapons and train in the same way. In the army, it is all about being together, as one. But today, and for the selected members of the Iron Spear, you will be treated as special. You each may have your own way of fighting, with your own weapon of choice. Today I want you at your best."

He waited impatiently until all of the soldiers had stopped moving. He then moved to a place where he could watch the ten elite warriors as well as the soldiers he had divided according to their chosen weapon. A wide space now separated all of the different groups.

He focused on the men near the red flag, who stood with bows in their hands and quivers of practice arrows on their shoulders. "Archers, select one among you." He then nodded toward the ten warriors. "Veterans," he ordered. "Choose your challenger."

Cora watched the elite warriors close in to confer. Then, one warrior stepped forward while the rest formed back into their evenly spaced line. The veteran they had picked was the huge woman, bigger even than Malgannis, who gripped a tall shield in one hand and held the hilt of a wooden practice sword in another. She had close-cropped hair, a square jaw, and her eyes were dark and fiery.

Meanwhile, from the group of archers, a bowman emerged. He was a middle-aged man with a whipcord frame and hawklike face. Keeping his eyes on the huge woman with the sword, he walked away from his fellows until he was well apart from them, close to the middle of the previously empty space.

"Approach," Malgannis called to the woman.

The woman with the sword unhurriedly walked until she was fifty paces from her opponent. She turned, rotating her body until she was presenting her side, with her tall shield blocking a large portion of her body. The point of her sword came up.

"There is only one rule," Malgannis said. "Bring your opponent down. If you are the man – or woman – still standing, you get a black stripe on your cheek. This is a mark to bear with pride. We will continue until there are two hundred of you, and then you will fight each other, rather than the ten veterans here. At the end of the day, when we are done, we will see who among you has the most marks of pride."

Cora watched closely as the lean bowman grabbed an arrow from the quiver on his shoulder. He nocked the end of the shaft to the string, and then kept his attention focused on Malgannis.

"Begin!" Malgannis bellowed.

The instant he heard the shout, the archer lifted his bow. In one swift movement he sighted along the arrow shaft and pulled his string to his ear. He loosed.

The huge woman lifted her shield and the arrow struck against the hard surface with a crack. With her fiery eyes resting on her opponent, she began to walk toward him.

The bowman calmly grabbed another arrow, fitted it, and drew his bowstring. He sighted and the string thrummed. The woman lifted her shield but the archer had tricked her, and the blunted arrowhead struck her upper thigh. The loud smack the arrowhead made when it hit her leg was audible to all. The woman stumbled, and her knee bent halfway.

The bowman was already sighting along another arrow. Cora couldn't believe how quickly he could fit, draw and release.

The huge woman straightened and lifted her shield; this time she managed to block. She lowered her head and charged. The bowman loosed an arrow but she managed to weave, and he missed her altogether.

When she reached him, the outcome was inevitable. The bowman had courage, and managed to strike her across the head with the haft of his bow. But she slammed her wooden sword into the leather armor on his chest, the breath left his body with a whoosh, and a follow up blow across the back brought him down.

The huge woman was left standing on the sand, panting as she lowered her sword. She didn't smile, but she reached out a hand to the groaning bowman on the ground.

Gritting his teeth, the bowman let her pull him back to his feet; Cora was glad that he didn't look badly injured. The huge woman gave him a rough slap on the back and he smiled shakily as he limped away. She then returned to her place among the other nine elite warriors, until she was standing just as she had been before.

"Next!" Malgannis roared.

The next contest was different again, as another bowman faced one of the archers from the elite group. The two opponents ducked and lunged, straightening to bend their bows, loosing blunted arrows at each other, forcing some of the onlookers to dodge when the shots went wide. In the end, the veteran's arrow struck the aspirant in the center of his forehead, and he toppled over like a felled tree.

The white priests came over and crouched beside the prone man. Cora held her breath, only releasing it when they got him back onto his feet and led him away.

"Next!" Malgannis cried.

Another archer from the group of aspirants – a small, wiry man – faced a stocky veteran with limbs like tree branches, holding a mace. This time it was the veteran who struggled; the archer was both swift on his feet and incredibly fast to draw his bow. The stocky man with the mace lunged from place to place but began to tire, unable to catch his opponent. When an arrow hit his throat all he could do was clutch his neck and crumple. The archer got a black stripe drawn across his face. His companions grinned and clapped him on the back. The white priests dragged the gasping veteran away.

Cora watched archer after archer, seeing some get black stripes, but many more hit the ground. Malgannis then moved onto the swordsmen.

The battles were never tedious. Cora sometimes didn't know who she wanted to win, even as she admired them all for their courage and skill. It was difficult to watch at times, but she no desire to leave, and it also made her think.

She remembered the assassin and his long, sharp dagger. She again felt that sensation of smothering, and her sheer terror when she had woken and there he was, looming over her.

Cora might not have the strength of these warriors, but she didn't plan on being defenseless like that again.

"Next!" Malgannis cried.

Chapter 40

THE NIGHT WAS QUIET and misty, with trails of white vapor between the trees. The warmer weather brought the scent of moss and pine needles rising from the ground, but at this time, a few hours before dawn, there was still enough cold to hold men in a deep slumber.

The sentry stamped his feet in an attempt to banish the numb sensation in his toes. He blew on his hands and paced, back and forth, along the length of the perimeter he had been designated to watch. His black and crimson uniform was too thin for this particular watch.

A nightjar called. A few moments passed, and then a corresponding trill came from a different section of the forest. The sentry stopped his pacing.

He stood completely still, head cocked as he stared into the trees. He turned to glance back toward the military camp, looking past the thin screen of trees, through the fence of spiked poles, toward the milling horses and the collection of tents behind them. Thoughts visibly crossed his face.

Another nightjar call made the sentry's head snap forward once more. The sentry took two steps backward.

Then another swift sound was over in seconds, a drawn-out hiss that cut through the stillness of the night. A corresponding slapping sound caused the hiss to suddenly stop.

The sentry's body jerked. He wrapped his hands around the arrow shaft sprouting from his neck. As he gurgled, he tried to call out, but the gush of red liquid prevented him. Almost silently, he sank to his knees and toppled to the side.

Malgannis sat with his back against a tree, peeking around the wide trunk. Like his men, he had blackened his face with soot. His only armor was a leather breastplate; the rest of his body was clad in soft clothing to keep his movements quiet.

He had identified this gap in the enemy's defenses, where the removal of this one sentry exposed the camp to a surprise attack. He now focused on the fence of spikes and the horses behind it and watched as black shadows raced from the trees to head toward the fence. Reaching their target, Malgannis's men worked together, pushing and pulling, until they had opened a wide gap between the poles.

Malgannis heard a horse blow, stamping its hooves as it gave a soft snort. The enemy had put horses on the edge of their camp so they would stir and alert the camp to trouble. The idea was sound, but a large group of animals could be both a blessing and a curse.

As Malgannis continued to watch, a wiry older man in black clothing hurried up to the gap in the fence. One benefit of having such a special group was that it attracted those with unique skills. The wiry man gave a quick glance around and then entered.

The wiry man, a horse expert from Vestria, reached the hobbled horses. He laid a soothing hand on the nearest horse and although Malgannis held his breath, whatever the horse expert was murmuring was working, and the creatures didn't whinny. The horse expert began to take off the hobbles, removing them one at a time, swiftly working his way through the group.

A figure appeared between two trees, approaching from the direction of the camp. He reached the latrines, just a stone's throw from where the horse expert was working.

As the newcomer fumbled at his trousers, an arrow sped out from somewhere near Malgannis. Two arrows followed right behind, peppering the man's body. He gave a low cry and clutched his torso as he fell forward.

Malgannis watched the camp. He began to count his breaths. One. Two. Three.

He decided that the cry hadn't been heard.

"You all right?" a loud voice called. "You fall or something?"

Malgannis suppressed a curse. He cupped his hands around his lips and the loud call of a nightjar came from his mouth.

It was time.

Aside from the quieter clothing and minimal use of metal, there was no way to completely muffle the rush of men pouring in from the forest. Malgannis put his head down and ran. He leaped over a ditch that lay between the trees and the fence of spikes. A few men in front of him worked to widen the existing gap in the fence and Malgannis jumped through.

Malgannis and half a dozen others reached the horses. More men were still coming in behind. The time for silence was over.

"Iron Spear!" Malgannis roared.

"Iron Spear!" his men shouted back.

The startled horses whinnied. Malgannis and the others around him began to slap at the animals' flanks. Around them horses neighed, adding to the commotion. When one of the horses at the front reared, startled by all the noise, the rest began to bolt. With the Iron Spear along one side of their group, the horses raced off in the opposite direction—through the camp.

"Iron Spear!" Malgannis cried. "Attack!"

Malgannis's men gave a series of answering cries and came right after the horses to wreak havoc in the camp. Pathways between the rows of tents now made it easy to disperse throughout the area. A few campfires still crackled at the junctions, enabling archers to light up their flaming arrows. Soon flames streaked through the sky like comets, bringing fire and destruction to place after place. Some of Malgannis's archers simply stood by a campfire, lit up an arrow, loosed it at a tent, and repeated.

The sentries from the perimeter began to appear, seeking out the source of the commotion. But they weren't a cohesive force, and when they came in ones and twos they discovered scores of skilled warriors with soot-covered skin, ready to take them down with a variety of weapons. More of the enemy came running out of the tents, wild-eyed and fearful, to meet the same fate.

Malgannis faced up to a burly Vailander with an axe, blocking twice before countering with a thrust that dispatched his opponent. He turned and immediately fought a scar-faced swordsman with the pale skin of a northerner. He found his opening and slashed his enemy across the torso.

More of the enemy appeared; now they were emerging from their tents in numbers. Unlike the raids Malgannis had conducted at the border, this was the main camp, and it was immense. A larger force would never have got in, but now it was time to go before they were swallowed by bigger numbers.

"Iron Spear!" Malgannis called. He was using the name intentionally; he wanted the enemy to know who they were, and importantly, to fear them. "Pull back!"

All around him, the men with soot-covered faces and limbs took up the call. "Pull back!"

In a brief lull, even as some fighters grappled and others ran, Malgannis took in the scene. Most of his men were leaving. But not all.

He spied a huge bearded warrior with a war hammer. With his shaggy hair the warrior might be from Rumandy but he could also have been from Vestria or Aranor's north. Despite all his companions calling out the retreat, his eyes were wild as he smashed his heavy weapon into enemy after enemy.

"Keep fighting!" the warrior with the hammer called to his companions. After bringing an opponent down, he growled at one of his companions nearby. "Stay and fight! Kill them all!"

Malgannis burst into a sprint to get to the shaggy-haired warrior. "Soldier," he barked. "Soldier!"

The warrior brought up his hammer but then lowered it, the haze in his eyes clearing for a moment when he saw who it was.

Malgannis didn't initially speak, but simply held the warrior's gaze. Then, after a moment, he spoke firmly, "It's time to pull back."

The warrior was big enough to crush Malgannis's skull with a casual swipe of his hammer. And yet, as Malgannis stared into his face, he reluctantly nodded.

"Yes, General," he said.

Malgannis heard a series of shouts. He looked past the man in front of him and saw a surging tide of enemies rushing toward him. He grabbed the warrior's arm and got them both moving, running back the way they had come.

As he jumped through the gap in the fence and then leaped over the ditch, he heard the enemy slow when they hit the fence. He sprinted hard until the cries of pursuit fell quiet and at last the comforting shadows of the forest swallowed him up.

Malgannis shifted into a ground-eating lope, and his Iron Spear raced along with him, interspersed among the trees, almost as silent as the mist that clung to the ground and shifted around their bodies. He felt an intense surge of satisfaction. It was close, but he had pulled them back just in time. The attack had been a success. The enemy would fear them.

Already he was planning. He worked out his next moves as he ran, with his men around him, flushed from exertion but also victory. He had an idea for a different kind of attack—an ambush along a constrictive route between two steep cliffs, where the enemy would have to travel if they wanted to get to Adin.

He would spend the following day digging. This wasn't going to be just any ambush, he would use spikes and ditches. His archers would force the enemy to run from his ambush and then, when the cliffs were above them...

He was determined to use every opportunity, employ every trick, and to keep fighting, even as Baelock Fain led his army toward the capital. He would never forget what he had seen so far of Aranor's north.

His men were proud and knew their strength. At every battle, in every raid, there were those of his men who wanted to fight to the end, even if it meant their own lives. Malgannis job was to keep them fighting in the way that counted the most.

The enemy camp was now distant behind them. Malgannis opened his mouth to call out. "For Aranor!" he shouted.

And all around him, as they ran, the Iron Spear took up the call.

"For Aranor!"

Chapter 41

ERIK WAITED OUTSIDE Fort August. The tall palisade of vertical black planks stretched on and on, farther than he could see in both directions, as it enclosed the several structures inside. He was tense as he watched the closed gate, which was too sturdy for anything but a battering ram.

It was a clear, starry night. From multiple places in the fort, smoke rose up in steady plumes that grew thicker as time passed. Panicked voices shouted. The moon changed color from yellow to red. Erik saw his first tall flames, leaping and dancing from somewhere inside the palisade. He heard a great crashing sound. With hundreds of Moranian soldiers in the garrison, the shouts grew louder and more frequent. Some voices called for buckets of water, others cried for help. When the fire was done, Erik doubted if there would still be a fort left standing.

"Be ready," Erik said.

He turned to look at the sixty strong men he had brought from Aranor, but his gaze also took in the far greater number of freedom fighters from Vestria. This was their land, their town, and they were taking it back.

"Soon they'll have no choice," Erik said. "They'll have to flee. When that gate opens, be prepared to knock them down and bind them."

He glanced at Thorne, who gave him an enigmatic look as she held a thick wooden club. "Don't worry," she said. "We'll be ready."

Thorne had only just finished speaking when Erik heard the clatter of wood against wood. A groaning and clanking came from the gate.

"Hurry! Open the gate!" someone shouted from the other side.

A moment later, the gate began to move, revealing the chaos inside the fort as it opened outward. Flames cast garish shadows as men tried to push past each other to get out of the burning fort. The gate opened wider and Erik opened his mouth.

But Thorne was first. "Now!" she cried.

As the fort's occupants poured out, Thorne sent her club straight into a man's head. He fell with a sickening thud. Meanwhile her compatriots used their own weapons to tear into their enemies. Soon the people inside the fort inside no longer tried to get out. But their eyes were wild, and all of them were coughing. Fire and billowing smoke rolled their way. The heat must have been unbearable.

Thorne hurried past the bodies to go up to the gate, and grunted as she tried to push it closed. A handful of other fighters went up to help her.

Erik watched it all in shock. He hurried up to Thorne and grabbed her shoulder. "What are you doing? What's happening?"

She shook off his hand. "You weren't there when they took the town."

Erik grabbed the gate, trying to keep it open. "You can't do this!"

"Hold him," Thorne ordered.

A burly Vestrian took Erik by the arms and another man helped to hold him back. With a loud crash, Thorne and the others shoved the gate closed.

"Captain? Erik?" Norris's voice cut through all the shouting and clatter.

"Let us out! Please!"

Pleading voices came from the direction of the gate. Erik heard another fiery crash as timbers fell. The crackle of flames tore through the fort. Erik's throat was burning from all the smoke.

The two men holding Erik released him, but Thorne's firm stare made it clear what would happen if he tried again to stop her. Erik turned toward Norris and gave her a slight wave of his hand to indicate that he was fine.

And yet he knew he wasn't. He and his men had thrown oil into the fort. They had tossed torches over the palisade and launched fire arrows.

He walked over to Thorne, whose lips were pressed tightly together. "I didn't sign up for this."

"You—" she broke off and coughed. Her mouth twisted; she was tasting the same smoky air that he was. "You did."

"If you still want my men, you will open that gate."

"Choose your battles. This isn't one you are going to win."

With a shake of his head, Erik left her and returned to Norris's side. He glanced at Norris. His lieutenant was red-eyed and a sheen of sweat coated her face.

"This is their land," Norris said quietly. "Remember what you said, about Adin falling like Helmsford? Ask yourself how you would feel."

Eventually, Erik couldn't hear anything from the other side of the gate. He and his men stood apart from Thorne's group, and none of them spoke or looked at each other as they watched. Crash after crash came from the fort. The flames had finally conquered it.

Thorne and her countrymen stood shoulder to shoulder as if witnessing a funeral rite. Finally, Thorne turned away, squeezing the arm of one of her companions before she headed over to Erik. She stood directly in front of him, legs apart, and cleared her throat.

"Tomorrow we head to Ballina, to free the Red King. We need you, it is true." Before Erik could reply, she held up a hand. "But you are in Vestria, Erik. Don't forget that you also need us."

✦

It wasn't until Erik reached Ballina that he realized the size of the task ahead of him.

Vestria's capital wasn't as big as Adin, but it was still a sizable city. The seat of the Red King crowned a hill with a wide paved road climbing up to meet it. A circle of craggy peaks behind the city loomed tall and forbidding in the low light of a clouded afternoon. The black walls were tall. Four immense corner towers with conical roofs thrust their points into the sky. Sturdy gates looked like they must have been built by giants.

Although Thorne had described Ballina to Erik, he had never visited himself, and was daunted by its scale. Half of the city's population lived in the outer town, a sprawling collection of huts and shacks that spilled down from the walls to cover the rest of the surrounding hill. And yet the amount of space between the walls was still immense. Thorne had spoken about broad avenues and city squares, a huge theatre and no fewer than five temples. The Red King's palace wasn't as lofty as the palace in Adin, but it was a crimson structure of three stories in a horseshoe shape, with two wings enclosing Ballina's most famed landmark: Victory Square, where over the years a balcony enabled the king or queen to give speeches to the city's populace.

Erik was dressed in farm clothes as he walked alongside a wagon, holding the halter of a mule. He felt naked; he and his men didn't have any of their swords or armor. Waygather's local farmers had helped them with their disguises. Meanwhile, their weapons were hidden under dozens of sacks of potatoes.

As Erik approached the gates, he looked up to scan the two gate towers on either side, and saw the black and crimson flag of Morania flying proudly from the top of each tower. Meanwhile, the road he was following, and the crowd inching forward, was being funneled toward the guards who questioned everyone entering.

Events had moved swiftly since Waygather. Erik and Thorne both knew that they had to get ahead of any tales about the fire at Fort August. The smell of smoke had still been in the air when they left the town behind.

"Stop staring," Norris whispered from the other side of the mule.

Erik turned his head to see Norris glancing meaningfully at him, and realized he had been showing too much interest in the Moranian soldiers.

"Sorry," he mouthed.

Erik saw that Thorne was about to be stopped, just ahead. Two soldiers headed over to her, but watching from behind, Erik couldn't see much more. He saw the taller of the Moranians, a soldier with a squashed nose, bark at her in a harsh voice. She scowled and growled something in a defiant tone. The tall soldier's eyes widened.

Then the Moranian burst into laughter. Thorne grinned back at him. He waved her through.

Now it was Erik's turn. He tried to remind himself that he was a farmer, doing something mundane, and simply bringing his goods into the city. The mule took some dragging before its lumbering footsteps resumed, and then veered off into the wrong direction, jostling another cart before settling. Norris called an apology to the merchant they had struck.

"She said you're with her," the approaching soldier said, nodding toward where Thorne was leading her cart through the city gates. His nose looked like it had been broken a dozen times. "By the gods, she's got a mouth on her." He shook his head. "I hope for your sake you're not related."

"His wife," Norris said with a grin.

Erik glared at her as the Moranian laughed.

"Well, let's just say I don't envy you," the broken-nosed soldier said. He nodded toward the cart of potatoes. "Now, where is it?"

As the Moranian's smile fell, he was suddenly serious. Erik felt a chill. "What?"

He became irritated. "You know what I mean."

"Erik..." Norris tried to get his attention, nodding toward part of the cart, closer to Erik's position.

"Oh." Erik turned and grabbed a small sack. "This?"

The broken-nosed soldier reached out to take Erik by the shoulder. He squeezed hard enough to hurt. "You know something? I think I prefer your wife. Get in there. Next time, try to be a little more subtle."

Erik handed the Moranian the sack. The man swiftly peered in, before nodding that they could continue.

But then the Moranian noticed something. He cocked his head, staring past Erik's shoulder. "What's that?"

Erik turned and saw that when the cart had jostled the merchant's wagon, the load must have shifted, altering the arrangement of sacks. He could now see the glint of a buckle and the leathery length of a scabbard.

Erik knew he had to think fast.

"Let me show you," Erik said. Heading over to the cart, he waved at the tall, broken-nosed Moranian to come with him. Now suspicious, the tall soldier walked past the mule and over to the sacks of potatoes. Erik reached down, fumbling between the sacks until he felt the hilt of a blade. "It's gold," he whispered.

Erik motioned the guard closer still, and as the Moranian's head bent down, Erik drew the sword from its scabbard. He pulled swiftly, flashed the steel, and thrust the blade straight into the guard's torso.

Pushing hard, Erik also wrapped his arms around the Moranian to bring him in closer. Then, Erik sank to a crouch, bringing the broken-nosed soldier down to the ground with him. Glancing around, Erik pulled off his cloak and laid it over the body, which was still hidden by the cart.

"Help me," he hissed at Norris.

Together they quickly picked up the cloak-covered body to place it in the cart. Erik then began to heft the sacks, rearranging them again until eventually he stopped to regard his handiwork. The body was mostly covered.

"Come on," Erik said.

With a strong jerk, he got the mule moving. Risking a look back, he saw that the other fighters disguised in farmer's clothes were stunned as they watched him. They all had their own carts to get into the city.

Erik scanned the area, in front of him as well as behind. He saw more soldiers, searching and inspecting, asking questions. None of them had noticed their missing companion. The cart rolled forward.

And then Erik was in the city.

He almost froze when he heard a loud challenging voice, but glanced back to see that a different soldier was addressing the merchant behind him.

"Keep moving," Norris muttered.

"I know," Erik replied.

Erik's back itched, and his tension didn't ease until he and Norris had left the gates behind and were in the city proper. And then Erik knew he had a new challenge, one he would need Thorne's help with. He saw her up ahead, giving him a questioning look, wondering if there had been trouble.

Norris gave a low whistle. "That was too close."

Erik glanced at the cart. “What are we going to do now?” he asked Norris. “Any ideas?”

Norris thought for a moment. “Thorne made herself clear,” she said. “This is her land. She wants to see bodies. Let’s go and tell her we’ve got another one for her.” She gave a crooked smile. “She’ll be pleased.”

Erik have a short laugh. “Sure she will. Now let’s see. I’m the captain. You’re the lieutenant. You can be the one to tell her.”

Chapter 42

ADIN LAY AHEAD, nestled like a vision among the curling ribbon of the Sylvan River. Malgannis's men cheered. After all they had seen, the normality ahead of them was heartwarming. Smoke snaked from chimneys, wagons crossed the drawbridge, and blue and gold flags flew proudly from the towers at the palace.

Malgannis smiled along with them. The Iron Spear had done well, and he was returning to the city not just for provisions, but to reward his warriors with some rest and respite. But when he glanced back at his group, his smile fell as he realized something. He had recruited a hundred skilled fighters. A third of that number was gone. The huge woman with fiery eyes, who had been among the first to face an opponent on the sands of the parade ground, was no longer with them. Nor was the small, wiry archer who could loose arrows even as he darted from place to place, leaping around like an acrobat.

Yet for each fallen fighter, Malgannis's Iron Spear had taken scores of the enemy. Malgannis had made Baelock cautious as he marched toward Adin, for any narrow place might mean an ambush. Most importantly, the enemy was no longer willfully attacking towns and villages—for lurking in wait, ready to strike, might be the Iron Spear.

Malgannis thought about the coming days as he led his band down the King's Road toward the drawbridge and the city's main gates. He would replenish the Iron Spear's numbers from the army. After some training together, he would lead his fighters back out again. He worked through who might help him, running names and faces over in his mind. There were those among his existing number who made excellent leaders. Others had the skill and patience to be teachers. He needed more archers and perhaps even a few engineers...

As Malgannis crossed the drawbridge he passed through the towers where the tall walls of gray stone opened up at the city gates. He saw people waiting just inside the city: women with children and older parents, all anxiously searching the faces of the fighters behind him. Malgannis had already issued the necessary instructions, and as the Iron Spear began to disperse, the fighters waved to each other and headed off to stay with their families, lodge at the barracks, or get an ale at one of Adin's taverns.

Soon Malgannis was alone, walking along Adin's main avenue. He scratched at the stubble on his chin and slowed, before stopping altogether. The market ahead of him was busy, with city folk crowding the stalls and stopping to share gossip. No one gave him any attention. He remembered coming this way before, and who he had been with.

"Malgannis."

Hearing his name – his real name – Malgannis turned around, to see a familiar figure standing directly behind him. Cora wore her gray cloak with the hood covering her head. Her brown eyes were hopeful as she searched his face, although he wasn't sure what it was she was hoping for.

Malgannis's eyebrows slowly came together. "Someone tried to kill you, and you're out in the city alone?" He made a show of searching for guards; clearly she had none. "You have a recognizable face, girl."

As he inspected Cora, he wondered that people weren't stopping and staring at her. With her bright eyes, high cheekbones, and dark, shining hair, she was striking, even if she hadn't been the queen.

"Girl?" Cora demanded.

Suppressing a curse, Malgannis realized what he had just said.

✦

Cora waited for Malgannis to answer her as they stood in the streets. He looked tired, like he needed a good meal and a soft bed in Adin Palace, not a night at a tavern spent over meat and grease and too much ale.

"Girl?" Cora repeated.

"Sorry," Malgannis muttered. "I'm just surprised to see you, that's all."

"You would rather I hadn't come?"

He considered for a moment. "Yes," he said. "You should be safely at the palace."

She hadn't wanted to wait to see him, intentionally meeting him before he was caught up again with his men. "Well, I am here," she said, "so we may as well walk to the palace together."

"I was going to find an inn," he interrupted.

Before Malgannis knew what was happening, Cora had linked her arm with his. He had no choice but to walk at her side as she turned him and they headed together toward the market. She saw the crowd thinning up ahead, toward where they would travel along the main avenue toward the palace. "No inns, Grandfather."

His bemused frown made her smile. "Grandfather?"

She glanced at him as they strolled. "I have been thinking about it. We know you're my great-grandfather, but that's too wordy, so we need something else. There is only one man I ever called Father. So there you have it. Grandfather seems best."

"I prefer my name."

"And yet your name is a famous one. Out here in the city, Grandfather it shall be."

Cora saw two young men walking in the opposite direction. Both were handsome and around her age, dressed in doublets and leggings, perhaps the sons of merchants or craftsmen. The eyes of one of the young men traveled to her, and then he looked shocked and stopped in his tracks. He squeezed his companion's arm, and he also came to a sudden halt.

Malgannis hadn't noticed them, but then after seeing her, they both looked at him. When he finally glanced their way and they saw his face, they exchanged looks and hurried away.

"News travels fast," Cora said, picking up the conversation when they were alone. "You have done a lot for morale. You and your Iron Spear."

"It still might not be enough."

"Malgannis, take credit where you can." With a smile, she corrected herself. "Grandfather, I should say."

As they walked, Cora was trying to appear cheerful, but in truth, she couldn't understand what she was feeling. She kept imagining Malgannis with his men, sharing stories of their exploits, raising their full mugs and slamming them together, toasting fallen comrades and lives saved in narrow escapes. He had always told her who and what he was. He was a fighter. He wanted her to remain safely in the palace, but if she did, she would barely see him.

Watching his face, she chose her words carefully. "I saw how you selected your fighters. Your men are the best."

Malgannis raised a curious eyebrow. "They are."

"You probably don't know this, but when it comes to fighting, they say you are as good as any of them."

Malgannis grunted a laugh. "We both know that's not true."

Cora looked at him again. "And yet that is what they say."

He was clever enough to know she was trying to lead the conversation. "What are you getting at, Cora?"

“I’ve been thinking,” she said. “I want to be able to protect myself. I know you’re busy, but perhaps you could find time to teach me?” She ventured a smile. “I am the queen, after all. I know you have your men to worry about. But perhaps you also have some time for me?”

His frown wasn’t the response she wanted. “Cora... I’m tired.”

“You think I can’t stop a man from killing me? That I’m too weak?”

“I don’t think you’re weak. There are different kinds of strength. The reason it’s not worth the time is just that. Time is the one thing we don’t have enough of.”

Cora disentangled her arm from is. Stopping in front of him, she lifted her chin and met his eyes. “What if I were a man?”

Malgannis spoke in a weary tone. “If you were a man, your father would have taught you to fight from the age of a child, and we wouldn’t be having this conversation. Listen, Cora. I taught my own daughter to fight. It takes years to be any good. I’m sorry your father didn’t do the same for you. We don’t get to choose our fathers. As you said, you’re the queen, which means you have guards at the palace to protect you.”

When Cora next spoke, her voice was soft. “But I’m not asking them. I’m asking you.”

Malgannis’s expression became uncomfortable, like he wanted to be anywhere else. Even as she watched his face, Cora felt a strange clenching sensation deep within her chest. Her end was coming. And the man she had come to depend on was doing everything he could to prove himself to her—everything except remain by her side.

“You are not a fighter, Cora,” he said bluntly. “Not that kind of fighter, anyway. Now leave me be.” He stepped away from her. “I think I’m going to find a tavern after all.”

Cora forced her blank mask onto her face. “I understand. I’ll see you when you have time.” She wondered when she would see him next—or if she would see him at all. “One thing I didn’t tell you... why I came to meet you. There are always rumors. One of them said you were dead. I’m glad it isn’t true.”

She met his gaze and nodded, before she turned and left him where he stood.

✦

Cora stood in the middle of the weapons room in Adin Palace, her focus moving from one object to another. She saw pole arms on one wall – she struggled to remember their names: halberds, bills, glaives, and pikes – and an array of swords on another. A variety of bows hung side by side, from a tiny crossbow to a composite bow as tall as she was. The room smelled of wood, old leather, oil, and iron, and while its walls were busy, the rest was bare, with only a few sparse items of furniture in the corners. More of a museum than anything else, the weapons room had always been a place that interested Patrick and her father. Cora had rarely visited.

Various swords hung up on the wall. She spied one that interested her, a two-handed sword with a long hilt and a slightly curved, single-edged blade. As with the other swords on display, it had no scabbard. Reaching up, she unhooked the weapon, until she was holding the sword by the hilt. She brought the blade to a vertical position. It felt good. She took a few swipes, cutting at the air. Perhaps it was too light? Men on the battlefield wore armor.

With a sigh, she let the tip drop, until the sword was pointing at the ground. What was she doing? Despite everything: the mark on her arm, the pain that kept her awake at night, and her constant worry, part of her still couldn't believe that no matter what she did, she was doomed. She was going to die in little more than a week, and there was nothing she could do about it. Any sword she held would only be a gesture, an attempt to be someone other than who she really was.

"My Queen."

She turned to see Hailsham standing at the doorway with his hands clasped behind his back. Bald, smartly-dressed, and with a perpetual look of concern on his face, he never revealed any judgment, and if he was wondering why Cora was in the weapons room with a sword in her hands, she knew he would never ask.

"My Queen," he repeated. "There is an elderly man from the city asking to see you."

"What does he want?"

"That is the problem," Hailsham said. "He will not say, only that he wants to speak with you in person. I told him that if he wants to meet you, he must reveal his purpose, but he refuses."

Cora frowned. "If he won't say what he wants, then he won't get an audience."

"Of course, Your Majesty. Usually I would not bother you with this, but he has been coming in every day." Hailsham bowed and departed.

As soon as he left, Cora reached up to return the sword to its former place.

"It takes time to learn, but I am willing to teach you."

Cora turned to see Logan watching her as he entered the weapons room. She felt color rise to her cheeks, but he didn't look condescending or surprised. Despite his athletic frame, he didn't convey Malgannis's aura of deadly force, but she remembered her father saying that in his day he had been a fair swordsman.

After hanging up the sword, Cora faced him. "Our enemy may be here in a matter of days. But thank you, Logan. If we somehow survive, I will gladly take you up on your offer."

"Tell me something. Are you prepared to stand up on the walls, even without training?"

"Of course I am."

"Then let me speak with the weapons smiths." He gave the display of swords a quick glance. "We may not have time for you to learn, but a queen should have appropriate arms."

"I would appreciate that." She hesitated, but the time felt right, and she cleared her throat. "Logan... Do you think you would make a good king?"

"King?" He laughed and shook his head. "I have no plans to be king, Coraline. You will easily outlive me." He became serious. "My hope is for a child—"

He was interrupted by the sound of hurried footsteps and they both turned. The sound was that of boot heels on the hard wooden floor, so Cora knew she wasn't hearing the soft tread of Hailsham or one of the other stewards. When she saw Lord Byron's stout figure, clad in a crimson tunic, she grew anxious; his face was always easy to read.

"My Queen, My Lord," he said in a swift greeting. "Hailsham said you were here." He held something up: a scroll with a broken black seal. "We found a boat, drifting on the Sylvan. In fact we couldn't miss it... the vessel came all the way to the city, running on the current to the midst of our battle fleet. The man inside it was dead. He had this with him."

Cora inspected the scroll, but other than the black seal, she could tell nothing about the contents.

"Give it to the queen," Logan said, nodding toward Cora, even as she held out her hand.

Surprising Cora, Byron shook his head and instead held the scroll out to Logan. "I am afraid, Lord Kane, that in the first instance it should probably be you who reads it."

Frowning, but obviously perturbed, Logan took the scroll, and Cora watched as he swiftly began to read. As he digested the scroll's contents, she saw his changing expression. At first his brow creased, then his eyes widened, until his obvious shock grew as he looked horrified.

Logan lowered the scroll, but for a long time he stared into the distance with an unfocused gaze.

"Tell me," Cora said quickly. "What is it?"

Logan handed her the scroll, but spoke without waiting for her to read. "The message is from Guylan Wren, my senior steward. He says an enemy fleet has been sighted and approaches the island of Fastness. Battle is expected. Survival is uncertain."

Cora looked from Logan to Byron and back again. "Could there be a mistake?"

"There is no question," Logan said. "The ships all fly the same flag—red on a black field."

As the realization sank in, Cora thought the implications through. Adin was depending on Aranor's fleet to help with the city's defense. When the enemy came, the battle fleet could move about at will, changing position on the Sylvan River and raining arrows on any force attempting to besiege the city.

Meanwhile, Fastness was one of the most important parts of the kingdom. Much of Aranor's wealth came from the island's silver mines, and the port city of Coron connected a dozen busy trade routes. Fastness was also her husband's home.

Cora turned to Logan. He always kept such cool composure that it was frightening to see him so anxious. "How many ships?"

It was Byron who answered her. "Wren says at least thirty."

She realized she had a choice to make.

Should she send Aranor's battle fleet to Fastness? Or should she abandon Logan's home – and his family – to a terrible fate?

"My Queen," Byron said gravely. "I hope you realize, you cannot send our fleet to their rescue."

Logan stared at Lord Byron. "What? She has to."

"This is the capital city," Byron said firmly. "The seat of the queen. Adin falls, and Aranor falls. The fleet is needed for the city's defense."

"To lose Fastness would deal the realm a mortal blow."

"A grave blow. But not a mortal one."

"Coraline," Logan said, "we must send help. Listen to me. This is not just about my home. If the enemy holds Fastness, they will always be able to threaten us from land and sea. They can blockade our ports and cut off all trade. Graven Callow's army can lay siege to Adin and simply wait." When Cora didn't immediately reply, his tone became desperate. "Please. At least ask Lord Morgan."

"We can't," Cora said. "He is away with the Iron Spear."

She thought about their last encounter. *You are not a fighter, Cora.*

"The decision is mine," she said. "I need some time alone to think."

"But Coraline—" Logan began.

He trailed off as she walked away, heading toward her personal quarters. Another of Malgannis's maxims came to her.

Remember, every decision ultimately lies with you.

She had an impossible choice to make.

Chapter 43

A HOT, FIERY SUN cast its burning rays on a city of black stone and low-set houses. The sun peeked from the ring of sharp mountains before it climbed and gained strength, lighting up the broad streets and winding alleys. Bright daylight soon revealed white sheets of paper stuck to walls in the busier junctions. All of the posters were freshly made.

The message in Ballina was simple: get to Victory Square at dusk. The city's governor, General Bannon, who led the Moranian occupiers, would show the Red King to the people, so that they would know he was alive and well.

Of course, General Bannon planned to do nothing of the sort. Soon soldiers in black and crimson uniforms were racing through the city, tearing down the posters wherever they found them. Raised voices came from the Moranian patrols, calling out to deny the rumors. The Red King was safe and well, they said, but he was not about to leave the dungeon. There would be no gathering in Victory Square. Curfew was being brought forward. After sunset, all residents were to remain in their homes.

General Bannon even went to the palace's most prominent balcony in the afternoon, and when a few people milled in the square, waiting for him to speak, he announced that they were to spread the word, there would be no event taking place at dusk. Additional forces were called to Victory Square, ready to disperse crowds before they could gather.

Some city folk went to the dungeon. "Where is our king?" they shouted. Stones were thrown, and when the guards displayed their weapons, the mob only became angrier. More than a few Vestrians went home to dig out their own real weapons: wood axes, hunting bows, and blades with sharp edges.

General Bannon took another dozen soldiers from his reserves and sent them to the dungeon to support the guards there. All of his men were now deployed; there weren't any reserves left.

The city's governor and chief occupier was in a difficult position. Bannon had kept the elderly king alive as a hostage. But now, how could he leverage his hostage to calm the populace? If he displayed the Red King on the balcony and showed he was as well as could be expected from an old man stuck in a cell, Bannon would be doing the dissidents' bidding and showing his weakness for all to see. He would also be performing the one action that would guarantee large numbers of people congregating outside the palace, which was the last thing he wanted.

On the other hand, if Bannon threatened to kill the Red King, he might tip the city over the edge.

It had taken some organization, a lot of risk, and days of hard work, but Erik, Thorne, Norris, and their growing number of insurrectionists had successfully executed the first stage of their plan. Erik couldn't say it was all his plan, but the core of it was his. Now it was time to see how it all unfolded.

The plan moved onto the second stage.

In late afternoon, with the city on high alert and the mood of expectation rising up through the streets, the liberators had a few select street urchins and market vendors put out a rumor. The Red King wasn't being presented because he had just been rescued. He was, even now, somewhere in the city.

Everyone wanted to know if the Red King was in the house next door, or perhaps across the street. The rumors became more elaborate as the stories gained their own momentum. The Red King was in the cellar below the mason's guild hall. He was buried in a pile of hay, on his way down the road to freedom. The priests were harboring him in one of the temples.

As the sun began to fall toward the horizon, the streets thronged with curious city folk who watched each other's faces with sudden interest. They were all thinking the same thing: any one of them could be an insurrectionist, fighting for their collective freedom. People who would normally keep their heads down left their houses and exchanged gossip with their neighbors. The occupying soldiers tried to send people back into their homes, but they couldn't be everywhere, and their numbers had been thinned by the forces required at the dungeon and Victory Square. Becoming fearful, the Moranians struck out with weapons as they tried to move people on. Some city folk fought back. Others rushed to their aid.

The hot day led to fiery tempers. The city felt like a bundle of dry tinder, ready to combust.

As dusk approached, at all five of Ballina's temples, bells started to peal. The time had come. The plan moved onto the third and final stage.

The one place the citizens weren't congregating was Victory Square. The city's famous landmark and meeting place was instead full of soldiers, keeping any and all Vestrians away from the palace. As the temple bells rang throughout the city, a formation of soldiers waited, fearful and expectant, for the rush of the mob.

But the mob wasn't what came to greet them. This part of Erik's plan meant that most of the occupying soldiers were all in the one place. When the soldiers outside the palace heard the loud sound of marching, filling all of the avenues that emptied out onto Victory Square, the figures that appeared in a constant stream weren't civilians. It wasn't a crowd come to see the Red King.

It was a well-trained force, with sixty veterans from Aranor and hundreds of Vestrian soldiers who had gone into hiding after defeat at the ruins of Leventhal. They were equipped for battle, clad in armor and wielding sharp steel swords.

The Moranians were expecting a rabble, not a determined enemy. If General Bannon had planned for what was actually coming, he might have pulled even more soldiers from the city's towers and walls, and perhaps the liberation would have resulted in failure.

But when they saw Erik and Thorne's strong force enter the square, the occupiers turned and fled. Moranian soldiers streamed out of the city. The palace fell. Bannon found himself in chains.

By nightfall, Ballina was liberated.

Erik was pleased. His plan had worked. And yet his thoughts were already turning to his next steps. Remembering Waygather, he realized that if he wanted things done his way, he had to lead.

He didn't stay to see Willem the Red King – the real one, who had never left the dungeon – presented to his people.

Instead Erik took his men, along with some volunteers from Vestria, and left Vestria altogether. He was surprised when Thorne said she wanted to come, but she knew how high the stakes were, and what they needed to do if they didn't want the Moranians to return to her homeland with twice the numbers.

Erik knew he had to maintain the initiative. He had to attack. He had to do whatever he could to help the queen... Coraline... the woman he thought about far too much, whose face was never far from his mind.

After the liberation of Ballina, his destination was Harven, the capital of occupied Rumandy.

✦

Just two days had passed, and yet Vestria felt like another world.

Perhaps it was the change in landscape. Rather than hills and lakes, grassy plains and craggy mountains, Erik's vision was instead filled with dark swamp and skeletal trees. Everything was wet, from the dull grass to the submerged logs. Everything was dragging, from the sucking pools of mud that never liked to relinquish a foot, to the vines snaking from the branches overhead. Even the sky was oppressive, constantly threatening a storm, with the sun gone as if it never existed.

"I've never been to the Gray Marshes," Norris said as she trudged along beside Erik. "Never wanted to, if I'm honest."

Even as Norris spoke, it began to rain, in a misty drizzle that Erik knew wouldn't stop for hours.

"I wonder why?" Thorne asked from the other side of Norris. She indicated the landscape. "It's got its own charm."

"I suppose it does, if you look at it in a certain way," Norris said thoughtfully. Water trickled down her face while she spoke and her blonde hair clung in tendrils to her forehead. "How about you, Erik? Been here before?"

Erik stared up at the sky. At least the grim crossing meant that he had no trouble getting his group moving quickly. None of them wanted to spend any longer in the marshes than necessary.

"I've been here," Erik said. He wiped water from his face as he walked straight through a pool of mud. His feet were already wet; there was no use going around it. "They say that after Malgannis defeated the Vailanders, they flooded the plain on purpose so it could never be a battlefield again."

"Oh?" Thorne's eyebrows went up. "I didn't know that."

"Well, it's only what they say," Norris said. "It's not like we can ask Ironclaw himself." She glanced over at Erik and noticed something in his expression. "You all right, Captain?"

"Fine," said Erik.

"What about the dead?" Thorne asked.

"They took them away." Erik rested his gaze on a nearby hill, where a rusted breastplate sheltered some old bones from the rain. "Most of them, that is. Except for the Vailanders."

Norris squinted to take in the scene farther up ahead. "By the gods," she said. "Is that what I think..." she trailed off.

Past the next section of swamp, bones lay strewn across the hills as if scattered in the wind. Erik saw spines, rib cages, and thick leg bones. Just a stone's throw away, a sword lay half buried, with only the hilt and part of the browned blade still visible. When Erik's foot brushed against something, he glanced down and a broken skull rolled over to reveal a pair of empty eye sockets. An upturned helmet lay submerged in a black pool nearby. A spear was entangled in the vines of a distant tree.

"Whose idea was it to come this way?" Thorne asked.

"It's the quickest route by far," said Erik, even as he picked up his pace. He looked behind him, at the hundred or so men and women he had with him. His soldiers from Aranor had come a long way and looked tired, but he also knew how determined they were. He realized that the rain would soon come to an end. A golden circle peeked from the clouds as they pulled apart. "Let's just get through this part."

He focused on where to place his feet, and tried not to look too hard at the carnage left behind after a vicious battle. A wide bog forced him to go around it, but then as the terrain climbed, he and his companions left the bones and rusted metal behind.

When Erik finally led his group to the crest of the hill, he brought them to a halt. He focused on a wide ribbon of road, distant but reachable before the day's end.

"That's the road," Thorne said.

"It's still a while to Harven," Erik said. "But it will get us there fast."

"Or we keep our distance," Norris said, looking worried.

"You want to stay in the swamp?" Thorne asked incredulously. "And here I was, thinking you were a city girl. But if you really prefer it out here..."

Norris's eyes narrowed at Thorne. "I'm being cautious. I don't actually want to keep off the road."

"Sorry, Norris, we don't have time," Erik said. "The road's the fastest option."

Norris rubbed her jaw. "Are you sure, Cap'n? We're in occupied territory."

Erik watched the road and considered for a moment. "Nothing of consequence is accomplished without risk."

Thorne snorted, and she and Norris exchanged glances.

"Who have you been talking to?" Norris asked.

"Come on," Erik said.

He led his group down the hill, up another rise, and across the plain. The dry ground underfoot made for much faster going. Soon enough, Erik found hard road under his feet and was feeling hopeful to know he was on his way to Harven.

"What's that?" Norris asked.

Erik stopped. A column of dust clouded the road up ahead, soon revealing a group of horsemen heading his way. He scanned the area. Grass spread out on both sides of the road. There was no place to hide.

"We're in trouble," Thorne said.

Erik realized that the approaching riders were mounted soldiers, armored Moranians in black and crimson uniforms. In comparison, Erik's group was a dirty, motley collection of warriors without uniforms or insignia. Erik's men had weapons, mainly swords, but in a fight, the Moranians on horseback would easily be the victors.

"Well?" Thorne asked urgently. "What do we do?"

"We wait," Erik said grimly. He glanced back at his men. "You've been trained to fight men on horseback," he called. "If they charge, you know what to do."

As the Moranians neared, the leader raised his hand into the air and called something back. The riders began to slow, stopping altogether as they reached the section of road where Erik was waiting.

The officer, a lean Moranian with tattoos on his face and neck, sat on his horse and stared at Erik. The tension dragged out. Neither of them spoke.

Erik looked around at his group, and then back at the officer. He continued to wait.

"Well?" the officer finally demanded.

"Well what?" Erik asked.

"You're not going to explain? What took you so long?" The officer sounded exasperated. "You mercenaries are all the same. No discipline at all. Come on, then." He yanked at his reins to turn his horse. "Harven lies this way."

Chapter 44

CORA STOOD ON THE PALACE balcony and watched the city that spread out in front of her. Her gaze took in the houses, the buildings, the temple, the streets and markets. From her height, she could see where the Sylvan River opened up and the mighty ships of the battle fleet bobbed on the water, ready to defend Adin from attack.

She had a decision to make.

If she sent the fleet to help Fastness, Adin would lose a crucial element in the city's defense. And yet, if she didn't send the fleet, Logan's home would be ravaged, his family killed. Aranor would lose access to the sea and may never get it back. Baelock Fain would control everything except for Adin and the lands immediately surrounding the capital. Adin's population was sizable. Without support from the regions, the people would starve.

If Fastness fell, the war would be lost.

"My Queen." Hearing a sober voice, Cora turned to see Hailsham approaching. She felt a surge of disappointment when she saw he was alone. "I am afraid I do not bring the news you want."

"He is still not back yet?"

"Everyone knows to alert you as soon as we hear of his return." Hailsham hesitated. "I came to discuss something else, Majesty." He looked like he was struggling with what he wanted to say, which was unlike him. "Lord Wallace. Perhaps a few words..."

Cora's mouth tightened. "Erik is alive."

"I pray that is so." Hailsham said with a nod. "Majesty." He bowed and left her on the balcony.

Cora began to pace. She occasionally looked out at the city full of people she needed to protect, and glanced toward the powerful ships of Aranor's fleet.

It wasn't just Adin she was supposed to safeguard; she had to think of Fastness too. She had already abandoned one of Aranor's regions. Even Malgannis didn't know that she was the one who had destroyed the Bridge of Willows. She didn't have the courage to admit it to anyone, not after what Baelock Fain had done to the towns and villages of the north. Part of her knew she had saved the army, and that if she hadn't done what she'd done, Adin would have already fallen, but that didn't make her feel any better.

"Coraline!"

A rush of footsteps made her turn. Logan came racing toward her, and he held another scroll in his shaking hand. Cora saw the same paper... the same black seal, broken to indicate Logan had already read the contents.

"Another message. Fastness still holds the harbor. Wren says my son is in the midst of the fighting. He doesn't think they can last longer than another few days. He requests immediate assistance."

Cora knew in her heart. She couldn't wait any longer. She had to make a decision. Surely she could just divide the fleet, send half to Fastness and leave the other half in Adin?

"How many enemy ships? Does he have firmer numbers?"

"More than thirty."

Cora tried to breathe evenly. "How did the enemy find thirty ships? How is that possible?"

"Wren says they fly the colors of Morania but they are foreign ships with gray sails. From across the Sea of Mirrors."

Cora watched the ships of Aranor's battle fleet. "How many do we have?"

"Thirty-six. Please, Coraline," Logan said. "My family is there."

Cora couldn't wait any longer. She had to make a decision. "Do it. Send the fleet. Give the order."

Logan gave a sharp nod. He was almost running as he left her. Past him, she saw Hailsham's anxious face; he was watching Logan from inside.

Cora could only pray she had made the right choice.

✦

"General, you need to see this."

Baelock Fain tilted his head and frowned; he was a canny enough reader of men to know that the inquisitor was nervous. The stocky man's florid face was pale and he had a fidgeting, jittery manner. He kept wiping his hands on his leather apron, which drew Baelock's attention. The inquisitor's hands were stained red, as if he had drenched them in wine, telling Baelock that he hadn't stopped to wash them before coming to make his report.

"Very well," Baelock said. "Lead the way."

The inquisitor bobbed his head and Baelock followed him across the muddy road toward the village smithy. As Baelock walked, the hem of his cloak dragged in the dirt. The smell of burned wood clung to the air, along with the underlying stench of death.

The smithy, a structure of thick beams up ahead, was one of the few buildings still standing; the rest of the village had been razed to the ground. As Baelock took long strides, he stepped over a body, one of several that lay in the mud where they had fallen. He didn't see any reason to move them. In fact, he intentionally left signs of his passage behind.

He didn't plan on spending long in the area; he hadn't even bothered to find out the village's name. Its location was the important thing; he was currently at the southern limit of the Witherglen, the great region of forests in Aranor's east, and with every passing day he was taking his army closer to Adin.

"The hinge is broken, General," the inquisitor said apologetically. He yanked the door hard and held it open so that Baelock could enter.

The stocky inquisitor again took the lead. As he headed deeper into the smithy, he continued to wipe his hands on his leather apron, glancing back at Baelock and becoming increasingly apprehensive. At last he came to a halt, and indicated a table he had repurposed.

"He is dead, General."

Baelock's gaze rested on an older man who lay on his back, staring without seeing up at the ceiling. He had black hair, parted on the side, and still wore the fine clothing he had been clad in when the inquisitor commenced his work. The top half of him was fine; there wasn't a mark on his face or torso, and he still possessed the perfect use of his arms and, importantly, his hands. But his boots had been removed and the lower half of his trousers had been roughly cut away with scissors to reveal his feet and lower calves. This was where inquisitor had concentrated; the dead man's feet were ruined; there was barely anything left of them, other than shredded skin and thin bones.

The man was Guylan Wren, and he was the steward and administrator of Fastness.

Baelock spent a few moments looking at Wren's body, and then turned to the inquisitor. His eyes narrowed. "I told you to keep him alive."

The inquisitor wrung his hands. "His heart gave out. He must have had a condition."

"He took a great deal of effort to capture," Baelock said. "A third message is now out of the question." He glanced meaningfully at the body. "Obviously."

Baelock wondered what to do with the inquisitor, but was interrupted when a soldier came to the door. The young Moranian was panting; he had evidently just been running.

"General," the soldier said quickly. "News just arrived. Aranor's fleet is leaving."

The inquisitor's shoulders slumped with relief.

"Excellent," Baelock said. He turned toward the inquisitor. "Get the door open for me."

The inquisitor shoved the smithy door open and Baelock left him to cross the road again, ignoring the bodies, the smell, and the burned out husks that had once been houses. He climbed up a hill, taking swift steps. The forest swallowed him up, and then he took a narrow track toward an immense field on the other side of the cluster of ancient trees.

The sentries were all in place, rigorously patrolling. Trenches had been dug. Defensive spikes formed a perimeter. Dominating the field were rows and rows of tents and huge numbers of men and horses. In the distance, twenty wooden structures on wheels, vaguely pyramid-shaped, stood side by side in the most protected part of the camp.

A soldier saluted. Baelock ignored him. He was pensive as he crossed the field to travel toward the camp.

Aranor's fleet was leaving. Victory was near. His army was strong and ready.

As Baelock Fain, he had come close to victory. If it weren't for Malgannis, he would have won. Now, as Graven Callow, the same man with the same face, but a larger, more powerful army, he would finally have the prize he sought, while having his revenge at the same time.

Approaching the camp, he watched his men as they moved about. He had given them a cause, the end of an order imposed by a foreign nation, the so-called Code of Aranor. The thrill of victory, the ability to take what they wanted and dominate another person completely, that had done the rest.

A Vailander would soon be the ruler of the world. The nations of the south had once made slaves out of the people of Vailand. Aranor had enslaved the rest of the world in shackles of a different nature. No one people would systematically exploit another anymore.

It had taken him two attempts, but he was now on the cusp of completing what he had started all those years ago. And this time, in this second life, he was able to enjoy the act of torturing his greatest enemy. Every time he caused someone pain, he always thought about what effect his actions would have on Malgannis Vandryden.

Gods, it felt good to be alive.

In the distance, Baelock caught sight of a funeral pyre, blazing away with some men standing nearby. The sight reminded him about the place he tried hard not to think about. He would do anything not to return to hell. He had been there once, and that was enough.

His plan was to spend his life accumulating power. Then, he could put his energies toward finding out how the black priests managed to live forever. Perhaps he could become a black priest. Or a servant of darkness. Anything to stay in this world and avoid the next.

As he entered the camp, his thoughts were interrupted by a cluster of soldiers talking, and he overheard their words.

"...Iron Spear hit them hard. Killed them to a man." The soldier speaking trailed off as he saw Baelock. Instant terror reached his eyes.

Baelock had stopped walking. "Enough about the Iron Spear. They are just men. We have the most powerful army the world has ever seen. And today, we begin the final march to Adin."

Baelock focused again on his twenty wooden towers on wheels. His siege weapons were complete. It was time to advance on Aranor's capital. The towers would be dismantled for the journey and reassembled outside Adin.

He raised his voice to address all of the soldiers in the area. "Do you hear me? We leave today. Our enemy is soft. Aranor's end is inevitable."

As his men gave a cheer, Baelock walked away. He lowered his voice, speaking now for himself as he imagined his final confrontation with Malgannis Vandryden. "And you, Ironclaw? Are you ready? I am coming, and nothing you can do will stop me."

Chapter 45

HARVEN WAS A BLACK, brooding city, fashioned of massive blocks of stone and the dark wood that came from the nearby forest. A wide moat flowed under the tall walls, but the water was thick and dark, like the swamps of the Gray Marshes. Rumandy's capital was far enough north that the warmth of spring had yet to reach it. The skies were gray and the sullen people were wrapped in thick clothing. Rubbish and waste filled the gutters, the markets displayed scant pickings, and soldiers played dice up on the walls. The occupation had smothered the city for months.

Erik found himself facing a desk in an immense rectangular building, a hall being used as a recruitment center for the various mercenary groups joining Morania's army. At the back of the hall, Erik's men stood and waited where they could be inspected by those who might be willing to pay them to fight.

"Name of company?" the official asked from the other side of the desk.

"The Unseen," Norris replied.

Erik give her a slight frown, but knew better than to make any other reaction as the official made some marks on a paper with quill and ink. This wasn't the time for Norris's humor; the name was a little too close to the truth.

The official seated at the desk in front of them was a fussy Moranian, bald and skinny, with half a missing ear. A thin scar traveled from below his nose to cross both his lips.

"You will be joining the Fourth Mercenary Division," the bald official said. "Pay is two coppers per week per man."

"How about the fighting?" Erik asked. "Any news?"

"We'll send you to Vestria. There's been some trouble there."

"I was asking about Aranor."

"You'll be too late to plunder Adin, if that's what you're asking. Graven Callow is at the Witherglen, last I heard. Going to be at Adin in days."

"I see," Erik said.

He tried not to show any emotion on his face, but a vision came to him of Cora, standing on the lawn outside Adin Palace, utterly alone while a horde of savage fighters poured in through the main gate. Among them, at the front, was a helmeted warrior. As the horde rushed the palace, the warrior pressed down on Cora's shoulder until she was kneeling. He lined up his sword blade with her graceful neck and then brought his weapon above his head...

"Name? Your name?"

Erik returned to where he was with a jolt. "Arek."

"Arek," the official repeated as he scribbled. "Arek of the Unseen." His hand stopped moving and he looked up. "Second?" He became impatient. "Your second, in case you die. I need to know."

"Oh," Erik said. He glanced at Norris.

Norris cleared her throat. "Morris."

"All done," the official said. "You're just in time. The Fourth Division leaves tomorrow."

Erik reminded himself that he had a secret purpose. As he had been in the hall, he had been surreptitiously inspecting the area. Realizing his moment to get the information he needed was about to pass, he put on a puzzled frown.

"What about our advance pay?"

"Advance pay?" The bald official pursed his scarred lips and looked up.

"A signing bonus," Erik persisted.

The official snorted. "There is no signing bonus."

"Then we walk," Erik said, indicating his men. "I'll take my men and leave."

"Fine," the official said wearily. "If you want to leave, leave."

Erik allowed himself to show his worry. "Early pay then. One copper per man. Take it out of our next earnings. With some of it for you."

The official tilted his head, frowning as he pondered. Erik had a feeling that he had almost achieved his goal.

"Look," Erik said, pleading. "My men are hungry. Give us half of our first week's earnings. When we get the other half, I'll give it straight to you."

The official's eyes became calculating. If he agreed, he would get close to a hundred coppers for himself. "You know what you're asking? You realize that next pay you won't get anything at all?"

"Like I said, my men need to eat."

The bald official shook his head and shrugged. "Fair enough." He hastily scribbled something on a piece of paper and handed it to Erik. "Take this to the paymaster. At the end of the week, I expect my money promptly, understood?"

Erik took the paper and then looked around. "Understood. Where can I find the paymaster?"

"He's a big man, wears a gold earring. There's a small building with a metal door, across the road from here. You'll find him there."

Erik nodded and walked away from the desk with Norris at his side. She remained silent until they were far away from the official.

"What are you doing?" she muttered.

Erik spoke in a low voice. "There are more mercenaries in Harven than there are Moranians. By a long margin. Graven must have them all in Aranor."

"What of it?"

Erik smiled. "Mercenaries don't fight if they don't get paid. I want to know where they're keeping the gold."

✦

The mercenaries were leaving, one group at a time, dispersing and going back to their homes in Nara, Kor, and places even farther.

The Moranians pleaded with them not to go, but every mercenary captain took one look at the burned out building where the gold had once been kept and demanded reassurance that they were still going to get paid. Words weren't enough. Where was the coin? They wanted to see it. The theft was plain for all to see, and the mercenaries started to pack up. As they departed, they cursed the company who had done the stealing, but there was more than a hint of admiration at the audacity.

The mercenaries weren't expecting to be met on the road.

Erik sat on a fence bordering a nearby pasture. When he saw a group of warriors heading his way, he called out. Some of them recognized him, most didn't, but they all wanted to hear what he had to say.

"Do you still want your share of the gold?" Erik would ask. "Not later, not paid week by week, but all at once, today?"

They knew he had the gold. He knew they wanted it. "What's your proposal?"

"There's a city there." Erik nodded toward Harven. "It's full of people desperate to be freed. You can have your share of the gold we took. You can have it today. All you have to do is help us destroy the Moranians."

More often than not, Erik's words were greeted with a calculating look and a cold smile.

✦

In the end, once they realized what was happening, the Moranian occupiers of Harven fled. The mercenaries had their reward, and Rumandy's capital returned to the control of its own people, who wouldn't let their city be taken again.

Erik stood on the battlements with Norris. The night sky opened up in front of them, filling their vision with countless glittering jewels. The moon was high and full, like a silver pool against the black behind it. Far below, the moat under the walls reflected a sludgy, slick version of the moon, marred by bits of flotsam and half-submerged debris.

Erik had his gaze on one of the starry constellations. "The Southern Ring," he said. "That way lies Aranor." He glanced at Norris. "I think it's time to go home. We've done what we can here. We need to get back to Aranor. There might still be time to help."

"The men will be pleased," Norris said. She turned to stare directly into Erik's eyes. "Erik..." She shook her head. "I can't believe what you've done."

"What we've done," Erik said, reaching out to grip her shoulder. He let his hand fall as something occurred to him. "One more thing. See if any of the mercenaries want to fight with us." He thought of the journey ahead. This time he wouldn't need to cross the Gray Marshes. He would be able to take the road. "Only those with fast horses."

"I'll see to it," Norris said with a nod.

"Oh, and Rosie?"

"You do remember my name," Norris said with a smile. "Yes, cap'n?"

"You'll want to see Thorne before we go."

Norris reddened, and her mouth worked soundlessly. Erik smiled to himself as she uncharacteristically left the walls without a retort.

He continued to smile as he found himself alone. He focused on the circle of bright stars that indicated the way south. It was time to say goodbye to Thorne, to leave the people of Rumandy and Vestria to pick up the pieces left behind after defeat and occupation. He was desperate to get home, as soon as humanly possible.

He pictured two brown eyes, high cheekbones, and dark, braided hair. He tried to think about Cora not on her knees as Graven raised his sword, but instead with the familiar look of determination on her face as she stood tall and defiant on Adin's strong outer wall.

Malgannis would be with her. He would slow down Graven's advance and make sure that Adin held.

Erik was vaguely aware of someone walking up the stairway to the walls, past Norris in the opposite direction. He heard a mumbled "My Lady", but it was distant, and he didn't give it any special notice. Instead, he stood close to the drop below and thought about Cora as he gazed at the stars.

"Arek of the Unseen," a voice hissed.

Erik jerked his head and there was the bald, skinny Moranian with the scar across his lips. The man's eyes were ferocious, and Erik noticed one key difference. Where before he had been missing half an ear, now his other ear was missing altogether.

"Enjoy the afterlife," the Moranian said.

Erik was too shocked and too off his guard. He tried to fend the man off but the Moranian reached out and shoved him. Hard.

Erik's heels hit the low wall on top of the battlements. He stumbled and began to teeter. His eyes went up as he tumbled back, looking up at the sky.

He heard Norris cry out. "Erik!"

But there was nothing she could do. Erik's stomach shot upward as he fell. His limbs clawed at the air. The sensation of plummeting felt like it went on forever.

His thoughts darted around. Flashes of remembrance came to him. He wished he had been braver. Why had he always held himself back?

He should at least have told Cora he loved her.

He struck the water. The smacking sound was like a thunderclap. Pain filled his senses. He felt something inside him break.

Everything went black.

Chapter 46

CORA STARED AT THE NAKED SKIN on her arm. She contemplated the swirling, grasping green and black tendrils and the redness that mingled with the bruised coloring.

Only three days remained to her.

She knew every letter of the agreement she had made, the contract she had signed in blood. In just three days, as midnight passed on Commemoration Day, her life would end.

The mark would spread to cover her entire body. It would creep across her shoulders, down her back and chest, and up her neck and face. Like evil fingers choking her, the green, black, and red stain would spread until no part of her body had escaped it. Then, the lord of the underworld would claim his price, and she would die.

Section by section, she carefully unrolled the fabric of her long-sleeved dress until her arm was once more covered. Then, unable to help herself, she left her private chambers altogether. She traveled the corridors and the carpeted stairs, always climbing. Guards nodded to her. Stewards bowed. Her movements were followed; at all times someone knew where she was.

Cora had grown up in Adin Palace. Every inch of it was familiar to her. At the end of a carpeted hallway, she found a tiny stairway behind a door. This time the wooden steps were only wide enough to allow one person up or down at any time. The clatter of her shoes filled the dark space. Her calves were soon burning. She was in a tower, gaining height as she ascended.

At the top of the stairway, another door greeted her. She opened the door and wind slammed into her face. The bright midday sun made her blink, and then she almost felt giddy at the vista she was presented with.

She was up on the palace's highest point, a special place called the observatory. Girded by a stone rail, the balcony was big enough for half a dozen people but no more. Her position was so lofty that she could see all of the city, with its tall walls and red-roofed houses, its wide streets and narrow lanes, its markets and grand temple. The Sylvan River opened up in front of her, curling around Aranor's capital, easily in view.

And there, on the rolling landscape where the King's Road descended toward the drawbridge and Adin's main gates, she saw at least twenty huge siege engines, towers on wheels, even taller than the city walls, with moveable sections of planks that could form ladders and bridges. From her high position, she took in the vast number of Moranians, Narans, Vailanders, and Kors, as well as mercenaries from nations farther still. Spread out on the hills, they were so numerous they looked like swarming ants.

Cora watched Aranor's unfolding doom. There were so many of them. She couldn't see how the city would survive.

She tore her eyes away to focus on Adin's walls and the battlements on top. Her people were up there: every able-bodied man and boy over sixteen, as well as a great number of women, all ready to defend their families and homes. Malgannis had given the order. He had been in charge for so long now that everyone followed his command without question. At this point in the conflict, they needed to demonstrate numbers. When the enemy looked at Adin and saw how many defenders were on top of the walls, they needed to feel the terror that Cora felt now.

As she returned her watching the siege towers, she was experiencing so many mixed emotions that she could barely think. Among them was guilt. She had sent the battle fleet away. There were no agile ships to defend the city from the water and prevent the towers from making their approach.

"My Queen."

Cora turned. Lord Byron's face was anxious. With the jewels on his fingers and his bright silk clothing, he would stand out. And yet when many other lords had fled, Byron had remained.

Cora smoothed her expression. Her hair may have loose strands and tangles, but she was the queen. She couldn't show her fear. "Lord Byron?" She inclined her head.

He twined his fingers in front of his paunch. "The city will be surrounded by the end of the day. I regret to inform you that this is your last opportunity to leave. A fast ship awaits at the docks. I have spoken to the captain and—"

"I'm not leaving," Cora said.

"Please, you must. If the city falls, your father's dynasty—"

"Will end," Cora finished. "I am the last of the Vandryden dynasty. I am adjusted to the concept, Lord Byron." She softened her tone. "Thank you. I know you're only trying to help. But I am not leaving."

"Yes, My Queen." Byron gave her a bow this time, a deep one from the waist. "Please allow me to say, it has been an honor. I honestly believe that in the circumstances you inherited, no one else could have achieved what you have. Whether or not the people know that, or the history books reflect it, I know it."

He reached out and clasped her hands within his. He then turned to depart.

"Byron?" Cora asked.

"Yes, My Queen?"

She hesitated, but there was something else; she was worried. "Is there still no sign of Silvia?"

"No. I'm sorry. I gather the palace staff are all searching for her."

Silvia hadn't been there to greet Cora in the morning, and after asking around, she hadn't been seen since the previous afternoon. The simplest explanation was that like so many others, she had fled the city. Cora missed her. She had to hope that she was safe.

"I hope she got away," Cora said.

"As do I," Lord Byron said. He turned to leave again.

"Lord Byron?"

"My Queen?"

"Thank you."

"It has been my pleasure, Queen Coraline." He gave her another bow with a flourish, and this time he left her on the balcony alone.

Cora returned to the events unfolding in the city's surrounds. It was strange seeing the pastures by the riverside devoid of all life. Usually sheep and goats nibbled grass by the water's edge, children played under the trees, and a few bowmen on horseback followed the watercourse, heading out to hunt. Night and day, merchants and farmers and general folk filled the King's Road in a mass that tightened as it reached the constriction of the drawbridge.

Now, between the walls, the glistening river below, and the enemy army, not a single person moved. Even the livestock was gone. The King's Road was empty. Only the river's sparkling flow continued.

Cora spied movement as the drawbridge began to lift up, for the first time in her memory. It rose slowly, inexorably, its end pulled higher and higher by the chains connected to the towers at the city gates. When it reached its apex, to line up vertically with the gates themselves, a loud clunk resounded throughout the city, reaching even her ears.

Adin was now cut off from the rest of the world.

No one was coming to Cora's aid. Baelock Fain's fingers were wrapped around the Queen of Aranor's throat, and now he was going to squeeze.

Cora shivered. In a shaking voice, she whispered to herself. "I feel so alone."

"There's no need to be," said a rumbling male voice.

Cora heard footsteps, sensing movement, and then Malgannis was beside her.

He watched her face and his eyes were clearly concerned. She wondered what he saw there. It was only then she realized, that unlike the way she was with Lord Byron and all the other lords and courtiers, she hadn't smoothed her expression.

"Child of my heart," he said softly.

He opened his arm to pull her in close to his side. His height meant that her head was under his chin as he kissed her on top of her head. She remained in his embrace as he took her hand in his. Cora closed her eyes. They held each other for a long time.

Then she opened her eyes, glancing toward the city's surrounds. He turned as well, but without releasing her hand, and she was still leaning in to him, wrapped in his arms. Together they watched the swarm of advancing soldiers and the siege engines as they moved into position.

Neither of them spoke. Cora heard and felt his breathing. He no doubt sensed her tension. They shared the closeness of each other, gaining comfort, as the scene of horror unfolded.

Gradually a shadow descended on the city and its environs as clouds gathered to obscure the sun. The brightness of the day shifted to gloom. There was no thunder or rain, just a smothering blanket of gray that ate up the blue until there was nothing left of it, and it felt like night was approaching, even though it was still hours away.

The mass of soldiers moved about. Cora's vision was filled with horses and flags, fighting men and tall, ugly wooden towers. Cora knew from Malgannis: this time there would be no raids, no sorties, no surprise attacks from secret allies. The next move belonged to Baelock Fain.

"A message, Your Majesty."

The messenger, a young olive-skinned man in blue uniform, hurried up to where Cora and Malgannis stood by the rail. He displayed a piece of paper, sealed with a circle of red wax imprinted with the letter 'V'.

Cora drew in a sharp breath. She exchanged glances with Malgannis. "You open it."

He took the paper and broke the seal, unfurling the scroll. Cora watched his face as his eyes moved swiftly.

"You may leave," Malgannis instructed the messenger, who bowed and departed. Cora bit her lip as Malgannis waited until the young man had gone. He then met her gaze. "He gives Adin three days to surrender. On the fourth day, he says he will burn the city to the ground."

Four days. The number resounded in Cora's mind. Four days. She knew she didn't have that long.

"Commemoration Day is in three days," she said. "In four days I'll be dead."

"I'm sorry, Cora," Malgannis said. "He must know. It's the only reason to wait."

Something occurred to Cora. There was only one other person who knew the truth. She felt sick to her stomach. "Silvia."

"We don't know—" Malgannis began.

"Who else could have told him?"

"That black priest, for one," Malgannis said. "Keep your head, Cora. Silvia might have simply fled the city."

"What are we going to do?"

Malgannis stared toward the army outside the city. "He wants me to suffer. For me to see you die, along with all your people. He wants us to despair, before he crushes Aranor forever."

Cora's thoughts were spinning. "Then we should attack him." She bit her lip again, watching Malgannis. "Shouldn't we?"

Malgannis had never looked so serious as he shook his head. "It is a lost cause. We need him to bleed numbers on the walls before we can launch any assault of our own."

The realization was stark and terrible. Cora was out of time. There was no longer any uncertainty. She knew how the next three days were going to unfold, in a state of tension, with Adin under siege, culminating with her death.

"But if we can't attack them until they attack us, then what do we do?"

"I'm sorry, Cora. I don't know."

Malgannis returned his attention to the enemy as she watched the thoughts work on his face. He knew as well as she did that when their young queen, the last Vandryden, died unexpectedly, the people would lose all hope. He would try to boost morale, but Aranor was being beaten, blow by blow.

"There is only one thing we can do," Malgannis said. "Before I tell you what it is, you have to understand that I have no issue with the consequences for me personally. None." He let the silence drag out. "Our only option is a terrible one."

She summoned her courage. "Tell me."

✦

Cora was alone, standing in front of a tall rectangular mirror. Her new suit of armor was bright and shining, the color of polished silver. She checked herself over, lifting one arm above her head and then the other, making sure that she was well-protected. Her hands explored her torso, the individual plates that jointed at her hips, and her legs. She touched the helmet that covered her face, stunned at the artistry of the smiths, who had created tiny slits for seeing and breathing that meant she could see, but left no part of her head unprotected.

Malgannis always said that armor made all the difference in a fight. It separated the wealthy from the poor on the battlefield and the bodies of those without armor, or with minimal protection, vastly outnumbered those with thick steel covering every inch of them. An armored warrior, fighting from horseback, was a fearsome thing indeed. And while Cora might be new to swordsmanship, few could match her when it came to skill with riding.

When she took herself into battle, she didn't intend to fall right away. She wanted to make a difference. Time and time again, from the books she had read, the soldiers she had spoken with, and again from Malgannis, she had heard that soldiers would throw themselves into battle in support of their king or queen, in a way they never would for an officer. Victory might be a dream, but perhaps it was a dream she could realize.

The helmet felt stifling, but Logan had said she would get used to it. Nonetheless, Cora placed both hands on the side of her head and lifted it, breathing with relief to get the enclosing metal off. Placing the helmet on a nearby table, she focused on the other item that rested nearby.

The sword was long, with a ridged metal hilt that could be held in one or two hands. The blade was curved to aid fighting down from above, as she was likely to do on horseback. Presently, a scabbard covered the sword, but she now took the scabbard in her left hand and sword hilt in her right, pulling to reveal the sharp steel.

She heard the slight whisper as she drew the sword from the scabbard, displaying more and more of the blade. She was tense; she knew the sword was sharp. She inspected the blade and then completely removed it from its enclosing sheath. Finally, she set the scabbard down and stood in front of the mirror, holding her new sword in both hands. She remembered all the times she had watched her brother and Erik, and moved one foot forward and the other back, turning to present a smaller target. The tip of the sword went forward, toward the mirror, as if preparing to defend her from an imaginary opponent.

"You cannot be serious."

Cora's eyes moved in the mirror and there was Lexen Crow, standing directly behind her. Fire flashed in her eyes. For an instant, she had to resist the temptation to whirl and strike him down. But she had made her bargain. In fact, the priestess at Patrick's camp had told her that the only person who could release her was him. Not that he ever would.

Lexen wore the same black robe with the hood over his face. As he watched her, an incredulous expression filled his face, but then he coughed. Another cough wracked his body, causing him to bend over. He straightened and scowled. Sweat beaded on his forehead. His intense eyes were as red as they were white.

Cora allowed her sword to fall. "Always we meet when the sun is shining," she said to the man behind her.

"I hear many whispers. You intend to attack?" His tone was scathing. "I thought you were no fool, Coraline. You have three days. If you die before then, our pact is void. Malgannis goes back to where he came from."

"I know that, and so does he," Cora said simply. "It was his idea. And for me, it is better than waiting to die."

The black priest spoke in an icy tone. "You are doing this for him?"

"I'm doing it for him, and he's doing it for me. Malgannis says we have an outside chance, a very small one, but if I'm going to die, I would rather die fighting."

"Baelock's army is bigger and stronger. Here in Adin, you have tall walls. You are dooming your city to fall. Your people will—"

Cora's voice strengthened as she interrupted him. She turned to face him, rather than his image in the mirror. "Malgannis didn't hide the truth from me. Whether now, or after Commemoration Day, Adin will fall. The enemy won't be expecting us to attack, not with everything."

"But the risk—"

"What would you have me do?" she demanded. "It is the only plan we have."

Lexen opened his mouth but then broke off in a bout of coughing. He wiped at his lips with the sleeve of his robe. When he spoke, his voice was softer and his eyes were calculating. "He has such influence over you..."

"He is my great-grandfather," Cora said, "and he is a hero. I trust him."

"A hero?" Lexen's eyebrows went up. After a moment, he shook his head. "No. I would not use that word. An influential figure, yes. A man of the sword, undoubtedly. But he is not the noble figure you think he is."

Cora's brow furrowed; she was confused by the change of approach. "Malgannis?"

The black priest stared directly into her eyes. "Have you never wondered why he haunted the shadow world? His soul is dark. He chose to remain there, to atone for terrible deeds."

Cora's frown became deeper. "What are you talking about?"

"Tell me, Coraline, what happened after he defeated the forces of Vailand in the final battle?"

"They asked him to be king. He said no."

"What did he do next?"

"Baelock Fain got away. It took Malgannis a decade to track him down."

"That is the core of what happened," Lexen said. "Malgannis Ironclaw finally found his enemy by the coast near the Sea of Kor, not far from a place with the name of Seven Elms."

Cora searched her memory. "Yes..." she said slowly. "Malgannis and his men surrounded Baelock Fain and brought him down with dogs."

"You know the story," Lexen said. "Malgannis never saw Baelock Fain put on trial and executed," he nodded in the direction of the city gates, "out there on those hills where his army now waits. With his lifelong quest complete, so the tale goes, Malgannis died in his sleep on the journey home."

Cora nodded uncertainly. That was the part that everyone agreed on. Malgannis caught his enemy, but the quest took too much out of him. He died quietly, content in the knowledge that Baelock Fain would at last be judged for the things he had done.

"However, in truth, there is much more to the events that took place at Seven Elms, some fifty-six years ago," Lexen said. "Before you ride out with Malgannis, to throw yourself against the arrows and blades of your enemy, you should know the truth about the man you wish to follow."

A large part of Cora didn't want the black priest to continue, but she knew that now he had begun, she had to know. "Go on," she said warily.

"Then listen carefully." Lexen paused for a moment. "Baelock Fain knew he had been found. As he fled, he put obstacles in Malgannis's path, in an attempt to distract him and slow the pursuit."

Lexen's stare into Cora's eyes was unrelenting.

"He left a woman cut and bleeding, so that her wounds needed tending. He nailed a vagrant by his hands to a wooden stake so that Malgannis and his men had to free him. Malgannis grew increasingly frustrated. His quarry was getting away. Baelock Fain's tactics were working."

Lexen's voice lowered, so that Cora had to lean forward. She couldn't help herself.

"And so, when it came to the next distraction, at Seven Elms, Malgannis did not stop. He kept going. He caught Baelock Fain. But..." Lexen moistened his lips, "he paid a price."

Cora had to summon her courage to ask. "The distraction... what was it?"

"Baelock Fain set a building on fire. A convent. Full of people. Many of them just girls."

Cora's vision swam. As Lexen continued talking, his lips curved in a slight smile, she imagined fire and smoke... the shouts, the horror and fear, and tasted bile at the back of her throat.

"Malgannis was in time to stop the flames," Lexen said. "He knew that the gates were nailed shut. He made a decision to keep going. He chose to let the place burn."

"I don't believe you," she whispered.

"It is the truth. When it comes to matters of death, of who dies and who does not, I do not lie."

Lexen's dark eyes remained on Cora as she began to run.

Chapter 47

AFTER A HASTY MEETING with some members of the council of lords, Malgannis was on his way out of the palace. He took long steps, taking himself along the main colonnade to the palace gates, past the lawns and gardens, on his way to the causeway that led to the city.

"Ironclaw."

When he heard the one word spoken raggedly, by a familiar voice, he stopped in his tracks. The moment he heard her call, it was like a fist grabbing hold of his heart and squeezing.

He slowly turned.

There she was, in a suit of armor, striding straight past the palace guards toward him. Cora's face wore naked emotion in a way he had never seen before. Tears had carved passages down her cheeks, but they were tears of frustration and anger, released by terrible feelings.

Malgannis stood and waited. She didn't use the name Ironclaw with him. Whenever people added the word to his name, it was to paint him with the brush of the ruthless general, out for vengeance, worthy of tales told in darkness by the fire. Cora was intelligent and chose her words carefully.

Seeing her expression, hearing her voice, there was only one explanation. Here, at the end of it all, she had finally discovered his terrible secret.

She knew.

His strongest emotion was regret. He felt he had given her something, perhaps hope, or strength, or simply a comforting presence. She had now lost the last thing she had left: her faith in him. He was disappointed in himself for the deeds he had done, but living with his sins was something he had been doing in both life and death. What he hated most was what he had done to her. In her time of need, she had no one.

"Tell me it isn't true," she said.

He didn't need to ask what she was talking about. Even as she stared at him with fierce anger, he could see some hope in her eyes. However she had found out, she was even now wanting him to deny it.

"The..." He couldn't bring himself to say it. "The fire."

"The convent," she said.

He held himself in tight check. There was no use consoling her. He had to atone for what he had done, and if he now had to live with this pain, the pain of what he had done to her, then that was what he would do. "It is true."

"How could you?" She asked, imploring him, even as she accused him. "How many died?"

He couldn't answer. He remained silent, unable to trust himself to speak.

"Say something," Cora demanded.

Malgannis shook his head.

"I trusted you." Her entire body was shaking. "I gave you everything!"

"I didn't ask you to," he said quietly.

"It doesn't matter," she said. "None of it matters. We've lost anyway. With or without you."

As Malgannis stood in front of his great-granddaughter, he knew that it was the last time he would see her.

Cora was going to die, because she had thought he was something that he wasn't, and given her life for his. Malgannis's homeland was going to fall, because he had failed to meet the challenge he had been given. He wasn't a hero; he had never been a hero. His role was that of a fighter, a warmonger, a taker of blood. Heroes only existed in stories. He had just happened to have his name end up in them.

He knew he had to find some words. "Cora..."

"Go," she snapped. "I don't care where, just go. Get out of my sight. Go and get yourself killed."

Cora turned her back to him and walked with angry strides back to the palace. Malgannis watched her for one final time, and he thought about when they had fled the defeat in Vestria, and he had held her on the saddle in front of him, in his arms, just like he had once held his own daughter.

And then she was gone.

✦

Thunder shook Adin Palace. The loud booms made the windows rattle. Some mighty goddess had the heavens in her hands, tearing the sky in half with the snicker of long jagged scratches. Rain dropped in a sudden torrent, pouring down with an ever greater intensity and volume.

Yet as she stood at a window, staring out into the rain, Cora heard another sound above the storm. She turned and saw Hailsham with one of the young maids, just inside the entrance to her private chambers. The maid, a blonde girl four of five years younger than Cora, was pawing at Hailsham, trying to prevent him from entering the room. The bald-headed steward calmly removed the maid's entangling hands. The maid kept trying to stop him. She now grabbed his arms, and she was sobbing, which was the sound that Cora had heard.

Hailsham's blue uniform wasn't as crisp as it usually was. His lips were thin and his face was gray. He said something to the maid and the girl's gaze went to Cora, her eyes widening when she realized that the queen had already seen them. The maid gave up on what she was doing. She wrung her hands and turned and fled, still crying.

Cora straightened. She waited as Hailsham approached. A strange feeling of numbness had spread throughout her body.

Hailsham drew a steadying breath. His eyes were red. Terrible memories came back to Cora. She remembered the only other time she had seen Hailsham like this, when she had returned from riding and he had stood with Silvia, waiting to give her the news of her father's death.

"Lady Silvia..." He broke off and moistened his lips. "Her body..."

Cora remained stiff and straight-backed. She felt a burning sensation behind her eyes and at the back of her throat. But she kept her face as blank as she possibly could. "Tell me."

"They... someone left it at the front gate. Please, My Queen. Don't see..."

"I have to," she said sharply.

She began to walk, and it was Hailsham who had to hurry to lead the way. The numb feeling never left her. She was vaguely aware of men and women bowing to her as she passed them. Some were in uniform, others in fine clothing. Either way, they saw a queen who was calm and poised, who would guide them through the storm.

As queen, you must always appear strong, even when you don't feel it. I wish the world weren't this way, I truly do, but this is especially true when you are a woman. Others may crumble, but you are their rock. For if you were to crumble, they would become dust.

She had to get Malgannis's voice out of her head.

Hailsham took her to a room. She didn't pay much attention to which room it was, she simply entered a small, square space with a high domed ceiling and red velvet on the walls. Her eyes went straight to the table that occupied the room's center.

A white linen cloth covered the body on the table, but there was no mistaking the figure of a person on her back, with the round shape of a head at one end and the small perpendicular protrusion of feet at the other.

Hailsham rested a hand on the cloth, without actually touching the body beneath. He turned to Cora, and there were tears slowly sliding down his cheeks.

"This is her," he said. "You know she loved you like her own daughter. Cora, no, I suggest you don't—"

Cora ignored him as she went right up to the table. She still hadn't allowed any tears to flow. Taking hold of the cloth at the corner, she lifted it up to reveal familiar flaxen hair with the occasional gray thread. She kept bringing it up, and there was the skin of Silvia's neck.

She moved more quickly, pulling the linen back to reveal Silvia's face completely.

Cora covered her mouth with her hand. The black bruises, purple welts, and the dried red blood told her a terrible tale. The cowards who did this wanted to know about Malgannis and Cora and how they fit together. Silvia had held out; she had tried to protect her, and this was the result.

"I'm sorry," Cora whispered.

"My Queen," a voice spoke from the arched entrance to the room.

"Not now," Hailsham snapped.

Cora's gaze went to the speaker, a shorter man with long brown hair wearing a blue uniform that matched Hailsham's. His name was Brody and he was one of Hailsham's under stewards. He had a lively sense of humor, and had always taken a liking to Erik.

Brody surprised her by pressing on. "She would want to know," he said firmly.

"Know what?" Cora asked.

Hailsham sighed. "Come," he said in a voice filled with sadness.

Cora followed Hailsham from the room. This time he took her close to the palace's main entrance, along a hallway that Cora knew led to an audience chamber. She still felt like someone else was walking on her behalf; someone else was nodding at the people who bowed to her. Voices were muffled. She noticed strange details: the golden thread in the wallpaper, the softness of the carpet, the constant chant of the falling rain.

As she entered the audience chamber, she saw a young woman with a square jaw, dirty skin, and her blonde hair in a pony tail. Despite how grimy she was, she was pretty. And yet she had the bearing of a warrior, with scars on her hands and a steady gaze.

Cora frowned. She looked familiar...

"My Queen." The blonde woman stood quickly when she saw Cora and bowed. "My name is Norris. Lieutenant Rosie Norris."

"You're one of Erik's officers," Cora said. As soon as she had the realization, hope flared in her heart. "Where is he?" She looked around.

"My Queen..." The blonde woman broke off. "I am the bearer of terrible news. He... Erik... he didn't make it."

Cora became utterly, completely still. It was as if some external force wrapped tight arms around her, holding her in place, supporting her so that she didn't need any strength in her legs to hold her up.

"You're sure," a distant voice said, despite the words coming from her lips.

"I was there."

"How...?"

"A Moranian, out for revenge. Pushed Erik off a great height. Erik fell to his death. We caught the man. He was happy to confess. We strung him up by his neck..."

She continued speaking, but Cora couldn't hear her.

As a queen, you must always appear strong...

"Thank you," Cora said. "All of you. I would like to be alone now."

Chapter 48

MORNING FOUND MALGANNIS waking up in a strange inn next to a strange woman.

He blinked. He ran his tongue over his mouth, grimacing at the foul bitter taste of too much liquor. At first, he could barely see; it was all a haze. Then, as he continued to blink, his vision gradually cleared. He stared up at a grubby ceiling. How did anyone manage to get so much dirt up on a ceiling? He inspected himself; he was fully clothed. Turning his head, he saw a plump woman with bushy, ash-colored hair, lying on her side with her back to him.

He had absolutely no idea what her face looked like.

The events of the previous night were a mystery to him. How had he come to be here?

Then he remembered. It all came back to him... what had happened, and why he was here.

Cora despised him, he knew that, and he deserved to be despised. He had let Seven Elms Convent burn to the ground, along with everyone in it, rather than be slowed in his quest for Baelock Fain.

Yes, she hated him. But surely, no one could hate him more than he hated himself.

He lifted himself up on his elbows. There, on a little table by his bedside. Sweet relief.

He reached over to grab the flagon. He lifted it to his lips and the burning liquid began to trickle down his throat, lighting up a fire in his stomach, even as it prepared to drag him back down into oblivion.

He had decided to live his life before ending it. What he was doing now, was this living life? It was what he had sought out, but right now, it didn't seem to hold much appeal. If he died, when he died, he didn't think he would be missing much.

He was sore everywhere. It didn't matter. The pain would be over soon.

He barely managed to set the flagon back down on the table before unconsciousness dragged him down.

✦

"Wake up! Lord Morgan, or Malgannis, if that's what you want me to call you. Wake up! I need the room."

Part of him wondered where he was, but a greater part of him didn't want to know. His eyes opened the slightest amount, revealing daylight that would have made him flinch if he had been able to move. Instead he felt heavy, from head to toe. His head throbbed. He wanted the woman to stop yelling and leave him alone.

Through the heavy fog, he heard the woman give a sound of disgust.

"Have it your way. But you're paying for this. I'm going to make sure of it."

✦

After the storm came sunshine. The flowers straightened, the birds trilled with glee, and the lawns were so green it was like they were glowing.

And yet Cora preferred the weeping flowers and the drooping branches of the willows, and so that was where she wandered. She felt untethered, more like the drifting clouds than the plants with their sturdy stems.

When Logan found her, it took his voice a moment to cut through and reach her. He had to stand directly in front of her until she met his gaze.

"Coraline. There is some old man trying to see you. He won't say what it's about."

"I know," she said. "Hailsham told me."

Logan reached out to take her by both shoulders. He squeezed. "We found them," he said. "I know it isn't much, but Silvia has been avenged."

Cora nodded. "Thank you."

"One of the stable boys told me everything," Logan said. "The boy has no one in the world except for his mother. She's not well, has the palsy. They threatened both the boy and his mother. All the boy had to do was convince Silvia to go into town, to a particular location, supposedly to talk to a healer who might help. The boy is sick with guilt."

"The mother?" Cora asked.

"She's fine. I've got some men with her."

"Who were they?"

"Moranians. Pretending to be from Nara but even the stable boy knew. Graven snuck them in long before we raised the bridge. They tortured Silvia and got a message to their master."

"Where are they now? The Moranians."

Logan's mouth twisted. "It's better you don't know."

There was a long pause, as Logan intently searched Cora's face. Uncomfortable, Cora glanced down at herself. Today she wore a blue dress that was so dark it was almost black. She opened her palm and watched her hand, to see that she was shaking.

"Coraline..." Logan said. "Look at me, please. I deserve that much." He waited until she was meeting his eyes. "What did Silvia tell them? Why is Graven Callow waiting until the day after Commemoration Day?" He paused, and when she didn't speak, he became even more urgent. "The Moranians... they said something about a mark."

He waited for her reaction and saw her swallow. When she didn't reply, he reached out and grabbed her arm. With a series of yanks, he pulled back the sleeve. He was breathing heavily, as first he revealed a blue swirl, then a purple finger that grew wider, until he saw that her forearm was a mess of twirling lines, welts, and skin that had the appearance of recent burning in fire.

"By the gods, Coraline. What bargain have you made?"

"It doesn't matter now," she said. "What is done is done."

She yanked her arm away from him and returned her sleeve to its former position. Even as she did, she glanced at him. As she assessed her own feelings about what Logan had learned, she realized that she was resigned to whatever came next.

Logan was going to be king. The choice about what to do with this knowledge was his.

"That man..." Logan said slowly, "who looks so much like Malgannis Ironclaw..." he trailed off.

Cora spoke softly. "It's him."

Logan was shaking his head, clearly disturbed. "Your father... he raised you in the light. And yet you pledged yourself to darkness."

"I did," she said.

His voice became crisp; he had made his decision. "The queen of Aranor can't be beholden to the black arts. Especially now, in our darkest hour. A monarch should be worthy of the title." He stared at her coldly, and she knew she had lost him. "I am sorry, Coraline, but that is my belief."

Without another word, Logan turned and strode away.

Chapter 49

THE WATER WAS ICY, run off from the mountains. Deep and turbulent, the river could be crossed, but it wasn't an easy feat to accomplish.

Erik patted his horse on the flank and led her down to the river's edge. The mare knew what was coming; she wasn't stupid, and knew she was about to be freezing cold. She balked, but Erik spoke to her in soothing tones, even as he patted her on the flanks and continued to lead her by the halter. The mare's foot entered the water and she shivered. Erik's own boot was soon submerged and he knew how his horse felt.

Still, this water wasn't as cold as the moat outside Harven's walls. Even as Erik gently pulled the horse into the clear blue river, he wondered if somehow the cold had kept him alive when he should have drowned. The impact of his fall had knocked him unconscious, he knew that much. He did have some hazy recollections of weakly thrashing around. He could still remember the moat's horrible stench and the taste that entered his mouth, along with a great volume of viscous black water.

Together with the discarded furniture, half-submerged logs, reeds, and the assorted rubbish generated by a large settlement, Erik had drifted half-drowned in that water for what felt like a long, long time. Part of him had wanted to close his eyes forever. His ears continued ringing. A terrible pain filled his head. His body felt broken. But somehow, he had survived the fall.

A current tugged at him, pulling him away from an entanglement of soaked linen, and he tried to move with the shift of the water. When he had at last been able to take stock of himself, he had turned his head and seen the distant walls of Harven, surprisingly far away. Somehow, he had entered one of the watercourses that drained liquid from the moat and went on to join a section of marsh, with tall reeds stretching to the horizon. He lifted his head. A long time later, he pushed himself to a seating position. Then, he finally stood.

He remembered Norris crying out his name. She would have searched for him, but clearly she didn't find him. She would have already left for Aranor.

He began the journey alone.

Past the marsh he found a road, and then he found farmers' fields. He was lucky. A farmer gave him the mare, as soon as the old man found out which side of the war Erik was fighting on. The horse wasn't as swift as some, but she was the sturdiest horse he had ever ridden, with stamina to match. On the journey back to Aranor, she and Erik slept side by side. They were always together, for they barely stopped moving. They drank water together and ate the same oats. Erik recovered as she bore his weight, traveling the road south, always south, toward home.

The mare shivered, bringing Erik back to the river, as her belly made contact with the cold water. He glanced at the ruins of the Bridge of Willows. When he was in Vestria, he had heard the story, but it stunned him now to see that it was gone entirely, the burned and ruined supports just a mess of timbers that filled the gorge. He tore his eyes away. The fast flow meant that he had to focus. His horse was getting her flanks splashed and she snorted, her anxious gaze going to Erik. Meanwhile Erik was more than waist deep, struggling to keep his feet on the stony riverbed.

"Easy, easy," he said soothingly. "Just keep your eyes on the other side."

Following his own advice, he kept his attention fixed on the opposite bank. Before he had entered the water, it hadn't seemed far, but now the bank seemed impossibly distant. To add to his difficulty, the stretch of gravel that would make it easy to exit didn't continue forever. If Erik and the mare went too far in the current, they would miss the opportunity altogether, and as the banks became steep walls and the river developed rapids amidst sharp rocks, they would drown.

Erik's feet left the ground, but he kept hold of the pommel, at the front of the saddle. The mare gave a whinny as her own feet scrabbled and then she was swimming, with all of her bulk submerged except for her head, the saddle, and the sloping top of her back.

"Come on. You can do it," Erik urged.

The fast current took hold of them as they entered the middle of the river. The mare kicked and snorted, blowing water from her nostrils. Part of her head dipped completely under and she lifted her nose up, her eyes wide with panic, showing the whites. The gentle part of the bank drifted past, far too quickly. Erik tried to keep his voice calm. All he could do was urge the horse on.

"Keep going," he encouraged, "you're a strong beauty, stronger than any stallion. That's it. Focus on the goal. You're so close!"

He sensed the jolt as her legs hit the riverbed, and nothing could stop her as she kicked herself forward to lunge out of the water. His boots struck the ground but it was the mare who dragged him up and out. He felt a surge of triumph.

He and his horse were both relieved to climb up the solid ground of the riverbank. But as he led the mare over the gravel, a strange sparkle made him stop. Something small and circular lay on top of the stones at his feet, something that was twinkling with inner fire, as the sunlight struck it at the perfect angle to draw his attention.

He crouched. A moment later, he reached out to pick the item up. Recognizing it immediately, his mouth dropped open.

He found himself looking at a beautiful golden ring set with a square blue sapphire. There was only one ring like it. It was Cora's ring. She had told him that she lost it. He turned it over and there was her name, written in tiny letters. He shook his head in wonder, and then put the ring into his pocket.

He became even more determined to reach Adin. Turning his head, he saw it: a curling, silver ribbon, descending from the high ground. All he had to do was take a straight path to meet it. The King's Road.

From here, he would have a fast ride to Adin. Cora needed him.

Nothing was going to stop him.

Chapter 50

MALGANNIS WAS SURROUNDED by people, behind him and on both sides, arrayed in long rows to cover as much of possible of Adin's outer wall.

And yet he was alone.

The city's defenders around him had taken one look at his face and given him a wide berth. Malgannis had climbed up to take this last look. Wind gusted into his face. He gazed out at the immense number of enemy soldiers preparing to destroy his homeland. He took in the sight of the twenty tall siege towers.

Chain mail covered his arms and torso. Steel plates formed a skirt to protect his lower half. He had no helmet, but he planned to don one, just before he left the city to walk alone toward the enemy force. He would raise his sword into the air, his intention clear to all.

If his life was a story, and Malgannis was the hero, then Baelock Fain would answer his challenge.

Of course, Malgannis was no hero.

He knew he would never get a chance to fight. Baelock Fain, the man with two lives and two names, was anything but a fool. He might defeat Malgannis in combat, or he might not. No one would ever know, because arrows would fill the sky. Malgannis wouldn't get half way to the enemy before he died under the onslaught. And then it would be over.

Not many could say they were going to experience death for a second time. Even fewer could say that both times, they were well aware of their impending death, including its manner.

Today, Malgannis was going to die again. He would go back to where he deserved to be.

One last time, he forced himself to remember.

✦

Ten years.

Where had the time gone? Malgannis was forty-eight when they offered him the kingdom of Aranor. He knew he couldn't take it up; he couldn't become king, not while Baelock Fain still lived. But even then, he had thought his quest might take him a few months... maybe a year... perhaps two or three.

Malgannis felt old. He was old. He had missed ten years spent at his son's side, as Alfred took on the burden of being king. Instead Malgannis had traveled the length and breadth of the known world, always one step behind his quarry. He had crossed the Sea of Mirrors half a dozen times. He had ventured into the icy north, where the locals referred to even Vailand as the south. Rumors sent him to Kiora, but then his hunt proved fruitless. Baelock Fain was in Gila, posing as an exiled noble from Odfeld. Then he was at Inadris, a long term guest in the city's finest tavern.

One thing Malgannis knew was that he had often been close, within a day or two of catching up to his enemy. Baelock left a trail. Innkeepers' daughters murdered, just for Malgannis to find them. More than one of Baelock Fain's own Vailander bodyguards tortured, perhaps planning to betray their one-time king. Gold spent lavishly, no doubt blood-soaked plunder from Baelock's numerous conquests.

Now Malgannis was again close. And this time was different.

Baelock Fain had spent all his gold. His companions had deserted him, one by one. Even his horse had gone lame. Malgannis had found the animal whinnying in pain, wandering by the road.

Malgannis had eight strong men with him on fast horses. Among them were Aranor's most skilled trackers. Together, they had pursued Baelock Fain to Plura in Nara's north, where Baelock had been occupying an abandoned house in a close-knit town where the locals liked to gossip. The chase had begun, leading them across the mountains, through the east of Kor, and on a wild ride in the Forest of Asham.

Every time a member of Malgannis's company complained about the speed they were forced to make, he threatened to leave the man behind. He knew they were frightened of him, and he didn't care. If they didn't want to be with him, he would do this alone. As the hunt took Malgannis toward more settled places on the way to the Sea of Kor, one thought remained with him at all times. If he didn't catch his enemy before he reached Port Vein, Baelock would take a boat and vanish, and he would lose him altogether.

As Malgannis kept his eyes on the road ahead, wondering how much time he had before Baelock would reach the sea, the barks of dogs filled the air, along with the thunder of horse hooves. A breeze blew in his face, smelling of salt. The people at the last village had said he would soon find two landmarks. One was an old lighthouse atop a high cliff. The other was a convent, near a circle of trees. The trees gave the convent its name: Seven Elms. When he saw the convent, Port Vein would be just a few hours ride away.

For a decade Malgannis had hunted this man, who had proudly taken the title of butcher, who had razed countless towns and villages and slaughtered untold numbers of men, women, and children. One of Baelock's raids had targeted the village of Rathlee, Malgannis's home. The things the Vailanders had done to his wife and daughter...

He turned his mind away. The important thing was that at last he had his enemy in his sights.

He continued to scan the terrain as his horse raced along, lifting his body up and down with every movement. Captain Styles, a sturdy, loyal man who was tougher than his skinny frame suggested, rode just as hard at his side. Then, in ones and twos, came rider after rider, all moving with haste to keep up with their leader. At the front of the group, the lean hunting dogs barked as they led the way.

Malgannis reminded himself that if Baelock left the road, the dogs would tell him. But as he searched the landscape, he was looking for more than just a solitary man on foot, or places where his quarry might attempt an unlikely ambush.

Baelock had left distractions in his path.

There was the woman, Malgannis would never know who she was, but back when Baelock had still had a horse, he had left her by the side of the road, cut up and bleeding from the thigh and shoulder. Malgannis had reined his group in. Some members of his company had experience tending wounds on the battlefield, and had tried to stanch her wounds. She lingered, while Malgannis paced and worried, not only about her fate, but about his fleeing quarry. His men tried everything, but when she died, he and his men swiftly buried her before resuming their pursuit.

Then there was the wretched old man – a vagrant, Malgannis guessed – nailed by his hands to a stake. His moans were horrific to hear. He had cried out, over and again, for water. Malgannis and his men had pulled up. They had no choice.

At the same time, even as Malgannis felt pity for the vagrant, he decided that he would leave some of his men while he continued the chase with the others. But the nails were buried too deep. Malgannis couldn't leave his best tracker, his finest archer, his strongest swordsman, and his hunt master. In the end, it took six of them, working together, to figure out a way to get the vagrant's wrists out of the wooden plank. Once the man was freed, Malgannis left the youngest member of his group to help the wretch to the last village, a dozen miles behind them.

Baelock's delaying tactics were working.

As Malgannis rode hard and worried about what might come next, clouds began to gather overhead. The smell of salt grew stronger. The weather had been worsening as his group approached the frigid sea. In addition to watching the landscape, he began to glance anxiously up at the heavens. A storm could only hinder his pursuit, while helping Baelock to vanish.

Another concern was the haze gathering on the right hand side of the road. At first the mist was thin, just mere wisps here and there, and Malgannis could still see bushes and grass, trees and rocks dotting the terrain. The farther he and his men traveled on the road, however, the thicker the mist became.

From horseback at his side, Malgannis heard his captain calling.

"General," Styles said. "Can you hear it?"

Malgannis listened. As he rode hard, he could only make out the clatter of galloping hooves. He pricked his ears until he finally heard another, fainter sound, a repetitive rumbling. At first, he thought it was thunder from the gathering storm, but then he knew what it was: the constant pounding rhythm of a savage sea as it pounded upon rocks, wearing them down a hair's breadth at a time.

His sense of dread grew stronger the louder the sea became. He knew they were nearing Port Vein. Just a few hours and Baelock Fain would be on a boat. Malgannis was so close. This opportunity might never come again.

He had to go faster. Time was running out. He glared back at his men. "Faster," he growled. "Faster!"

A moment later Malgannis saw a tall, thin tower appear in the mist. The lighthouse was a good distance from the road, but without the haze, Malgannis would have seen it from much farther away. The cylindrical structure was tall and made of white-washed wood and stone, tapering until it narrowed at the top.

"Should we investigate, General?" Styles asked.

Malgannis focused on the lighthouse. The beacon was unlit and several planks were missing from the walls; the lighthouse had the air of an abandoned building. If a keeper lived there, as cold as it was up here in the north, he wouldn't allow drafts to come in through the holes.

Also, Malgannis knew Baelock Fain. Retreating to the lighthouse, where there was only one way in or out, was a foolish move, and Baelock Fain was anything but foolish. The man they were hunting would be heading for Port Vein, where he could disappear altogether. It was what

Malgannis would do.

"No," Malgannis said with certainty.

"Are you sure? We could rein in and let the dogs—"

"I said no." Malgannis repeated.

Styles gave an abrupt nod. "General."

The chase continued. As Malgannis rode, he cocked his head and sniffed; there was a new odor in the air. Wood smoke? He kept up his unrelenting gallop and searched the cold and misty landscape. The road here passed through a sparsely populated region. The hills were windswept, with long yellow-brown grass that was tough enough to withstand the elements and thrive in the salty air. Trees were few.

And so when Malgannis saw a circle of trees on a hill, the sight stood out. His eyes continued to rove. The smell of smoke became stronger.

Then he saw it.

Emerging through the haze was a bigger structure than any he had seen in a long time. His eyes were on a hulking, manor-style building with corner towers and high wooden walls.

"In the names of all the gods," Styles breathed. "That's the convent."

Malgannis's couldn't look away. He knew he had found another distraction.

Seven Elms Convent was on fire.

Malgannis slowed, which meant that he was still riding at a fast pace. He made out detail as he and his company neared. The convent was close to the road; he and his men would pass right by. Bright red flame sent spears into the sky that climbed higher and higher. A wide plume of smoke was so tall that the top of it merged with the storm clouds high above.

When he reached the convent, Malgannis didn't need to give a signal. He reined in, and his company pulled up behind him. No one spoke. He was aware of everyone arrayed around him sharing anxious glances.

Fire licked up three of the corner towers. Even as Malgannis watched, the smoke grew thicker and darker. He heard a crash from somewhere inside. Flames stretched, leaning out to reach the fourth tower. The heat must have been ferocious, for the fourth tower was burning in mere seconds.

Malgannis felt Captain Style's eyes on him, along with the eyes of his men.

"We know who did this," Malgannis said. He turned and gave an order to a slender young soldier, a man swift to follow orders and nimble on his horse. "Duncan," he instructed. "Ride to the gates and call out. See if there's anyone inside. Quickly."

The dogs sank down onto their bellies, panting after the long run. Malgannis watched and prayed to all the gods. The convent looked abandoned. There were no cultivated fields outside; there was no livestock; no one had come to try to put out the flames. Time felt like it was flying past. Malgannis kept picturing Baelock Fain, with his knife-sharp chin and deep-set eyes, his ghostly white skin and long black hair. In his imaginings, his enemy was on a ship, watching the retreating coast, safe and secure, planning his next identity.

Duncan was as swift as Malgannis had hoped.

"Report," Malgannis snapped.

"The gate's nailed shut," Duncan said.

"Did you call out?"

"Loud as I could, General."

"Hear anyone?"

"Not a soul."

"See anyone?" Malgannis persisted.

"No."

Malgannis watched the burning convent. It would take time to get the gates open. There was no doubt in his mind; to remain any longer would give Baelock Fain the time he needed to escape. The man had a vicious cunning; even now, he was torturing Malgannis with indecision. Almost certainly, Baelock had found the abandoned convent, set fire to the structure, and nailed the gates shut.

"It's abandoned. We keep going," Malgannis said.

"Sir..." Captain Styles spoke up. Everyone looked troubled. "It's a convent."

"I have given the order," Malgannis called, sweeping his gaze over not just the captain, but all of his men. "We keep going," he repeated. "Ride out!"

Malgannis yanked on his reins, turning his horse away from the convent. He dug his heels into the creature's flanks, and soon he and his company had left the burning structure behind them.

Baelock Fain was close. So close. If Malgannis didn't catch him now, he would hurt more innocents. Malgannis was determined. He knew he couldn't falter.

✦

It was Malgannis's decision to return to Seven Elms Convent. He led his company at a much slower pace as the blackened structure appeared out of the mist. When Malgannis reached the convent, he glanced at the circle of trees, and then returned his attention to the ruin as he reined in.

In the few hours since he had last passed by, there had been some recent rain, with storm clouds threatening more to come. There was no longer any flame, but smoke still climbed the sky and charcoal was a bitter taste in his mouth.

He slid off his horse. The animal ducked its head as it began to chew on the tough grass. The sky rumbled, but there was another, more distant thunder: the sound of a sea pounding at the bottom of the nearby cliffs.

"General?" Styles asked.

Malgannis focused on the forbidding wooden structure, which was too big to be a house, and too ugly to be a manor, almost like a fortress but without military purpose. The fire had done its work. Most of the convent was blackened and crumbled, torn apart as if a giant fist had pounded it from above. One of the four towers had crumbled into a charcoal mess. The gate was at an angle, half off its hinges.

The gusting wind carried the smell of the nearby sea. Malgannis's long, gray-streaked hair blew about his face. He felt tense, disquieted. As he stood with his legs apart, staring grim-faced at the convent, clouds again began to gather, almost directly overhead. He cracked his knuckles. Another rumble of thunder made a sound like tumbling rocks.

A new sound made him take his eyes away from the ruins, a whine, low by his knees. He crouched to give the dog a pat, meanwhile returning his attention to the convent.

He glanced toward his captive.

Baelock Fain glared back at him. The Vailander had been planted on the ground by one of the soldiers, and sat on the gravel beside a horse with his knees up. Manacles enclosed his wrists, with matching metal circles binding his ankles together. A steel collar encircled his neck, connected by chain to his wrists. His long black hair was wet and plastered to his face. His once-fine clothing was in rags. But the look of venom in his eyes, that was still the same.

"I didn't think you had it in you, Ironclaw," Baelock Fain said.

"General, let us depart," Styles said.

Malgannis ignored him. "Help me with the gate," he said. "I have to see."

He gave the convent all of his attention as he began to walk, and as he approached, his boots crunched on the bone-dry gravel.

When he reached the gate, he waited as his men pried off the timbers fastening it closed. The fire had taken hold, however, and the gate was already torn from its once-tight frame. The gate began to move, groaning as it slid across the ground until it revealed the opening it had once hidden.

Malgannis was the only one to approach the opening and look inside. He sensed that something was wrong, and the feeling only grew. Heat washed over him, but after the rains, it had died down enough to enter.

The first thing he saw was a gnarled tree, in the middle of the courtyard. The fire had been so fierce that even the tree was blackened. A rope swing dangled from a horizontal branch; the hemp was surprisingly unharmed compared to everything around it. Not far away, a rag doll lay on its side, giving him an eerie stare.

He walked forward. Smoke stung his eyes, burning with a different fire from anything he had experienced before. The convent's central courtyard was the most open part of it. The halls and living quarters all framed the center.

He spied an opening wide and whole enough for him to enter. He ignored the harsh scratching sensation in his lungs and the growing pain in his throat and ducked inside, to follow a hallway that opened onto room after room.

Time passed as he hunted for survivors. All he found were the dead women who had called the convent home. The last room was the only one different, but it was also the worst. He discovered a gray-haired woman with her throat cut. Nearby was a girl, bearing a similar wound. The fire hadn't reached either of them, but in her terror, the old woman had cut the girl's throat, rather than have her burn alive, and then she had sliced her own.

Malgannis ended up on the ground with the girl's head on his lap. She was a pretty girl, with pale skin, honey-colored hair, and beautiful, big blue eyes.

Chapter 51

TOMORROW WAS COMMEMORATION DAY, Cora's last day. She gave her life so that Malgannis could come back.

Malgannis. A ruthless man. A man with the blood of innocents on his hands.

She pushed herself away from the table. She didn't know why she had sat down; the plate of fruit, seeded bread, and cheese was untouched. Logan's last words were still with her. He knew she had made a pact with darkness. What happened next was in his hands.

She decided to head out to the gardens. They were the one place where it sometimes took the guards and stewards a reasonable time to find her. But as she began to leave the room, she realized that Hailsham stood watching her from the doorway.

"Hailsham?"

"Ah, Majesty."

Hailsham's worried face bobbed up and down. With his hands behind his back, he had clearly been waiting for her. As Hailsham made way for Cora to leave the dining hall, he nodded to indicate another man, seated on the bench against the wall outside.

Cora saw that the stranger was old, easily older than seventy. His shoulders were slumped and his hair was entirely white, with wrinkles carving his skin into countless furrows. He groaned as he put his hands on his knees to push himself to his feet.

"Sorry, Majesty," the old man said in a reedy voice. "Let me bow... Just a minute."

"Please, remain seated," Cora said gently. She tilted her head at Hailsham.

"This is Duncan," Hailsham said. "I have just learned that he is a veteran, and served Aranor bravely in the Great War." Coming in close to Cora, he leaned in to whisper in her ear. "We should at least hear what he has to say." With a start, Cora remembered about the old man who kept trying to see her. "This time, if he won't say what he wants—"

Duncan's ears must have been better than Hailsham's assumptions. "If I said what it was, Queen Coraline, you would never see me." He rested his cloudy gaze on Hailsham. "He should go, and then I will tell you."

Cora nodded at Hailsham. "Leave us."

Hailsham paused for a brief instant before giving her a small bow. "I will be in the next room."

As Hailsham departed, Cora returned her attention to the old man. She knew instinctively that she had nothing to fear from him. He deserved her respect for his service, and at least a few moments of her time, enough to find out what he wanted. She sat down next to him and turned toward him. "Please," she said. Duncan, she remembered his name was. "What is it?"

"Majesty," Duncan said, fixing her in place with his rheumy eyes, "The reason I couldn't say why I wanted to see you is simple. I have seen a ghost."

Cora's expression shifted into a scowl. She began to stand. "If that is—"

"Wait," he said, and his tone was surprisingly sharp. "It is true. I swear it in the name of the country I love, by all the gods. I have seen the ghost of Malgannis Vandryden."

Cora tried not show any reaction. She sat back down again. Her hands were clasped carefully on her lap. "You served with him?"

"I didn't believe it at first, but I would never forget that face. I didn't just serve with him, Majesty, I watched him die. That's why I had to come here, to see you."

Cora wondered what he meant by watching Malgannis die. She knew the histories. "You were there?"

"Yes, Majesty. I was."

"You didn't watch him die, though," Cora said. "You didn't actually see it. Malgannis died in his sleep on the journey back to Aranor, after the capture of Baelock Fain."

Duncan leaned forward and lowered his voice. "That's what they say, I know that." His eyes became unfocused "But that's not what happened. I've keep it secret, all these years, like they said I should. I knew why, and I didn't resent it. But I'm old now. And you're his great-granddaughter. You deserve to know the truth."

Cora almost didn't want to know. But despite thinking that she'd had enough of Malgannis Ironclaw, that wasn't what came out of her mouth. "Tell me."

"We caught Baelock Fain but there was a convent. Baelock Fain, he... he burned it. Malgannis blamed himself."

Cora focused on keeping her expression even. "Continue."

Duncan was no longer meeting her gaze, he was remembering. "He walked away from the convent, toward the cliff." The old man wiped at his eyes. "I followed him. He didn't seem well."

This time, Cora didn't trust herself to speak. She sat, tensed, and waited for Duncan to reveal the rest of his story.

"Malgannis... he stood on the edge of the cliff. We were high. Far below us, the sea threw itself at the rocks. You can imagine it, can't you? He stood much too close to where the cliff ended." Duncan rubbed his eyes again; Cora realized he was weeping. "He saw me then. 'Soldier', he said. 'See that Baelock Fain is brought to justice.'"

Duncan broke off. He took a long, slow, shaking breath.

"And then he stepped off the cliff," Duncan said. His eyes refocused, and he stared once more at Cora. "He killed himself, Majesty. I was right there. Saw it happen with my own eyes. The histories... the stories... they all have it wrong. The legend, the hero of Aranor, Malgannis Ironclaw, he couldn't live with what happened."

Cora's mouth was open.

Malgannis had chosen to haunt the shadow world. She remembered their conversation, when she had met him for the first time, in the flesh.

"Tell me, Coraline, what did the black priest tell you about me?"

"He said you were between worlds."

"And that's where I deserve to be."

He didn't want to leave the shadow world. He had to do his penance, rather than move on to the afterlife. If he'd had his way, he would never have come back.

"Why are you like this?" she had asked. "Don't you want to live?"

"I've had my life. I made my mistakes. I don't deserve a second life."

Cora was the one who had brought him back. He had said he wouldn't help her, but then there he was, rescuing her after the defeat at the ruins of Leventhal.

She remembered him holding her close, giving her comfort, allowing her time to grieve, as they traveled home together. Casting her mind back, she again heard him describing the terrain, making inane comments, filling the silence, letting her know he was there.

He had ended his own life. Had he suffered enough?

The only thing she knew was that she had to see him.

Chapter 52

IT WAS TIME.

Malgannis was as ready as he would ever be. All he needed to do was depart the walls, don his helmet, take his sword, and order the guards at the gates to lower the drawbridge. His men trusted him. They would obey his command.

Soon it would all be over.

From his high position he took one last, lingering look at his homeland. His great sadness was that the grassy hills he was looking at were covered in enemy soldiers. He turned to look behind him, at the red-tiled houses, the buildings of gray stone, and the elegant palace above it all. When the enemy came, it was all going to burn.

As his gaze moved across the battlements, something in his vision gave him pause.

There, amidst all the soldiers and the normal citizens dressed in whatever armor they could find, was someone walking toward him. He was a man in a black robe, with the hood back, revealing his close-cropped gray hair and pale, narrow face. His eyes were reddened and his skin was flushed.

Malgannis immediately recognized the black priest Cora had visited in the catacombs. As the robed man walked, the city's defenders saw who was coming and drew apart without letting the fabric of his robe touch them. The black priest traveled with a smooth, gliding motion. At last he came to a halt and stared directly into Malgannis's eyes.

"Lord Morgan," the black priest said in a voice heavy with irony.

Malgannis remembered his name: Lexen Crow. And yet that wasn't what Malgannis chose to call him. "Servant of darkness."

He heard a gasp from someone nearby. There were few bold enough to challenge a black priest. The people on the walls backed away, giving Malgannis and the black priest plenty of their own space.

Something occurred to Malgannis. "It was you. You're the one who told her."

"It was only fair to reveal the truth you tried to conceal."

"I was trying to protect her," Malgannis snapped. "She didn't need another disappointment. She needed to believe in something... in someone."

"And you thought that could be you."

"I didn't ask for it. I was fine where I was."

"Perhaps you were." The black priest sadly shook his head. "It is unfortunate that you have proven to be such a disappointment."

"It doesn't matter," Malgannis said. "I have disappointed her. I have disappointed you. I never claimed to be anything I'm not. Now, what do you want?"

"I know the hearts of men, and I can see that your mind is made up. You are going to walk out there, and you are going to die. When it comes to death, my eyes see clearly."

"Then we are in agreement," Malgannis said. He began to turn away. "Leave me to it, priest."

"Wait," the black priest said, resting his fingertips on Malgannis's shoulder. "Before you do what you need to do, I must ask something of you. The men still take your orders. Issue a command. Insist that the queen is not to join any battle."

Malgannis raised an eyebrow. "You care for her so much?"

"We have a bargain. The price must be paid." Lexen fixed Malgannis with his intense stare. "You will do it?"

"I will do what I think is best for her."

Lexen considered for a moment, and then nodded. "And that is not to die from a blade slicing through her body. Good. Farewell, Malgannis Vandryden. At least, unlike your nemesis, you still have your soul. He will conquer the world. But eventually, some day, he will go to hell, while you will at least be better off in the shadow world."

Lexen's robe shifted as he turned and then departed. Again, Malgannis saw the back of the black priest's neck. The tattoo was so familiar, a crescent with a horizontal arrow piercing it.

Malgannis pondered as he watched the black priest's back.

He had to know.

He continued to focus on Lexen Crow as the black priest descended the stairway that connected the battlements with the streets below. Taking a bearing, Malgannis made sure he knew which avenue the man in black was heading down, and then he hurried to follow.

Malgannis knew Adin well, and made sure to keep his distance as he ran forward, his eyes on the black priest, and then stepped behind a wall, peering to make sure he still had his target in sight. There were few people about; with an attack imminent, the streets had a ghostly, expectant feel. Shopkeepers were nailing planks over the doors to their premises. Many more places were closed than open. A few passersby glanced curiously at Malgannis, but anyone about had somewhere they needed to be.

Lexen rounded a corner, and Malgannis raced up to the intersecting wall, waiting a breath before he craned his neck to scan the street.

There he was, unmistakable among the city folk. The black priest moved purposefully, taking another corner into a narrow alley. Malgannis ran forward again. He now found himself watching from behind a fountain in one of the smaller squares. He swore. He couldn't enter the alley without a high chance of being seen.

As he waited, wondering what to do, he knew he had to make a decision. He was about to run to the alley when he stopped, poised on the edge of leaping forward. A man had exited the alley's dark, narrow entrance. He wore a casual brown smock and drab, gray trousers, slightly faded and worn, but there was no mistaking the thin face and close-cropped gray hair.

Exiting the alley, Lexen Crow glanced from side to side, then resumed walking. Malgannis followed him only a little farther, to a tall wooden door in one of Adin's main thoroughfares. As he was about to reach out to the handle, Lexen fell into a fit of coughing. It was some time before he gathered his strength and pulled the door open to enter.

Malgannis tried to guess what the building was; there were so many shops, houses, and craftsmen in Adin that at first he wasn't sure. Then he saw the symbol of the goddess Lura beside the frame: a golden leaf. His brow furrowed. There was a mystery here, and he intended to solve it. The black priest had just changed his clothing and entered an apothecary.

A few moments later Lexen left the building with a bundle in his hands. He began to walk away, and Malgannis was faced with a difficult choice. Should he follow Lexen to see where he went next? Or should he talk to whoever it was Lexen had just spoken with? The apothecary could close his shop at any moment.

When Lexen vanished once more into the alley, Malgannis made a decision.

He walked swiftly up to the doorway and pulled the handle to enter. With the skies so dark and moody, the interior was lit up by a trio of strategically placed lanterns. Bottles and flasks lined shelving along the walls. The aromatic scent of spices and herbs mingled strangely with several sharper notes he couldn't put a name too. Spying a portly man in a white tunic shuffling bottles around, Malgannis went right up to him.

"Do you know who I am?" Malgannis asked.

The plump apothecary looked startled. He was in his late forties, and from the golden rings on his fingers, his trade was relatively successful. "Lord Morgan..." He trailed off. "Err. Ahem. What can I do for you?"

"That last man who just came in. What did you give him?"

"Why... milk of the poppy." His brow furrowed. "Red pepper berry. Wormroot."

"For what?"

"Poor man," the apothecary said, shaking his head. "His body is ridden with tumors."

"You know him?" Malgannis asked, perplexed.

"Of course. He served with Lord Fowler. I always help veterans. He comes every day. Once the tonic is made, it must be consumed quickly."

Thoughts whirled through Malgannis's mind. Lexen was a veteran? He now remembered how he knew the tattoo. It was the sign of a freeman who had pledged his life to the service of a lord.

And yet Lexen was no former soldier. He was a black priest.

Something wasn't right.

Malgannis nodded his thanks and left. He scanned the street, but Lexen Crow was long gone. He continued to think as he walked, working to put the pieces together.

Lexen wanted to prevent Cora from coming into harm's way. He had tumors... some kind of degenerative disease.

Malgannis was barely aware of his surroundings as he tried to make the connections. He had always assumed that Cora was marked for death. She was cursed. She had signed away her life. Tomorrow, the mark would spread, until she fell down dead, and the bargain she had made was done.

And yet he had heard the stories. What was the exact wording that the black priest had used, when he had made her sign her agreement in blood?

Lexen's current body was once desirable—but now it was not. Cora was young and healthy.

Everyone said black priests lived forever.

Lexen Crow had seen an opportunity to accomplish two goals: to find an opponent for Baelock Fain, and to get himself a new body.

And now, Cora was the queen.

Malgannis lifted his gaze to stare straight ahead, although his eyes were unfocused. For Cora, it was a fate worse than death. The real her died, and someone else ended up walking around in her form.

His footsteps quickened, as he hurried toward the palace.

Chapter 53

IT DIDN'T MATTER how tired he was, Erik rode his mare hard and fast.

Adin was a city under siege. He was fortunate that his face was known, or the guards would never have lowered the drawbridge. He could see how desperate the situation was from the people he was seeing up on the battlements; among the trained soldiers were old men, women, and boys. With the streets of Adin empty, he crossed the city faster than he ever had before. His knuckles were white as he gripped his horse's reins and navigated the quiet streets.

At last he found himself in sight of the palace. He rode straight over the causeway connecting the palace's smaller island to the city, and then he was approaching the pair of palace guards in bright blue uniforms with golden embroidery on either side of the palace's main gate. When the guards brought their halberds into a warding position, he slowed his horse, allowing them to see him.

Erik knew he was dirty and unkempt. But he had made it. It was Commemoration Day, and Adin still held.

The older of the two guards, a man with black hair and a stubbled chin, called out, his face stern. "Halt!"

Erik drew up. His mare was blowing hard.

The second guard was younger, with a pockmarked face and a long nose. He tilted his head, and then his eyes gradually widened and he placed a hand on his companion's shoulder. "Wait," he said. "By all the gods... It's Lord Wallace."

The older guard's stern expression melted away as he realized. "Erik Wallace? Everyone thinks you're dead."

"The queen," Erik said quickly. "Where is she?"

The two guards exchanged glances. Both looked worried. When they didn't immediately answer, Erik spoke sharply.

"Is she well? What is it?"

The older guard rubbed his stubbled chin. He came in close so he could look up at Erik and speak in a low voice. "There's something happening. They're keeping it quiet." He nodded at his companion. "Neither of us is sure what it is, but it involves the queen. My Annie, she works as a maid. She said they're all worried about her. It's got something to do with Logan Kane."

Erik lifted his gaze to stare at the palace. "Where is Lord Morgan?"

The two guards glanced at each other again.

"You wouldn't know... Lord Morgan..." the older guard said hesitantly. "He's gone missing. There's a rumor he's been imprisoned, though I couldn't guess what for."

A hundred thoughts stormed through Erik's mind. Malgannis imprisoned. Something worrying happening with Cora.

He had a terrible sense of foreboding. Cora had never told him what it was she had done to bring Malgannis back from the dead. She had paid a price of some kind, and if Logan Kane found out...

"Lord Wallace?" The guard with the pockmarked face asked. "One more thing. It might help." He glanced at his companion, who nodded. "We were told to stay away from the dungeon yard."

"Thank you both," Erik said.

The two palace guards drew apart and Erik again kicked his mare forward. He passed through the gates and saw the palace up ahead, at the end of the colonnaded path, with lawns on both sides of him. He left the path to veer at an angle from the palace's main doors, heading toward the far side.

He saw more guards, but their mouths dropped open as they recognized him, and they let him continue without challenge. This was his home. He had grown up in Adin Palace. He had pushed himself beyond endurance to get here. No one was going to stop him.

The dungeon yard was well away from the palace, near the woods. He snapped at his reins, riding his mare hard until he saw the terrace and rose gardens on the palace's other side. Fountains and flowers sped by as he traveled through the lattice of yellow sandy paths, past one hedge, and then another. Soon he was on open grassland, with the woods at the limits of vision. He focused his attention on the distant cluster of buildings hidden behind a row of trees.

The dungeon was famous for once housing Baelock Fain. The Vailander had spent a number of days in a cell below ground, before he was tried in the dungeon yard and then executed by hanging on the hills outside Adin. The cells hadn't been used in Erik's memory, but as part of the palace complex the dungeon was maintained and kept in working order. As a boy, Erik and Patrick had explored the cells and pretended to lock each other up. Patrick had once dared Erik to spend a night in Baelock Fain's cell. Erik had lasted an hour. When it was Patrick's turn, he had changed his mind and stubbornly refused.

As Erik came close to the circle of ugly stone buildings, he saw a number of people in the dungeon yard. Whatever was taking place, they were keeping it secret from the public. He slid off his horse's back and tied the reins to a nearby tree. Now on foot, he approached the screen of trees.

Twenty or more people had gathered on the cleared space between the guard's quarters, the stables, the storeroom, and the dungeon itself, where Erik knew the barred iron gate led to a stairway that plunged underground. He saw three big, sturdy chairs with high backs and straight arms, almost like thrones. The three chairs bore two scrawny old men and one woman with long white hair pulled back from her head; when Erik saw their severe gray and yellow robes, he knew that they were judges.

Pacing back and forth in front of the judges was Logan Kane, the Baron of Fastness. He was giving a speech, emphasizing points by pounding his fist into his hand. Erik didn't know the small crowd of onlookers, but they were well-dressed; he guessed they might be from the baron's staff.

As Erik neared, he gained a better view through the crowd, and then he saw Cora.

He stopped completely, shocked into stillness.

Cora stood in the middle of everything, the focus of the three judges and the onlookers.

She was shackled.

Thick metal bands enclosed her wrists, connected to each other with chain. Manacles also fastened her ankles. Erik was so used to seeing her hair in a braid that it was unnerving to see her long hair bedraggled, and that she wore nothing but a plain white tunic with draping sleeves. As she hung her head, she didn't look determined or defiant. She looked broken.

He sensed movement. All of a sudden he had a huge man on either side of him, guards in the blue and red uniforms of Fastness. He felt a strong hand grip his left arm, and the other guard clutched his right arm.

"That is close enough, Lord Wallace," one of the guards said in a low rumble.

Erik tested their strength, but they easily held him in place. He could only watch helplessly, and do his best to hear what it was that Logan was saying.

"...and so she made a pact with darkness. She discarded her most cherished beliefs. She tainted her very soul." Logan thrust out an arm to point at Cora. "Our queen is not deserving of the title. She has brought shame on her family name and shame on our nation." He stared grimly at Cora and raised his voice. "Coraline Vandryden. In the names of all the gods of light, show us your mark."

Cora was thin-lipped as she shook her head. Logan kept his arm pointed at her, and then dropped it to stride over to her. He lifted Cora's arm above her head, and because of the shackles he brought her other arm with it. He roughly pulled her white sleeve down.

Erik saw the first green and black swirls, like the bruise marks left by someone's fingers as they squeezed her arm with force. The redness between the swirls was bright and fiery, the color of fresh arterial blood. The mark started just below her wrist and grew savage and evil as it traveled toward her shoulder, before continuing under the fabric of her tunic.

The people in the crowd gasped.

Erik realized he was shaking his head from side to side. He didn't want it to be true. And yet it all made a terrible sense. After her father's death, when Patrick became king, Cora was distraught. Then she sent Erik to meet a man at Mount Janus. It was only much later, in the Stony Mountains, that Malgannis revealed himself. But Cora, she had always known who he was. She had made a bargain. She had paid a price.

And now Erik understood; she had sold the most valuable thing she possessed: her life. Logan had found out. She was now on trial for what she had done.

Logan released Cora's arm.

"We can see the mark," Logan said loudly. "Is it true that you made a bargain with the lord of the underworld?"

Cora hung her head. "I have no reason to lie."

"Louder," Logan said. "Speak so we may hear you."

"Yes," she called.

"What bargain did you make?"

"I gave my life to bring back my great-grandfather, Malgannis Vandryden, to help us in our time of need."

"Your life?" Logan asked. "But then how are you still here?"

"I was given sixty days. Today is the last of those days. Imprison me or condemn me, the result is the same."

Erik's legs felt weak. She had to be lying. Surely she couldn't be about to die. It couldn't be true.

And yet she bore the mark, and why would she lie about such a thing?

His vision blurred. Cora's intense desperation had led her to do something terrible. And the worst part of it was, she had failed. Erik had assessed the defenders on the walls, and compared them to the enemy force outside. He had seen the siege towers and knew the horror they would bring. Adin was going to fall. Malgannis was missing or in prison.

Erik didn't know what Malgannis had done to incur Logan's wrath, but the baron was the new power in Aranor. Perhaps Logan thought he could make an agreement with the enemy and surrender. Erik had no doubt that when the trial was over, Logan Kane would be king.

"Who did you make this bargain with?" Logan called as he paced in front of the judges.

"With a black priest. I said the words. I signed the pact in blood."

Erik thought he saw movement in the trees behind the dungeon. Someone was watching. The figure wore a black robe and stood a distance from the others, in a place where he could observe without being noticed.

"Tell me, Coraline Vandryden," Logan said. "Do you have anything more to say?"

"Only that I have carried this burden for sixty days. Now, at the end, I have no reason to hide the truth. Tonight, I will die. Tomorrow, the enemy will come. Nothing will stop either of those two things from happening."

"Is this your final statement?" Logan asked.

"Yes."

Logan turned to face the judges. "Then I request adjudication."

The judges conferred, but it wasn't long before the scrawny old man in the center called out. "The mark says it all. Whether she tells the truth about this being her final day, or it is a deception, we will soon find out. What she has done is unholy. Coraline Vandryden, we sentence you to be imprisoned until you meet your demise. Needless to say, you are no longer queen of Aranor. Lord Kane will act as regent until a new monarch is named. Coraline Vandryden, you will remain in the dungeon until you are dead."

Before he knew what he was doing, Erik was calling out. "This is not justice," he shouted. "I have seen others trade their life force for a favor from a black priest. Why is what she did any different?"

Cora's head jerked around. She stared directly at Erik. "Erik?"

Logan scowled. The judge who had spoken called out. "Silence!"

"Erik!" Cora cried. "I'm sorry I didn't—"

"Cora!" Erik lunged toward her, but the strong guards from Fastness held him firmly in place.

Some more of Logan's personal soldiers came up to take Cora in hand, and as she cried Erik's name, they forcibly dragged her away.

Chapter 54

CORA STOOD ALONE in her cell. She was underground, but a thin shaft had been dug that enabled her to look up through the barred window at the circle of stars that made up the Southern Ring. Clouds passed over the night sky, but the moon was out, and she was able to clearly see the arm she held up to the window.

She had her sleeve rolled up. Her mark was impossible not to see. Soon it would be midnight. Her curse would come to fruition, she would pay her price, and the mark would spread.

The dividing line between one day and another approached. She began to pace the length of her cell, back and forth. There was a wooden cot against the wall, along with a stool, but she wouldn't be in any need of either item of furniture. The palace was far away, but the night was still and silent, and she heard a distant bell tolling the hour. She counted the peals until she reached the number eleven.

When the bells finished, she returned to pacing. She thought about her life. There was little else for her to do. But then she heard a nearby gate open and close. A soft whisper of footsteps came closer and closer.

Her head turned, and her gaze went to the barred iron gate that kept her in her cell. She saw a pale, narrow face, looking out from the folds of a black robe. Lexen Crow stood and watched her through the bars. His expression was contemplative.

"Come to watch me die?" she asked.

"The punishment is harsh," the black priest said. "A lifetime in prison."

"We both know that for me, a lifetime means less than an hour. I don't believe I will have time to find it difficult to be in a cell."

"Nonetheless, I have never thought of Logan Kane as a devoted follower of the white gods."

"He wants to be king."

"I thought as much." Lexen paused, clasping his hands in front of him. "I have come to say farewell, Coraline. I doubt our paths will cross again. Before I depart, tell me, was there any good in him at all?"

"None," Cora said. "Nothing has gone right. Aranor is going to fall. And he couldn't stop it."

"I understand," Lexen said. He looked down at the ground. "For what it is worth, I am sorry. I honored my part of the bargain. It was up to him to do the rest." He met her gaze. "Farewell, Coraline Vandryden."

She didn't say anything in reply. The black priest turned and glided away, until he was gone altogether.

She returned to the window. The stars had slightly moved position in the sky. She focused on the Southern Ring and returned to contemplating the turn of events that led to her being marked, and everything that had happened since.

She again heard bells. One. Two. Three.

She held her breath and lifted her arm to the starlight.

Seven. Eight. Nine.

The spidery tendrils wrapping her upper arm began to fade. Next were the curling sections of black and green near her elbow. Where the mark spread up toward her wrist it became lighter in color, and softened toward the shade of normal skin.

Ten. Eleven. Twelve.

With the tolling of the final bell, the mark faded completely, until it was gone altogether.

Cora felt a warm glow deep inside her chest. It spread from her abdomen to her heart and throughout her entire body. It made her limbs tingle and an upward tilt tug at her lips until it burst open and she was smiling.

She turned and saw two other smiling faces. Malgannis and Erik stood side by side on the other side of the barred gate, and the sight of them both almost made her laugh out loud. Another figure stepped forward out of the darkness, and she saw Logan also with them.

"It worked," Cora said. She wiped her eyes. "It worked!" She shook her head at Logan. "You were terrifying. I found myself half-believing you."

"He certainly fooled me," Erik said.

Malgannis unlocked the bars, but it was Erik who was the first to enter the cell. Erik rushed toward her and pulled her into his arms. Cora hugged him just as tightly back. She felt him breath in deeply, inhaling the scent of her. Tears welled in her eyes and spilled as she held Erik as close as she possibly could. With blurred vision, she looked past Erik's shoulder to Logan, but there was no resentment there.

"The black priest?" Malgannis asked.

"My men know what to do," Logan said. "He won't get away."

Chapter 55

LEXEN CROW WAS A CREATURE of the night. As he left the dungeon behind, he took long, gliding steps, his hands enfolded in the fabric of his black robe. Trees soon surrounded him as he entered the woods near Adin Palace.

Against the midnight black the emerald trees were strangely sinister, branches appearing more gnarled than they did at daytime. He followed the horse trails that countless royal families had used throughout the generations. Then it was time to depart the path and plunge into the thick forest where pheasants, deer, and wild boars lurked in wait.

But he was forced to pause. The scratching, tingling pain started low in his chest. He knew what was coming and put a hand on a tree's trunk for support. His lungs convulsed, and then he was coughing. The sensation was like fire in his chest. Liquid burned at the back of his throat, and he snatched a piece of white linen from a pocket inside his robe to splutter into the cloth.

The coughing fit finally subsided. He looked at the linen and even in starlight saw multiple large and small flecks against the white. Replacing the cloth, he reached farther into another pocket to withdraw a tiny glass vial. He removed the stopper and raised the vial to his lips. He tilted the little vessel to allow several droplets to fall to his tongue.

Instant relief flooded through his body. The scratching feeling in his chest was still there, but it was distant, and then it barely bothered him at all. He returned the vial to his pocket and kept walking.

He knew where he was going and headed deeper into the forest as soon as he saw the stone marker. Foliage grabbed at his robe but he pushed through, eager to be free of this city and its impending doom.

He reached a clearing and went straight to the base of a mighty tree. Kneeling, he scratched at the leaves below the tree's trunk. It took some time, but he uncovered the metal plate and used the handle to pry the lid open. He revealed a square hole, three feet to a side, with steep ladder-like steps leading down.

Once he was in the secret tunnel, he took a few steps down and then reached to a ledge by the side. He was relieved when he located the torch in the alcove, along with flint and steel. Once he had the torch burning, he continued to climb downward and closed the lid behind him. He soon reached level ground, but even then it still had a downward slope.

Lexen knew Adin better than any man, because he was older than any normal man. Long ago, when Adin was still a young city, Mad King Agar had dug the tunnel in case his people ever revolted and attempted to besiege or storm the palace, so that he would be able to take another route than the causeway. Adin had many secrets. Lexen knew them all.

Holding his torch high, he followed the tunnel as it took him deep underground. When the slope began to go up, rather than down, he knew he was leaving the area of the river, and tried not to think about the volume of water. The passage took a sharp turn to the left, and then another to the right. After stretching on for perhaps half a mile, he came to a set of stairs. He climbed until he came to another tunnel. A puff of fresh air caressed the skin of his face. A glimmer of natural light appeared ahead.

He found himself at an iron gate, and removed a key from his robe to unfasten the lock. The gate creaked as he peeled it open. He looked first left, then right. Closing and locking the gate behind him, he climbed four stone steps. He emerged out onto a narrow alley, where half of the iron gate was sunken at the bottom of the steps and it would barely merit a glance.

A temple bell began to toll.

He counted the peals, one after the other. Even as he walked, he couldn't help himself. Nine. Ten. Eleven. Twelve.

Midnight had come and gone. She would know.

Hurrying along, he followed the city streets, the hood of his robe over his head as he hugged the stone walls and took turn after turn. He rushed through the city, keeping to the shadows, wary of the few people he encountered out so late at night.

It was difficult not to feel both angry and frustrated.

His luck had gone from bad to worse. First, a horrific disease had taken hold of this body, and then his choice of a new body had gone terribly wrong. Faced with two options, both of them bad, there was nothing else he could do. Coraline was destined to spend the rest of her life in a cell. If he had kept to the bargain, and left this body – cursed as it was – to inhabit hers, he would be forced to face her fate.

He had no choice. He had released Coraline from her bargain.

Even now, he was only just coming to terms with the scale of his failure. He had been so close to achieving his goal, all to lose everything. In Coraline's body, he would have been able to surrender the city—and then perhaps even make an offer of marriage to its conqueror, once Logan Kane was rid of. Poison or a quiet blade could have dealt with Baelock Fain, sending him back to hell where he belonged. Lexen could have become a dark queen, tearing down the white temples and replacing them with black. Step by step, he could have changed the world.

He had no choice. He would have to start again.

At last he saw the next gate he was looking for, set into Adin's thick outer wall. He glanced from side to side, and when he saw he was alone, he fumbled in his robe for another key and shoved it into the lock. As he pulled the gate open, the jangle and groan set his teeth on edge. He entered, locked the gate behind him, and found another stairway leading down.

The stairs kept going, deeper, as he headed below the streets until he knew he was almost at the level of the river. At last he heard the splash and gurgle of water. He came to a set of steps cut into the stone, and at the bottom he saw the river pushing up against the stairway. A tiny boat bobbed on the water. He headed down to the vessel, climbed in, and unfastened the rope.

An archway in front of him was barely big enough to allow the boat to exit. He took the paddle and began to pull at the water, first on the left, then on the right. He ducked his head to allow the vessel through the archway and into the open air.

The current picked up pace. He felt the immediate change in the air as soon as he was in the open. He tilted his head back to peer up at the top of the walls, high, high above. The night was dark and clear. He saw torches on poles and knew that up there the city's defenders were waiting. But in his black robe, against the dark water, he knew that no one would see him.

The night was his domain. He grew confident, putting on more speed as he paddled.

Then he stopped.

There were shapes on the water, many of them. They were too small to be ships, and at any rate, he knew that Aranor's battle fleet had gone to Fastness. He realized they were boats. There were men in the boats, also staying quiet, also wearing black.

Something shot toward him out of the darkness. He saw a wooden vessel, much bigger than his own tiny boat. The bigger boat crashed into his. Someone reached out; a man put his hand on the gunwale. Lexen stared into the man's face to see the flat stare of a soldier, with a sword on his hip and a black cloak covering his uniform underneath.

"I've found him," the soldier called to his fellows. He lunged and grabbed hold of Lexen's arm. "We have been expecting you, priest."

Chapter 56

"WHAT DID HE TELL YOU?" Malgannis asked.

"Just come with me," Cora said.

Malgannis followed at her side as she led him toward the dungeon. The gray clouds had at last released Adin from their smothering presence, and in the light of day, even the ugly cluster of buildings they were approaching couldn't banish the sense of new hope.

As he walked, Malgannis couldn't stop himself from glancing in Cora's direction. Her shining hair was again fashioned in an elegant braid. Her brown eyes were bright, her skin was smooth, and her mouth was no longer twisted with despair. It was early morning but warm, and she even wore a sleeveless dress.

In all, she looked well.

But one thought was more prominent than any other. It was a thought that filled him with more joy than he had felt since the early years of his first life.

Cora was alive.

He knew that Adin was still a city under siege. Today the enemy was expected to attack. And yet the knowledge that she had been released from her curse filled every fiber of his being. He felt resolute and strong, as if he could do anything. Together, they had done it. Their plan had worked. The subterfuge had been difficult to execute, but everyone had come together, from Logan Kane to the captain of the palace guards. They had to make it believable. There couldn't have been any doubt in the black priest's mind.

Poor Erik. The lad had a shock. But in the end Malgannis had found him and explained.

"Majesty. General."

The guards outside the dungeon bowed to them both, before one of the pair turned to open the gate. Malgannis allowed Cora to lead the way, and as they traveled down the steps to head underground, he again caught a glance at her.

Her back was straight. Her bearing was regal, with chin held high and a determined expression on her face. She had grown. When he first met her, she had been so uncertain. Now, here she was, with Logan, Erik, and yes, even Malgannis himself, all acknowledging her right to lead.

She went straight to the only occupied cell. She waited for Malgannis to join her, and as they stood side by side, they both watched the man inside.

The black priest sat on a wooden stool, shoulders slumped as he glared up at Malgannis and Cora. His hood was back, revealing his face, and in the daylight, he simply looked like a sick man, with reddened eyes and sweat on his forehead. A series of low coughs rumbled in his chest, and he wiped his mouth with the back of his sleeve.

Malgannis knew that he wasn't just looking at a man, however. In one form or another, the black priest had lived much longer than him. He wondered how old he truly was.

"Queen Coraline," Lexen said. His gaze moved. "And Malgannis Ironclaw, the Great General."

"Tell him what you told me," Cora said.

"And you will release me?" Lexen asked, staring into her eyes.

"I give you my word."

He put his hands on his knees, pushing to climb to his feet. Through the bars, he now kept his intense gaze firmly on Malgannis.

"Then here is the truth," Lexen said. "In matters of life and death, I deal only with certainty, and I do not lie."

Malgannis glanced from Cora to the black priest. "What is he talking about?"

"Just listen," Cora said.

"I speak of you, Ironclaw. Even you do not know the full story of your own demise. But your queen offers me my freedom, and I have little else to trade."

"You need to hear this," Cora said.

"Are you ready?" Lexen asked.

Malgannis nodded uncertainly.

Lexen continued, "Then here it is, the full tale." He paused to take a breath. "Pursued by a relentless foe, Baelock Fain came to a place called Seven Elms Convent. He knocked and asked for water. The sisters opened the door, and then their fates were sealed. He pushed his way inside, although he did not yet know what it was he wanted to do to buy himself the time he needed to get to Port Vein."

All of a sudden, Malgannis couldn't breathe. He found himself taken back to the road to Seven Elms Convent, to the barking dogs and the thuds of horse hooves. The smell of burned wood reached his nose. He didn't trust himself to speak, and it was Cora whose voice he heard, as if at a distance.

"Go on," she said.

"Baelock Fain had his idea – he would set fire to the convent – and he began to drag anything flammable to the hearth. The sisters realized they were dealing with a madman. As anyone would, they tried to stop him. Baelock realized that in the little time he had, his plan would be too difficult to execute with so many women in his way."

Malgannis felt sick to his core.

"Continue," Cora said, even though her face was pale.

"And so Baelock Fain drew his sword and cut them all down. He killed everyone he found. One. By one. By one. He did it quickly and efficiently as he worked his way through the convent."

Malgannis's eyes became unfocused. He remembered the last room he had found. He had assumed that the sister had cut the girl's throat before doing the same to herself, in terror of the smoke and flames. He had been too overwrought, he hadn't looked for the blade that did it... and in truth, there wasn't one.

"Baelock Fain had what he wanted," Lexen said, "there was now no one to stop him as he set his fire and nailed the gates shut behind him."

Malgannis again heard the words of the man he had sent to the gates. What was his name again? Duncan.

"Did you call out?"

"Loud as I could, General."

"Hear anyone?"

"Not a soul."

"See anyone?" Malgannis persisted.

"No."

Malgannis covered his face with his hands and turned away. His eyes were burning but he didn't allow himself to cry. Cora gripped his shoulder.

He drew in a long breath, releasing it slowly as his shoulders shook. Then he took his hands away. He faced Cora.

"It doesn't change the fact that I kept going," he said hoarsely. "I left them to burn."

"You made a choice," she said simply. "You don't have to accept what happened, but you do need to recognize the truth."

Malgannis stared with glazed eyes at the stone wall. The people who had burned... they were already dead. He found himself having difficulty processing it. He cast his mind back and recalled the neglected lighthouse, and the way he had believed the convent might be abandoned too.

He no longer knew how he felt.

Hearing a jangle, he turned to see that Cora held the key to Lexen's cell in her hand. The black priest's eyes gleamed as she reached out.

A voice reached them, a loud male shout into the dungeon. "Majesty, General! The enemy is advancing!"

Malgannis had an idea.

"Cora," he said. He held out his hand for the key. "Will you leave me alone with him for a moment?"

Lexen glanced from face to face. "You gave your word."

"I don't want to hurt you," Malgannis said. "I just want to talk, and then you can go."

Cora watched Malgannis for a moment. She then nodded. "Of course. Be quick. We need you at the walls." She squeezed Malgannis's shoulder. "Great-grandfather... if it is of any value... to me, you are a decent man."

✦

Cora climbed up the long series of steps that rose ever higher until they reached the battlements on top of Adin's tall outer wall. She kept her gaze fixed up at the stairway's summit. Her back was erect. Her movements were precise.

She was aware of all the eyes on her. Up on the battlements, soldiers saw her approaching and nudged their fellows. Like a ripple in a pond, whispers traveled as word quickly spread. Women in leather aprons they were using as armor stared at her open-mouthed. Boys relaxed their nervous grip on their swords and spears to watch her climb.

With just a few steps remaining, Cora then saw Erik's broad-shouldered figure. When he turned to see what the commotion was, his eyes widened at the sight of her. Standing nearby, Logan gave her an encouraging nod. Even Lord Byron was up on the walls, wrapped in chain mail that some poor squire must have spent hours getting him into. His chin wobbled as he gasped at her.

Cora was wearing her bright silver armor. She had her sword on her hip. Her braided hair was tight on her scalp, but also decorated with tiny silver beads that sparkled in the morning light.

Where murmurs had once bounced back and forth along the battlements, and the defenders had milled as they shared their worries and fears, a perfect silence now fell upon the walls of Aranor's capital city.

All eyes were on Cora. The crowd drew apart to give her space as she walked toward the very edge of the battlements.

She stared at the approaching enemy, seeing the twenty siege towers roll down the hillside toward her, taking in the sight of the swarming infantry, the archers, the rows of knights. She raised her chin, narrowed her eyes, and stared defiantly at the rider who walked his warhorse at the very front of his army. Baelock Fain wore his plate armor and helmet. Beside him was a giant of a man on a draft horse.

Cora placed a hand on the hilt of her sword. She drew it slowly, deliberately, and the sound of scraping steel accompanied the motion.

Once the sword was in her hand, the blade naked for all to see, she turned and swept her gaze over the defenders. She took her time, making sure to reach them all.

And then she thrust her arm into the air. As she pointed her weapon directly into the sky, she opened her mouth to cry out.

"Aranor!"

The resulting cheer from the defenders rushed over her, like a wave that almost threatened to knock her over. The people around her took up the cry. It came from Erik and Logan and Byron, from the boys and women and old men. From the warriors of the Iron Spear, and from the soldiers who had been defeated at Inadris and Leventhal and the three border forts.

"Aranor!"

Chapter 57

BAELOCK FAIN WAS REVELING in his moment of triumph. The sense of power he felt, to be walking his horse at his army's front, was giddying.

Ahead of him lay Adin, the city he had dreamed of conquering since he first led his Vailanders south. Aranor's capital was revealed in all its splendor, beautiful and elegant, yet also vulnerable, like some of the proud women he had taken at Helmsford, who with their wealth and finery expected to be able to buy their way to safety and freedom.

At his side was Halvar, one of the few who knew his true identity, and would follow him to victory and beyond. On his huge horse, Halvar was a strong, indomitable presence. Even the Vailanders in the army were afraid of him.

The downward slope meant that the army had little trouble advancing toward the city. Whirrs and rumbles came from the siege towers; the wooden wheels were huge, but even so, a few fast scouts ran ahead of them to remove the bigger rocks out of their way. The sounds of marching men mingled together: the groan of leather armor, the clang of steel, the thud of boots, the clatter of arrows, the occasional call of an officer.

Baelock turned and held up his hand. One officer took up a cry, followed by another, and another.

"Halt!"

The army ground to a halt.

Baelock's plan was simple. A flat section of ground now separated his attackers from the river and the city's tall wall behind it. His strongest soldiers, veterans from Morania and elsewhere, would fill up the siege towers. The advance would begin. When his army neared the battlements, arrows would of course fill the air, but the towers would form a wall of their own, protecting those inside as well as his soldiers behind. The heavy bridges made of timber planks would slam from the tops of the towers onto the battlements. The attackers would surge forward to fill the top of the wall.

Baelock now scanned the battlements, wondering where Malgannis was. His spies had learned about the bargain the queen had made and her impending doom. Ironclaw would be a broken man, having lost his great-granddaughter, his last surviving descendant. After the death of their queen, the defenders' morale would be as low as it could possibly be.

Victory was inevitable.

Baelock opened his mouth to call out the attack, when he closed it again; something was happening at the top of the wall.

He saw someone in silver armor, a figure with a crown of dark hair filled with tiny sparkles that caught the morning light. She looked too slim to be a man, but she couldn't be...

The woman drew a sword and lifted her blade into the sky. All of a sudden the defenders cried out as one. "Aranor!"

With so many people up on the walls, the sound was loud even from where Baelock was standing. He heard another mighty roar. The words changed.

"For the queen!"

"The queen!"

Baelock's nostrils flared. She was destined to die. Malgannis was supposed to see her suffer. Had his spies given him bad information? Why else had he waited these four days? There was unrest in Vestria and Rumandy, rebellions he needed to tend to. He had waited for nothing.

He clamped down on his irritation. Nothing had changed, he told himself.

Today, he was going to have his final triumph.

✦

Malgannis heard a great roar, from the direction of the city wall.

"Aranor!"

Malgannis was in the palace, and his shoulders were tight; he knew he needed to get moving. And yet he was on the palace's ground level, in the great hall, gazing at a painting.

The painting was of him.

He inspected the painting carefully. In his heart, he felt that it wasn't drawn of him; he was staring at another man. A man who hadn't spent ten years pursuing Baelock Fain. A man who hadn't let his obsession lead him into darkness.

Below the painting was a sword, resting in a pair of brackets to support it horizontally. It was a huge weapon, a great sword, and could only be wielded with two hands. A scabbard enclosed it, with wire of pure gold decorating its length, and a leather shoulder strap.

Malgannis had already checked the blade. The weapon was considered an important part of Aranor's history. Someone had been maintaining it. The edge was sharp enough to cut his thumb if he pressed hard.

There was something else.

Between the sword and painting, he stared at a pair of mailed gauntlets. The gloves were expertly fashioned, made of tiny interlocking rings, and they were as black as the deepest night.

Another powerful roar from elsewhere in the city made sweat collect on his forehead. He lifted the scabbarded sword off its brackets. Hefting its familiar weight, he settled the shoulder strap so that he was carrying the sword on his back. He felt inordinately strange, to be wearing the weapon once more. His sword fit him just as well as it always had.

He then pulled one gauntlet onto his hand, followed by the other.

He wasn't wearing armor, just a black vest with a long-sleeved gray undershirt. On his lower half, he had black leather trousers and his high leather boots. For the first time since his return, he had carefully combed his hair in a certain way, so that it was parted in the middle, with half hanging down to either shoulder.

Perhaps he did look like the man in the painting, with the addition of the gray in his hair.

The time had come.

✦

Erik glanced at Cora. "They're going to come now." He bellowed to the defenders. "Here they come! Be ready!"

Cora tried to put on a fierce, determined expression. And yet when she swiftly scanned the battlements, she couldn't help noticing how thin the line was, how much their numbers were made up of the young and old.

In comparison, the enemy seemed unstoppable. Everyone in Adin knew it, just as Cora knew it. Baelock Fain's army had never lost a battle. Aranor had lost two kings and still failed to prevent the enemy's advance.

Cora realized she was terrified. But she knew she couldn't show it. Instead she kept both hands wrapped around the hilt of her sword, holding the point protectively in front of her.

Baelock Fain was clearly savoring his moment. He sat astride his warhorse, across the space of empty flat grass that separated his army from the river and the city.

But then something strange happened.

Cora heard another cheer from somewhere below her. The sound grew louder and louder. There were no words in it at first, and it became even harder to understand what was happening when she heard another noise: a grinding rumble. Around her the defenders were exchanging puzzled glances. Erik looked just as bemused as she was.

Cora's gaze shot to the side. The rumble was the sound of the drawbridge lowering. At the same time, the gates were drawing apart.

"Who gave the order?" Logan cried.

Another officer called out. "What's happening?"

The drawbridge passed the halfway point and continued to lower. Cora tried to understand why it would be moving. The enemy stirred but had yet to advance any farther. The drawbridge hit the ground with a thunk; it was now all the way down, connecting the city of Adin with the opposite bank of the river.

A solitary man walked onto the wooden bridge. He took purposeful strides as he began to cross to the other side.

Cora felt light-headed. She turned to Erik beside her; he was watching open-mouthed.

The black gauntlets. The long hair. The huge sword on his back.

Malgannis was on his way to the midpoint of the bridge when the murmurs became cheers and then roars that grew in volume until they must have been heard all the way to the palace.

"Morgan! Morgan!"

But then the words changed. Cora would never know who started it, but it was immediately taken up by all.

"Ironclaw! Ironclaw!"

Malgannis drew his broadsword and raised into the air. The cheers became frenzied. Everyone around Cora, no matter who they were, was shouting together. People were stamping their feet; boys were jumping up and down.

When he was halfway along the bridge, Malgannis turned. He met Cora's eyes. His lips moved, and despite the distance, she knew what he was saying.

"You will make a fine queen," he said. "Farewell, my love."

Cora reached out and grabbed Erik. Squeezing his hand, she cast him a quick look. "I don't understand. What's he doing?"

Erik was pale. "He's not wearing armor."

Cora remembered all of Malgannis's teachings. Armor was everything, he had said. It separated the rich and the poor, and at the end of a vicious battle, the living from the dead.

Cora heard Logan's voice. "He is facing his enemy," he said, and his tone was grave as he glanced at her. "One last time."

As Cora watched, the chant from the city continued. "Ironclaw! Ironclaw!"

And yet Cora was unable to prevent the tears from streaming down her face. Malgannis reached the end of the bridge. He walked alone toward the enemy.

Behind him, the city roared.

"Ironclaw!"

Chapter 58

EVERY MAN FACED DEATH on his own.

And yet few were so fortunate as to hear such a wondrous departing noise, the sound of a multitude calling out as one.

"Ironclaw! Ironclaw!"

The roar of Adin's defenders was deafening. It didn't matter what they were all thinking. Was their general, in truth, a descendant of Malgannis Vandryden? Was he a secret relation of the queen, which meant effectively the same thing? For those who didn't know Morgan's face – which was most of them – their awe was even stronger.

Ironclaw was here. He had returned in the flesh to save his homeland in her time of need.

"Ironclaw! Ironclaw!" They cheered over and over.

Malgannis again raised his black fist into the air, but he never stopped walking. He was now on the grass, his focus on the enemy as he approached. For once in his life, his thoughts were clear.

If the battle went ahead, how many would die, on both sides? If he could stop if before it began, how many would be saved?

Throughout his life – both his lives – he had been instrumental in causing so much death, had instigated so many collisions between men with weapons. He wanted this time to be different. He would do this on his own.

A solitary figure, he walked until he was directly in front of the immense host preparing to assault the city—his city. He then came to a halt and thrust the point of his great sword into the ground, to leave the hilt quivering. His meaning was clear. There would be no mistaking his challenge.

Siege towers loomed over him. Knights prepared to charge. Archers could easily pepper him with sharp arrows until he was a bleeding mess on the ground. Flags fluttered from tall standards: flags of Morania and Nara, Kor and Vailand. The mass of infantry seemed countless.

Malgannis glanced back at the battlements to focus on the woman in silver armor. Cora stood right at the edge of the battlements, with another figure beside her. Erik was close by her side; they were in their own space. He thought about Cora and all she had done.

He didn't need to tell her. She knew he was proud of her.

Could he still save her?

It all depended on whether he would get his chance. Without armor, he felt naked. He wore only soft cloth; there wasn't even a leather breastplate on his chest. A wind gusted toward him, blowing at his long hair as he waited. With his sword still quivering in the ground, he stood with legs apart and waited.

He stared directly toward Baelock Fain, the distant man in plate armor, who sat astride his dappled gray warhorse. Malgannis ignored the huge warrior on the draft horse. His eyes were only for his enemy. What happened next would turn on Baelock's decision. Malgannis would either face his enemy, or he wouldn't.

He glanced at his hands and cracked his knuckles. Another gust of wind made his black and gray clothing snap and ripple. At any moment, Baelock Fain could give the command and arrows would fill the sky.

But Malgannis knew the man in front of him. He was arrogant. And here Malgannis was, unarmored, without any support from elsewhere.

The temptation must be hard to resist.

✦

Baelock Fain knew that a multitude of eyes were watching what he was about to do next.

As he sat astride his powerful warhorse, he thought about all the stories he had heard since his rebirth, tales of Malgannis Ironclaw and his turbulent life.

Even in Morania people wanted to know about Malgannis's youth, the period when he had learned about history, strategy, and combat from his father. They wanted to know what his wife had looked like and how he had first met her in a vineyard. They told of the raid that killed his wife and daughter, his desire for vengeance, his rise through the ranks, and his assumption of ultimate command in the struggle against Vailand. Most favored of all was the tragedy of his late life, when he had finally captured his despicable Vailander nemesis, only to die in his sleep on the way home.

No one wanted to know about Baelock's sister, and her capture by slavers at the age of thirteen. No one told stories about his quest to unite the tribes of Vailand, and his seizure of his destiny to become the first king of Vailand. Even now, no one knew that Graven Callow and Baelock Fain were one and the same man.

And here they were, calling from the walls.

"Ironclaw! Ironclaw!"

Baelock Fain's mouth tightened. Malgannis stood in place, legs wide, clearly defying Graven Callow to answer his challenge. His great sword quivered in the ground, the hilt swaying back and forth. Baelock knew that sword.

Malgannis lifted his chin. He punched his fist into his palm. Baelock also knew those black gauntlets. Early in the Great War, when Malgannis first became a general, they had given him his epithet.

Baelock heard a loud call from Halvar, the giant next to him. "Archers!"

"Wait." Baelock held up a hand.

He continued to watch Malgannis. They were evenly matched in height. Malgannis was a little wider, and perhaps stronger, but Baelock was leaner and faster.

There was one great difference between them.

Baelock had always been the younger man, ten or twenty years Malgannis's junior. Now, when Baelock gave Malgannis his appraisal, he saw a beaten man with gray in his hair. His shoulders weren't as square; his back was ever so slightly stooped.

Baelock Fain's eyes narrowed.

How could he have not noticed before? He prided himself on his cunning, his attention to detail, the fact that he was always one step ahead of his opponents.

Malgannis wasn't wearing armor.

Instead, he wore a black vest over a gray undershirt, dark trousers and high boots. The wind was up, whipping the material against his chest. Baelock inspected the older man's frame carefully until he was certain. Malgannis's sleeves were loose; there was nothing hidden under there. Even if Malgannis had a metal plate buried under his vest and somehow molded to his body – something Baelock had never heard of – he wore no helmet, no bracers, no greaves. His head was unprotected as was his waist and legs.

In contrast, Baelock was encased in steel. No one could see his long black hair, his deep-set eyes, or his thin-lipped mouth. Every portion of his body was protected, from his mailed gloves to the interlocking plate armor that covered the rest of him.

In spite of everything, Baelock and Malgannis had never actually fought each other one on one. Baelock felt his blood rising in anticipation. He forced himself to remember the dogs that swarmed him in a pack, snarling and biting as they took him down, just a mile from the docks at Port Vein. He again felt the noose that enclosed his neck, on the hills outside Adin, not far from where he was now. In his mind, he experienced the sensation of falling, and then the snap as his neck broke.

Malgannis remained in place, not far from the end of the drawbridge, which was still lowered. The tension continued to grow. Baelock's neck felt warm, and then his face, and his anger became rage at what this man had done to him.

Baelock heard Halvar's baritone voice from his side.

"If you want him for yourself, take a lance," Halvar said. "Ride him down."

Baelock slid off his horse. One heavy boot, and then the other, struck the ground with a thud. He reached over to his saddle and drew his sword from its scabbard.

"No," he said. "It is time he met his end. I am accepting his challenge."

Chapter 59

MALGANNIS HEARD A ROAR from the direction of the enemy before he caught any movement. He focused on the ground up ahead, and then he saw Baelock Fain walking toward him, his naked sword held in both hands.

The defenders on the walls of Adin answered with their own powerful cry.

Malgannis stepped forward to grab the hilt of his sword and yank it out of the ground. He shifted his posture, bringing one foot forward, the other back. The point of his sword went up.

Baelock Fain had answered his challenge.

Malgannis remained where he was, waiting for his enemy to come to him. Every sense was telling him that what he was doing was wrong. He heard his father's voice, lecturing him on the importance of good armor. He remembered all the narrow escapes, all the times he had almost been killed, only for the sharp steel of the man trying to kill him to be blocked by his plate or chain. A voice inside him told him to run, that it wasn't too late to escape.

He stayed where he was, as the tall warrior in black armor strode steadily toward him, growing larger and larger in his vision.

At last, Baelock Fain came to a halt. He kept his sword held casually, with some distance still between them.

"Why?" Baelock asked, and Malgannis easily heard his Vailander accent. "You are a warrior as much as I am. You know how this will end."

Malgannis focused on the black eyes he could see through his enemy's helmet. Baelock Fain. Graven Callow. Both were the same man.

He ignored the question. "How many have you killed?"

Baelock paused for a moment. “Why count? I will soon be king of the world. What value should I give the lives of my enemies?”

“The fires of hell are calling you,” Malgannis said, still holding his sword ready. “The lord of the underworld wants you back.”

Malgannis knew he had struck a nerve when he saw Baelock’s eyes flash.

“Do not pretend your soul is pure,” he snapped. “You and I are the same, Ironclaw. We are opposite sides of the same coin.”

Malgannis watched his enemy carefully, prepared for his body to make the slightest move. “You take lives. I save them.”

“By taking still more lives? There is nothing between us. We will both do anything to accomplish our goals.”

Even now, Malgannis wanted final confirmation. “You cut those women down. In the convent.”

“They weren’t the first.” Baelock lifted the point of his sword and shifted his posture. “Now, prepare to die, Ironclaw. For a second time. At least this time you will die by the sword, rather than take the coward’s way out.”

Baelock Fain suddenly lunged. He batted Malgannis’s blade to the side and thrust, fast as a snake, toward Malgannis’s head. By the gods, he was quick. Malgannis couldn’t believe the man’s speed. He was barely able to step back and once again protect his body with his own weapon.

Baelock spun his sword deftly and cut down from overhead. Malgannis crossed his weapon in front of his face to block the blow. Steel clashed against steel. With the blades locked together, Baelock gritted his teeth and tried to push Malgannis from his footing. But Malgannis held fast, and the muscles in his arms strained as he attempted to shove his opponent in turn.

Eventually both men drew apart, panting after the exchange. Malgannis watched Baelock’s eyes and feet. In turn, Baelock circled round, looking for an opening.

Malgannis launched into a flurry of blows. With both hands gripping the hilt of his huge sword, he brought it down time and again. Baelock blocked and stepped back. Malgannis advanced. Baelock pushed Malgannis’s steel to slide it away from his body. Malgannis cut from above once more. Baelock brought his blade up to ward off the huge sword, but there was too much strength and momentum crashing down on him. The broadsword scraped against the armor on Baelock’s shoulder.

Now it was Baelock’s turn. He roared and came at Malgannis, who retreated from the onslaught. Each time the two weapons smashed together, Baelock’s lighter blade came closer to Malgannis’s head or torso. The tip of Baelock’s sword lashed toward Malgannis’s chin, and he ducked his head back, feeling the sharp metal cut the air in front of his face.

Malgannis stumbled and barely managed to deflect Baelock's next blow. He tried to regain his footing, even as his arms came up to block, and again his opponent's weapon missed him by a hair's breadth.

Finally Malgannis managed to get his feet steadily under him. His arms were groaning, but he smashed down hard to knock Baelock's thinner weapon back. He followed by kicking with his boot, bringing his foot forward as hard as he could to slam it against Baelock's knee. Armored as Baelock was, Malgannis didn't cause his opponent any pain, but Baelock almost lost his balance.

Malgannis scored his first good blow. He sent his broadsword crashing against Baelock's helmet. The clang sounded like a temple bell. Baelock was momentarily dazed, and Malgannis followed up by hacking at his enemy's waist, near the armor joint, but once more his strike was deflected by the steel.

Baelock's sword was down, and Malgannis saw the opportunity to bring all his strength to bear. He brought his sword down in a vertical arc toward Baelock's neck and shoulder. But Baelock saw the danger, and at the last instant brought his sword up to knock the blade away.

Baelock took two steps back, visibly panting.

And yet Baelock's eyes were fierce, and he kept his sword point up. Malgannis wasn't just breathing hard, his chest was heaving. His arms were on fire; the muscles in his legs were burning. A buried part of him wanted more than anything to lower his sword point, which was the one thing he could never do.

"You're old," Baelock said, and Malgannis could hear the struggle for breath in his voice. "I've taken your measure, Ironclaw. You know how this is going to end."

Malgannis saved his own breath, taking the precious time to recover as much as he could.

Baelock repeated the style of attack he had begun with, moving from stillness into whipcord speed, every motion a blur. He thrust, weaved, and then slashed, forcing Malgannis to turn, time and time again. Malgannis knew how he looked to his opponent. He was obviously fatigued. Every time he blocked with his blade, his movement was slower than the time before.

Baelock changed style again. Now he was the one hacking from above, forcing Malgannis back. The grass became churned up to mud around them. Malgannis had traveled a hundred paces and back again. Baelock roared and chopped down with his sword like an axe. Malgannis blocked with his blade horizontal. Once more, their weapons were locked together.

This time, Malgannis's legs were heavy. His arms felt wooden and numb, as if they too were weighed down. He clenched his jaw as Baelock pushed down. He knew he had to disengage or part of him would crumple.

One of his legs gave out underneath him. All of a sudden he was on one knee. He kept his sword frantically held above his head, as his enemy's steel inched closer to his face.

Steel slid against steel. Baelock disengaged and with terrible speed and skill, he thrust the point of his sharp blade into Malgannis's shoulder, near his neck.

Malgannis gasped.

From the walls of Adin, he heard a collective cry.

✦

Cora was gripping Erik tightly. His hand clutching hers was painful.

She couldn't watch. But she also couldn't look away.

"Please," she whispered.

Malgannis was on one knee. He was swaying. Silence filled Adin's surrounds. A dry wind blew into Cora's face.

The once-indomitable warrior who had rescued Cora at Leventhal, who had fought at Martenhal, and had led the Iron Spear, was beaten. The evidence was clear for all to see. His sword was down. He had given up on trying to protect himself. After Baelock's deep thrust, he looked like he was about to tumble to the side, regardless of what his enemy did.

Baelock lifted his sword for a finishing strike.

"It's over," Erik whispered. "Farewell, my friend."

But then Baelock Fain took a step back in shock. Malgannis straightened, returning to his feet. His sword was up, held in both hands. He returned to fighting stance, and began to circle his opponent.

From everywhere along Adin's outer wall, a powerful roar from the onlookers shook the heavens.

✦

Baelock's wide eyes spoke volumes. Malgannis gritted his teeth and stood, even as blood welled and then began to stream down his shoulder. He returned to the position he had been in when the fight commenced.

"This isn't over," he said.

Malgannis began to take sideways steps, goading his opponent, even as he searched for an opening. Baelock came forward with his sword, and Malgannis blocked. Again, Baelock probed, and Malgannis repelled his opponent's weapon.

Even as Malgannis fought, thoughts also fought each other for space inside his head.

As he hacked and thrust, he thought of all the towns and villages burned, the bodies strewn across the mud, the wells poisoned and the fields spitefully salted. Images came to him: the youths of Aranor, up on the walls of the border forts, peppered with arrows; the pillar of smoke from Helmsford; Cora's face when she told him about Silvia.

He remembered his wife and daughter. The faces of the three women shifted from one to the other, until he was left with his last sight of Cora. He had to do this for her.

Fire had returned to his limbs. When the two swords came together again, there was no weakness in his attack. He weaved and found a hole in his opponent's defense. Seizing the moment, he slammed his broadsword once more against Baelock's helmet.

Baelock retreated swiftly. In the few moments he had to himself, he yanked off his helmet and tossed it to the side, gasping. Malgannis could now see his enemy's flushed face and wild eyes. When Malgannis charged, Baelock was forced to raise his sword to protect himself and retreat still farther.

Soon the two men were once more circling each other.

"Listen, old man," Baelock hissed. "I am not going to hell. Not today."

Malgannis was keenly aware of the gaping wound in his shoulder, just below his neck. He knew wounds. His was grave. And yet he was able to put it to the side of his mind, even as he felt liquid soak his clothing.

"All of the dead," Malgannis said. "Today they are giving me strength. With the dead behind me, I can't lose."

Baelock attacked. Malgannis weaved and blocked, and initiated his own attack, which his enemy countered again. The two swordsmen danced together, weaving and ducking, slashing, thrusting, blocking, and warding away. Multiple clangs sounded again and again.

Now Malgannis saw that Baelock was tiring. The Vailander was breathing just as hard as Malgannis himself. His sword point wasn't kept as high.

Malgannis saw a gap. He pushed Baelock's sword aside with his weapon, before charging with his shoulder. Baelock lost his footing and stumbled. Malgannis thrust the tip of his sword into Baelock's armpit.

Malgannis's blade penetrated a few inches and Baelock gasped. The two men came apart again, both of them with blood streaming down their sides. Malgannis wasn't the only one with the occasional stumble in his stride.

Baelock sliced three times in quick succession, forcing Malgannis to turn quickly to meet each blow. Then Baelock pushed Malgannis's blade to the side, exposing his chest.

Baelock's next slash was like a red hot poker drawn across Malgannis's torso. The sharp edge of the Vailander's steel carved through Malgannis's clothing and opened up a gash that traveled across his ribs and abdomen.

All the strength in Malgannis's legs vanished. He wasn't even aware of crumpling. All he knew was that he was on his knees. His sword lay on the ground a couple of feet away.

He glanced up. His vision was blurred. Baelock stood over him.

"I will see you in hell, Ironclaw," Baelock said.

Baelock Fain raised his sword and deliberately pushed it into the very center of Malgannis's torso. Malgannis gasped and looked down at the sharp steel embedded in his own chest. Baelock Fain withdrew the blade. Blood filled the void his weapon left.

But then Malgannis pushed down on the ground. He got one leg under his body, and then the other. Scanning the ground, he saw his sword lying nearby, and reached to pick it up.

Baelock took two steps backward. His mouth was open. He could only watch in shock as Malgannis returned to his feet. Pain filled Malgannis's body, but he lifted his sword and he knew he had the strength to keep going.

"You have forgotten something," Malgannis said. "I never sold my soul like you did. I was brought back by the sacrifice of someone else. Someone who cares about me. Tell me, who cares about you?"

Baelock attacked, thrusting toward Malgannis's face. Malgannis easily swatted his opponent's sword away.

"This whole time, I still owned my soul, unlike you," Malgannis said. "And it was a surprise to me, but it appears that my soul is of value."

Chapter 60

"YOU STRIKE A HARD BARGAIN, Ironclaw," said the black priest.

Malgannis snorted. "I'm sure you say that to everyone who runs afoul of you."

"The lord of darkness has long wanted you," Lexen said. "And so now, Malgannis Vandryden, you finally offer your soul."

Malgannis knew that Cora had long gone. Underground as he was, in a deep, dark cell, no one would hear him, but he kept his voice low. "You can give me what I want?"

"Are you certain you know what it is you are giving?"

"I am."

"You will burn forever in the fires of Abaddon. Forever is a long time, Malgannis."

"I am well aware of that."

"Why now?" Lexen asked. "When you were in the shadow world, nothing could tempt you."

"I chose to stay there. To atone."

"And now?"

"I have something more important to do."

Lexen studied Malgannis's face. In his black robe, with his pale face and his hands clasped in front of him, he looked every inch the sinister servant of darkness that he was.

"I can see that you are determined," Lexen finally said. "Very well. The lord of darkness agrees to the bargain. I can give you the strength you are asking for, the endurance to keep going, but for this day only. When the day ends, one way or another, you will be dead. And when you die, your soul goes to burn in the underworld."

"And she must not know," Malgannis insisted.

"She will not know from me."

Malgannis thought for a moment and then nodded. "I agree to it."

✦

"This is not possible," Baelock breathed.

Malgannis roared and attacked. Baelock fell back from his furious assault. The two weapons clashed.

Malgannis kept the pressure on, even as Baelock was fading fast. Both men had red liquid streaming down their torsos. The blows between them were sluggish, but it was Malgannis who had the strength to endure.

Baelock's sword went up to block, but Malgannis had feinted. Malgannis saw the opening he needed. He thrust his broadsword into Baelock's torso, and the steel plate was unable to stop his weapon from penetrating.

Baelock screamed.

Malgannis pulled his sword back to attack again, this time slamming his weapon onto Baelock's arms. The Vailander couldn't keep hold of his sword; his hands reflexively lost their grip; the weapon went flying.

Baelock fell onto his back. Malgannis towered over him. He stared down at the Vailander, who glared up with venom in his eyes.

"You sold your soul to come back to life." Malgannis cast a quick look over the two forces facing each other. "To gain so much power that you could find a way never to return to hell." He returned his attention to his enemy. "I sold my soul to stop you."

"So I will see you in hell after all, Ironclaw."

"With pleasure," Malgannis said.

Malgannis took his sword in both hands and thrust it through Baelock Fain's chest, pushing until it penetrated all the way through his body. With a groan, he then pulled, feeling the strength leave his limbs even as he yanked his broadsword free.

Baelock Fain convulsed. He coughed and blood came from his mouth. Then his eyes glazed as he died, until he was staring sightlessly at the man who had killed him.

Malgannis stood panting. Other than his breath, there wasn't a sound to break the stillness. He felt himself begin to teeter, and thrust out a leg to catch himself. He turned slowly to face Adin. His sword fell out of his hands.

As he gazed at the people prepared to defend their homes with their lives, he had to believe that he had saved them. He had finally realized that he was the only one to judge his own actions. He had chosen to end his life and haunt the shadow world, to pay his penance for the convent. If he had saved his great-granddaughter, if he had saved the city, he would have done a good deed. Something before he went to the fires of hell.

He stared toward the city with hope in his eyes. It wasn't just any city, it was his city, filled with his people. He was Aranor, and Aranor was him.

His vision began to blur. He blinked, trying to focus on the woman in silver armor. He raised his arm.

He collapsed.

✦

The silence continued. The two armies faced each other across the Sylvan River.

Malgannis turned. Cora knew he was looking at her. He raised his arm.

And then he fell.

"I'm going to him," Cora said. She began to race toward the stairs that led down from the battlements to the streets below.

"It's not safe!" Logan called after her.

Cora reached ground level in moments. "A horse!" she cried. "Give me a horse!"

She was soon pulling herself up onto horseback. Digging in her heels, she spurred her mount on and went straight through the gates. She rode over the drawbridge, swiftly reaching the end. The two fallen figures both lay near each other, in the middle of the section of churned up mud and grass.

Cora threw herself off her horse. She glanced at the armored figure of Baelock Fain, whose glazed eyes stared back at her, but then she ignored him. Rushing over to Malgannis, she crouched beside him. Leaning over him, she smoothed the hair away from his face.

Tears poured down her cheeks. Droplets dripped down from her and struck his exposed skin. She searched his face, but already the life had left him. Reaching out, she closed first one eye, and then the other.

There was movement all around her. She was aware of a flurry of activity.

"Is he...?" Erik asked from nearby.

"He's gone," she whispered.

She glanced up. The enemy army was stunned; it was clear to all. They had just lost their general and commander. Cora sensed their mood; they were uncertain. The giant on the draft horse had yet to call out or make any sign of movement.

She returned her attention to Malgannis. His face had relaxed. The tightness had left his jaw.

"We need to get him back to the city—" Cora began.

"Wait," Erik said. "Something's happening." Glancing up at him, she realized he was beside her, staring back down the river. "Look."

Cora turned her head. She saw white sails and graceful prows, along with high wooden sides and oars giving the warships additional propulsion. As she straightened and joined Erik's side, just a little farther away from her, she saw Logan, his eyes filled with hope as he stared in the same direction.

"It's the fleet," Logan said in awe.

"But there's too many..." Erik said.

Cora knew at a glance that this was a far greater number than the thirty-six ships she had sent to aid in Fastness's defense.

It was Logan who answered Erik. "Blue and red. The colors of Fastness."

"Look!" someone nearby called.

Cora saw a young soldier in the uniform of Aranor pointing as he shielded his eyes. She watched, stunned, as a column of soldiers followed the curve of the river to approach the city from the far side. She saw the blue and red of Fastness as well as Aranor's blue and gold. The ships of the fleet had unloaded their cargoes of soldiers. The column would reach the city gates in moments.

Glancing at Erik, Cora noticed that he was open-mouthed, staring in the opposite direction, toward the King's Road. "Wait. By the gods. Is that...?"

Following his gaze, Cora couldn't understand what she was seeing; all she could make out were shaggy figures, dressed in furs. As the newcomers traveled the King's Road toward the city, there were so many of them that she couldn't even guess what nation they came from. A short stumpy man with a braided beard led them, carrying an axe in his hands.

"Is that the Harrmen?" Logan asked incredulously.

Erik shook his head in disbelief. "And there is Cedric Nine Lives himself."

Cora's attention moved again when she saw two riders leave the column of fresh soldiers from the ships. The two riders galloped at speed, quick to approach Cora's position. With his ebony skin and handsome features, the younger of the pair looked familiar.

"My son, Kinley," Logan said, pleasure evident in his voice.

The pair of riders pulled up and the baron's son gave a bow as he breathlessly addressed Cora. "Majesty. When we met the fleet on the open sea, we knew there had been subterfuge. We loaded up with every man who can hold a sword, and we are here to fight with you."

"You come when we need you most," Cora said. "And for that I thank you."

"We also bring news," said the older captain who rode with the baron's son. "You have been cut off here and will not have heard. Vestria and Rumandy are liberated. The two nations have combined their strength and formed an army, which now marches on the Moranian capital." He glanced toward the enemy army. "I will warrant that if they haven't heard yet, they will at any moment."

"Look," Erik said. "A flag. They want to talk."

Cora returned to Malgannis. She crouched down at his side again, bending to kiss him on the forehead.

"Thank you, great-grandfather. Wherever you are now, be at peace."

Chapter 61

CORA AND LOGAN watched together as dusty men exited the catacombs. Each shook his head and said the same thing. "Nothing. No temple. No sign of anything."

Logan glanced at Cora. "What do you think they got out of all this?"

"The black priests?"

He nodded.

"I don't know," Cora said. She was pensive as she waited for the next soldier to come out of the tunnels. "Perhaps what they have always wanted. Death."

He gave her a sidelong look. "Now, about what I was saying."

"I told you. You don't have to do this."

Logan smiled, but his tone was firm. "My mind is made up. Every age has its heroes. I am not one of them. But at least I can do the right thing. Malgannis had his time. He even had a second roll of the dice. Now, Erik is the new hero. This war would still be going if it weren't for him."

Cora shook her head. "To hear him talk of it, he had no role in it at all."

"He is modest," Logan said. "It is a good trait."

"He is much more than that," Cora said softly.

"Coraline..." Logan said seriously. "Listen to me. I have many years of wisdom. I have had a marriage before, to a woman I loved. You have not experienced the same joy, and it is one of the greatest joys we are offered. Life can be wondrous. It can also be short. The two of you deserve each other."

Cora turned her head and there Erik was, giving the men instructions, insisting they keep searching. When he noticed her eyes on him, he looked right back at her. When he smiled, it lit up his face.

"Logan," Cora said. She met his gaze. "You are a kind man."

"And you are a good queen, Coraline Vandryden. I will follow you until the end of my days." He smiled. "Which is sure to be long before your time, my dear." His smile fell as he became earnest. "Be free," he said. "Marry the man you love."

✦

Not far from Adin Palace, between the rose gardens and the woods, a stream flowed past banks of lush green grass. The recent arrival of summer had littered the lawns with flowers in as many shades as a rainbow. White clouds drifted across the brilliant blue sky.

Cora and Erik stood together by the water, which was so clear they could see the stones and pebbles down at the bottom. Together they watched the stream slide lazily past.

"It has been a long time since I've been here," Erik said. "In truth, it feels like forever."

Cora had made sure to get Erik alone. She turned to look at him, inspecting the face that she knew so well. Reaching out, her hand went up to his cheek, slowly approaching until her fingertip brushed against his scar with the lightest of touches. Her hand fell back down again.

Erik immediately touched his own cheek, pressing his hand against the vertical line that traveled from below his right eye toward his chin.

"Don't hide it," Cora said softly, with a smile. "Remember, to me you wouldn't be you without it. I've never known you any other way." His hand fell away. She focused intently on his gentle brown eyes. "Will you tell me about how you got it? I don't mind if you don't remember. You can just say that. Please. I want to know."

He was silent for a time before answering. "There is no great mystery. My mother came to visit me at the orphanage. She told me she was very ill. She gave me my last name and said she was sorry she couldn't raise me. She also gave me some money, but the other boys found out, and we fought. They got the silver, and I got this."

"Did you see her again?"

He shook his head.

"What happened to her?"

"I don't know." He stared at the ground for a moment and then looked at her. "My family is here."

Cora smiled. "I'm glad you told me. Thank you. There is now nothing between us but the summer breeze."

Erik frowned, confused by what she had just said. Then he started. "I can't believe I forgot. Here." He grinned at her and took something from a pocket, before presenting it. "Look. I found it below the Bridge of Willows."

Cora couldn't believe what she was seeing. Erik was holding up her ring, her golden ring with the square blue sapphire. She couldn't help herself. She took it and looked at the inside of the golden band—there was her name, written in tiny letters.

"How...?"

"It was in a lonely place, but the sun was making it sparkle so that I couldn't miss it."

She smiled, and then passed him back the ring. "Could you hold it, for a little longer?"

"Of course," he said, puzzled as he took it back.

She cleared her throat. "Did you see me speaking with Logan?"

"Yes..." he said uncertainly.

"He wants to divorce me," she said simply.

Erik scowled. "What? How dare—"

"Erik," Cora said. Rather than keep her expression smooth, she allowed her emotions to show on her face. She smiled at Erik and continued to gaze intently into his eyes. "It's what I want."

"Why?"

She didn't say anything.

"Why are you looking at me like that?" he demanded.

"Perhaps if you think, you might realize," she said. Her eyes narrowed slightly.

"You know who you remind me of?" Erik asked. "He used to do that. That flat stare. Like I'm a complete fool."

Cora couldn't help herself. She laughed. "Well, sometimes you can be." She leaned in to whisper up into his ear. "But I still love you anyway."

Erik drew back, stunned. "Cora..."

"The time is right," she said with a smile. "We'll be married in the summer. Now," she held out her hand, "you can give me that ring."

"But..." Erik was still perplexed, almost lost for words. "How could... how could we be married? I'm a commoner."

"Malgannis once told me something," Cora said. "He said his grandfather was a commoner. His father was a lord. And his own son became king. He said it is all a show, like a play at the theatre. Marry who you like, he said, as long as the audience claps at the end."

"When did he say that?"

"When I was no longer cursed. And I had just discovered you were alive."

"But the council of lords—" Erik began.

“Malgannis also said something else,” Cora said. She smiled, but there was also steel in her voice. “‘You are the queen,’ he told me. ‘You make the rules.’”

Without giving Erik a chance to reply, Cora reached up, touched his chin, and leaned in to kiss his lips. He continued the kiss, and pulled her in, holding her close.

It was a long time before they broke off. She held up her hand, and he gave her the ring to put on her finger.

Holding Erik’s hands, she glanced at the river. “We used to swim here as children.”

“And then you stopped.”

“I began to develop as a woman. It wouldn’t be seemly, they said.” She smiled mischievously. “Perhaps we should go in now.” Her eyes twinkled. “Or it might be better in darkness. Although,” she mused, “darkness wouldn’t be good. I wouldn’t get to see you. And you wouldn’t get to see me.”

“Cora!” Erik exclaimed with a laugh.

She kissed him again, and then murmured once more into his ear. “Remember. I am the queen. I make the rules.”

Chapter 62

MALGANNIS STOOD ON a graveled road, near a circle of elm trees. His legs were apart as he faced the burned out husk of a building. As he focused intently on the ruins, he cracked his knuckles.

Storm clouds were gathering, dark, sinister shapes that took all the light away. He heard a whine, and looked down. A lean dog was by his knees, looking up at him. Malgannis scratched the creature behind the ears.

The dog panted happily, and then scurried away. Malgannis rested his gaze once more on the forbidding structure, with its blackened corner towers, crumbling walls, and gate hanging off its hinges. He was supposed to do something, but he didn't feel right. This place was supposed to have some hold on him.

But he was just looking at an old, burned out building.

He felt a warmth.

He turned his head to look in all directions. Color was coming to the shadow world. A bright light had an origin nearby, and cast a glow so strong that soon it was all Malgannis could see. He turned and found himself staring at a door-shaped rectangle of pure, solid white.

A figure stepped through the door.

The figure was smaller than him and glowing. With measured steps, the figure approached. Malgannis blinked, warding the light with a hand, trying to make out what he was looking out. The figure stopped in front of him.

The girl had big bright eyes, the shade of the bluest blue. Her skin was soft and her hair was the color of honey. Malgannis looked to the convent and back at the girl. She smiled.

"You're here to take me to hell?" Malgannis asked. "You don't look like a ghoul."

"No, Malgannis. I am not here to take you to hell," the girl said.

"Why not?" he demanded. "I sold my soul."

"Let us just say you have those who love you in heaven, and they interceded on your behalf."

"The lord of darkness is expecting a soul," he said.

"And although he only has one, he is happy with the one he has got. Now come. Let us leave this place."

Malgannis frowned, uncertain. The blue-eyed girl smiled again.

"Take my hand," she said, holding out her palm.

Malgannis took the girl's hand in his. He felt a tingle spread through his body. All of a sudden, he was light. Everything that had weighed him down was gone.

"You mean...?" He broke off; his eyes were suddenly wet.

"Yes," the girl said with a smile. "Your wife and daughter are waiting for you."

He had missed them more than life itself. He was going to see them again. They were going to be together once more.

The girl led Malgannis to the doorway made of pure white light.

"Are you ready?" she asked.

"I am."

Together, they stepped through.

* * *

BLOOD AND EMPIRE

Power is never granted... it can only be seized.

BLOOD AND EMPIRE begins best-selling author James Maxwell's epic fantasy series, THE GATEWAY SAGA—a gripping tale of ambition, sacrifice, and defiance in the face of destiny.

Young seamstress Bethany dreams of becoming a diviner, one of the select few able to navigate the mysterious gateways that unite the empire. But without wealth or education, and only her mother to raise her, she is on a path to disappointment.

Then Bethany meets Charlton, a cleric, who offers her books and guidance, and she glimpses a life she had thought unreachable. Her problems grow, however, when her ambitions draw attention and her father re-enters her life, confronting her with a past she still needs to come to terms with.

As invasion threatens the empire, and intrigue and betrayal create fault lines amongst the highest circles, Bethany must learn to master both powerful forces and herself, in order to confront the darkness within her own bloodline—and save the empire from itself.